D0986476

Julia Bell is a writer, editor and tutor based at the University of East Anglia. She is the co-editor (with Jackie Gay) of *Hard Shoulder* (1999), which won the Raymond Williams Community Publishing Prize in 2000, and she co-edited the *Creative Writing Coursebook* (2001). Her first novel, *Massive*, is to be published in 2002.

Jackie Gay was born in Birmingham and travelled in Europe, Asia, the Far East and Africa before returning home to write. Her first editing job was with Julia Bell, on the prize-winning anthology *Hard Shoulder*, and her first novel, *Scapegrace*, was published in April 2000. She is currently working on her second novel.

England Calling
24 Stories for the 21st Century

Edited by
JULIA BELL AND JACKIE GAY

PHOENIX

A PHOENIX PAPERBACK

First published in Great Britain in 2001
by Weidenfeld & Nicolson
This paperback edition published in 2002
by Phoenix,
an imprint of Orion Books Ltd,
Orion House, 5 Upper St Martin's Lane,
London WC2H 9EA

A CIP catalogue record for this book
is available from the British Library.

ISBN 0 75381 332 7

Printed and bound in Great Britain by
The Guernsey Press Co. Ltd, Guernsey, C.I.

Acknowledgements

We would like to thank the following people for their advice and feedback during the preparation of this book: Penny Rendall and Emma Hargrave at Tindal Street Press, Julian Jackson, Alan Beard, Annette Green, Ashley Stokes, Tina Jackson; and Anna Zaluczkowska and Tim Moss at Lumb Bank.

Contents

Introduction

There is no future in England's dreaming
Sex Pistols

What does Englishness mean to you? To any of us at the turn of the century? It's the question on the lips of newspaper journalists, magazine editors and commentators from Northumberland to Cornwall. And how many generations of English people have felt there is no future in the concept? For some, being English is an embarrassment – a shame – associated with empire, imperialism, stoicism, stiff upper lips; others feel uncomfortable taking pride in being English because of the associations with nationalism, yobbishness and an inability to hold our drink.

But this England, this Englishness, is changing. No one can seriously deny that. At the start of a new millennium we live in a country which is restless, uneasy, questioning and devolving. English politics is showing signs of breaking free from Westminster following the devolution of power to Scotland and Wales, but what is happening to the cultural life of the country in the wake of these developments? It is one of many ironies that a flourishing regional culture depends on funding from central government; nevertheless, there are plenty of examples of excellence outside London. Cornwall has its own Tate Gallery, so does Liverpool. Salford has the Lowry Centre, Birmingham the CBSO and Manchester the Royal Exchange. Popular music – somehow always more anarchic than other art forms – has always had strong regional roots. But there is still a metropolitan bias, especially in literature.

Some of this distortion may be due to the concentration of publishing in the capital, but it also seems that for English writers, London – and just about anywhere else in the world – offers a grand canvas, whereas a novel set in, say, Bradford or Exeter is seen as necessarily provincial and limited. Why? Is it that we don't take ourselves seriously, that we have to be first in line to mock attempts to define ourselves through regionally based literature, to get in there before someone else has a go? Or is it that we genuinely feel our lives to be uninspiring? This self-depreciation, the rush for the irony button, is still a very English trait – what better way to show off your stiff upper lip than to be self-mocking? But, given the current pace of change, it may be that the comfort-zone of self-mockery is something we need to grow out of.

In an essay for the *Times Literary Supplement*, Ferdinand Mount remarks that in England, 'Tight central control – of industry and commerce, of politics, of personal behaviour, of national boundaries and a lot else besides, is giving way to a free-flowing, unbuttoned openness. You may think of all this as welcome, stimulating and long overdue. Or you may find it alarming, headlong and decadent . . . But it would be hard to pretend that nothing has changed, or that the changes were trivial and not worth remarking on.'

We have not arrived at this juncture by accident. The last thirty years of government – Mrs Thatcher's war against society and Tony Blair's devolving New Labour – have left, and are leaving, indelible marks on the landscapes of our country. Punk and Thatcherism, not the Second World War, are the key cultural and historical reference points for many English people and – despite 1980s stagnation and repression – sooner or later this generational shift was going to show through. In the 1970s, sporting a mohican in Carlisle or Canterbury was the ultimate act of rebellion. Now middle-aged ladies dye their hair pink for a laugh, a night out. Pubs are open all day, high streets bristle with balti houses and Bollywood video shops as well as dotcom companies and

Starbucks, and the national anthem is ousted by Fat Les's version of 'Jerusalem'. These new freedoms, however, may yet prove to be illusory. Our much vaunted parliamentary democracy is undermined by focus-group ideology; by a powerful corporate economy which has a more direct influence over our lives than any government policy; and by a reductive, reactionary tabloid culture.

England Calling is an attempt to mark out some of this ground, both geographically and socially. We wanted to gather together writers from every corner of the country and from a broad cross-section of society. These writers are not only telling stories of the landscapes of England, but peeling back the layers of Englishness in the process – Englishness as it is now: multicultural, messy, survivalist. Writing about landscape inevitably raises political and social questions, because social change is writ large in the topography of England. Here we have history jostling with industry, towerblocks and cobwalled cottages, pubs and Euro wine-bars, claustrophobic suburbia, the weather, the sea, the moors, the roads and nuclear reactors. Cities and whole swathes of countryside are modified and reconstructed so quickly that they become unrecognisable almost overnight.

The stories in this book illustrate a nation questioning its identity in the face of these changes; and they suggest that one way of orientating ourselves in new times is through fiction. Previous literary responses may have been, as Ian Jack said in *Granta* 56, the 'literature of farewell', but we think these stories move forward from mourning the loss of greatness. There is something saltier about these pieces: a boldness, an attitude, flashes of soulfulness. Perhaps we are returning to qualities identified as English in much earlier times – Voltaire paints a picture of us familiar even today: independent, prickly, coarse, innovative, sentimental, patriotic. Or perhaps we are at a point where we can, once again, write stories which reflect upon and redefine our identity.

A girl who wilfully forgets who she is, couples who can't

agree on the truth, a woman snipping her way out of her stifling marriage: these are all stories of identity. The identities revealed may not be comfortable ones, or even very secure, but here English writers have the confidence to examine who they are, to question it, rather than mourning the loss of an Arcadian vision they never felt part of in the first place. We may not yet have the cultural confidence of our neighbours in Scotland, but the possibility of the whole of England becoming a country of discovery, to be reclaimed and revitalised by its writers, is the premise for *England Calling*.

We asked our contributors to write stories set in their England. Here we have David Almond writing about South Shields; Alan Beard on Birmingham; Julie Burchill on her Brighton; Lesley Glaister on urban and rural Yorkshire; Harland Miller on York; Alexei Sayle on London and Pavan Deep Singh on the Black Country.

Stuart Hall, the renowned thinker on race, culture and Britain's post-colonial traumas, has challenged the nation to reimagine Englishness itself 'in a profoundly more inclusive manner'. He asked, 'Is Britain going to accept its diversity and become more humane?' We hope so; that is the England we dream of. England's history is shameful and glorious, its people are black, gay and disabled as well as white Anglo-Saxon, its landscapes are devastated and breathtaking – sometimes at the same time. These are the contradictions we live with on this packed island, they are what we must make our future from. Devolvement of power allegedly places more responsibility for our own government in our hands, but before we know what we want, we have to know who we are.

We believe that fiction is a good place to begin exploring these questions; that literature is democratic, that ordinary lives – whether in Crewe, Ipswich or Peckham – are fascinating, that culture is interesting in itself. David Almond says, 'Stories stop us from being individuals. They make us a community; they hold us together.' This volume hopes, just for the space of these pages, to bring us together for a snapshot. A picture of England – this turbulent, rebellious, mongrel nation – at the beginning of the twenty-first century.

Julia Bell and Jackie Gay, September 2000

The Day You Lost Her
Julia Darling

The day you lost her you caught the number one bus that glides through Newcastle like a knife through butter, from east to west and back again. You thought she had gone to school, and that everything was in its place. Your coat was buttoned up and the papers in your briefcase were crisp and white.

She arrived at the school gates in her blue shirt and trousers, and stopped outside. She looked at the building with its temporary windows and battered doors, and it seemed to shrink. She thought of stars and universes and how the sky went on and on, and she just turned round, amazed by the ease of it. And as she walked away from the barking teachers with halitosis, who spoke of nothing but exams, and the carping bells and bumping corridors, each pace was like a knot untying, and she sang and didn't care who heard.

You had lost her once before; up on the sand dunes of the East Coast. She was six years old. You ran through the whitened tufts of sandy grass, slipping in the soft sand, calling her name over and over again. The sea grimaced with greyness and the wind blew your footprints away. You found her crying by a rock pool, crouched in her pink coat, asking you where you'd been. Her face was walled up by your absence. You hadn't looked after her properly, she said, you never do.

She was walking past tight terraced houses with gardens of pruned roses, and then some shops. She stepped into the darkness of a pet shop that sold snakes and caged birds, and breathed in the warm smell of vipers. A man with hooded eyes was pouring seeds into plastic bags. The snakes were all asleep, coiled in the corner of glass cases, trying to be invisible, and the birds hunched on their perches dreaming. She ran her hand over a glass aquarium and the man said, 'You'll smear the glass. Can't you read the notice?' And she put her hand back in her pocket, and she thought of the rock pool she had looked in when she was six; the scuttling crabs, the glint of something precious under dark stone.

You were looking at people on the bus. Working people, with lists in their bags, and mobile phones, and washed hair and pressed trousers. People with diaries, like you. You were thinking about books and the man you had arranged to meet. That's your job. Making beautiful books. Your Newcastle was arched and elegant and redeveloped. It had forgotten its dirty past. Its buildings were sprayed clean and its quayside was polished and smelt of fresh coffee.

Her Newcastle was darker than yours. Its alleys beckoned her in. It had doors behind doors. It was clockless and itinerant, and she could hear it calling from drains and bars in a voice that was drunken and whispering. She looked for her reflection everywhere.

She also got on a bus, showing her bus pass to the driver, who considered asking her for ID, but who was going to Marbella the next day and couldn't be bothered. She climbed upstairs where the air was stale and the seats were burnt with cigarettes and some of them were broken, and she sat right at the back and lit up a Marlboro cigarette and she felt like the queen of the world up there, racing down Jesmond Road, past the Dene, with her fag held up high. She loosened her blonde hair from its bobble and she pulled a mirror from her bag and considered her face with her cheeks sucked in, and it seemed different to the face she had the day before. She was glad not to be sitting in assembly with a headmaster making a moral point which was pointless.

You were standing in Northumberland Street waiting to meet the man who was a photographer. A busker was playing the flute, and there were women everywhere with shopping on their minds, like it was a religion. Women whose children were scared of them, with their fat leather purses and mantelpieces weighty with family history. Women who made a pound of Cheddar last for a week. You felt superior. You imagined that you and your daughter were close and loving. That you understood her.

Her bus turned the corner and she gazed down at the street where you stood, but she didn't see you. She saw all the things you wouldn't buy her and she thought that if she had a thousand pounds she would have plastic surgery, to eliminate you from her body.

You were meeting the photographer in the Tyneside Tea Rooms. He was late. He had large hands and a craggy face, and he carried a plastic bag. He was a recovered alcoholic and he sipped his water as if it was a penance, and he talked about his photographs of birds up in the Farne Islands. He trembled a little, and his shoes were very clean but his teeth were awful. You ordered a coffee and he had a black tea and a mineral water. He said, 'How's your daughter?' and you told him, 'She's fine. She's at school. She's a teenager.' But he wasn't really interested. He wanted to talk about the nesting terns and money.

She was getting off the bus, where the big clock is, and the paper seller who cried out as if he was in pain. She thought about trains and where they could take you. She had eighty-nine pence and she didn't know what to do. She stood by the station and listened for clues. She remembered a man called Ollie who lived in the flats nearby. She had met him once with a friend. He was a musician. She quite fancied him, except he talked of nothing but bands and guitars.

In the tea rooms the seats were red velvet and the tea came in a tarnished teapot and the menu hadn't changed for

3

years. The photographer was giving you pictures to look at of birds that looked vicious and unkind. You were fingering your mobile phone in your pocket and wondering how long you needed to spend looking at photographs. Somewhere behind the steam and the clatter of pensioners having their mid-morning coffee you could hear pigeons, cooing and moaning.

She was ringing the bell of the flat, and there was a drunk staggering up the alley behind her. Once he worked at the ship yards and somehow he had got stuck there, and he talked to himself about ships and love. He asked her for money and she gave him ten pence and he turned it over and over in his hands as if it was a trick. His eyes were like un-cooked eggs. 'I built ships,' he told her. 'What do you think about that?'

'Nothing,' she said. Just then Ollie looked down from the window and she shouted her name and he told her the intercom wasn't working, then he ran down in his underpants and opened the door and the drunk stuck out his chin and swayed like a mast as Ollie pulled her inside.

The photographer was saying that Newcastle was being butchered. 'Have you seen the Co-op?' he said. 'They've sliced off the side as if it was a cake. They're building a leisure complex. That's what's happened to co-operation, it's turned into leisure. You should do a book about that.'

And sometimes you think that we talk about this city as if it's a person. A person that's trying to change, but who is fettered by historians and poets, who want it to be theirs.

'You don't come from here,' said the photographer, as if you couldn't understand.

'My daughter was born here,' you tell him.

She was walking up the stairs behind Ollie's naked white back, and they went into his flat which was green and empty with a mattress on the floor. Ollie put on the kettle and she told him she was wagging off school, and he grinned and put on some loud music and the TV, and somebody banged on the ceiling below them. Ollie was dancing about with a garish look on his face and she lit her last cigarette and watched the smoke gathering in nostalgic layers. On the screen someone was shooting pigeons and Ollie put on a T-shirt and remembered he had to sign on. 'But you can wait here for me,' he said. 'We could spend the day. Me and you.'

'Cheers Ollie,' she said in a voice that was not her own. A Newcastle voice full of river and sky.

You said goodbye to the photographer and wondered if you should kiss him or not, like French people do, but his teeth put you off so you shook hands with him instead, in an English fashion, and you said that you'd phone him soon. He sloped off down the street and you walked down Pilgrim Street to your office. You were hoping that Janice would be doing something, not fiddling with paper clips with a surprised look on her face that made you want to scream. The streets were full of the sound of demolition and refurbishment. A woman selling the *Big Issue* stepped towards you. 'I've already bought one,' you lied.

Ollie had left her alone and she didn't like it. She had run out of cigarettes. She wished he had a telephone. She glanced out of the window and through the buildings she could see the bridge. It was heavy and old, she thought. She looked in Ollie's fridge. Inside there was margarine and a can of lager. She opened the can and drank it in the bathroom, looking at herself in the mirror. It tasted of metal. She walked out of the flat, not locking the door, and back down the stairs into the alley. She thought about begging. It was still early and people looked busy. A woman selling flowers saw her and thought, what a lovely girl and why wasn't she at school?

Janice was typing very slowly and you were looking at a fax from Germany. The phone rang and Janice answered it in slow motion. She said, it's for you, without finding out who it was. You took the receiver crossly, knocking a book off the desk. It

5

was a teacher from the school, with a voice like marmalade. 'Your daughter isn't at school,' she said.

'What do you mean, she's not at school?'

'She's not ill then?' said the teacher.

'She left this morning,' you said. 'She was in her uniform. Where is she?'

'Exactly,' said the teacher. 'That's what we'd like to know.'

She was outside the public library. She was getting fed up. She wandered inside, smelling the stuffiness of books, which reminded her of you. The foyer was filled with Newcastle ephemera; postcards of bridges, and black and white mugs. It was warm in there. She went to the reference library which was full of old men asleep behind newspapers. She picked up a magazine called *Astrologers Monthly* and sat down by a radiator. She read that her life would be turned upside down; that Saturn was ascending.

You were furious. You told Janice to deal with the fax from Germany and you rushed out of the office without knowing where you were going. You found yourself searching for her, and bits of her city leaked into yours. You saw a group of goths smoking in Old Eldon Square and suddenly the city was full of windows and doors that you couldn't open. You remember the argument you had the night before. 'You're hopeless,' you'd said. 'You don't try hard enough. Take some responsibility.'

She was bored with astrology. A man came and sat down next to her. He was reading a book of poetry. He was thin and restless and she asked him the time and he said that he hadn't a watch. He said, 'Do you want a coffee?' and she followed him into the library café. He bought her a coffee and an iced cake, and they sat at a small plastic table. She told him that she was fifteen and he said that he'd had a breakdown, but that he was better. 'What is madness?' he said.

She liked him. He was the opposite of the hectoring

teachers. She told him she hated the system, and he agreed. He said they were bastards. She told him that she never wanted to go back to school, and he said the same thing happened to him. One day he just stopped going. He said he wanted to hitch-hike north, to see the northern lights. 'Can I come?' she asked.

You were trying to think which shops she liked. You were harassed and hot. You saw someone you knew and you crossed the road to avoid them. Yellow buses drove past you deliriously fast, and there were huge people everywhere carrying too much shopping. It's all you could do not to call out her name.

'It's all up here,' he was saying, tapping his head. She noticed his fingers were covered in tiny scratches and burns.

'Did you hurt yourself?' she asked him, and he shook his head and glanced down at his hands with a worried look. She had drunk her coffee and eaten her cake.

You walked into the library. You didn't expect to find her. You ran through the aisles of fiction, thinking about books and how useless they were. Just pages and pages of stuff. You were thinking your daughter was more important than books. You'd got your priorities all wrong. You hated books. You saw a book about Druridge Bay that you published ten years before. Photographs of sea gorse, sea-coaling people with eyes like charcoal, almost indivisible from the shadows of rocks and water.

'I'll meet you in ten minutes,' said the man. 'I've got to get my prescription from the chemist. I'll be back,' he said, 'and we'll head off up the West Coast of Scotland.'

'I haven't got any money,' she said.

'Money isn't important,' he told her. 'We'll get some. You and me.'

And then you found her. You glimpsed through the forests of books and saw her, hunched up in the library café. You ran up to her, shouting her name. People turned and stared. When she saw you she shrugged.

'Why aren't you at school?' you asked. She told you she couldn't be bothered. 'You're coming home with me,' you roared. 'Put on your coat.' And she did, but when you look back on what happened later, that was the day you lost her. The day when she didn't want to be found.

Bleeding Statues
David Almond

The statue first moved in February. It started to bleed in March. It was a statue of the infant Jesus dressed as a shepherd boy, naked but for a goatskin loincloth and sandals. He had a staff in his hand, his hair was golden and there was a ring of seven stars around his head.

Mrs Miller bought the statue in the Catholic Truth Society shop in Edinburgh. She said there was nothing to show that it was special at the time. She simply bought it for its beauty, for the infant's piercing blue eyes. There were a dozen others on the shelf, each as lovely. They'd been sent in bulk from a North African mission factory and were being sold at a bargain price. Right from the start Mrs Miller loved this statue above all the others in her house, even though, in Felling's damp northern air, the gilt and paint began to crack and the cheap plaster beneath to crumble.

The Millers lived on Watersyde, the broad roadway that curved through Leam Lane estate. They'd been rehoused, like so many others, from the ancient terraces at Felling Shore. The estate at that time had just been completed. There was still the taste of builders' dust in the air and many of the gardens were littered with builders' rubble. But each of the houses was inhabited at last, the pubs and the clubs and the shops were open, the pond in the park was stocked with minnows, there were tiny saplings tied to stakes on the verges and it was clear, after all the years of building, that the people

9

of Leam Lane had become the first inhabitants of a little new town within our town. It was another parish too: St Aloysius, with its church of bright brick and shining glass and the thin steel steeple that soared into the sky.

It was Mrs Miller's neighbour, Mrs Dodds, who was the first to see some movement. She said it was the merest glimpse, from the corner of her eye, just as she was lifting a cup of tea to her lips. She said nothing about it at the time. She tried to dismiss the memory, but the image returned to trouble her for several nights afterwards. The next time she visited she made sure that she faced the statue. She stared into those piercing blue eyes. Mrs Miller set off on a long, familiar tale about her son in South Africa and her daughter lost somewhere in London and the carelessness of her husband. All he did was drink and work and clean that bloody scooter of his and it was like he didn't care about anything that might happen to any of them.

'And I'm at the end of my tether,' she said at last. 'Just can't think what to do.'

Mrs Dodds put her cup down. She reached across the table and patted her friend's hand.

'I'd hate to bring more trouble, Veronica,' she said. 'But I'm sure I saw that statue move.'

At first, the moving statue was known only to a small circle of women from Leam Lane. They gathered together in the afternoons in Mrs Miller's kitchen. They held rosary beads and scapular medals, and they wore headscarves and mantillas. The statue on these occasions was placed at the centre of the kitchen table between a pair of candles. The women prayed to Our Lord and Our Lady and the saints for guidance. Then, under the direction of Mrs Dodds, they stared at the statue and waited for it to move. She said that they would see a kind of trembling or twitching. The statue might shift and shiver. Soon Mrs Miller herself began to see more clearly. Yes, she would say. Watch closely. The hands might appear to flex, the feet to lift, the head to tilt. The stars around the head might begin to move, and to slowly spin. Do you see? Do you see? And more and more came back the answer, Yes.

It was discovered that the statue was most likely to move at dusk. As Mrs Miller said, 'As darkness casts its cloak upon the world, so the light of Jesus burns more brightly.' This caused no difficulties in the dismal days of early February but, as March and spring approached, it became obvious that new arrangements must be made. Husbands were the problem: husbands coming back from work, needing to be cooked for and fed; husbands who had been told nothing about the marvellous events in Mrs Miller's kitchen; husbands who could easily scorn this gathering of wives around a tawdry foreign statue.

The women spent a long afternoon in anguished prayer. They knew that they should seek guidance from those better versed in these matters, but they were reluctant to go to their new priest, Father Connor. A pale, thin, Ampleforth man, he seemed so stern and humourless. All he seemed to think about was making sure the church windows fitted properly or the plaster was smooth. He'd had the builders back time and again for finicky jobs with doors or skirting boards. One Sunday in the pulpit he'd raised his finger at the congregation and said they'd have to dig deeper in their pockets if they expected to have the best silver chalices and leather-bound hymnals. He had none of the benign and caring touch of Father O'Mahoney. No wonder so many of the Leam Lane folk kept going back to the old church.

But there was a suspicion too that the Irishmen would be of little help. Mrs Hanlan had filled in as housekeeper for O'Mahoney once when Mary Corey was having her veins done, and she'd found him to be a faithless old bugger when it came to the miraculous. She'd even heard him dispute the verity of Lourdes itself, saying it was as much the brainchild of the French tourist industry as the work of God and His Immaculate Virgin Mother.

The women prayed again, this time focusing their prayers directly at the image of the infant Jesus.

'Give us guidance, Lord,' murmured Mrs Miller.

And then she leapt with fright and the women scattered as Mr Miller's scooter puttered to a halt outside.

Mrs Miller blew the candles out and prayed again. He took such a time to get the scooter in the garden shed. He came in at last and dumped his helmet by the statue. He sighed and rubbed his head, lit a Capstan and stared at her. He'd known something was up, he said. Wilfie Mack had given him the whisper. He laughed. Bloody women, eh? So what was going on?

Mrs Miller cried. She said all they'd ever had was trouble. First there was Michael going off to South Africa, then Vera running off to London. And it was like he didn't care, just didn't care.

Mr Miller sighed again. There was a bottle of brown ale in the cabinet. He snapped the cap off and got a glass.

'What's bloody going on?' he said.

'We've got a moving statue, Tommy.'

He took a long swig of brown ale. 'Which statue?'

'That one there.'

He stared at the statue.

'If you look at it for a long time it starts to move,' she said.

He looked down and rubbed his head again. 'You need a doctor,' he said. 'You know that, don't you?'

She wiped her eyes. 'I'll see the priest first, though.'

They stared at the statue for a while, then she went to put the chips on.

Mrs Dodds said that was it, the decision had been made for them. Tommy would be blabbing it and scoffing it in every bar from here to Felling Square. If they didn't get some expert help they'd not only be a laughing stock but they'd have brought great offence to God and great peril to their souls.

The two women cried and prayed together.

'God is testing us,' said Mrs Dodds. 'This is a time for faith and courage. We have to go to Father Connor with the truth before the liars and the mockers get to work.'

She squeezed her friend's hand.

'Just imagine. You could nearly think that in coming back early your Tommy was being guided by the hand of God.'

And they laughed, and they cried a little more.

It happened that they didn't need to go. Late that Sunday evening, Father Connor himself appeared at the Millers' door. He was getting to know his parishioners, he said as Mrs Miller guided him in.

She gave him tea and Battenberg, and her hands trembled so much she had to pour with two hands. The priest sat back in his chair, gazed about the room and remarked on the abundant evidence of her faith.

'I hear you're a great pilgrim,' he said.

'Yes, Father. I've been to Lourdes and Knock. I'm saving for Fatima. I go with the parish once a year to Walsingham.' She caught her breath. 'The old parish, I mean.'

'A great thing, to travel. I burnished my own faith in Rome. A year in the Vatican itself.'

'This is a change for you then, Father.'

He smiled. 'May I smoke, Mrs Miller?'

'Oh, Father, you can't know my Tommy. Kipper Miller they'll be naming him soon.'

She rested an ashtray on the arm of his chair and asked if he wouldn't like a glass of sherry with his smoke.

'It's a difficult thing,' he said as she took the bottle and a glass from the cabinet. 'The establishment of a new parish. So many demands, so important to build a firm foundation.'

'Yes, Father. It's all so much work for you.'

'I'm aware that I may seem at times . . .' He flicked the air before his face and looked away. 'But I see for myself, and am informed by Father O'Mahoney, of the goodness and devotion of my parishioners.'

'I'm sure you will build a fine parish, Father.'

'Thank you, Mrs Miller. We will all have our part to play.'

He was silent then. He smoked and drank. Mrs Miller felt her heart fluttering and her face burning. She lowered her eyes before Father Connor's gaze. She searched her heart for faith and courage.

'There are rumours, Mrs Miller,' he said at last, 'of idiosyncratic events.'

And Mrs Miller leapt with fright and wept and trembled, and she showed him the statue and told him the truth.

The rumours worked their way quickly to St Patrick's. The tales grew in the telling. It was said that Leam Lane had received a visitation from the Holy Ghost, that there were apparitions of the Virgin. One story told of a miraculous well that had been exposed during the building of St Aloysius. When Father O'Mahoney was asked to confirm or deny the truth of the reports, he simply dismissed them as notions suitable only for children, idiots or the lapsed.

It was suggested, however, that when he spent a whole sermon railing against the idolisation of film stars and pop stars, he was making subtle reference to happenings in Leam Lane. He reminded us of the anger of Moses when he descended the mountain with the Commandments in his hand and found his people returned to debauchery and the worship of false gods. We must hold fast to the simple tenets of our faith: communion, prayer, confession and the Mass. Those who strayed in their pride from the body of the church would soon be lost in the gloomy regions of falsehood and sin.

Once Father Connor had visited Mrs Miller in her home, though, the wild rumours were replaced by the facts. Father Connor said that although he himself was unable to discern any movement, he could not in all humility deny that this movement might be discernible to others. Such events were known to illuminate our history. They were both a demonstration of the workings of God in the world and a means of fortifying the faithful. As long as those who gathered in Mrs

Miller's house retained their allegiance to the one true church, he saw no reason to contest their sanity or to condemn the fervency of their devotions. Though he would keep a fatherly eye on these proceedings, he could not take it upon himself at this stage to curtail the possibilities which, after all, are implicit in our faith.

After such a clear statement from the pulpit, the voices of the liars, the rumour-mongers and the mockers were stifled, and Mrs Miller's house quickly became a little place of pilgrimage inside our town.

There was a particular interest in bringing children to kneel before the statue. At that time, growing up seemed almost of necessity to involve abandoning the faith. It was believed that God had chosen to work through this humble infant form in order to speak directly to the young and to hold them closer to Himself. I was taken myself several times. The statue was now kept in Mrs Miller's living room. It stood on a wooden pedestal at the centre of a small dining table. Ranks of candles burnt around it. The table and the floor beneath were covered with prayer cards, scribbled devotions, requests and thanks, flowers, little offerings of coins and sweets. The infant's pale skin bloomed, his golden hair and the stars about him gleamed. His blue eyes gazed out at us and glittered gently in the candlelight. Those visiting for the first time were heard to gasp with joy at his simple beauty, his air of calm.

Each time I went, he moved. I stared, and after some time he began to twitch, to shift, to shiver. His head appeared to tilt, his hands to shift. At times it seemed as if he were just about to step towards us, to speak. One evening, the woman at my side turned to me.

'Can you see him move?' she whispered.

I shrugged and told her that I could.

She raised her rosary to her lips and kissed it.

'I can't,' she said. 'Just can't. And I try and try.'

Her eyes shone with tears.

'Tell me what you see,' she said.

I began to mutter something about it being just a trick of the light, a result of staring for a long time, that if you stared at anything in these conditions . . .

Her hand closed tightly over mine. I felt her thin, cold, trembling fingers, the rosary beads biting into my skin.

'Oh, pray for me,' she whispered. 'You will pray for me, won't you, son?'

As the news spread, Mrs Miller's house drew pilgrims from the wider world. They came in cars and on motorbikes and on the number 82 that stopped just outside Mrs Miller's door. Coach trips were arranged by Legions of Mary from miles around. An ancient priest appeared from Consett – Father Muldoon, who was given lodgings by Mrs Dodds. He was deaf and almost speechless and he spent his days slurping tea from a saucer in the kitchen, but his presence helped to confirm the orthodoxy of the whole proceedings. There were regular visits from a pair of shy Poor Clares. There was particular interest from Blyth, where similar events featuring a statue of the Virgin had taken place before the war.

The story of the Leam Lane statue appeared in the *Gateshead Post* and the *Evening Chronicle*, with photographs in both of Mrs Miller, Mrs Dodds and the statue. Mrs Miller had doubted the correctness of allowing the Infant to appear in print, but Father Connor told her that if God was giving us a sign, it was a sign that should be noticed by the world. He even mused that one day, perhaps, given time and prayer and a continuation of the movement, Leam Lane might draw visitors as Fatima or Lourdes did. Then he sighed, laughed bitterly and stared out at the sleet.

There was talk that the *Daily Mirror* and the *People* were on their way, but there was little surprise when the reporters didn't show. As Mrs Miller herself said, If this was going on down south the buggers'd be there like a shot. The Deuchar Arms did a roaring trade. The manager pinned the newspaper cuttings to the wall, ordered extra deliveries of drink and provided a range of tasty Pilgrim's Pies. He lost the custom of Tommy Miller, who took to drinking in Finnegan's way up towards the Heather Hills: the only place, he said, where he didn't get pestered by nutters about the bloody statue and his bloody wife.

The time of tribulation began with the rows between the priests. Father O'Mahoney accused Father Connor of filching parishioners, of encouraging his flock to follow erroneous ways, of allowing extraordinary and perilous practices. It was said that he had demanded a diocesan inquiry into the whole affair, and there was indeed a visit from one of the Bishop's right-hand men, a silent Jesuit who spent an evening in the living-room doorway taking notes.

Groups of students with long hair took to gathering on the pavement, trying to hand out Communist Party leaflets. They carried placards saying GOD IS DEAD and SMASH THE IDOLS.

Then there were the tricks played by the BBC, whose reporters seemed to come in a spirit of innocent inquiry, but when the affair was highlighted towards the end of *Look North* there was no mistaking the sardonic nature of the soundtrack, nor the contempt of the sociologist who said that while activities like this might be fitted for the dark, damp parlours of Felling Shore, they could surely have no place in the housing estates of the new North.

On the evening of the broadcast, after the final pilgrims had departed and Father Muldoon had been escorted to his bed, Mrs Miller and Mrs Dodds knelt together. The Infant shifted and trembled in the candlelight before them. They heard Tommy tumble in and totter up the stairs. Soon he was snoring loudly just above. Mrs Miller prayed for him. She prayed for Michael in South Africa and she prayed for a word or a sign from Vera. Then the women focused on their common difficulties.

'Lord,' they whispered. 'Give us guidance in this matter. Show us how to proceed.'

They prayed into the early hours. Often they held each other's hands for comfort and encouragement.

'Give us guidance,' they repeated. 'Show us how to proceed.'

Mrs Miller was almost sleeping when her friend gasped with joy or pain.

'Veronica! Oh, Veronica! He's weeping blood.'

The doubters said that what looked like blood running from the eyes was simply something in the cheap paint melting. The heat of the candles, they said, of the bodies packed into that little room. Those who saw real blood smiled gently and shook their heads. They pointed to the Infant's unchanged, piercing eyes. 'How can blue run red?' they asked. The believers looked at each other with joy. How can blue run red?

Until now, the word 'miracle' had been resisted. Under instruction from Father Connor, Mrs Miller had insisted on talking of a 'sign' or an 'event'. But now the word began to be whispered and to flow with ease among the pilgrims. It was said in hushed tones, with joy, yes, but also with apprehension, with trepidation. The pilgrims stared through the candlelight at the moving boy, at the blood congealed on his pale cheek.

What was the significance of this? What did the Infant wish them to know? What had they been brought to see? Mrs Miller said that they should be satisfied with what had been shown to them. The Infant was evidence that God was at work in His world. What else was needed? He brought us to Him by action, now He shows through His tears of blood the pain we cause Him. Our purpose was to worship Him, to submit to His will, to bring our children to see the Truth.

I was taken again to see the statue. He continued to move. There were thin, muddy-looking trickles over his pale cheeks. The house was packed. The Women's League provided tea and biscuits. In the kitchen a group of men drank whiskey and talked of the seven stars, their significance. They remind us of the seven deadly sins, said one. The seven last words, said another. No, gathered about an Infant's head, they tell us of the age of seven. They remind us that we must become as infants again if we are to enter the Kingdom of Heaven. The men sighed. All these things, they agreed. So complex and so difficult. They bowed their heads and prayed for guidance.

As I passed by, one of them tugged at my cuff.

'What do you think is meant by this?'

His hair was slicked back with Brylcreem, he wore a heavy, striped suit that he must have owned since the war. A St Vincent de Paul medal was stuck in his lapel.

I shook my head.

He held me, gazed into my eyes. 'You're closer to Him than us,' he said. 'Hardly more than a child yourself. What does He say to you?'

I shook my head again, tried to move away, but he held me.

'I don't know,' I said, staring back at him. 'I don't know how to put it.'

The others in the group were watching me.

'Are they things that we could hear too?' asked one.

I raised my palm, tugged away, pushed through the people into the garden.

It was just a few days afterwards that the news of the first cure came. Margaret Sloane – seven years old, afflicted with awful eczema all her young life – had been made whole again.

Now the great newspapers did come. The affair filled a whole page of the *News of the World*. Opposite a photograph of the Infant and the headline, 'Bleeding Jesus of the Council House', Barbara Windsor tugged at her bikini top to show a massive cleavage. The *Mirror* focused on the origins of the statue and covered it with 'African Magic at Home in the North'. It printed a photograph of Doubting Tommy knocking back the drink in Finnegan's. The *Guardian* ran a piece called 'The Fag Ends of Superstition?' next to a smoky photo of the men in the kitchen, with another of Mrs Miller and Mrs Dodds smiling shyly beneath.

The Jesuit came back. By now there were more cures:

Daniel Myers of whooping cough, Valentine Carr of shingles, Dominica O'Callaghan of an apparently irreversible melancholy nature. Requests had been granted for the conception and safe delivery of babies, for success in examinations, for fine weather when most needed, for many safe journeys, for loving family reunions. The Jesuit stared at the statue for many minutes. He leant forward and fingered its cheeks. He cast his cold eye over the silent pilgrims. He drove off and was seen moments later entering Father Connor's vestry.

That Sunday the Bishop's letter was read out in St Aloysius and in the surrounding parishes. As he entered the pulpit, Father Connor looked down upon the faces of Mrs Miller and Mrs Dodds, sniffed, wiped his steel-framed glasses with his handkerchief and calmly laid the letter on his lectern. He said that more money was needed for the purchase of candlesticks and altar boys' vestments. He was to begin arrangements for a parish visit to the glories of the Vatican.

He read the letter. It made direct reference to events in the house in Watersyde. The Bishop said that it must be his purpose at all times to restrain the possibility of misdirected devotion and to curtail all signs of hysteria. He was unable to give support to the pilgrims or credence to the object of their attentions. He called upon all visitors to the house to attend daily Mass in their own parishes, to gaze upon the objects of devotion in their own churches, to take guidance and comfort from their own priests. We must hold fast to our faith and continually affirm our allegiance to the one true church. He wrote his letter in the love of God. His blessings to us all. Amen.

Father Connor lifted his eyes from the page and stared through the clear windows to the sullen sky. He seemed about to speak but he simply muttered, 'It's enough,' and returned to the altar and the Mass.

Father O'Mahoney visited for the first time that evening. He didn't go through to the statue but sat in the empty kitchen, waiting. Mrs Dodds found him when she came out to make some tea. She brought Mrs Miller out to him. They prayed together to St Aloysius and St Patrick. He told her that God would see great faith and strength in her and that there was great love for her in Heaven.

He held her hand as she cried.

'I'm so sorry, Veronica,' he said.

That same night, as she lay in bed, she heard the turbulence downstairs. Tommy, in a stupor, wouldn't wake. She waited for silence, then went down.

They'd smashed the statue into little pieces. They'd left their placards: GOD IS DEAD; SMASH THE IDOLS; SET THE PEOPLE FREE. She sat all night amid the debris, then as light came back she collected the broken pieces in a brown paper bag. She picked up the tiniest flakes of paint, swept up the finest dust. She was sitting with one of the seven stars resting on her palm as Tommy woke and came down at last.

He stared into the room, into the mess.

'See what they've done,' she said.

She listened to his rushed breakfast. She heard him in the shed outside. She heard the puttering of the stupid scooter on the garden path.

He came back in, with his helmet in his hand.

'I'm so sorry,' he whispered, and he looked at her. 'I'm so sorry, love.'

An awful morning. Mrs Dodds came, and some of the other first women. They sat stunned, staring at the empty table. They dreamt of their lovely Infant, they touched his fragments and his dust.

'We'll keep Him safe now,' they said. 'We'll keep Him secret.'

They huddled close, said hushed prayers over him.

Low, dark clouds outside; sleet splashing down on Leam Lane. They heard the back door opening: another of the women, a disobedient pilgrim, Father Muldoon come for his tea.

In the kitchen Vera slipped off her coat, rested her suitcase on the floor. She smoked a cigarette, waiting for Mrs Miller to come out from her devotions.

Then she went into the inner room.

'Mam,' she said. 'Mam. Look, I've come home.'

Castle Early
Harland Miller

York

'Can ah 'elp yu, pal?' said the new landlord.

'Hmm . . .' I came round. I'd been day-dreaming. My chin resting in my palm, eyes lost in the grotto of optic reflections behind the bar. 'Oh yhea, sorry,' I said. 'Yhea, ah-lava bottler Newky Brown please – frum t'fridge please,' I added, just as he opened one from the shelf. 'S'ahl right,' I said, catching his reflex of cold displeasure. 'Ah'll drink that un.'

I gave a lazy stretch. The pub doors were yawning to the evening sun and I'd been standing within a bright stripe of dusty yellow that had warmed my back and made me drowsy. I slid over my change, took my bottle and glass – a packet of nuts in my teeth – and sought out the old-world alcove at the rear.

Being a sombre area, avoided by revellers, it was, as usual, empty – not even the chess man, old Mr Morrison, was at his board tonight. As I entered, the sunlight seemed to drown in the swirl of antiquarian atmosphere. My own inner cadence seemed equally quelled so that now, I thought, I might enjoy a few moments of tranquillity before Flo arrived. Not that Flo shattered my serenity any – not that I was even serene – but with my first draught of ale this sequestered nook where old men played chess seemed to soothe me. Lull me into a time-honoured play of quasi-Dickensian characters in which I was merely one. I let my mind wend along the unexpected and life-changing events that long-lost rellies and shady benefactors might bring. A pleasant yet ludicrous pastime, made all the worse when at its height it collapsed, leaving you once more teetering on your beam ends. I steadied myself in the reflection of a dimpled warming-pan.

There are no shady benefactors, I thought to myself somewhat dramatically. Only pariahs, greasing the slippery slope with their wares. I saw myself just as I was – plain poor, though not needing pity. I needed a break, that's all. A leg up in life. Money I suppose.

'Cash.' I said the word out loud: 'Cashhh,' extending the last letters out. The sound was like the reprimand in the rustle of strict skirts – skirts that brought admonishment closer. Then a familiar swish, accompanied by the jingle of shrunken goat bells that I knew, without seeing, were sewn by lilac thread to the hem of Flo's clothes.

'Hiya,' she said, appearing in the doorway. By a trick of the light, she was as yet a silhouette and I couldn't see her face, but I could tell by the way she'd said hiya that she was smiling inanely. Smiling despite having counselled herself not to. In her mirror, getting dressed – don't smile. In her car, listening to music – don't smile. In her self-conscious steps coming here . . . The counsel actually came from goth band frontmen, from whose lyrics she drew much meaning.

I'd met Flo at the Ouse Bridge secondhand record and book exchange. She was browsing through LPs when I'd come in enquiring out loud if they had a copy of 'Emma', the Hot Chocolate record, except I wanted the cover version by the Sisters of Mercy. 'I think it's a B side,' I said. I wasn't a massive Sisters fan, but I wanted the record for the soundtrack to a short film I'd made after my best friend – Chris – had killed himself. He'd liked Hot Chocolate and the film began with 'Emma', a song about an unfulfilled life and subsequent suicide. I don't know if Chris liked the Sisters of Mercy, but I thought ending the film with a version that sounded – going purely on one listening – to have a kind of fitting emptiness about it might be good. I wasn't sure.

Flo reflexed at the mere mention of the band's name and, as the shopkeep was uhhm-ing and ahrr-ing, she interjected with a sudden outburst of her specialised knowledge.

'It *is* a B side,' she said. 'It's on the other side of –'

The grateful shopkeep – obviously a jazz buff with no head for goths – said 'Ah right. 'F wee gorr it then, shud jus' bi in there under S.' He pointed to the tiers of 'Rock' along one wall and returned to his jazz rag.

Essentially shy, Flo had gone back to her sifting, though by now she was too curious about me for it to hold her any. After all, I didn't correspond at all to what a goth would/should look like. Though I had potential – tall, skinny. Absent-mindedly I murmured the names of records that to Flo were gospel truths. She shot me glances that lingered, just falling short of something she seemed to want to ask me. Making a big thing of tossing back her long black hair, she rapidly scanned columns N, O, P and Q, which brought her right next to me.

Distractedly she flicked through Rs: Rainbow, Rod Stewart, Roxy Music. I was aware of her black nail varnish and fingerless lace gloves catching on the clear plastic record covers. Meanwhile, I was getting nowhere. Many of the albums were duplications of one another. I could tell she was itching to get me out the way and look herself, so when I picked out a wrong twelve-inch and began studying the listings she burst out, 'No, no, not that one!' And seeing how she meant to take over, I stepped back as her busy fingers deftly took up the search. She became silent and I had time to take her in. High black boots, black skirt, black corset contrasting with the paleness of white skin. Her breasts, I now saw, were very large and I found myself looking down her milky cleavage. Intuitively perhaps, she chose this moment to speak, and turning to me she said, 'Are yu just gettin' in t' th' scene?'

'Uh –'

She repeated: 'Are you just getting into the scene?'

'Er –'

Suddenly it seemed important not to disappoint her. She turned back to the records, waiting for my answer. Even the shopkeeper glanced up to see what I was going to say.

'– Er – to be honest wi' yer' – I lowered my voice a bit – 'I am just getting into the scene, yhea.' And I shot the jazz buff a look, returning him quickly to his paper.

She nodded and I perceived that my admission, though false, had kindled a new confidence in her breast.

'They ant god it,' she said, turning to me with finality. Eagerly she surveyed me, nakedly transforming me into the scene. I was beginning to feel depressed at the turn events had taken when she said, 'I've got it at home.'

It was, in a sense, a statement of intent, only it had come out too fast and we were both now wondering what to do with it. I was gloomily imagining myself in her room – a kind of shrine I fancied – and ending up sitting surrounded by records. Much like when my niece would take me gravely by the hand to inspect her Gonk collection.

Flo, on the other hand, was unconsciously blowing out one pan-white cheek then the other, as though slooshing from side to side what her parents would say when they opened their big posh door at the end of their long gravel drive to be confronted with me in tow.

I spoke first. 'That's – great.' Then hurriedly, 'So mehbi we could jus' meet up some time then y'know, for a drink . . .'

'And I can do y' a tape,' she cut in, relieved.

That was three months back. Since then – though I'd been unmasked as a non-goth – we'd carried on seeing a fair bit of one another, neither of us really knowing full why. Perhaps we were each other's summer. We didn't do much, neither of us liking each other's friends. We'd meet up in the chess room of the White Horse where it was safe – neutral.

'Hiya, Flo,' I said as her face emerged as though from dark water. The sudden greeting bombed my ruminations, and my reverie – not yet dug in – lay in tatters around me.

I half stood to kiss her but she was already delving dutifully for her purse in a large floppy bag sewn with mirror fragments. It was the way our greetings often got off – not so much on the wrong, but on no footing at all. While she rummaged I felt a fool half standing so I sat back down. On the table yesterday's candle wax had hardened into a pearlescent pattern. I chipped at it with my nail.

'You weren't at home,' said Flo, producing her purse, 'so I thought you'd be here.'

I nodded. 'Here I am.' Then thinking this sounded glib I added, 'I thort yu'd know tu cum 'ere.'

It'd been a hot half-mile up the hill from my place and she was sweating like a racehorse. Summer was hard on goths. She looked at me pleasantly, smiling with her blue eyes as if to say, I don't mind, I'm happy whatever, and in her hand she was proffering a crisp fifty-pound note.

'Drink?' I asked, moving imperceptibly to receive the fifty and clearing my throat.

'Jack Daniel's and Coke,' she said, sitting down and arranging her skirts.

Flo had an allowance from her father – who owned a brewery – the smallest denomination of which always seemed to be a new fifty. It never occurred to her to break them when she went to roughish pubs – not that the White Horse was rough, but most people's pockets were out and they usually bought drinks with towers of coins, slid like draughts pieces over the bar.

But then again Flo never went to the bar. Neither did she play chess. It was an understanding between us that when we were together she paid for everything. I cleared my throat a lot, but always took the cash – the sound of the word 'skint' had recently seemed to pronounce on my character and, cruelly, some of my friends had of late begun to call her my Cash Flo.

'Yes pal, kun 'elp yu there?' said the new landlord.

I ordered drinks and while he addressed the optics I said, 'Mr Morrison not in?'

He shrugged. A long map of sweat tapered down his shirt. He called to someone out back. 'Hast Mr Morrison bin in, Gill?'

'Yu wha'?'

'Morrison! Youth that plays chess at back?'

'Oh 'im, no, not bin in for daze,' came a woman's voice.

Setting down the drinks – even though I'd obviously heard – he said, 'No, iz not bin sin. Four fiti, pal.'

I handed over the note. 'Zee ahl right yu reckon?' I asked as he checked the fifty up to the light. Squinting, the landlord shrugged and pressed his lips into the full extent of his concern, which wasn't for trade, as old Mr Morrison made one pint last the whole night. The length of a chess game. Occasionally you'd see him – come last orders – carefully carrying an unfinished board to the bar for safe keeps. Above the bar was a stuffed weasel in a glass case that the taxidermist had seen fit to recreate making off with an egg. The new landlady – Gill – appeared in the doorway beneath it.

'It's just not like 'im,' I said to her.

'He knows the way 'ere,' she said.

I put the change from the fifty in my pocket and made my way back.

We got slowly steamed. With no one else around, Flo and I had the easy ability to make each other laugh. Half aware it mightn't last, we always drank too fast as though to keep ahead of what might come close on its heels – sex for one.

We'd not yet fucked or, shall I say, made love or aligned our bodies in any way that was intimate. But it wasn't like she was shy about sex; no. In fact – especially after drink – a boldness would come over her. Standing in the middle of the room, with a certain hang to her body, she'd fix my eye and slowly, one-handedly, undo the hooks at the front of her corset. Snapping her thumb and middle finger over the buttons, almost like a jazz siren slowly counting time. But as I say, we'd never fucked or made love. Sex acts, like blow jobs, were performed with rather exaggerated posture, as though demonstrating to a class – OK, this here's the penis, see now how I'm gonna take it in my mou-oouw-mm-mouth. Thus, I rarely came to be between her thighs. If my cock did chance to brush her lips in the silent language of *Is this OK?* she'd clamp me between her thighs and simulate an urgent fucking till I came – often, I believe, faking her own orgasm, but I couldn't be sure of this and we were a long way from being able to talk about it.

That night though, owing to the absent Mr Morrison and the balmy evening keeping everyone else out front, and, as I say, we were making each other laugh, and through drink, laughter turned to intimacy. Intimacy to daring. Daring heightened by the chance that Mr Morrison might any minute appear – my hand up Flo's skirt, hers burrowing down the front of my trousers.

'Hey c'mon,' I breathed, jumping every time I heard a sound, 'we can't do this here.'

'No,' she said grinning, 'but – I know –' and removing her hand from my flies – her many silver bangles jingling – she wriggled her fingers through a hole in my trouser pocket, ripping the seam wider till she was in.

Then very humdrum like, while lightly stroking my erection, she says, 'Hasn't the weather kept fine though?'

The booze had slightly inured me to Flo's caress and I found myself thinking again about Mr Morrison. One suit always pressed and worn, long grey hair and beard. He seemed to have no one in his life, maybe a sister somewhere but as far as I knew he lived alone. Inevitably that had turned people against him. 'He's weird in ee,' they'd say, telling their children not to play near him. And I'd shrug and wonder how he kept up the little twinkle in his raggedy countenance. It was odd but I somehow relied on it, that little light, so that without it – if it had grown dim I mean – or gone out . . .

'Wha's wrong?' whispered Flo. She nodded towards my crotch. 'Gone soft.'

I averted my eyes from Mr Morrison's unoccupied seat.

'Nothing really,' I said. 'Giz a kiss. Giz another . . . An' another.'

She was giggling now and I was hardening in her hand again.

'Yu whan nuther?'

'Kiss?'

'No. Drink?'

'Let's jus go back,' she breathed, her eyes widening to her own boldness.

'Right,' I said, and I downed my pint even though it was warm and I didn't need it.

In the main bar the new landlord was upending chairs on tables. He didn't look at us as we staggered out, nor did he say goodnight. When the cat the old landlord used to feed came in, he stamped his foot at it and it scarpered.

Lately, I'd begun to feel a little self-conscious about the way I lived, and I wondered if somehow the new landlord had got wind I was a squatter – in one of the old Georgian houses just down the rise. In its time that house would have been grander than anything he could imagine; it'd gall his kind to think of me not paying any rent.

I didn't give a fuck though. I loved the pub, the alcove and Mr Morrison and all, but the new landlord was *persona non grata* as far as I was concerned – bordering on corpus vile. And I wasn't going to let the surly image of him upending stools come between me and Flo. She'd slunk down against my chest, and as we stumbled and jogged down the hill she was holding on round my middle, the way you see a boxing trainer hold one side of a pummel bag – only Flo was giggling and the shrunken goat bells were jingling. When we reached the squat, a certain quiet descended upon us. We stole down the basement stairs where it was cooler than the street. I don't remember at what stage the door down there had become an impasse of junk, but for a while we'd been using the window as the entrance. Normally Flo could negotiate it, but being so drunk, I had to lift her on to the sill where she could let herself down. On the other side was the back seat of a car – a sofa that doubled as an easy landing.

It was dark inside and when I dropped through I half landed on top of her. She began to laugh and I began to kiss her laughing mouth till her giggles transformed into hungry sounds of encouragement. I was readily positioned between her thighs. Her skirt had ridden up and the goat bells were muted in the folds. A saliva bubble caught in the back of her throat accentuated her tiny gasps as my fingers wrenched the gusset of her knickers aside. She fumbled my zip and got my cock out. In a press-up position I eased down, pushing out my pelvis till the head of my cock was touching her lips and the lace of her knickers was rubbing one side of my glans. I tried to be as gradual as I could about it, as though any slip – a sudden lunge – could wake us both out of this. Gradual, I thought, grad-ual, grad–jew–ull. And the muted goat bells agreed. Flo held her breath and then, like fingers wriggling through a hole in my pocket, I was in. Her body tensed but she made no attempt or utterance to stop. Instead, she continually shifted on the back seat, small creaks of leather easing the passing of her virginity.

And, after what seemed like an age – in which I seemed to have sobered up some – we began to find some semblance of rhythm. My jeans were undone but not down and I didn't want to stop to remove them, even though it felt tight down there – uncomfortable. Flo hadn't really got me out properly and my foreskin – all the skin around my cock – was skinned back, trapped at the base of my cock behind the tangle of pants and flies. This proved to be a mistake or, should I say, this proved to be *the* mistake. I don't know when it happened exactly.

The doctors said it was unusual for the skin to be ripped so badly. And why, they wondered, hadn't I stopped? I didn't know. I do recall – my senses, though stultified by desire and alcohol had noted it – some new stress, giving way to some new sensation – not altogether pleasant. I assumed it was Flo's virginity.

The phrase 'split your banjo' was used by a jovial orderly in an attempt to lighten my concern. It's odd that it hadn't seemed so serious at the time, merely consistent with the general ructions around us. At the height of our fucking, a glass globe containing a plastic rose in water fell to the floor and smashed. Some empty beer bottles began to roll across the tiled floor picking up momentum as they went. I didn't hear them stop because a bicycle, propped somewhere, fell and the handlebars hit Flo on the head. She screamed, I came, and when I pulled my cock out it was covered in blood.

Looking at it, bathed in the orange street light filtering in from the window above, it took a few moments to see that the blood wasn't a virginal residue left by Flo, or even menstrual. It was too thick and fresh, and also it seemed to be somehow pumping out like an underground spring. My mouth was dry as I heard my voice saying, 'Ha-have you come on, Fl–Flo?'

She raised herself up, rubbing her head, and she looked at me puzzled for a second then our eyes met down at my crotch. Her hands covered her face and I heard the muffled 'Oh my God' between them. Blood was pissing everywhere. It was like I was weeing – powerless to stop. In rapid shock I made to try and back off from myself, to limbo out of my skin.

I could hear my voice and it seemed to spin round me getting louder. Then I realised I was screaming. I remember thinking, I'm passing out. I shut my eyes tight and pushed with clenched fists for some surface above. Bursting through, I breathed out, 'Holy Shiiit!' Blood was splashing out faster. It was on Flo, on her hands, on her face, trembling in red pools in the hollows of her thighs. I ran down the hall, yanked on the bathroom light, winced in the brightness. Just inside the door was a full-length mirror on a chrome stand, chucked out by the local boutique because it was cracked. Blood was spurting on to it. Two invisible karate blows took the back of my knees away. I hauled myself up using the side of the bath. Shakily I turned on the taps, full blast. I thought, get in the bath, that's best place. Get in the bath – it's contained. I needed to clean the blood away to see what was going on down there. So far I hadn't really felt pain, just this rubbery state of shock. But, as I tried to undress, the pain began – a worrying shooting pain in my scrotum, into my stomach. I got in the bath with my jeans on. I remember thinking – clear as a bell amid the turmoil – will I ever be able to use it again?

As the warm water lapped me, I groaned and let my head back. I closed my eyes. It did feel better to be in the bath and by and by I became calmer. What's happened? I thought. What the fuck has happened down there? As yet I still couldn't bring myself to look. I just lay there, vaguely conscious of the aggressive whirring of the Xpelair.

Into the incessant motor of the fan a pulsing grew, a deep pulsing that rose in the steam, throbbing a vein in my temple and pulsating behind my eyes. I felt like my life blood was pumping out. I reckoned I was losing too much, and that frightened me. I drew in a breath and, forcing my eyes open, started a nervy preamble down from the ceiling to my crotch. The second I saw the water I gasped. It was piranha-like – blood red – something like a rock suicide. When I recovered from the shock I saw that, despite the pulsing which was in my head, the bleeding had actually slowed down a bit. The underground spring effect wasn't pumping so vigorously now and it only sent occasional bubbles to the surface.

I felt a bit like crying but something held me back. I swallowed thickly and looked around. The whole bathroom was red. Every surface was splattered. Reflected in the mirror, behind the splashes that had dribbled to a translucent red veil, I saw Flo coming up the hall. She seemed to be in slow motion, unaware I was watching her – only I wasn't really, my eyes were just staring out that way and she didn't look real behind the red veil. Our eyes met in the mirror. She was fully dressed and clutching her bag in front of her crotch. The sight of her fully dressed and holding her bag like that made me feel suddenly worse.

33

'Are you all right?' she said, her eyes leaving mine and following the riotous splashes around the room to the red water and quickly back. 'Shall I . . . call an ambulance?'

'I'm fine,' I said. Funny how you say such things. 'I'll call –' I forgot there was no phone in the squat.

'Shall I –'

'S' OK. Flo –' I cut in. 'Jus' leave, ah'll – ah'll be fine. I jus' need y' know –'

I saw that she'd tried to clean the blood from her face with a paper hanky that she still had scrunched up in her lace glove. She remained a moment more, smiled weakly and left.

I don't know how long I lay there. The water got cold. I hauled out. The bleeding had slowed significantly. With difficulty I struggled out of my wet jeans. There was no towel but I found a hardened flannel that had been stopping up a leak under the sink. I softened it in cold water and wrapped it carefully round my cock and went to my room and with my stained body got into white sheets.

Three days went by. I'd done nothing. I lay in bed staring out the window, watching the troubled sunlight blitzing nettles in the overgrown garden.

Thus time passed. I'd think about having a look downstairs and try to raise some feeling for it, in my limbs, then capitulate. Occasionally a sound such as an ice-cream van would reawaken me to what I was supposed to be doing. I had no clock but I'd be amazed to see how much further the garden had grown into shade. I cast around. Normally I liked to keep the squat tidy – my room anyway – but all about lay various bits of things I'd used to swab the bleeding. Each one bore testimony to its slowing up till, eventually, it stopped and began to scab over. But the scabs didn't look great – they were like congealed brambles.

I'd still not told anyone. I didn't know the other people in the squat that well. There was Andrew Kidney – the New

Zealand guy who'd broke the squat – for some reason I thought I should try talking to him. He had a motorbike and I listened out for it, but it never came. Sometimes he could be gone days. Once, while dozing, I thought I heard Flo's voice calling in at the front window, but I wasn't sure and I didn't call back. The congealed brambles were hardening. It looked all wrong. The white sheets were flaked with the dried rust that had rubbed off my body. On the fourth day I decided I had to go to Outpatients. I found my jeans in the bathroom where I'd left them. They'd dried hard in the heat. No one had been in and the bath was still full of the bloody water which had darkened and begun to smell. In the pocket of my jeans there was still change from Flo's fifty so I got a cab.

The packed waiting room was sweltering. I'd have gladly swapped injuries with anyone there: broken arm, broken ankle, cut finger, bee sting. *Bee sting!* for crying out loud. I wanted to tell bloody bee sting to get the fuck behind me in the queue. I'd been there nearly an hour and, despite the heat, a cold pit sank in my stomach as I heard, 'Miller?'

'Uh yhea.'

'Harland Miller.'

'Yhea.'

'Room four please.' The receptionist indicated the direction, holding a clipboard in the air.

The doctor was a young woman – foreign, maybe Eastern.

'Good morning, Mistaar – mistaar – Miller. And how can we help you?'

'I – er – I uhm –'

She raised her eyebrows. 'Yes?'

'I've uhmm' – my hands made a roly-poly motion out in front of me – 'I've split my willy,' I said, conducting the words out quickly with my hands.

'Oh.' She was slightly taken aback. Not too much, to her credit. 'Uh huh, I see, well! Please take a seat. I'll be with you in a moment.' She began studying the form I'd filled in, and without looking up she said, 'If you could just pull your trousers down and we'll take a look.'

She expressed her eyes towards me professionally. Fingers browsing like a rare butterfly.

'You can get dressed again.' Lathering her hands, she raised her voice above the gush of a tap. 'You'll need stitches there and we'll be keeping you in overnight. Is there anyone you can call?'

'Hmm?'

'To bring you some things – and you'll probably need to be picked up, there'll be some little pain walking, not much, but you might want to take it slow at first.'

She said more in her clipped English, but to me it flowed melodiously, lulling me into a hamper of relief in which there was many delicious things to savour. This chair, for instance, what a comfy chair it was, and soap and the joy of towel-drying your hands, sunlight falling in strips across the wall; all of this was much better with a penis that was going to be OK. My worst fears – fostered over the three days of limbo – I now realised were ridiculous. She'd not panicked and there'd been no talk of cutting it off – none.

'Can I call my girlfriend?' I said.

She looked at me then, just a look while handing back the towel, a look she couldn't stop, as if to say, *indeed!* I was oblivious and wanted to kiss her, despite her professional distance, and it never occurred to me that she might be repulsed by my sex organ. As I beamed, I took the full meaning of her look and her *indeed!*

Back in the waiting room, looking round at what Flo's parents would have no hesitation in calling losers, I began to worry again. What would it look like after the op? Not something a girl would want to put into her mouth, that was for sure.

'Harland Miller? This way please.' I went with an orderly through a labyrinth of corridors and swing doors following signs that said Urology Ward in three different languages. 'Nearly there.' He pointed down one more corridor. At the far end two charwomen had mopped the floor into a glassy surface, across it a hasty banner read 'Good Luck Sue'.

'Sister's leaving,' said the orderly. There'd been drinks in paper cups and the two cleaners were both still wearing party hats: St Trinian's-style straw boaters – Kiss me quicks, Squeeze me slows. Sunlight filtered their chatting figures into silhouettes. As they leant on their brooms their long shadows lengthened down the glassy corridor like gondoliers with their poles.

We passed a door open into a TV lounge. Inside were mainly old men, all of them with problems downstairs, some with problems upstairs. One man stooped for a magazine – the movement was difficult for him. My bed was shielded from the rest of the ward by a white curtain like a windbreak on wheels. A nurse took over and patted some things. 'Put these on please, this is your bed.' She fingered her name badge. 'I'm nurse Rhodes or Sally if you like.'

'Sally's nice.'

'And how yu like to be called?'

I shrugged. 'Cun call me Harland – 'f y' like?'

'Harland! 's unusual iznit. Where's that from then?'

'Whitby, I think, it's on me ma's side anyroad, shiz from there.'

'Sort of old-fashioned really.'

'Oh yhea, there's plenny in the cemetery.'

We were both surprised that her polite small talk about my name, intended to steer clear of aught heavy, had ended so quickly in the graveyard.

'Now, Harland, just some questions.'

She asked me lots. What did I eat? How many times did I go to the toilet? When did you las—

'OK, that's great. Doctor Joseph'll bi along tu see yu in a minit.'

Laid out on the bed – bearing the indentation of her hand like a blessing – was the outfit worn by all. I put it on and felt assimilated. It was almost Moonie-like in that sense – when I say Moonie I mean the cult – mind you, it did have rather a large hole at the back. I got into bed. The sheets had the texture of Flo's money.

I must have dozed because I was awoken by the curtain ripping round. Sally was there again and with Dr Joseph. He smiled. 'I'm going to be operating on you tomorrow, just wanted to see you'd settled in all right – hmm?'

'Yhea fine thanks.'

'Just need you to sign this . . . thaaat's good. See you tomorrow then, bright and early, don't you be going anywhere now.'

I tried to rejoin in spirit. 'Oh no, I'll try not to,' I said, thinking, Don't you be going anywhere now with that gorged, butchered penis of yours, don't you be sticking it in Flo's mouth now.

They slipped through the curtain to the next bed.

'Mr Morrison! You haven't eaten much.'

Mr Morrison? I thought. I sat up. Mr Morrison. The movement of the curtain created a small chill through which I found myself eye to eye with . . . with . . . I hesitated. 'Mis-ter Morrison?' I said. He raised a smile and nodded, not half as surprised as I was.

'I heard you come in,' he explained. 'Thought it be you, thuz not many Harlands about, is thu.'

'But . . . what yu doing here?' I was so used to seeing him in the rich setting of the chess room, I had trouble fixing him in the bleached-out ward. He seemed to be just parchment, a paper apparition with a thin, dry voice. In front of him, instead of an absorbing chess problem, a dish going untouched. And they'd cut his beard off.

'Oh! That's nice,' said Sally, taking up his tray. 'You two know each other.'

We nodded.

'That's lovely. Someone for you to play chess with, Mr Morrison.'

*

38

That night, after tea, Mr Morrison set up the board and began talking. I noted that it was his own personal set, exquisitely carved, apparently there weren't two like it. He said he didn't go far without it and it was, in a manner of speaking, all he had. He talked more, a lot more, on and on without pause, and all about himself. I'd never heard him speak so much. He'd begun at the beginning with lots of 'when I was young' and 'not much older than you are now'. He quoted Mark Twain and talked on and around and all in parables and similes, so that as he wearied, I didn't know much more about him than when he'd begun. Of his illness he made light but he gave me a tip. 'When you go to the toilet, son, when you wee –'

'Yhea?'

'Do this! See if you can stop it – then start it again – try and control the flow. Hold it for a few seconds – then release. Do it, because as you get older you need that muscle. That's why you see so many of us older blokes with pissed pants, and blokes don't pass on information. They're too scared of illness and death, so we say nowt. Women talk all the time. They bleed, son, have babies, they're hard, resilient creatures, men are weak –'

'Uh huh.' I looked up.

'Check!' he said.

I looked down. 'Oh! Right . . . thanks,' I said, 'for the tip I mean, I'll try it.' I laid down my king, knowing I couldn't win now. Three or four more moves, at the most five, but I was beat.

Mr Morrison nodded. 'Aye, good,' he said, seeming tired by this last effort of talking. 'No point in dragging things out.'

'No.' I smiled and, as my king rocked, Mr Morrison pressed down on the arms of his chair, taking the weight from his sitting position. He grimaced, then easing himself down again said through slightly gritted teeth, 'You did well, son.' His nostrils flared at some unexpected twinge, then he let out a long sigh.

39

'I'll gi' yer wun las' thing,' he said, and for the first time I noticed his shallow, hampered breath.

'Yes.'

'Always castle early,' he breathed. 'If you're going to do it . . . don't wait till it's too late.'

I helped him into bed and plumped his pillow. Sighing down, he tried for a wink but it was caught away in an unexpected wince of pain. 'Phwooo cha bas – !' He closed his eyes.

'Can I get you something?'

He nodded, but as I waited he said nothing and presently I saw he was asleep.

'Mor-ning!' Activity round my bed. Curtains ripped round.

'Turn over please.'

As I turned, the sheets were pulled back – BANG! – A shot in the bum.

A booster. A trolley docked next to me and I was rolled on to it. Immediately we began moving. The rest of the ward was still asleep and we went swiftly in silence. Halfway down it I realised something. After the curtain had been folded back? In that little chill? It had barely registered at the time but – I twisted round and caught sight of Mr Morrison's bed – it was made.

'Easy there,' said the male orderly, placing a restraining hand on my shoulder.

'Just lie back,' whispered a nurse.

The sun was up but it hadn't yet reached the protractor-shaped windows set up high in the thick Victorian walls. 'Where's Mr Morrison?' I asked, but it was as though I hadn't spoken. If they responded at all it was to push me faster down the corridor. I was really on my way now; striplights passed by on this medicinal highway, just like the broken white lines of some nightmare journey in a dream. My heart began to race. We were all in a lift. The doors opened. We'd arrived. A face loomed in. 'Right, Harland, I want you to count to ten.' A needle was introduced into my arm and I began . . .

'Hiya, y' all right?'

'Oh, is he awake?'

Slowly, through the jangle of cutlery, jingle of goat bells, I made out a blurry white form busying over me – nurse. Between nurse's uniform, flashes of black at the foot of the bed – Flo.

'Hiya.' I blinked to bring them into focus.

'And how's Harland from Whitby feeling?' It was nurse Rhodes; she was holding up a covered plate. 'Like eating something maybe?'

Just the smell made me nauseous. I shook my head. 'No thanks.'

She tutted. 'Maybe a bit later.' She bent down to slide the tray back into the trolley.

'Sally?'

'Yes?' She looked up, frowning.

'Uhm, how er . . . did it . . .'

'Everything's fine,' she said. 'Oh bugger this thing.' She gave the tray a shove. 'There! Gotcha.' She stood up. 'Yes, Doctor's very pleased with you. He'll be along to see you later.'

'Flo!' I burst out, beaming with relief. I didn't know what to say so I just said, 'Hiya, *babe*!'

Flo turned to me, her blue eyes pleasant and wide, saying *isn't that great* – they were almost brimming with an inappropriate kind of pride. I smiled back.

'God, Flo,' I said. 'Damn, I'm sorry babe but av jus' – am bustin' fu t' lav.' She smiled without getting up, still sitting trapping me in. 'Er – yu'll av t' move, hun.'

As she stood I eased my legs out from beneath the sheets, my gown rode up, and between my legs wrapped in mummy cloth I saw my willy. Flo caught it too. I looked up. 'God! Tom and Jerry,' I said. It did look like an anvil had landed on it. I lowered my feet to the floor and as the gown repaired down, blood dripped on to the white tiles. 'Whoa, shit –

Sally!' I called. She looked over and I nodded her down at the blood.

'Oh – 's OK, you've had stitches, haven't you?'

'Yeah.'

'So, there'll be a few wee drops.' She turned to Flo pushing off with the trolley. She said, 'He'll live.'

I slumped back on my bed, feeling weak. My eyes came to rest on the clean white plain of linen on the next bed: tucked, plumped and cornered.

Suddenly remembering, I mumbled, 'Mr Morris . . . Mr Moh? Where's Mr Morrison?' I called.

Sally's back tensed. She stopped and reversed the trolley back a bit, then in a low voice said, 'Mr Morrison died last night.'

Out the corner of my eye I saw Flo reflex and turn from Sally to me and back.

'I'm sorry . . . You knew him, didn't you?'

Flo's head was still going between us. I nodded.

'Did you know him well?'

I shrugged, feeling a sudden hoarse thickness at the back of my throat. At length I said, 'I don't know, yeah . . . maybe?'

'Mister Mr Morrison?' asked Flo.

On the way out of the ward with my things, limping a bit, we passed Sister's office. Sally was in there, drinking from a paper cup left over from the party. I waved and she started when she saw me, spilling a little juice down her chin. 'Hey,' she called, wiping it away and waving for me to stop. Then she was standing in the doorway. In her arms was Mr Morrison's chess set. Oddly, I'd known it. I'd heard it a fraction beforehand – just the familiar rattle of the chess men when she'd picked up the box – the sound she made when she shook them and said, 'These were going down to the bereavement office.' She held them out to me. 'But I think he would have liked you to have had them. To be honest, there doesn't seem to be anyone else.'

Outside the hospital grounds I smelt reprieve in the late summer air. I breathed in deep. Castle early, I thought, and as we walked off – goat bells jingling distantly – Mr Morrison's chess set was digging into me in a way that I didn't mind at all.

The Quick and the Dead 2
Joolz Denby

Bradford

The café in the shopping centre is pretty crap really; well, very crap to be honest. The centre isn't up to much either, come to that. It used to be, years ago, but the big out-of-town complexes put paid to any dreams of retail heaven for the low-level chain stores that clump wearily round its inside edges, like wilted wallflowers at the youthie dance. Sometimes whoever runs the place tries to mod it up by having little stalls in the main aisle, flogging posters or make-your-own-name bead bracelets or livid-coloured water gel you can put in glass vases for flowers. Sometimes brightly painted young lasses in corporate uniforms try and get you to sign your soul away to the leccy board. Or fat, dispirited blokes try and offload insurance on you as you 'sorry, sorry' straight past them.

The café never ceases to fascinate me, though, rather in the way a dead jellyfish fascinates children at the seaside. You can't believe a thing like that could ever have been *alive*. It was meant to be a modern, genteel replacement for the old utilitarian café on the balcony floor where, in the old days, various representatives of Bradford's disaffected youth hung out, ratting up their punk coiffures and spending all afternoon gossiping over cups of cold, weak coffee and singed teacakes lathered with not-quite-off butter. But all that was swept away in a burst of early nineties enthusiasm; the café concession was sold to a catering company and relocated beside the

44

escalators on the ground floor, next to the cheap jeweller's and opposite the posh frock shop.

In the café area itself, there's a circle of glass display cases full of beige cakes, which have apparently been knitted from extruded polyester, and teetering stacks of yellow cheese sandwiches foaming with cress. These grease-sheened cabinets are drawn round the till like covered wagons grouped against an Apache attack, defending themselves against the sprawl of untidy tables blobbed with grazing customers.

Next to the escalators are two curious green-painted gazebos, like garden furniture gone AWOL, each with a couple of tables in them. They're raised up a step so they give the impression of two little bandstands. It's very disconcerting sitting in them, or indeed near the escalators at all. People riding the crawling metal stairs hang over the rubber handrail and gawp at you while you stuff greasy food in your face. They point you out to their turnip-headed mates who are gormlessly picking their noses and flicking the results over the handrails. *Fookinell*, they go, *look at that . . .* It doesn't take much inventiveness in a sartorial or body-art way to be an object of interest in the shopping centre. Really.

Normally, I sit near the cakes; out of the way, peering myopically at whoever's in. As bad as the escalator folk, in my way, I suppose. I used to know the previous manageress, Shaz, until she left for better things. We'd talk for hours, sitting in the designated smoking area, while she puffed on a Benson and constantly surveyed the area as if it were a potential war zone – which, actually, it is. I liked Shaz. She always laughed uproariously at any quip I made and told me I was a scream; how can you not like someone who does that? But she left, so it was no more free hot chocolate and gossip, unfortunately.

That Saturday, the café was pretty full. My usual bolthole was occupied by a big fat Heavy Metal lass in a sleeveless, neckless, modified T-shirt with a screaming skull design that showed her greying bra straps and the tiny Celtic motif tattoo that swam ineffectually on the great ham of her arm. I have no quarrel with fatness; but it makes me irritable to see a tiny tat on arms that could encompass greatness, that could boast swathes of heroic ink. As my friend Steve used to say, *If in doubt, go flat out.* Admittedly, he was referring to motorcycling but it applies to tattooing as well.

I took the spare table in the left-hand gazebo.

I was not alone. The other table was occupied by at least six or seven girls; prostitutes from the Lane. I knew they were on the game. They had that night-pallid, drug-waxy complexion that looks so luminously decayed by daylight; their make-up was applied archaeologically, layer over layer over layer. It scummed in the hairline of their tightly scraped-back gelled hair that exploded in topknots of crispy perm curls. White, black, Asian and every mix possible, they all had the same style. Old mascara crumbed in the corners of their pulled-back eyes, and their lips were unsteadily outlined in deep plum and filled in with the remnants of a mauvish nude colour, mostly bitten off or coffee-ed away. They smelt of cheap, fake-designer scent and mildewed leather. Their cigarettes laid a thick bluish pall in the air like a sea fret at dawn.

They were listening to a thin, beaky Asian girl dressed in a grubby, rose-pink shalwar kameez, her tatty, gold-fringed dupatta trailing to the floor, a whey-faced baby in a mango-yellow snowsuit lying prone on her bony knee. She was telling a tale and her audience gasped, tutted and bridled appreciatively as she spoke. Sometimes one of them would take the baby from her and pass it round the group, wreathed in fag smoke; sometimes they would pass the storyteller a lighted cigarette. Their beautiful eyes were glowing with attention, like seals; huge, round and liquid. Their faces were brilliant, engaged. I kept as still and quiet as I could and shifted imperceptibly towards them so I wouldn't lose a word.

'Take the babby, Marie. There, little bless, isn't he *cute*. Oh, I could weep when I think about what I'm to tell him about his auntie when he grows up. I mean, what can I say? Awful.' She bridled and sighed heavily, rearranging her dupatta, dragging on her ciggy; her accent that sing-song hybrid of Yorkshire and Karachi, but mostly Bradford.

'I mean – even this . . .' She plucked at the shiny imitation silk of her kameez, lifting a pinch of the skirt to show the others who murmured in sympathy. 'This were hers. You knew Pinkie, everything pink she had. Clothes, shoes, undies; all her room were pink and all. All good stuff, I couldn't bear to chuck it out. We're just the same size too; well, that's sisters, isn't it? Only a year between us but I tell you, she looked after me better'n our mam ever did – pathetic *she* were, oh yeah.' She puffed furiously on her fag for a second, unshed tears glittering in her long eyelashes.

'I knew he were up to summat that night – I did, you know. We was so tired; we'd had a pizza and I were watching a vid. Pinkie went off to bed, knackered she were, said she were done in. *I'm off up now, Sal, don't you stay up all night now, you need your kip* . . . That's the last thing she ever said to me, that is, the last thing, the last . . .'

Sympathy swept round her listeners like a wave, like a salt breeze through sand dunes. They made the ritual noises of concern; *ey, poor thing, ooh, awful*. They clicked their tongues and waited while the girl fussed with her clothes and settled back again.

'Anyways, see, first I heard was him knocking on the door, like. *Lerrus in, Pinkie, lerrus in*. Well, I thought, I'm not having him in here, bothering her int middle of the night – coz I knew it were him, I knew it were. So I goes t'door and opens it ont chain a crack and gives it: *Bugger off, Naz, she's sleeping*. Well, he goes fookin' mental, right? Starts mekkin' a right racket so I gives it, y'know, *Shurrup, you'll wake her!* But 'e just stands there int rain, that stupid yellow car parked all crooked outside like he just dint care. *That bloody banana car*, Pinkie used to call it. She thought he were a right idiot, honest – just another lad, y'know?'

47

The girls nodded, inhaling fiercely, recrossing their legs and hugging themselves. Their expressions and the set of their bodies showed that they knew all right; that sort of lad, all mouth and trousers . . . She wobbled her head and stuck out her jaw, acknowledging the shared experience of punters and their inexplicable ways.

'So, he's going fookin' nuts outside and y'know the trouble we've had with neighbours and that, so I goes, *All right, come in but shurrup, right?* And he does, soaking wet and a right funny look on his face, like kid with a new toy. Grinning, like. So I goes, *You're not staying, she's in bed, let her alone, she don't wanna see you any more, geddit?* But it's like he's not hearin' me, y'know? Like I int there, and he starts talking but to isself almost, just going on and on and then I realise, see, he's whizzin' off his block and I think, oh shit, I should never have let him in.

'Honest t'God, I didn't know what ter do for t'best, so I goes, *Naz, Naz, you gotta go, go on.* But he don't hear me and I can't shift him – he's a big lad – so I then thinks, OK, I'll get Mo ont phone, get him ovver, like. He'll be mad, but otherwise I'll never get shot of this 'un. So I goes for t'phone and Naz is still on about how much he loves Pinkie and how she's like a film star and so beautiful – which she were, she were – and how she's ter marry him, and come off the game, an' they'll go 'ome and have a family and all that . . . Course I'm thinking *Oh yeah, she'd love that, her, a load of brats and stuck out int middle of nowhere wi' t'fookin' mother-in-law, really.* And before I realise it, like, he's off up the bloody steps.'

She paused, taking a sip of coffee, and I realised she knew, they all knew I was listening. There was a long moment then, a long considering moment while they all said nothing in a meaningful way. Then it passed and her odd, flat voice started again, reciting the story as if she were making it into an old ritual tale like the ones recited by storytellers in distant market places, the chants ringing through the smoke of the dung fires and into the sapphire of the icy desert night. A story like the wind, coming from a far place, ancient and terrible, that you feel in your body instead of just hearing.

Except this was Bradford: urban, grimy, western, and this girl wasn't speaking of Alexander and Roxanne, but of herself and the sharp, cutting pain she needed to dull by repetition, so she could distance herself from its savagery, so she could *live* with it. I knew from the sound she'd told this part over and over, and that the women had heard it all many times but that it didn't matter, they wanted to go with her through the journey of it.

'Y'see, I thought – she thought – I mean, *everyone* thought he were just an idiot, a lad wi' too much money wanting a bit of a wild time, that he'd pack it in and get wed t'some village lass his folks got for him, y'know. Go all religious, like they do. He were nowt, nowt to her; she just took his money like any other.

'I heard the bang, see, then I knew. I knew what he'd done. I screamed, screamed me head off and he come staggering down t'stairs all shaky like, wi't thing in his hand. I tried t'get past him, t'get to her, but he took hold of me and said, *I wanted to show her I were a man, I just wanted her t'love me* . . . Then he were off, and I ran upstairs.

'Oh, oh, it were awful, awful I tell you; blood all ovver, blood and stuff all soaking inter that big pink satin headboard, blood all ovver everything and her poor head, all the back gone, all her 'ead – oh, awful – and the stink, the . . . But I thought, see, she might still be all right, she might – so I rush back downstairs t'phone and dials 999 like they say to do, but they wouldn't have it, they wouldn't come, like, and me begging them. They kept sayin', *Calm down, Miss, just calm down*. But I couldn't, I couldn't and they wouldn't come. Just some fookin' trouble ont Lane, y'see, that's what they thought. Oh, I know, one of t'coppers as good as said it. Just some fookin' prossies on the Lane. But it were Pinkie, Pinkie, an' she were dead, he'd shot her dead.

'It took them more'n half an hour t'come. Coppers and ambulance. I were frantic, I tell yer. I kept phoning and running ter look out the window and running t'street – I couldn't stop shaking, I threw up and everything. It were awful, really; just awful. Then they come and took her away t'Infirmary but she were dead. All that blood . . .

'He got off 'ome – his family sent him off the next morning, Mo said, on a plane, back in Pakistan that evening. Coppers did nowt. *You lot*, they kept saying, *you lot don't mek it easy for yourselves*. Well, what d'they expect? Honestly. So that were that. Now . . .'

This was the moment we'd been waiting for. The women leant forward, supple, intent, while Sal adjusted her dupatta again and took the baby back on to her knee, where it lay immobile in its stiff padded suit like a doll.

'See, he's back. Oh yeah, come back last week, Mo says. It's bin a year, like, he's safe enough, he reckons. So last night, he comes round, like before, int middle of t'night, in another stupid car. Me, I nearly had a fookin' heart attack when I sees who it is – not that I hardly recognised him, all smartened up and dead thin. Looks ten year older, and all, no word of a lie. So he starts on wi' the *can I come in for a minute?* business and I thinks, oh yeah? What's *he* want, I'd like ter know. So I lets him in, dead cold, like. Just stands there with me arms folded and gives him daggers. 'E's nearly crying, see, and I wanna know what he's up ter.

'*I want yer t'know*, he gives it, *I want yer t'know that I'm right sorry about what I done. I were a kid then, a kid – and the drugs and – I'm changed now, I'm different, see; I seen the error of me ways like, I go to t'mosque – I'm getting married, and I . . .*

'*Oh*, says I, *sorry now are yer? You killed Pinkie, you killed my sister and you dare come back here* . . . You should have seen his face, dreadful! Then he gets all shaky like, and he fishes around in his pocket then brings out a big handful of gold jewellery, real stuff from 'ome, like, earrings and necklaces and such, and gives it, *Here, tek this, tek it, there's more, Sal, more – and tickets for back 'ome, whatever you want, anything only . . .*

'Only keep yer mouth shut, is what I think he's on about. Only it isn't. It isn't.

'Only forgive me, Sal, forgive me. Tek the stuff, tek it. I'm so sorry for what I done, so sorry. I can't live wi' it, I can't, I dream of it, I dream of 'er at night, I wake up screaming. I'll do anything, anything, only, Sal, please, for the love of Allah, forgive me.

'Oh my God, oh my God – I knew what it were then. Blood money. Blood money for my Pinkie. I give him such a look, oh, such a look. I could have killed him dead wi' a look like that. *Get outta my house*, I says, *get out and don't you never come back, see? Forgive yer? Forgive yer? For murdering my sister? Never. Not ever. You get out and stay out – and tek your fookin' blood money wi' yer!* I did. I did. And he went, crying his eyes out like a kid, the bastard. Forgive him! Hah! Never.'

The others breathed a chorus woven of *no!* and *he never!* and *fookin' hell, Sal, y'do right*. Sal sat back, her face an ivory mask, bouncing the baby on her knee. She looked at me sharply and took a cigarette from her pack.

'H'excuse me, have you gotta light?' she said, leaning across to me while the others, who all had lighters, looked away.

'Er, no, sorry, I don't smoke. Sorry.' Too many sorrys, but it didn't matter. She smiled slightly and the others let their collective gaze drift back to me curiously.

'That thing in yer lip, does it hurt?' she asked judiciously, pointing at my labret stud.

'Does it . . .? No, er, at least, not now, not at all.'

'Well, you're braver'n me, *I* wouldn't do it, I hate pain, me.'

The others nodded, their skinny eyebrows raised to crescent moons. I was dismissed and they went on picking the carcass of the story.

As I walked back up the Leeds Road, the golden afternoon light casting long, fingery shadows over the fruit and vegetables, bags and fabrics, plumbing supplies and old fridges that tumble out of the clusters of little shops, a phrase kept dinning in my head. A proverb from a place where these things are better understood than in this cold, cramped island . . .

Revenge, it goes, *is a dish best eaten cold.*

Getting the Fear

Tina Jackson

Leeds

This is what it's like.

It's an ordinary day. You're at work, features editing on a high-minded independent which you produce on a shoestring out of a biscuit tin. You're a workers' co-operative; this means that at any time sorting out the fire alarm can take priority over your deadlines. The computers are made out of plastic cups and bits of string. The typesetting machines are museum pieces. You joke that they're made out of baked-bean tins but they were probably current before baked beans were put in tins.

You work in the low-rent end of Leeds, well away from the chichi arcades. Your office is beyond Kirkgate Market, under a railway bridge, squeezed in between the Aids Advice Centre and the back of Back to Basics, which is where the hippest of the club crowd spend their weekends. Along the road there's the lesbigay pub the New Penny, a goth shop that sells hair dye and PVC trousers, and a takeaway where you get your mushroom and tomato toasted sandwiches. These are your staple diet; you have them every lunch hour with a packet of Seabrooks cheese and onion. Crinkle cut.

You never have a day off. One week there is a bug going round and the art director finishes a page, goes off, throws up, comes back and starts cutting and pasting the next one. The next day it's your turn.

You do it for love because there isn't any money. Week in,

week out, you put your paper out because you believe in old-fashioned things like freedom of speech, social justice and human rights. You are willing to work all the hours God sends.

So there you are, at your overflowing desk in your ramshackle cubicle, frantically writing stuff and scowling at the news editor's Brillo-pad hair in the adjoining partition. You wonder if he'll still think you're a fluffbrain with lipstick after he's read your women in prison feature and the piece on Yasmina Khan, the new literature officer at Bradford City Council.

The phone rings. As it does hundreds of times a day. You pick it up and say the paper's name. You're on automatic pilot. There's a voice on the line and you sit there stunned as you realise it's not talking to you. It's threatening you.

– This is Combat 18, it says. – We're watching you, you left-wing scum, we've got our eye on you and things are gonna start happening.

You've heard of Combat 18, but only recently. You know they're a paramilitary branch of the BNP. The '18' stands for Adolf Hitler's initials, first and eighth in the alphabet. 'Combat' speaks for itself. They're the sort of people who used to go Paki-bashing, before they realised the Asian community would fight back. Now it's your turn.

You put the phone back in its cradle and you're shaking. You interrupt the news editor, who hates being interrupted, to tell him what's happened. He looks at you as if you're the kind of person who stands on a chair and screams if they see a mouse.

– That sort of thing happens all the time when you're fighting the system, he says airily. The news editor is a veteran anarcho. He probably wishes that we printed the magazine on hand presses, standing up to our knees in sewage. A bit of confrontation is like a bar of chocolate to him. His idea of a sex symbol is Astrid Proll. He has never forgiven the *What's On* editor for introducing club listings, or you for writing about pop culture. He never admits that you do it in a liberationist, equal-ops kind of way. He probably doesn't bother reading it. So you are still a fluffbrain in his book, which doesn't make you feel good. But now you're a frightened one and that feels much worse.

Later, you tell some of the other workers what happened. You are taken more seriously because they are nicer than the news editor and it has happened to one of the other women. The same morning. She thought it was a crank call but now she is frightened too.

You don't want to lose face by going to bits in the office. You don't want other people beside the news editor to think you are a fluffbrain. So you keep it together. You try to think of a few gags to cover your fear. But no one has ever phoned you up and threatened you before. You think someone is following you all the way home. When you get there you phone your best friend in the whole world and it just spills out.

She takes you very seriously. Combat 18 have just been in the news for firebombing another radical paper and breaking the presses at the Anarchist Press. But these were in London. You knew about them but it hadn't occurred to you that it might happen in Leeds too.

You wish your friend was here. But she's in London. You wish the man you love was here, but he's in America and he's fallen in love with someone else. He hasn't told you this yet, but you can tell. When he calls, he's different. It's not your fault, you can tell from his voice, but his voice is different from when he loved you. You know without him saying so that he can't be there for you, so telling him about the call would only make you feel more desolate, like you're trying to hang on to him by getting his sympathy. You sit on your sofa with your arms wrapped round your legs and you don't feel safe in your flat, which has always felt so safe before. You just feel very small and scared and alone.

The part of you which has not grown up thinks, why me?

But it isn't just you.

Over the next few days, some of the others get calls too. You get a couple as well. This is Combat 18, they say. It's always the same voice: martial, unrelenting, chilling. *We're watching you*, it says, *and somebody's gonna get hurt*. But it's just phone calls. You wait for something to happen and it doesn't, it's just another phone call. You tell the police, who don't approve of you, especially not after the 'Pigs Might Fly' headline you put on a cover story about going up with the police helicopter, but they come round and listen. Keep us informed, they say. That's about it.

The calls go on. They're still the same and very frightening but somehow not so bad because you're not the only one. But then you realise what that means and it's worse, not better.

The callers always phone the women workers. You get another one which says almost the same thing as usual, but adds that he's *gonna kill you*. The news editor still looks as if he's above it all and doesn't know what you're so worried about, but everyone else is edgy. The male members of staff – guess who excepted – make a point of answering all the phones in gruff, masculine voices.

You think about it all the time. You look over your shoulder when you leave the office, particularly when you go under the railway bridge. It is always in the dark because you always work late. You try to leave with another worker. You only feel safe when you get outside Marks & Spencer's. You try not to go out at lunchtime because you don't want to be seen leaving the office, although everyone takes turns getting the mushroom and tomato toasted sandwiches. You try to sneak in quietly in the morning. You avoid anyone's eye on the bus, because you think if anyone looks at you it's because they've got you in their sights.

If Combat 18 actually saw you all they'd realise your lot couldn't punch their way out of a wet paper bag. Weedy, intellectual lefties; soft skinhead gayboys; pretty drug messes from various clubland scenes; a woman with Aids, another with MS. The toughest thing you have in your armoury is Diva, the outspoken butch who writes a brilliant column on the Out page, but she only comes in the office every few days. And her attitude is only in her writing.

Your being a soft target doesn't deter your persecutors. They might have an equal fight with the industrial, shaven-headed boys from Nail Records up the road near the Corn Exchange, who got bricks through their windows for stocking anti-racist records. But they save most of their venom for you, because you write words and publish them and words are the most powerful things in the world.

You get used to it, and you get angry. Every weekend while you're at home, Combat 18 come and paint swastikas outside of your office. Every Monday morning, in the co-op meeting, you decide whose turn it is to paint out the graffiti. When it's your turn, you feel defiant as you stand outside with a big brush and a pot of paint. You make lots of brave jokes about it. You feel like, *Come and have a go if you think you're hard enough*. You definitely don't feel like a fluffbrain. Even the news editor appears to enjoy the blitz spirit which has taken over.

You keep a lot of PO boxes for various groups, and people come in all the time to collect their post. You don't always know who they are, but they pay good money to have a PO box so you have to let them in. So one day when someone asks to come in and get their post, and you don't recognise him, you let him in. He's followed by two other people and you don't recognise them, either. You're not quite on your own, there's the printer out the back, but you have to stay where you are because of the phone. The three men pick up their post and start poking round the office. You ask them not to, but you can't follow three of them round at once. One of them goes behind the partition but comes straight out again.

Later that afternoon, you realise the news editor's contacts book has been stolen.

Much later, Combat 18 call again.

– We've got your numbers, said the voice. – Now things are really gonna start.

You call the police. They take this quite seriously. They come round and ask a lot of questions. They tell you not to let the PO box people in any more. The contacts book was full of numbers of MPs, local councillors. You're desperately glad they didn't take your book, which has all the contributors' names in it: the soft lefties, the sweet clubbers, the gentle gayboys, the fiery dyke, the women with Aids and MS.

Then there's a film released. It's called *Romper Stomper* and it's about right-wing violence. There are demonstrations when it's shown in Bradford. People want to get it banned, saying it glorifies the far right at a time when there's a resurgence of extreme activity. The film critic gets an advance copy on video. You take it home and curl up in the corner of your sofa. You watch it.

It is the most frightening film you've ever seen. It's not a good film, not well plotted or concieved or conceptualised. It's just brutal. It shows exactly what happens when someone gets beaten up, how someone is kicked and punched until they are nearly dead, until they are a bloody pulp, until their bones are shattered beyond mending, until their eyes are ruined and they are spitting blood and teeth. You're used to screen violence which is flash and extreme and quickly over, but this is relentless. It goes on and on, and because you know this is what Combat 18 would do to you or the other workers, it's personal.

When you get into the office on Monday, you write an editorial about it. You tell anyone who might be interested that while people were picketing the release of the film this is what could be happening on your own doorstep.

Two days later is press day. This means you stay in the office until the paper is finished. The typesetters go home and it is just you and the art director, making sure that each page has all the headlines and captions, no faults anywhere. If there's a word wrong, the whole line has to be cut out, reset and pasted back in. You spend half the time processing the film in the darkroom; you wear tatty clothes on Wednesdays because the chemicals spatter you and ruin anything decent.

It's pitch black outside and there are no street lamps near your office. You're in your partition proofreading copy when something heavy strikes the glass window. Then there is a hammering on the door. Something tells you not to answer it. Then the phone rings. You pick it up.

– This is Combat 18, says a familiar voice. – We're outside. You better watch it.

They do the now familiar Seig Heil and put the phone down.

Your heart is pounding. You go round to the art director and tell him, very calmly, what has happened. Then you pick up the phone and dial 999.

The police take you seriously.

– We're on our way, they say. – Straight away. Lock the door and don't let anyone in until we arrive.

Somebody is outside. They're throwing stones at your window. They're shouting at you. You're terrified.

The art director bravely locks the door. You prowl around with metal chair legs for protection. You wouldn't know what to do with them in a fight but having them in your hands makes you feel better. The art director is brilliant. He does what he can to reassure you, which doesn't help much, but helps. He's got trendy round glasses and a First from Cambridge, and he does the Class War newsletter from the office in his spare time. He doesn't let on how scared he is, but you know he is, very.

The police arrive. They arrange for you to have a special tap put on the phones so they can trace calls. They tell you to let them know of any developments.

It doesn't stop you from having to leave the office in pitch darkness and walk down the deserted street to the bus stop, because you have to get the paper out that night whether

Nazis are banging on your doors or not. Every step of the way is like walking on broken glass, until you're outside Marks & Spencer's where it's light and there are other people.

That weekend they don't just graffiti the outside of the office. They smash the door and windows in.

You get a steel door. The police insist on this. The windows are reglazed. You don't have the money to pay for this. The next weekend they can't do the door, so they break the windows again. You can't afford to get them reglazed a second time, so you leave them boarded up. It's like working in a bunker: a war zone.

You phone the news desk of the liberal broadsheet newspaper, the one you read. You want someone to know this is going on. You hope they'll be interested, supportive even. They're not all that interested. You keep telling them, *please, listen*. Eventually they ask you to write something, not for the news, where you think it should go, but for the media section; they don't run it. There was something London-based on the radio that we had to cover, they tell you when you ask why your piece didn't go in. Oh, London. You're off the map, north of the Watford Gap.

You keep the metal chair leg under your desk. You jump whenever the phone rings. You hold your breath whenever anybody answers it. You've lost nearly a stone since all this started. You live on fags. You realise it's starting to get to you.

The man you love phones up in the middle of the night one night and you tell him. He's just got back from America and he's terribly upset and shocked, but not in the way you are when the person you care about most in the world is living through this. You can tell the difference. He says he'll call you the next day and at what time. You sit next to the phone and watch it ring and ring and ring. Then you sit in the bath and cry until you are empty.

Everything is awful. You only get out of bed because someone has to get the paper out. You lie there in the dark and think, *why?* You look at your body and wonder why. You wonder why all the time.

Your best friend in the world is wonderful. Over and over she says, leave, just leave. Come to London.

Workers start to hand in their notice. They can't take the fear. Once you've got the fear, it grows.

You stay. You feel responsible for something. You feel you have to prove something.

Business is terrible. You have no money. The printer is one of the people who leaves, and his print shop subsidised the paper. You can't afford to pay yourselves any wages.

Soon there are hardly any of you left. The news editor leaves. He says he's disillusioned with how apolitical people have become these days. You feel some satisfaction that you've managed to hold on longer than he has. You don't know what happens to him afterwards. The art director gets a good job designing for the local paper. It's the sort of thing his idealistic former self would never have done, but you can't blame him.

You're out of the office on a job when one of them buzzes the bell, barges past the clubs editor and starts Seig Heil-ing and smashing things up in the office. But you are there the day the police detective runs in to warn you that Combat 18 are round the corner, tooled up, waiting to come down en masse and destroy you. They don't come because they get a tip-off that the police are aware of them, but you spend the day strung out, waiting for the worst.

Waiting to get beaten up.

Waiting to be beaten.

Waiting.

After that, members of the extreme left come to sit in your office, armed with baseball bats, boasting about their own ultraviolence.

You hear them plotting actions to take place in London during the largest anti-racist march the country has ever seen.

During the march there's a riot. People are hurt. Some of them are the police, most of them are innocent. You hear the word infiltrators. You remember the gloating you heard in your own office and you feel sick.

The next day, a shaven-headed bloke in an army jacket approaches you. You're by Leeds Town Hall, nowhere near work, on your way to visit a friend who lives at the back of the university. You don't know the man but you would have said he was a meathead, not a crusty or a trendy. He calls you by your name. You run away.

Shortly afterwards, you leave. You feel awful about going. But you can't stay any more. You're not the only one.

You go to London. Your best friend moves abroad. You're given a room by a friend of a friend who's so sympathetic he tells you to pay when you've got some money, and not to worry. You spend a month being the quietest mouse possible so as not to disturb him. You bump into the man you love in the local pub, back from Los Angeles for a while without letting you know. He's so shocked to see you that you know it is irreconcilably over. You bump into a magazine editor, who is one of the kindest and cleverest people you've ever met. You tell him why you've moved. He gives you work. He is black and gay, and although he doesn't write about politics, everything he writes is political. You're more grateful to him than you've ever told him.

It is only a matter of weeks before your old paper folds.

It's months before the addresses from the news editor's stolen contacts book are printed in Combat 18's newsletter. When this becomes known and pillars of the local community receive death threats, it's taken very seriously. Questions are asked in the House of Commons. The CID come down all the way from Leeds to interview you.

They ask you what a nice girl like you was doing writing for a paper like that.

Eventually you get a full-time job for another paper you feel you can really believe in. In time, Combat 18 turn their attention to football hooliganism. A television documentary shows how near they were to killing another journalist and how dangerous they were before their leader was caught and imprisoned.

It turns your blood cold.

Years pass.

Over three weekends, nail bombs explode in Brixton, Brick Lane, Old Compton Street. Right-wing extremists claim responsibility. Combat 18 are one of them. There is carnage. The entire country is shocked to the core. You hear of papers getting death threat letters.

Your editor tells you that there's been a phone call to the office, threatening to kill someone.

You're like jelly for the rest of the day. Everyone who knows you says, *this isn't like you*. But you think, it's started again, and your body remembers getting the fear. The news editor – kinder than the old one – walks you out of the office. You check for murderers in the skip outside.

You make a joke about it the next day. But you let voice-mail take all your calls and you keep glancing behind you as you walk to work.

Most of the time you don't know it's there. But once you get the fear it sits on your shoulder for the rest of your life.

Wrong Footing
Lesley Glaister

Sheffield

The day after the last time she saw him, she went to Stanedge
Edge. Grey rock reared up against her, against the rock-grey
sky. The wind blew salty water from her eyes.

The night before was as frivolous in her head as the
daffodils she'd bought. A crinkled crush of them yelling their
throats out from the vase. White vase on a pale blue cloth.
She'd zested lemons and folded salmon steaks in foil, chilled
Chablis in the fridge, thawed a raspberry meringue. It was a
meal for spring and in the city spring was what it was.

The thing with fish, you mustn't overdo it. Everyone knows
that, but still, how awful to get a raw bit, a cool sliver still
translucent. That's what *she* thinks, though he likes sushi
and has even eaten steak tartare. The very thought of it makes
her heave, blood leaking into sticky yolk. And he likes violent
films, not *likes* exactly, he says, but he goes to see them
anyway. The time she hid her face in *Reservoir Dogs* he
laughed at her and rolled his eyes. She had to seal her lips
against the nag – death's not a joke, et cetera.

Not that he's violent. Not at all. Just full of appetite and
relish. More than that, of *hunger* for something just out of his
reach. He used to be a climber. Took a fall in Chamonix, a
shattered hip, a blood clot on the brain. He's OK now. No
climbing though, just the walking, walking, walking and
never getting there.

That last evening she wore a long pale skirt, a silky sweater,

64

clingy white. He liked the way it clung. He liked her blonde-
ness, it turned him on, he said, the contrast, the red sexiness
of her under the cool façade. *He* called it a façade. He liked to
cram his mouth with her or slide his hand up her leg under a
restaurant table, hook a finger inside her underwear, watch
the struggle on her face to retain her cool.

First time they met was in a railway station queue. A slow
queue, everyone heading off all at once. She was behind him.
Noticed first the mud flaked round his boots. Then the blue
day-pack on his back and one white hair curling through the
black. She wondered, does he know about that one white hair?
He turned and she flushed, caught staring. He smiled. His
eyebrows met in a black starburst above his crooked nose. His
eyes paused on her a moment.

'Got the time?' he said.

She nodded at the clock behind him. He smacked his
forehead with his hand and grinned. 'Oh yeah. You going far?'

'London,' she said. 'You?'

'Edale.'

'Walking?'

'Yeah.'

'Lucky you. I'd rather be walking in Edale than sitting on a
train to London,' she said, though not with any truth.

He bought his ticket and moved out of the way for her. As
she waited for her ticket, he leant in. 'Got to run,' he said, 'but
if you ever fancy a walk . . .' He pressed a card into her hand
and headed off. When she'd bought her ticket she looked for
him but there was no sign. Or yes, there was a sign: a wriggle
of mud, tread shaped, to show the way he'd gone.

She bought a newspaper and a cup of tea. Examined the
card. His firm did something with software and his name was
Jeff. But he was not her type. She dreamt out of the train
window till Chesterfield, then unfolded the paper and let it
go.

A Saturday morning, three weeks on. April now, the world

frisked green outside her window and the sun through the glass was hot. She thought about a walk, maybe driving out to Padley Gorge and breathing in the air. She rang a friend or two, but they had other plans. She thought about the man. Jeff. His card still in the pocket of her London jacket, hanging in the wardrobe. Nothing to lose, she thought, rang him and got his answerphone. His voice, remembered, made her gulp. She put the phone down. Of course, on a day like this, he'd already be out. She practised a message, witty, non-committal, rang back prepared – but this time he picked up the phone, wrong-footing her.

'Oh, er, I thought . . . It's Meg,' she said.

'Meg?'

'We met at the station weeks ago, you said . . .'

'Oh,' he said, an interested cadence in his voice. 'The ice maiden.'

'*Sorry?*'

He laughed. 'Cool, I mean, you looked unrufflable.'

She hesitated, uncertain whether she should take offence. 'I don't know about that, anyway . . .' If he could see her. Her face was red now, far from cool. She considered banging down the phone.

'Well?' he said.

'You said about a walk.'

'Oh yeah.'

'I'm just . . . it's just such a great day.'

'Now?'

'Not necessarily, it just made me think.'

'Yeah, I'm just off anyway. Sure, you can come along.'

When they got out of the car he looked down at her shoes. 'Haven't you got boots?' he said.

Out on the moors the wind was cold, much colder than the city breeze. The smell was raw, air scraped over heather, hoarse. The shoes, fine for streets and parks, were useless; they filled up with scratchy bits and she jarred her ankle on tangled roots. The wind swore in her ears, turned her earrings to ice. He walked fast and they didn't say a lot. Her attempts at chat were torn from her mouth and flung away. She lagged behind and surreptitiously looked at her watch. Getting near to time for lunch. She thought that they must stop soon, find a cosy pub. She cheered herself with thoughts of a log fire, scampi, half a pint of beer. But he hunkered down behind a lip of stone, opened his pack and brought out sandwiches and a flask.

'I didn't think . . .' she said.

'I always bring too much.'

The bread was thick, not quite stale, and the filling some kind of meaty paste. Drinking coffee from his flask lid felt intimate and she was careful not to put her lips quite where his had been.

When she got home, she kicked off her ruined shoes and ran a bath, deep and hot, to soak her aching limbs. She poured herself a glass of wine and lay and watched the world get dark, wondering how she felt. And it was virtuous.

She never thought they'd meet again.

But he rang her. He took her shopping and supervised the purchase of some proper boots, gaiters, a cagoule. And the next Saturday they walked twelve miles, through bogs and brambles, stumbling over the bones of sheep and parts of aeroplanes crashed in World War Two, forcing themselves upwards to where the wind was like a knife.

'What's it called?' she said. 'This hill?'

'Bleaklow,' he said and she huddled into her hood and nodded. That sounded right.

This time she'd brought the sandwiches, ham and Brie, and her father's hip flask with a drop of malt. That he liked. He laughed and swigged and kissed her with his whisky lips. They pressed together, cagoules flapping in the wind. He tried to get his hand in but she was all zipped up. No way she wanted icy hands on her up there in that bleak place.

He came back to her flat that night. He looked too big and real against her apricot walls and cream settee, after her imaginings. He liked the place and took his shoes off before she had to ask, before he walked across the deep carpet to the fire. She grilled lamb chops with redcurrant jelly and he ate with gusto, admiring the way she cooked the meat, the wine that she had bought. He made love to her with gusto too, admiring the smoothness of her skin, stunning her with pleasure.

He was a different man indoors. He cooked, he laughed, he even wiped up crumbs. He teased her in bed, he drove her wild. He sometimes made her beg. She told her friends he *could* be the one. But for one thing: the walks. Too long inside and he would start to prowl. A smell came off him like the moor. Walking was what they did. Saturdays, Sundays, any holiday. Even if the sky was coming down. She lost some pounds and found new muscles in her legs and told herself this as she struggled behind him up rocky paths, or slipped up to her knees into an icy stream.

She mourned long drowsy mornings sipping coffee, picking croissant crumbs off sticky skin. He didn't like to waste the light. Grabbed a quick bowl of cornflakes, a swig of tea and was out the door while the birds' songs were still wet in their morning throats. Sometimes, mutinous behind him, watching the frantic to-fro of his legs she thought he would be better off with a dog.

But at night, between the sheets, she took it back.

Her birthday was in August, on a Saturday. He wanted, of course, to walk. Taking it easy was her idea. They compromised. A walk on Stanedge Edge, then lunch in Hathersage. It was a thick grey day, no breeze, not even high up. Every available inch of cliff was colonised by someone on a rope. He stopped and hailed an old mate, talking routes and gradings, listing climbers' names, some of them dead. You could be dead, she thought, thinking of his fall, wincing against the egg-soft smash of skull on stone, the wait of hours for help. The touch and go of it. And now he walked and walked and never reached the place he sought.

And, she saw it then, he never would.

They stopped and watched a hang-glider, its flimsy arc hovering, the little insect-man, comic in the air. She squeezed his hand. He turned quite fiercely. 'Do you love me?' he said. The glider swooped, her belly too.

She looked down at her shiny boots, her feet too hot inside. 'Yes,' she said, 'of course I do.'

In the pub he had steak and she had prawns and over a pint of beer she felt better, warmer, as if something had been sealed. Later he kissed the curve of her white breast. 'I love you too,' he said.

The rain poured down that night, the thunder grumbled distantly. His breath was quiet beside her. She reached across and squeezed his sleeping hand.

In the morning he showered and dressed ready for a proper walk. He settled on Kinder Scout, spreading a map to show her on the bed where she still lazed.

'Listen,' she said. 'I'll give it a miss today I think. Feeling a bit, you know.' For weeks she'd dreamt of saying that, of having a day off, doing nothing much, mooching about, reading the Sunday paper right through, meeting a friend for lunch – but she didn't want to let him down.

He looked at her a minute and she nearly took it back.

'In that case,' he said, 'I'll . . .' He unfolded the map a little more, enlarged his plans. 'Sure you're OK?' he said and went off jauntier than he'd been for weeks. She heard the door bang, lay back down and considered the expression on his face. Could it have been relief?

When he got back, sun-reddened, dusty, she ran him a bath and served roast pork with apple sauce. They made greedy love for hours. He hadn't minded her staying home – nice to have her to come back to, he said.

After that day, she would sometimes walk with him and sometimes not. Never again in the cold rain or the nagging wind, but if the sun shone and she was in the mood she went. When she didn't go with him he walked further, she suspected, certainly he came back worn out, relaxed, as if he had temporarily walked something off. For a few hours he would seem at peace. Until a certain look came into his eyes again, a far-off focus, a restless smell.

As winter came she rarely walked, preferring to stay beside the fire, eating buttery scones and reading through a stack of books, or meeting friends for lunch.

They never lived together, though some of his things moved in: a dressing gown, a stack of maps, a tin of shaving foam. Winter nights at weekends smelt of woollen socks drying on radiators, and the entrance steps were littered with the tread-shaped worms of mud.

It was March. The days were lengthening. She hadn't walked with him despite the sun. She'd stayed home, shaved her legs, worn her pale skirt and silky sweater, the one he loved her in. She had prepared salmon and filled a vase with daffodils. The sun lit up the glasses. The wine waited in the fridge. He didn't come. It was because of the light, she told herself, because the evenings were drawing out, the walking time extending. But after half an hour she knew something was wrong. She poured a glass of chilly wine and shivered. It wasn't going to work.

He did come late, apologetic, a spray of pussy willow in his hands. They ate and drank. The fish was perfect, neither overcooked nor raw. He admired the food, her figure and her hair. But when she told him what she thought, he nodded and breathed out. 'Yeah.' He crushed a meringue crumb flat between his finger and thumb, brushed the dry white powder off. 'We're not . . .'

'Suited?' she finished. And it was what he meant. And that was that. He stayed a while. Drank some coffee, ran his finger on the map to show her where he'd been, packed up his dressing gown and left. Oh, he did kiss her first.

Next day she saw the dawn. The sky was soufflé pale. It was Sunday. A day for lazing, but she couldn't laze. She went out for papers, croissants, brewed a pot of Java coffee, but it was no good. She rang some friends but they were all busy – or busy being couples anyway. She put on her cagoule, threw her boots into the car and headed out of town. Wind buffeted the car, the trees were still bare, sore and fattened twigs swayed and scraped the wind. She put her foot down as the road rose slick and wet between the dull cushions of the moor. On the grey tooth slash of Stanedge Edge the climbers were fluorescent specks against the rock, roped and chalky, childish bright.

Out of the car, the wind tossed her heart away. She didn't walk the path they'd trod, she walked the other way, stumbling over heather roots, wet eyed. The peat sucked her feet, the slurp of it beneath her, the greediest sound she'd ever heard. She tied her hood-string tight against the wind. When she stopped to get her breath, black water seeped up round her boots.

A man hailed her. Just for a second she thought it was Jeff and her heart did a painful chisel stab. But it was not Jeff. She waited while the man caught her up. He was breathless, a drop of moisture on his nose. The wind batted about them, rustling her hood so it was hard to hear his voice.

'Stick to paths,' he said.

She frowned. 'I'm not doing any harm.'

'This bog, it's treacherous. Somewhere round there' – he jabbed a fleecy finger in the air – 'sunk under, there's a car. A whole car. A few weeks back it were. Some berk off-roading. Got stuck. Before the tow truck got here – it had gone.'

She stared at the place he pointed at. Black wet with spiky grass, patches of luminous green.

'Just stick to paths,' he said again. 'Good day.' He turned and bustled off.

She felt the earth give beneath her, gazed at the surface of the moor. A car down there – metal, glass and rubber tyres. Maybe a radio thrubbing out a silent tune. He never said, she thought, whether there was anyone in the car when it went down. What else was down there? Whole trees perhaps, lost wedding rings, aeroplanes crash-landed in the war and sucked below before a soul could see. And bones. Bird bones, sheep bones, the bones of men and women strayed from the path – oh, maybe centuries ago.

A grouse scuttered up and shocked her with its cry. The land was wild about her, and the sky. She found the path, went back to the car and sat. OK, maybe she cried. She put the heater on, sipped coffee from her flask and watched the tiny humans climbing upwards, gaudy against the grey.

Diamond White

Kevin Sampson

Birkenhead

The weekend's the weekend, it's great – but Monday afternoons are the best time to drink in there. There's characters in this pub at the best of times, I absolutely fucking love the place, but on a Monday in particular there's a certain solidarity that takes you beyond ordinary conviviality. I do – I love Spud Murphy's. Especially on a Monday.

For a kick-off it's 99p all day for a bottle of Diamond White. Now, in no way at all am I an alkie – I don't even think I get that particularly drunk, even when I've been on an all-dayer in there. But Diamond White is a potion that does the job for me. It really does. There's an INXS song – or is it REM? All those initials and Michaels, I always confuse them but I'm sure it's INXS; anyway, they've got a song called 'Comfortably Numb'. That's how I am on Diamond White. It's a lovely feeling, I can just stand there at the bar and I'll have a gab with anyone. A few of the girls in there give me bad looks if I'm gabbing on to their fellas for too long. I suppose they feel a bit threatened, but they should know I wouldn't make moves on anyone who's come in there with his girl. I'll say hello and ask how's it going, but that's it. Anyone who knows me'll tell you that.

That's the trouble with me. I'm a friendly girl, I am talkative and I will just start nattering to someone at the bar, I suppose. And I will lay with them too. I have to like the fella, but I'm not at all prejudiced by looks or age or anything. If I

73

can feel a real rapport with a fella and it seems like we can both be nice to each other then I will take him back. Some of them are very nice and won't let me pay for my drinks. Some men give me money too – a fiver or a tenner, they just slip it into my pocket but I never ask for nothing. I'm not at it. That's where some of the girls who come in Spud's have got me wrong, but I don't have much to do with them anyway.

To be honest, those sort of girls, the out-and-out townies, only really come here of a Friday and Saturday night. It's so packed in the bar by nine o'clock that I tend to try and get out of there by that time anyway. I might walk up to the Obby, but more often than not I'll just go back to the flat. Sunday is always a really good session anyway, and then it's Monday again. Spud Murphy's Mad Mondays. Fuck knows why it's called Spud's. It says the Charing Cross on the sign outside.

What I like about Spud's is all the mad characters that come in. Especially in the afternoons. There's all sorts. Up until about four o'clock it's the usual faces. Danny the Brickie's always in here, always full of stories. No one can testify to seeing Danny actually laying a brick in his twenty-odd years of adulthood, but he's always got a few bob. He's a pure gent, Danny – treats you like one of the lads, but in a nice way. He's gentle. Big mad beaming red face from the bevvy. I'm always pleased to see him.

And then there's all the Wardies. There's hundreds of them, all from Rock Ferry, all mad alkies. Big Wardy – that's as opposed to Fat Wardy, and there's a few of them to choose from – he's always good for a little sing-song. You can always tell when he's going to start off. There's that sort of drunken shine to his eyes and he'll pop one finger in the air as if to say, here we go, then. It's always something dead maudlin, too. 'Danny Boy', for a laugh, if Danny the Brickie's in there, or 'The Crystal Chandelier' – that's another one of Wardy's.

After four it starts to liven up. All the robbers and smack-heads come in with their day's haul. If you come into Spud's at half four on a Saturday you can buy your Sunday joint, a

Lacoste polo shirt and an Irvine Welsh omnibus for twenty rips. That's the thing with this lot – they know what sells. Long-life batteries. Boxer shorts. A good read. Zap, they're gone like that.

I don't mind the bagheads, me – live and let live, eh? Someone like Danny will tense up when they start coming in trying to sell you this and that but, really, where's the harm? You can say no if you don't want nothing. I wouldn't lay with a smackhead but they're entitled to be treated like human beings, aren't they?

Danny always takes the piss out of me when I go on like that – Milly Tant, he calls me. I suppose my dress code, if I have one, veers towards a sort of eco-traveller look, if anything. Like today, I've got on a pair of extra-baggy, pale tangerine bottoms, almost like a Buddhist's tracky bottoms they are, and I'm wearing my big floppy pullover with holes in the elbows. I couldn't find it, at first. I can understand them not wanting me to wear it. It's minty as fuck. And my hair's in braids at the back. It's wild. I'd be the first to admit it needs a good shampoo and condish. I smoke cherry-flavoured rollies, I light incense candles and that. I'm a bit of a scruff, I suppose, bit of a hippie. But I know I turn heads. Fellas always want to gab to me.

That's where I'm lucky with Sven. Now Sven *is* a fucking hippie! The first I knew about him or the Cross or any of this – my Spud Murphy's life such as it is, I suppose – was when I woke up in the flat, in his bed. He'd slept on the couch. He said I could stay as long as I wanted. Said, no pressure, help with the bills if you can, when you can. Come and go as you please. He's sound, Sven. He's an ugly old cunt, but he doesn't half bring some girlies back. I don't fancy Sven at all. I like him though. He really looks after me. Sometimes we lay together. It just seems like the right thing, at the time. He never asks me no questions though, nothing. I'm lucky. I see a lot of girls who get a really hard time off their fellas, whether they're with them or not.

*

John from Skelly's always the first one in after five. All the local traders and businessmen come in. Fuck knows how they make a living around this part of town. The Cross, like, Charing Cross, round here used to be where it was at. It was the posh end of town. Fat Wardy told me that. But everything changes, doesn't it? Things have improved at night-time since Yates's opened up, but in the daytime it's dead. John comes in for a brandy and a moan, then Silent Peter from the model-train shop – he just stands at the bar and from ten past five until eight o'clock he doesn't say a word. Then he says, 'See you tomorrow, then,' and he's off. He got wild on Christmas Eve. I hardly knew any of them, back then. I might've kissed a few of them, with it being Chrimbo. Might've gone with one or two. Silent Peter come over and tried to neck me. I laughed it off without hurting his feelings too much, I think. He started trying to offer me money and then he just started crying. Christmas Eve of all times. Poor fella.

The most interesting times – not to say anything against the regulars who I fucking adore, but life's all about chance and variety, that's what I think – and what I love is when a visitor comes in, a businessman or whatever. Most of the time it's just spontaneous, or I'll start off gabbing to the fella if I don't know his kite. But I must say that once or twice I've felt a bit weird. Someone'll come over and, all shamefaced, say something like, 'Are you Sven's friend?' or 'Sven said I might find you here.'

It can be quite unsettling at times but usually, if they're nice, I don't mind. If they're interesting and they're nice I'll go with them and do what they want. It doesn't harm anyone, does it?

More often than not, they've got a tale to tell anyway. I love hearing people's stories, even if they're just telling you about their jobs or their kids or whatever. It's not unusual for a fella like that, when it comes down to it, to end up just sitting there having a gab. There was this one fella from Bradford – I'm sure it was Bradford. The first time he came into Spud's he came over all suggestive, talking dirty and telling me how he couldn't wait to do this and that. He didn't really give me the creeps but I wasn't exactly looking forward to it, either. I just thought that I might as well. But when we got in his car and drove down to the place he just started blurting out all his problems and that and I ended up having to comfort him: there, there, there, and what have you. He came back a few times, like, just to get things off his chest. I never seen him again after that.

Just standing here outside the pub now, wondering whether to go in or not, takes me back to the last time I was here. It seems weird now, just to think how long ago that was. That was one fella I got totally wrong. And the rest! The day he walked in was the last time I had a drink in Spud's.

Something about the man hit me straight away. I felt sort of knocked back in my seat, dizzy, like – I didn't fancy him though. Nothing like that. He had a muzzy for a start and he was just . . . *stuffy*, you know? He was strait-laced and proper – nothing like the other sort of business-type fellas that go in there. And he looked at me really . . . *intently*, like. It wasn't a sex-starved look, I can handle that. It was more a pitying look; a deep, searching look as though he was trying to see what was inside of me.

He just came over with his own drink – the pub was almost empty, anyway, but he goes, 'May I join you?'

Not, *Can* I join you? – like I say, very stiff and proper and he didn't offer to buy me a drink or nothing, either. I just shrugged. Inside I'm thinking at least it's someone to have a gab with and, fair enough, we got talking quite easily. It was more him asking me questions – what did I do for a living, how did I like Birkenhead, what're my friends like, that sort of thing, which I'm more than happy with usually. But it was his looks. He wouldn't take his eyes off me. And his eyes were moving all the time, moving all over me. *Raking* me. It was quite spooky. I remember when I told him that I don't do drugs – nothing hard at least, anyway – he sort of closed his eyes and took a deep breath and rocked backwards slightly. It was more than just being relieved or whatever, there was nothing casual about it. The bloke was . . . he was *thankful*. My first thought was that he wanted to take me without a johnny and I'd just presented him with a clear bill of health.

And sure enough he starts asking about boyfriends and that and asking me if I get out much and do I go to the pictures. It was more than just chit-chat. I thought he was a nice enough sort of man, probably even a kinky type, and I decided I'd make it easy for him.

'Have you come here in your car?' I said, maybe a little bit flirtishly, which I hate in myself. He said he had.

'What sort of car have you got?' I asked him. Again, flirty. Stupid, really, I suppose. When he told me I made some comment about it being a nice car and asked if we could go for a ride. Again, he seemed sort of relieved. I think he was just pleased to be getting out of there. I could tell he didn't like being in Spud's.

It's always in the back of my head that fellas like this could turn out weird, but I always try to make it so that people see us together in Spud's and people see us leave. Maybe that's a little bit why some of the townie girls think I'm at it. They hear the stories, like, put two and two together and get five. Who's counting anyway? It's best for the punters in Spud's to see me leave with the fella, get a good blimp at him. That way, unless the guy's trying to get himself nicked for something, there's not really going to be a problem.

I sometimes let them drive me past the Four Bridges, round behind the Spillers warehouses. It's supposed to be condemned land, there's loads of signs saying you can't take cars past a certain point, but I love the tranquillity of the docks. There's something about the silent dark depths of the water down there. I often ask myself whether the water in those docks ages like we do. Or has it just been there for ever? The stillness of the deep docks makes me calm inside. Comfortably numb. The way the surface of the dock waters is just there at foot level, a footstep away – it says it all for me. There's nowhere I'd rather be, apart from Spud's.

But I didn't take this bloke down the docks. Something instinctive told me he wasn't after that. At first I thought we'd go to the old Wharf pub site, what there is left of it. The car park there is a nice spot, although the disused buildings are used as a shooting gallery, on and off. Smack's back in a big way. People've taken me for a baghead before, because I suppose I talk in that way when I've been on the cider, that blissed-out slurring drone of all addicts everywhere. I'm tall too, which makes me seem thin. I know I've got a good body, though. I'm quite pale as well.

I remember the stink of ciggies when we got in his car. Your clothes always stink of ciggies when you've been on an all-dayer in Spud's, but you don't notice it on yourself. It's just that his car was so clean. We headed off towards the Wharf and he was saying what a nice warm evening it was, mind if we have the windows open and that – that sort of chit-chat. Light. He asked if I was in a hurry to get back or did I fancy going for a drive. Just down to Moreton Shore or West Kirby or something. Just hearing those names made me feel faint again. Not the names themselves so much – you hear them all the time. But it was the way he said them, his voice – there was a warming sensation. It was something nice. Something secure.

So we drove down Corpy Road and up on to St James roundabout and over through Bidston on to the flyover. The tip's been filled in now, pretty much. That old landscape of foragers and speculators has gone with the wind now. Tip Rats, that's what everyone used to call them. As we drove past I remembered . . . well I *didn't* remember, really. What I had was the *sense* of a memory, a recollection that stayed just out of range and couldn't quite be engaged.

The man had stopped talking. I figured he was trying to decide whether or not to go through with whatever it was he had in mind. Perhaps it was his first time. Whatever, he was edgy as fuck, stealing little glances at me and taking those deep breaths, like he was steadying himself all the time. I liked him well enough by now. I felt safe with him. I really didn't mind if he wanted to do something.

He seemed to fight back whatever he was going to say and just stared straight ahead, carried on driving. We went straight across the roundabout at Moreton Cross, past the Big House and on towards West Kirby. I could see a spangle of tears in the corner of his eyes and, when there were enough of them, they trickled down his cheek. He made no attempt to wipe them away.

I would've asked him what was up but, what was happening was, I was starting to feel really, like, disembodied myself. We were driving past the Grange, the pub, and I just started to feel really woozy. I've only ever had an anaesthetic once, but it reminded me of that. The bit just after you come out of an anaesthetic. In fact, no – the bit just before you conk out. Your last thoughts before you go under seem perfectly well formed, well within your own control and then, suddenly, they make no sense, you can't rein them in, you can't develop whatever you were thinking to the next logical phase. You're unconscious. Sensations like these were starting to wash over me as we went over the little humpy bridge outside Meols station.

I felt utterly exposed now, naked, totally dependent on this man in the car. I turned to him, bewildered, not wanting him to see that I was scared. He turned into one of the roads that leads down on to the prom, I forget which, and he drove us along the front, right next to the sea, drove us along for a few minutes and then he just killed the engine.

'Are you OK, baby?'

I must have opened and shut my mouth but no words came out. He leant over and put his arms around me. I just sat there, letting him envelop me.

'It's OK, poppet.'

Poppet.

'You're home. Everything's going to be all right.'

I turned to look at the man. More and more images and sounds and snatches of familiar things were invading me and taking me over. I closed my eyes and tried to line it all up. Home.

So here I am again. I can hear Fat Wardy from outside the pub, mutilating some old rebel song. I can't wait to see their faces when I go in there. That's if I *do* go in there. I've been stood here half an hour, changing my mind, changing it back, turning away, walking back again.

I still can't really get my head round the whole story – how I'd just, like, disappeared off the face of the earth. And I was so close all the time, too – that's the thing that sort of distresses me if I think about it long enough. Christmas time, it was. Good job, too, because that's how they came to miss me so quick. I was due home from uni. I know I was a bit stressed about a few things – we've pieced that much together – but there was no hint of this. I don't even know whose party it was or how I came to be invited or anything. I was gone nearly six months. Dad spent that entire time trying to find me. He gave up his job, took early retirement, everything.

It's wrecked my head a bit, all this. I don't know what I think. I need more details, otherwise . . . I really do not know who I am. I do know that I liked it in there. Liked the buzz, liked the people, liked my life. I've started talking to some of my old friends, friends from uni and that, and it's starting to seem like I *didn't* like my life back there. I'm not really supposed to talk to them too much. Not all at once. I'm supposed to be taking things easy, but that's like saying there's something up with me. I know there isn't. I can almost get a grasp of what it was. It's not an illness. It's nothing like that. The closest I can get is like when you're a kid and you just shut something out that you don't like. You will it to be otherwise. I think I did that. I really do.

I know that if I go inside, now, that'll be it for me. I should probably just turn around, walk straight back to Conway Park and get on the first train back to Meols. I told Mum and Dad I just needed to go for a walk, get away from the house for a bit. On my own. I could see the little look that passed between them. That's only natural. They just want me to be OK. I want the same too. I do. I should just turn around right now and go on back to them. But I like it in there. I like the Diamond White.

My Horizons
Jane Rogers

Cheshire

Roses

Melanie must have noticed I'd put the roses behind the washing machine. She banged the back door.

'For God's sake, Mum. Why don't you *tell* him?'

'Tell him what?'

She throws her schoolbag on the table, looks in the fridge then the cupboard, takes two bags of crisps and goes up to her room. From upstairs she calls, 'Don't get cheese and onion again. They stink.'

What would happen if I told him?

'Teddy, I think I've gone off roses. They seem so forced . . . Really, I prefer smaller flowers: sweet williams, for example, or freesias –'

He would look up from what he was doing, mildly irritated. 'What?'

'Next time you buy flowers, Teddy, could you get something different?'

'Different?'

'Than roses. I mean, they're nice, it's just I'd like a change –'

'Have you taken leave of your senses?'

'No –'

'Other women'd eat their hearts out for a man who brought them flowers.'

'Teddy, I know how lucky I am, all I'm saying is –'

'I know what you're saying. It's incredible. It means nothing to you, that I've been giving you roses, week in, week out, for twenty years.'

'It does mean –'

'You don't think about my feelings. You don't *think*. No, a little whim floats into your head, Oh I'd like a daffodil this week –'

'I didn't mean to hurt your feelings, of course the roses mean something –'

'Should have told me twenty years ago. I could have saved a fortune.'

'Teddy, please – I'm sorry, please buy roses again –'

I'll fetch them in before he comes home. Midweek I can leave them. I used to just hope they'd die. Put them on the windowsill above the radiator and turn it up. Forget to put water in the vase. But the quicker I got rid of them the more he bought. In the old days it was one bunch a week. Now it's two or three. Always when he comes home at the end of the week. An Interflora midweek. Then again if he shops in the village on Saturday; and if he's away he sends more. He knows, he must know I'm getting rid of them.

'Tell him.'

Things look simple when you're Melanie's age – I remember that. I remember shouting at my father: 'Hypocrite! Hypocrite! Hypocrite!'

Birds

When I was at primary school a girl in my class told me if you see one thousand birds together then it's God. I used to wait – heart hammering against my ribs – when a big flock flew over. Trying desperately to count them; forty-one, forty-two, forty-three. And they'd be over me already and winging away, the higher ones flying slower than the ones below, so I couldn't tell which I'd counted. Their positions were shifting relative to one another, I began to feel giddy like the earth was tilting too and their individual shapes were clotting together as they moved on, becoming denser and denser, going into one dark moving mass flying towards the horizon and I could never get anywhere near one thousand. It was impossible. Sometimes in the holidays I'd stay in the garden all day. Waiting for one thousand birds.

I know I'm lucky.

Teddy's a good man. For example, he's generous. He buys me jewellery – diamonds, and that was before he could afford to. Perfume. Silky things. A silver rosebowl. Golden slave bangles. He says you should never buy someone the sort of thing they might buy for themselves. I used to prefer smoky, swirly stones – opals, pearls. But he says they don't suit me, I should have clear, bright colours. Diamonds are best for blondes, he says. I wear the jewellery sometimes. If we go out together he likes me to dress up.

He won't take me to Lyons with him. He told me that last night; he's going for a week. Quite right too. I made life awful for him last time. I kept him awake all night with my claustrophobia because the window wouldn't open. I hate those hotels; they control your air supply, they air-condition and centrally heat. My lungs were flapping like a trapped bird's wings, I couldn't get a breath. I'm no good at those dos anyway, my face goes stiff so I can't smile.

'You could make an effort to be civil,' he said through his teeth. But I couldn't. My head was empty as a bucket.

I should be delighted that I don't have to go to Lyons. But no. No, I feel terrible. My stomach's in a knot, I'm anxious, I feel guilty. What sort of a wife am I, if I can't even support Teddy in his work? It's all arranged for Melanie to stop at Jill's; there's nothing to keep me here, I should go. On my own I'll only pace about, waiting for the phone to ring with news of accidents, disasters – I should go. But Teddy doesn't want me to.

'You don't enjoy it, do you?' he said. 'And I can do without you hyperventilating at three o'clock in the morning.'

Of course.

'You need to get a grip,' he said. 'Really, you need to learn to relax. Take up yoga or something.'

He forgets, I used to do yoga. But then I couldn't get to the class because I had to take Melanie to her wind band practice on a Thursday evening. We said I'd go if he came home in time to take her. But he's a busy man, he can't promise to be home by seven.

This house is not a prison. It's nice outside – the view of the hills, sometimes I don't even mind the sound of the planes. I do the gardens, I grow all our vegetables. Only Teddy's rose garden I leave to him, he likes to feel that's his special project. I think we're happy when we're gardening. On a sunny Sunday afternoon when shadows lengthen across the lawn, Teddy calls, 'Tea? Or G and T?' and goes indoors before I can reply, and comes out with clinking glasses. Then I straighten up and we wander round together, looking at the new beech hedge, the delphiniums I managed to preserve from the slugs, the raspberry canes in their new cage, the borders, the lawns. He's laying a crazy-paving path around his rose garden. I admire it, he admires my leeks. I think we're happy, like lords of the manor.

But inside, Teddy's the one with ideas but I'm the one with time. Take the dining room. I said, 'Why don't we paint this room? A nice soft green, for example, with pale curtains so that at night with candles you get a glow – '

'Green?' he said. 'In a dining room? Have you taken leave of your senses? Green's the last colour you want in a dining room – cold, bilious. That snot-green jumper you wear, by the way, it doesn't do anything for you. What's needed is a stripe in here, something a bit formal – and echo it in the seats of the dining chairs –'

So I pored over the wallpaper books and swatches of cloth

and paint charts; in the end I chose a deep red and grey stripe on white, and white and grey for the chairs. It looked stiff when it was done.

'Well, the curtains,' he said. 'It needs a bit of flair. There's your chance to be creative. The curtains will make all the difference.'

I didn't know what he wanted. I got dark red velvet. It matched the stripe. It made me think of a funeral parlour. Teddy sighed and said it was a predictable choice.

We've been married a long time. It's not simple, in the way it looks to a fifteen-year-old. You have to compromise. Teddy is a charming man, everyone says so. Full of energy, powerful. I was always flattered that he liked me. I'm not the sort of woman he likes; sharp, sexy, confident. I'm a wishy-washy blonde, a person who tries to please. I don't have a firm grip.

I know he has affairs. The first time I found out I broke my heart. It was two in the morning, I was pregnant and the baby hadn't kicked all day. I tried ringing the friends he said he was with. I remember the feeling – a quick, cold blade, it slit me open the way you'd gut a rabbit. But I wasn't surprised. Shocked, shaking with shock, but I had known it was coming. Didn't I know when I met him? He was not the type to be faithful.

He says two things. 'One, I always come back. Two, I only give roses to the woman I love.'

'As if I cared!' I screamed. To begin with I screamed a lot. I threw things. I made him sleep in the spare bedroom. But in the end, what's the point?

'You're only hurting yourself,' he said. 'You know I love you.'

He doesn't tell me now and I don't ask. I know he won't leave me, although sometimes I wish he would.

A View
A friend of my mother's lived in a house where there was a

brick wall between them and next door. Her kitchen was an extension at the back of the house, the kitchen window faced the brick wall slap bang, five feet away. Her husband covered the alley between the kitchen and the wall with clear plastic roofing, so the kids could keep bikes and roller skates there. My mother's friend got a huge poster from the travel agent's and she stuck it to the wall opposite her window. It was of Switzerland, an alpine meadow, bright green flank of hill starred with white, yellow, gentian flowers, and a blue blue sky above. 'At least I can look at a view now, while I'm washing up,' she said.

Better than looking at a brick wall, I thought then. In zoos, do you ever notice the paintings at the backs of cages? Icebergs in a blue sea for polar bears. Jungle-bright trees for monkeys; a jagged mountain for the hawk. Someone told me once that the animals can't see them because they're two-dimensional. You have to be human to read pictorial representation.

I always thought I would go back to work. So did Teddy. But there was Melanie, and moving down to London when Teddy changed jobs – then up to Cheshire when he was promoted – I didn't have the contacts. We're a bit cut off here really. I mean, it's handy for Ringway and the M6, of course, that's why Teddy chose it. But there's nothing in the village, I'd have to go all the way into Manchester, and the rush hour traffic's terrible. Anyway, Teddy was abroad such a lot, it would have been difficult. He's got too high an opinion of me, really, that's the trouble. He thinks of the magazines I used to work for. I decided at one point I should take anything, just to get me out of the house again. I answered an ad for a local estate agent, to take photos of the houses. Such lovely big houses they have round here, half-timbered, rolling lawns – lovely.

Teddy reacted badly. What they were paying me would barely cover my petrol costs. Didn't I realise what an insult it was? If I wanted to take photos, why didn't I take real ones – artistic ones, like I used to? He didn't work the hours he did for me to be at the beck and call of some poncy little sales-man. How would I get pictures in on time when I couldn't even get Melanie into a routine? Why didn't I consider *his* feelings?

He said I needed to feel more useful, which was true, so I should do a course in word-processing and he could bring home work from the office for me. Then they wouldn't have to employ another secretary – I could do it, and be paid, all in the comfort of my own home.

He was quite right, I was hopeless with time. Melanie developed asthma that winter, she was off school a lot – and we were having new central heating in, they took up all the floorboards. Between the workmen and Melanie and cleaning and cooking, the day was gone, and it wasn't till nine in the evening that I got a clear run at the typing. But then Teddy would come home.

'You still working? You're just not on top of it, are you? I was thinking we'd have a pleasant meal and a drink, and relax together in front of the fire – but I might as well have stayed at work if you're going to be at that all night.' At ten o'clock he'd say, 'Haven't you finished *yet*?' And at ten thirty, 'I'm going to bed. But this won't work out, Sylvie. I mean, one of the girls in the office would have polished it off in half the time.'

I wanted to do it – I did – but I never got on top of the time. There was always something; taking the car to be serviced, or Melanie to the dentist, or the cat to the vet, or Teddy's suits to the dry-cleaner. Overseeing the men who were landscaping the garden, shampooing the carpets after the central-heating mess; I don't know, I was always busy. We did a lot of entertaining then, at weekends – I always cooked, but even so. I know there are these superwomen. I'm just not one of them.

*

A Day Out

Things change. He's started saying, 'Have you taken leave of your senses?' I begin to feel I have.

When Melanie was away at summer camp I went down to London for the day. I'd planned it, looked forward to it. I went to the Hayward and the Tate, then to the theatre to see *Oleanna*. Men in the audience stood up and shouted at the end, I couldn't believe it, I was thrilled. On the way back the motorway was almost empty, just the odd flash of light swooping past in the dark. Nearly home, I stopped at that road the planes fly over, the one at the end of the runways. It was very late, no one about. I got out of the car and watched as one plane after another came roaring down the runway towards me. They lift off the ground impossibly late – just when you think they never will. They lumber up into the air and then – away! To tiny twinkling lights as far as stars.

It was early morning when I got in.

'There you are!' shouted Teddy. 'Have you taken leave of your senses?'

'No, I've been to London. You don't normally come home on Tuesday nights.'

'But I did. And I didn't know where you were. Have you any *idea* how worried I've been?'

'But I wasn't expecting you. Teddy – I went to London, I'm back. It's not a big deal.'

'Yes it is, yes it is. You never even thought to phone to let me know what you were doing – anything could have happened to you. Anything.'

'But you're away for days – weeks – I don't worry about you.'

'That's the difference between us, isn't it. You don't think about anyone but yourself.'

Last year I was ill. In the summer. Melanie was staying with my sister, Gail, down in Brighton. Teddy took her, he had some work down there. But he was coming back on the

Saturday because he'd planned a dinner party. I'd already done the shopping and made salmon mousse and a citron ice cream.

Yes. It was very hot. The ground was baked hard and I'd been watering. The hose attachment was threaded and wouldn't screw on to the tap properly. I tried and tried to fix it on and every time the force of the water blew it off again. So I filled the watering can and did the watering by hand. Silly, really, in such heat. Anyway, I fainted. Teddy found me in the garden when he got back.

They took me to hospital and did some tests, it turned out I am anaemic. Pernicious anaemia, they call it. When Teddy visited next day he brought armfuls of roses. They took up all the vases on the ward. I was embarrassed, the nurses kept teasing me about the other women feeling jealous. And he gave me a letter, asking me to read it when he'd gone.

Darling Sylvie,

When I came home and found you lying there in the garden I swear my heart stopped. I know I have sometimes hurt you but never never meant to, and I promise now I never will again. Don't forget, you have always been the most important woman in the world to me. Get well soon, my darling, and don't ever go away from me. I love you.

Your Teddy

xxxxx

I imagine the nurses getting hold of it. Passing it round the ward.

'Ah!'

'Ooh!'

'Isn't it romantic!'

'Ooh, she is a lucky girl.'

I scrumple it in my fingers into a tiny, hard bullet.

*

Now the house is quiet, all mine. Melanie is at Jill's, Teddy is in France. I have emptied all the vases into the bin.

As he was leaving he said, 'I'm worried about you Sylvie. Now Mel's getting older you need to widen your horizons a bit. Spread your wings.'

Get a grip. Relax. I sit in the dining room and think about my horizons. Stripes are like bars. What if I left him?

That's such a twisted thought, it spirals like a corkscrew. How could I leave him? He loves me really. He would follow me, he would leave no stone unturned, he would beg me to come home. And what could I do? No job no house no money no value to anyone in the world but Teddy. Where could I go?

Melanie's swift confident contempt. 'Get a life, Mum. Get a life.'

I can't think how. I have colluded in this one.

An Ocean

The week is passing very slowly. There are immense amounts of time. I find myself watching it, like the ocean. I am not doing the cleaning or the shopping or taking back the faulty video. I have not taken down the curtains and sent them for dry-cleaning, which would be convenient this week when there's no one home. I have not even posted the urgent letters Teddy left me to post. I have become lethargic as a castaway in a wide warm ocean, idling through swaying waters, gazing at blurred shapes. I think maybe I will come to the surface, in the quiet and the space – float up, recognisable, with intention.

After all, I *could* go out. This house is not a prison. Any more than that woman's kitchen that faced a blank wall. Nothing to stop her going out through the door and flying all the way to a real alpine meadow. If she really wanted to escape.

Sometimes things come through and you didn't realise they were the point of what was going on. Having a baby was almost like that, I thought, although I know that sounds absurd. But you're all taken up with pain; it keeps coming, pain and pain and pain, filling up your head, engulfing your body. And then, quite astonishingly, a baby pops out – which wasn't in your consciousness at all, only pain was, and the baby is a by-product, a free gift, an astonishingly literal object that the pain has deposited as its tide pulls out again.

I thought of asking Gail to stay this week. She's filming in Manchester, she could come back here at night, we would drink red wine and laugh together. But I mentioned it to Teddy.

'Please don't,' he said.

'But Teddy. I haven't seen her for over a year.'

He shakes his head, walks to the window, stares out. 'Sometimes you are so insensitive.'

What have I forgotten? He had an affair with Gail last year, she told me; then he came over all maudlin and guilty when I was ill. That's why I mustn't invite her, because he feels ashamed. I don't mind. Gail doesn't mind. She'll screw with anybody.

He goes heavily out of the room. I am so stupid. Why did I tell him? If I invited her here without him knowing it would be all right. But now he knows he has to imagine her sitting at his table, laughing with his wife – her sister! Maybe even exchanging confidences about him.

We wouldn't because I'm not interested. But there's no point in saying that. I've already said too much, I've upset him and he'll make me feel bad all evening; and then he's leaving tomorrow. I follow him downstairs.

'Teddy? D'you want me to hear your speech tonight? I'll get supper first, what would you like? I won't ring Gail, I promise.'

I tell him his speech is very good and he smiles and pats my cheek. 'Why don't you try on that new black basque I bought you?' He dims the light and starts to undo his shoes. 'Oh, and next week if you're at a loose end you could call in at the office for me and pass those tapes to Gloria.'

I could.

But I won't. Time is passing. Surging, welling up around me, breaking over my head in great rhythmic rollers, buoying me up, tossing me about. I leave my dishes on the dining table, they mark where I have been like driftwood. When I've spread pâté on my cracker I slide the knife under the edge of a strip of wallpaper. It's well stuck, doesn't come away easily. Give it a yank. There is plaster under the stripes. Of course, indoor walls are plastered. I was expecting to see the bricks.

Today energy is coming into me. It is time's, it is the ocean's. I can feel it centring in me, focusing. It is drawn into me out of the waves and cresting rollers, it is rounding and rounding like a waterspout, a hurricane, a whirling dervish of salty energy. I go outside and mow the lawns; dig potatoes; tear up weeds. I make a bonfire and burn all the fallen leaves. Flocks of birds – hundreds, a thousand? – wheel and circle overhead, getting ready to migrate. I am making the place clear. I go to bed early, in preparation.

And today I have been pruning. I am not allowed to prune. Teddy says I must leave it to him but the garden is going wild. Today I have been pruning. Yes. He had all the garden tools sharpened. So nice to use. The little secateurs, the big shining shears. I got carried away, really; I got quite carried away. The planes roaring overhead seemed to be cheering me on.

I pruned the raspberry canes, the flowering shrubs, the bushes by the side of the garage; and then I pruned his roses. Prune back hard in autumn. That's what the gardening book says. Prune back hard for vigorous spring growth. I pruned them right back to the earth. I used the shears for speed.

And when I heard the car on the gravel I didn't stop although perhaps I should have done. It was already dusk and I wasn't expecting Teddy home, you see, he wasn't due back till Sunday. I heard him calling me and for some reason I didn't want to reply. He came out of the house again and into the rose garden. He was leaning forward, peering into the darkness.

'Sylvie?' he shouted. Then, 'My God! Have you taken leave of your senses?'

He didn't see me standing there, he was bending down, trying to see if any stems were left. The shears were so sharp I could have done it with one snip. I believe I could have done it, but I didn't move an inch. He straightened up. 'Mindless vandalism!' he shouted, and he marched off back into the house.

It's getting chilly now. He's drawn the curtains over the lit windows, he's shut himself in. Although my teeth are chattering I'm very glad to be outside. I can see perfectly well in the dark. I've started on the beech hedge.

I'll stay here for a while, I think. With my shears. It seems the best solution. To snip my way out.

Watching the Picture Bloom

Andrea Ashworth

Manchester

A whoosh of spires and green, pleasant land, then a whack of factories and gloom. It's the end of my first term at Oxford, time to head home for the holidays, and I am churning in the belly of the coach as it slithers its wintry way north. Chimneys huddle against rain under a tin-pan-lid sky. I can feel the drizzle seeping, sly, beneath my skin, making my soul soggy.

At Birmingham I am dunked in the greasy-spoon purgatory of Digbeth station café. Washed up, wobbly kneed, in a crowd of lonely gents and lost-looking ladies. They all emerge semi-sentient from buses, before shuffling in line for stewed tea – cups of stillness they sit down to sip.

'Manchester,' the loudspeaker sputters.

Folks lug their bags and themselves back on the bus.

'Manchester!' the driver yells over the engine's hubbub, before the door groans shut.

Jammed in, feeling clammy, I hear someone humming. Is that me? Under my breath wander half-baked nothings: scraps of school hymns I still find myself crooning to lull my mind when worries come bubbling up or memories swell.

Manchester is just a city. A big, day-after-day city, full of people whose lives tick along, clockwork, never exploding.

Nothing to be afraid of.

Besides (I catch myself humming again), these days I am

just passing through. Like JAIL on the Monopoly board: *Just Visiting*.

Jumbled on my knees I have a menagerie of books, dog-eared, with velvety spines and pages furred from flicking. Wherever I go, I lug an obese and elaborate library. It's a first-aid kit, equipped for all twists of emotion. Strips of poetry are soothing plasters. Novels inflate into snug, silky, pure-air cocoons. Newspapers, alive with the friction of here and now, are smelling salts, pungent with ink and the glorious-terrible stink of the world. My nose is stuck between pages. Paper castles I am forever surrounding myself with, close as skin. My tissuey armour.

Getting closer, my chest and my guts begin to go funny – and my knees, my toes, my fingers, even my skin, which feels raw, peeled, inside out. The greatest distress belongs to my eyes: I peer out the window and, with soot on my mind, I see nothing but grey. The coach halts at a rainy junction in the thick of Manchester. Red, gold and green: the traffic lights used to stand out, glowing, to my greedy, child's eyes, like fabulous lollipops. Now I look and look, dying to drink in some colour.

On a darkening street in Manchester, I knock on our old front door, then go woozy at the sight and scent of my mother, all eye-catching, gregarious curls and Chanel No. 5 and magical ankles in her liquorice-strap heels.

Mum.

She used to kiss me, when I was little, before sleep. She would bend down and kiss me and her hair would sigh, gorgeous-smelling, across my face. After that, I would be able to float off – unbruised by that lullaby worry, 'If I die before I wake' – because my mother's fragrance was a whisper of heaven.

'God bless, angel.' Flowery lips press my forehead.

Revelling in the kiss – burning, delicious, above my closed eyes – I breathe back in the dark: 'Gobbless.'

Then I fall into the nowhere of my pillow.

In Oxford, some nights are punctured by noise that yanks me awake, my forehead on fire. My ears throb, wrapping themselves around the sounds of a party in the next staircase, adjusting to the new acoustics, the clatter and screech of carefree commotion, of people not fighting and desperate, not out to hurt one another, but fired up by fun. I can practically feel the spirals inside my ears melting, remoulding to take in the new shapes of noise in the night. My head calms down from its simmer, and I sink back into sleep, wrapped in the feathery softness of my duvet and my life. My own life.

Waking up in Manchester, I peel out of bed and wash in the frosty bathroom. Then – reining in thoughts of the other city, stashing feelings behind my tingling face – I go downstairs. The curtains moan on their rails as my mother heaves them apart. I sit with her on the settee while the sky curdles from its deepest grey to a paler dullness.

Nervous shafts of sunshine glimpse through. The kettle gurgles then revs up, excited, before bursting into its boil.

'Nescafé,' my mother murmurs, handling the gigantic jar I have brought home for her. She looks at me, fond and sad. 'You shouldn't go spending all your money on me, love.'

Invisibly, I wince; I whisk through buckets of the stuff with my friends in Oxford.

'Don't be silly, Mum.' I give her a kiss. Then I unscrew the lid and burst the paper drum-skin with an extravagant plunge of my finger.

Pop! The aroma leaps up and I giggle. A whiff of optimism rushes through us both: my mother and me.

But the feeling soon stales into dismay, knowing we will be nursing mug upon mug of instant coffee, all the nerve-strung day.

My hands cup the hot ceramic and I look down, mesmerised by granules that sizzle and dance and slowly dissolve.

My mother is chattering on about this and about that, about

neighbours' foibles and vegetables' prices, about anything and nothing. At last, she stubs out her cigarette and coughs as if to clear something bad from her throat. She tells me that, tonight, she will whip up a bit of spaghetti, like, with a nice, real meat, Bolognese sauce.

'We'll be having a visitor,' she adds, very quietly.

'Dad,' I say.

'How did you know?' My mother glances at me, then her eyes glaze and drift off.

'I just knew.'

It hurts to look at her. There are no raw cuts, no bad rainbow shadows staining her face, but I can almost see the wounds behind my mother's eyes.

Evening slumps over our house.

Inside, my mother is dolled up and grinning in her best dress and lipstick. Motown is grooving, full belt, under the needle. My sisters' voices play in sweet, no-squabbling tides against the music's intense heartbeat.

'Everyone home!' My mother is so thrilled she can't stop making mince pies, which she pulls out of the oven in exorbitant, lovesick numbers. She bows her face to breathe in their tipsy, promising steam, half closing her eyes. 'We're all going to be together for Christmas.'

I sit in the dark on the stairs and wait for the bang on the front door.

'Come on, Andy,' my mother shouts, after she has ushered him in out of the cold. 'Come on, love.'

She insists that I put on my mortarboard and gown. 'Your – what d'you call it?'

'Subfusc.' I have to pass the flibberty phrase over my tongue, in front of my stepfather. He is dressed in his pinstriped suit. The same suit he was wearing last time I saw him: standing in court, charged with grievous bodily harm to my mother.

'Everything's packed away,' I say. I don't want to pull the

99

stuff out of my suitcase; don't want to balance the mortar-board on my head or unfurl the gown under our roof. Like opening an umbrella indoors, it feels like bad luck.

'Show your dad,' my mother urges, her eyes on fire. 'Go on, give us a twirl!'

I go up and sigh into my black matriculation gown and mortarboard. I come down and stand there, shoulders sulking, at the bottom of the stairs. A drooping bat.

'You look grand, Andy.' My stepfather shifts forward to stick a kiss on my cheek.

Peering through the tassels that dangle from my mortar-board, I wonder if the others can sense me resisting – because I love my mother, because I am afraid – the urge to paw away the wet lip-print that is stinging my cheek.

'Thanks.' I swallow and speak up: 'Thanks, Dad.'

Dreaming of a smooth Christmas, my mother had decided to splurge a few pounds on a really fancy Advent calendar. In the shape of a happy, big house, it hangs on the wall, some sweet treat lurking behind each window or door. In the mornings – after dusting and Hoovering and ironing – my mother turns to it for a surprise.

Today her long fingernails pluck open the next cardboard flap. From behind the cheery red and green door she teases out a gold-wrapped cube of dark, dark chocolate.

'You have it, love.' She presses the ingot into my palm.

Later, when my mother is upstairs in the bath, splashing gently, humming Christmas carols, I sneak over to lift the hallowed, chocolatey house off its nail.

There, behind the bright, red and green calendar, a blush of blood – *my mother's blood* – still hovers, in spite of scrubbing, on the wall.

There are a few last little Christmas things I need to fetch, I tell my mother, as I pull on my coat. I have to get out into the air, away from the sickly sweet house nailed on the living-room wall. Outside, I look up from the cracked pavements, the hedgerows and chimneys of childhood, and I feel deserted – by Oxford and by oxygen. Back here, the sky doesn't surge on and on, suggesting infinity. It is not blue and big as a dream.

Sooty smudges for clouds, with no brightness behind them.

My chest corkscrews, my pulse clobbers, my breath shallows out. I have a panicky sense that it is about to evaporate, my other world. Ornate gates, opening on to grand quadrangles, secret gardens. Oxford's night sky, a celestial brain, lustrous and winking. Gargoyles. Sublime stone carvings. Spires like fingers, pointing, promising answers.

It might all disappear, while I am here.

Every morning, I zip out in the whipping, mean weather and come back with satsumas.

'A bloody avalanche of satsumas!' My stepfather chuckles at the invasion of shiny, fresh orange.

My sisters and I rip into the fruit, unleashing zesty squirts inside our house. We undress their squishy flesh, taking care to keep the peel in one piece, then clutch their waxy, bright suits and think of a wish.

Christmas Day promises to come and go without tears.

My mother has eased a thin layer of icing, fresh-fallen sugary snow, across a shop-bought slab of fruitcake. Coming up with a sprig of real mistletoe, my stepfather has set it down, just so, in the midst of pure whiteness. We are all oohs and aahs until he takes a carving knife to the cake. Each wedge tastes of boiled coins and cardboard. Our jaws have to trudge through stodge.

Still, my mother marvels, this year the tree's fairy lights have flashed happily on and off, on and off, on and off, without faltering or blowing a fuse. Also, none – not one – of the excruciatingly brittle, glittery baubles has plunged to splinters and dust.

'A good omen,' she murmurs. 'Isn't it a good omen?'

I strain to read in the flickering dark while we're all gathered around the TV in the evenings, trying to be a family. During the day, I steal the odd half-hour away from my mother, who doesn't like me to stray out of her sight. While buying potatoes and bread and tinned food for the family, I dash to the local library, just to stock up on the smell of the pages and the sight of the spines, the crowded party of authors' names. At night, in my old bedroom, I leave the door ajar, listening for familiar trouble. As always, I lie on my bed with a book, my arms tortured by pins and needles as I poise the pages in a small globe of lamplight. I slurp up words, words, words, all kinds of words, long or short, voluptuous or spiky, poetic or plain, as if to keep my blood thick.

Voices break out downstairs.

The house holds its breath.

Laughter.

It is hollow and it has edges like blades but, still, it is laughter. My mother and stepfather are joking around.

The voices rise and the voices fall.

I hold my breath, and I wait.

Once our house has stumbled on peace and drifted to sleep, after Manchester has grown quiet and dark, I pull back the curtains to spy on the stars. Clouds make the night look puffy and bruised. The sky is not rinsed clear and shining, as I have seen it in Oxford, but a few gems of worlds-away light are sparkling through. I know they are there. When I was little, it was God who lived in the sky; now it's Shakespeare and Chaucer, Michelangelo and Bach, a buzz of new beauty and high-falutin ideas that have me besotted. I gaze up in the dark and then I can breathe, because I know they are there, my gods in the sky. Glamorous, heady spirits, twinkling.

It's hard to believe, after I have kissed her goodbye and snailed all the way back to this city of ancient, insouciant spires, that my mother and I share the same sky. During term-time, I work hard and enjoy my friends and smile and smile and smile.

My mother's house is still on fire. No one, it seems, can stop the flames from raging.

There is a flashing, siren irony at the heart of her new job – driving an ambulance, looking out for the rest of the world's hurts, tending to other people's tragedies.

Night after night, sometimes several times in one evening, I brace myself to go and stand outside the red telephone box opposite the Bridge of Sighs in the middle of Oxford. I am not the only one: literally hundreds of students depend on that one scarlet kiosk to touch and be touched by the people they miss. Come my turn, I step into the smoky womb, dial with brittle fingers, then trace delicate spirals, rhythmic with tense wishes, up and down the telephone's black umbilical cord.

How will she sound? Gravelly, dazed with despondency? High-wired and chattering, willing herself on? Muffled and sodden, misery leaking out of her face? Will she be able to speak at all?

'I'll not do anything silly,' my mother has promised.

But the telephone purrs, unanswered, into my ear.

Pick up, pick up, pick up.

'Hello?'

The sound of my mother's voice makes me so deeply, so sharply happy it hurts.

Years have wheeled by and my head reels with old, unfading stuff – still brilliantly, still terribly vivid. Those photos not abandoned in the endless shifting from place to place, from one frenzied fresh start to another, are gathered into a scrappy gang in a bashed and rusted biscuit tin that was once festively red and emblazoned with gold letters: *Family Selection*.

The back of my neck prickles whenever I bring myself to squeak off the scratched lid.

Smiles, forced or fleetingly real, cluster around sinister gaps: a man's face, chopped out by my mother's flashing scissors in a trembling fit of heartbreak or fear or desperate decision. A woman and three girls, features poised on the verge of happy, huddle wishfully around someone who has lost his head.

'Smile!' we were ordered on those occasions when a camera came out. 'Smile!'

Hope, that's what you see when you look at the hacked and misted photographs now. Hope, with a hole in it.

Our new photographs are exuberant and glossy, with no holes.

We take them when we get together – my mother and sisters and me – in one of the happy, safe places we have each made into a home: in Oxford, in London, in Devon, in Paris.

'Give over, will you?' Our mother laughs, shy, under the Cyclops eye of the camera.

It's not that the machine might steal a wisp of her spirit, but that it could show up too much: X-ray her soul; spread a nasty verdigris over her face, conjuring old bruises; or come out crowded with ghosts who have muscled into the frame.

'One more,' we plead. *Flash!* 'It's good to have pictures.'

My mother and sisters and I bow over the blank Polaroid square.

We giggle, realising we're all holding our breath.

Hannah comes over to join us, watching the picture bloom.

'It's you, Mummy,' she laughs, heart-ballooningly beautiful; there is my baby sister, Sarah.

'There's Aunty Andrea – and there's Aunty Lindsey.'

I hold the picture up to the light and waft it about.

From the murk of the Polaroid my mother's blushing image emerges.

'Magic!' Hannah's five-year-old eyes widen as the colours ripen up, shining.

She touches my mother's fingers. 'It's magic, isn't it, Granny?'

'Yes, luvvie.' My mother smiles at the picture of her family and squeezes Hannah's small hand. 'It is magic.'

The Lookout
Alan Beard

Birmingham

Once I'd have said we were the most visited part of the city, here at its remotest edge. Helicopters coming out of the sky, ambulances to pick up the dead and bleeding, police to take down the details. The Time of Nick. Politicians arrived in black cars and walked the charred area, craning their necks to look up at the three towers perched on land that juts out into the city's reservoir. The TV crew that came to make a documentary about the crime wave had their cameras nicked. Social workers honked as they passed each other on their way in and out of the estate, particularly after 'Fanny' Adams let her daughter eat herself to death in one of the flats above us. She fattened with all the trouble around and ended up so big it seemed dangerous to get in the lift with her. Not that she came out much. Nor did anyone else if they could help it. Mugging, suicide, arson, burglary. There was an accident where a lorry came off the flyover followed by a car. Nothing to do with us, of course, but on our patch. We hardly watched them clear the debris, except for the younger kids, we were too involved in our own clear-ups.

Things are calmer now. You can't leave your door unlocked like my gran says you could in the old days, but it's nothing like it was. Now I can hang out outside (not that I do much) and watch kids rollerblade along the paths that loop down through the slopes of grass between the towers.

In our block we now have regular floor parties, with all the doors open and music set up in the corridor. When the lift at the end opens by accident, the people see us and often return later. Rachel comes, the thin, dark-haired daughter of Annie, a friend of Mum's. I call her my XYZ girl because of the shapes her elbows and knees make out of her limbs. She's rarely still, moving around constantly, tapping ash from her cigarette. You could say she's posing, but you can see she's trying things out – different clothes, or make-up, or hairstyles every time. She seems made for the towers, nimble – I've seen her on the stairs, up them like she's on fast forward – darting, but able to fade into the background, essential here.

Like me. I'm nearly sixteen, little, bowed. Eyes stuck to the floor. But I see everything, everyone. From the man who lives among the wheelie bins in the basement and helps the dust-men and cadges fags off them, to the couple that live on the roof, nineteen floors up, take drugs and tie themselves with long ropes to the air-conditioning vent in case they're tempted to fly.

I patrol. I am neighbourhood watch. Darren gave me the job. He's Mum's current boyfriend and supplies the area; not the heavy stuff, just blow, some whizz. People come and go all day, everyone calm and chatty, greeting me, my sister Melanie, seven, and Dave, the youngest, a crawler, and Darren's own – on their way to the kitchen at the back where Darren works with his heated knife and accurate scales. On nice days they sit out on the balcony and blow the white smoke into acres of blue sky they can see from thirteen storeys up (floor 12A).

Darren's never lived in a flat before and seems to like it. He points out the finer points that no one else has – the use of natural wood in a lot of the fittings, how solid and well designed the place was inside and outside, how it looked as he was driving back from one of his runs, lit up against the background of water. Most of all, like me, he appreciates the view. Mum says I spent my toddlerhood staring out at the sky, its huge rolling clouds or its far, far distances on clear days. Mum says my first words were 'fog' and 'sun'. It was only when I got older, taller, I was able to look down and see the city spread below, as far as you could see; distant blocks, taller than us, marking the centre. I watched for signs of life: a train sliding diagonally across a corner, boats moving along the canal glimpsed through the tops of trees; closer, the flyover that looks as if it's taking off and reaching out to us but then curves away, held aloft by concrete stanchions.

Darren's grateful to me for pointing out the landmarks – the GPO tower, a golden domed mosque, the parks that are gashes of green. 'People'd pay to see this,' is his verdict. Evenings are best – the sunsets (Darren and I grade them), which make the city outline look like a backdrop for a movie. And then the lights sprinkled as if to mirror the night above. When it's snowing he calls me out to look with him up into air full of smudges like ash, further up like millions of full stops.

All this is undoubtedly due to the draw he puts down his neck. I don't know what he'd be like without it. Darren smokes like smoke is air, like it is breath and oxygen, life he's tucking down there in his lungs, but he's always careful to keep it away from the kids, especially his baby. (I'm allowed to join in occasionally.) Mum likes this consideration, and how much of a contrast he is to her previous boyfriends, including Melanie's dad who may or may not be Nick, and mine who's 'left the area' (Mum). Darren takes an interest, giving me the job of lookout and childminder, and Melanie is encouraged to do her plays, set in fairy glens with wounded horses, in front of him and he says she is going to be a great actress.

He calls me 'kid' and lies on the sofa with his hair tied back in a ginger ponytail and 'not bad muscles' (Mum) sticking out of his T-shirt. He asks me about my homework. 'Conrad? He wrote *Heart of Darkness* which *Apocalypse Now* is based on.' He retrieves the old video in its tattered case next time he's in Blockbuster's and watches it with me. He loves the beginning and keeps rewinding to repeat the lines, 'Saigon, I'm still in Saigon.'

When Mum does have one of her mornings, less frequent now, Darren's usually there – putting on the kettle, seeing to David, warming his bottle, always remarking on the broad sky at the window, having the door open on nice days although we get no sun in the mornings and all below stands in the shadow we cast, sometimes falling all the way to the curve of the flyover, its top edge across the shirts of hidden drivers on their way to work.

Mum's friends come and visit again, staying for a spliff and a chat. Doing each other's roots – there's always someone in the corner of the room with tinfoil on her head. Chatting about old boyfriends – 'There was a fart in a colander. Remember him?' 'That bloke with hair like an orchestra conductor?' 'Oh aye, and how many orchestra conductors do you know?' Most feel Darren's good for Mum, but there are one or two dissenters. Annie says he's too soft. 'Soft as shit. Thinks your arse is a perfume factory and we all know who's been there.' 'So does he,' says Mum, 'I don't hide nothing.'

Dave, if he's asleep, is in the pram – one bought specially to fit the lift. Melanie's in her room playing with her dolls or with one of the kids brought along, while I hang about. They've got used to my presence and sometimes talk about me as if I'm not there. 'Such a shame about his acne, will it leave scars?' 'Bound to.' If Rachel's there with her mum, which she sometimes is, I get very embarrassed. 'Still,' they always add, 'he's so clever. Always reading, writing.' 'He never bunks off school.' Then they get on to the usual subjects.

One old boyfriend always crops up: Nick. Darren, who sometimes joins the group after he's shut up shop, likes to hear stories about him. 'Was he good in bed then, this Nick?' The women differ on this; those who knew him early – 'yes', 'strong stuff' to those who knew him later on – 'crap', 'wasn't interested'.

Mum knew him early on, she was into Arnie in his

Terminator days and what with Nick's bodybuilding and being 'quite handsome if a little gormless around the mouth', she fell for him. He was a new boy on the block and Mum was always quick with the new boys. He wasn't around long enough for anything really bad to happen, but I didn't like him being in the flat. I tried to tell Mum but she was impatient with my seven-year-old's attempt – 'You mustn't think someone's guilty because of a look in their eye.' Nick was obsessed with the weights he kept in their bedroom – I wasn't allowed to touch them or even look at them. I'd catch a glimpse of him sat on the bed in his athletic vest lifting dumb-bells that looked like toys in his hands. He began to growl at me when Mum was out. Luckily, he left for a woman down the corridor and from then on he worked his way around the block, zigzagging up and down the floors from one side to the other.

And then it began. He got kicked out by one woman too many and couldn't find anyone to take him in, not even Annie, and he began living in doorways and cupboards and spaces in the building, which would have been tolerated except he began to threaten people, write his name everywhere and throw things off balconies. He put a sweatband round his head and proclaimed himself king of the block. He threw rival males down the stairs and ran to kick them down another flight. No matter numbers. He was a gang unto himself, as the police found out – trying to hold him down and getting bitten and kicked.

Marjory, fantastically freckled and shrunken from having too many kids or something, says, 'I'd chucked him out and he was still coming round for his marital rights though he never focking married me. Once he's outside banging and shouting and Lynne lets him in and I tell Marcus to ring the police on his mobile. "They won't focking come," he says and I'm off to the back bedroom and get in the built-in and he's coming down the corridor with two or three kids on each arm, slowing him down, but he carries on like a focking giant the noise he's making. I'm hid and it's like that scene out of *Halloween* with him pounding on the cupboard door and panels getting knocked in.' She's glad he's dead.

Not so Annie: 'He was bad but he had a heart underneath. Inside. He came to my door once, early morning, drunk, froze, but he was polite. He had this thing that he'd made for Rachel, been up all night doing it. Tied elastic to a stick and made an elephant out of plastic and fabric and when you pulled the elastic the trunk moved. 'I want to give this to Rachel,' he said; he insisted and I had to get her up.' She looks at Rachel to confirm this story but she looks down and mumbles, 'Don't remember.'

You never knew what to do if you saw him, he'd spring out at you and, as Annie says, he could be polite but would want a greeting, small talk or he became affronted. Inside knowledge helped. For instance, though he didn't like me reading stories he pored over my 'Eyewitness Account' book of lions. He said he wanted to fight one. He respected wildlife, he said. One day, I was coming back from school, crossing the Green, and saw him sat half-naked in the centre where all the paths converge. He sprang up when he saw me. Behind him the sun made scratched, blinding circles on all the windows and I focused on Rachel's – fourth floor, left corner – to keep out of eye contact. He was breathing heavily, fists curled. I knew he didn't know who I was; I could have been Robocop stood in front of him.

'Nick,' I said. 'I've been thinking about those killer bees you warned me about.' (Once, in a paternal mood, he'd told me how to survive an attack – basically, don't run.) His face changed. It was always just one emotion, in this case puzzlement, followed by joy.

'You've seen some,' he said and his body relaxed. 'I knew it. Knew it.'

About this time, Nick got into an empty flat and invited two tramps to live with him, and the next day one of them was found floating in the reservoir quite near the sofa the

Fowlers had heaved in the day before. The other tramp (now our basement dweller), still alive but beaten, couldn't remember anything and Nick was shouting 'kings and warriors, kings and warriors', blood on his upheld hands. He was sectioned and finally out of our lives about the same time as Darren came along and the residents' association was set up and, gradually, things improved.

We heard Nick had escaped from the secure unit and, presumably making his way back to the block, had climbed into the electricity substation and electrocuted himself. The women speculate as to whether it was suicide or whether he expected to get some charge from the electric, to turn into the superman he wanted to be, and fly like a streak through the sky, stars scattering behind him.

So now I can hang out. Darren encourages me. I'm not with the cool guys, you understand, brake-driving at the far end of the grass, spraying mud at the cheering audience, but with the girls, girls who aren't cool enough to be closer to the scene. Among them, Rachel. At the last party we stood close and moved our heads in time rather than dance together to 'I Love You Stop', which her mother, sobbing over Nick (it was a year, to the day, since his death), kept putting on, again and again. Rachel said, 'You won't catch me crying over a man.'

Now, outside, she is sneering again – up at the cars – and holding her ears. 'Bloody big dating ritual,' she says. She says that in Peru the boys attract girls' attention by throwing stones at them. She can't see much difference here. I agree. I find it difficult to talk. A few days ago she was in Levis and boots but now she stands knees apparent, face like a crescent moon through the dark lick of hair that curls against her face. We talk about Darren. I tell her he's got a big load coming in today so things will be good. I tell her I've got the last of his homegrown – 'a creeper' – and we walk off round the block to see the reservoir and we smoke, leaning against the railings. I refrain from pointing out the moonlight and starlight broken across the top of the choppy water; instead I talk of my 'job' for Darren. How I have to know all the comings and goings as his lookout. She says, 'And now you're on the lookout for me.' She says she's been thinking deeply lately and maybe I could help her decide something. 'Yeah, yeah,' I say like a Beatle, watching headlights wind up the hill across the lake.

She says 'come on then' and climbs the rail on to the concrete lip of the reservoir. We run along it, her first, arms out like a bomber pilot. The dust and gravel we disturb tips down the side, crinkling the water. I follow the stripe of her upturned trainers. She follows the route round the reservoir to the culvert, then heads inland to where the trees would hide us from the thousand window eyes of the flats. We pass the substation with its yellow 'Danger of Death' sign broken in half.

I know where we're headed. For some reason, after the crash, they never cleared away the car which is now part of the landscape, bushes growing up through the engine. Inside, the seats are used by lovers or as a doss for those who need it or a place to sniff glue with your mates. A boy and a girl together only head there for one thing. As we get close we slow, listening to hear if someone else is there, if we could hear above the noise of the traffic that sweeps by above us.

'You know why we're here don't you?' she says.

'Well, I hoped,' I say. We get in through the doorless side into the back seats that she cleared of debris first. We can see the three blocks through the glassless back window. 'Darren thinks they look like those thin cigarette packets.' 'Will you shut up about him.' She makes some moves. We kiss, touch. Well, she kisses my neck but avoids my face except for one quick brush of the lips. Today she's wearing a sending-home-from-school skirt but she slaps my hand when it goes to the hem.

'You're not doing anything to me,' she says. 'This is my night. I want to see yours.' She had chosen me, I saw, of all males, for the fact of my compliance. She takes out my cock and examines it like a scientist, screwing up her eyes to see in the reflected light. She feels it grow in her hand and turns up her nose. She yanks and pulls at it and peels it until I have to say 'careful' and then 'you'd better get something'. She points it out the car but the stuff still gets on her hands. She gets out to wipe herself on the grass. I lie back.

'Put it away then,' she says. I'd been quite impressed seeing it grow bigger than I'd ever seen before, but I don't think she was. She tells me as we walk back through scrub, which in childhood I had pictured as African veld, that she has decided, and I helped. She was going to be a lesbian.

It's then that I notice what I should have before – an unusual amount of traffic coming off the flyover and heading for our estate. No blue lights or sirens but there are motor-bikes. I tell Rachel I've got to run. She runs with me, fast as I am, faster, knowing the quickest way and leading me round dead ends I would have taken. We're still too late. We stop when we see what's happening, emerging from the wasteland. We have our arms round each other, catching our breath, as Darren – not handcuffed but flanked by policemen – walks out and down the steps of Spencer Tower. I look up to see Mum at the balcony, screaming down at the tops of heads but with the noise around, motorbikes running, a crowd gathering, no one can hear what she's saying.

Coventry
Peter Ho Davies

Frank and I are waiting for Lady Godiva. It's five to twelve and we're sat on a bench in Broadgate opposite the big clock, waiting for the pubs to open. We've just been down to sign on and we need a pint.

'Come on,' Frank says, his eyes on the clock. 'Shake a leg, darling.'

A group of OAPs on a tour have begun to gather in front of us. Their guide, Lisa, is telling them all about Lady Godiva and her husband, Lord Leofric; how she rode naked through the streets of Coventry to protest his unfair taxes and how the peasants, when they heard what she was doing for them, ran indoors and pulled their shutters and sat in the dark until they heard her horse go by. 'The original poll-tax demonstrator,' Lisa calls her and the old people chuckle and repeat the line to each other. Lisa is seventeen, but dressed older in a two-piece blue suit which makes her seem more skinny and angular than when we sleep together on her days off. She wears a light blue sash with the tourist board logo. It flaps against her chest in the wind.

'Wouldn't mind a cushy job like that, eh?' Frank says, a little too loudly.

'You'd look like bleeding Miss World,' I tell him.

The clock strikes at last and for a moment even the few shoppers hurrying for their buses stop and look up. The doors in the clock-face slide open and Lady Godiva rides out on to the narrow balcony. She's painted bright pink apart from the yellow hair that falls over her shoulders. One thick rope of it runs down her back and spreads like a cape over the horse; the other falls like a sheet into her lap. She gets about halfway round, when another door opens above her and a huge leering face, almost as big as Godiva herself, leans forward. It's Peeping Tom. He stares out for a moment, covers his face with his hands and is drawn back into the darkness.

The OAPs ooh and aah and Frank complains for the umpteenth time that it's not very realistic. 'She's too pink,' he says. 'And nobody has that much hair.'

'You'd be pink,' I tell him. 'Bollock-naked on a horse.'

'The horse is shite, too,' Frank says, and there he does have a point. It's drawn around the balcony on rails, and it's not bad enough that it glides, but it totters, too, as it corners. The last chimes die away and we watch Godiva wobble back inside for another hour.

Peeping Tom, Lisa is saying, was the only one of the townsfolk who spied on Godiva. 'And he was blinded for his trouble.'

'Blinded by who?' one of the old women asks eagerly, and Frank laughs. Lisa looks over at us and glares.

'By her husband, was it?' one of the old blokes chips in, hopefully.

'Actually,' Lisa says above the laughter, 'the legend doesn't tell us. Just that he was struck blind. By God, I suppose.'

The old people look a little startled by that, and Lisa says, 'Excuse me,' and walks over to where we're sitting.

'Just piss off, wouldya?' she says to Frank.

'Ah, we're only having some fun, pet. We were just saying how well you're getting on.' He looks at me for support, but she never takes her eyes off him and I keep my mouth shut. The OAPs are watching nervously.

'Here.' She digs around in her pocket for a moment and then thrusts her hand out under his nose. She's holding a tenner. 'Take it,' she says.

'Put it away,' Frank says.

The note is new and it quivers a little in the breeze.

'Go on, Dad,' she says, more softly, and, gently, he plucks it from her fingers. He takes it in both hands as if studying it, and only when his eyes drop does she give me a look and I nod to let her know it'll be all right. She walks slowly back to her group and I watch her go. She has her hair tied up, but one loose strand flickers across her neck. The old people are still looking worried, and I feel like calling out to them, 'It's all right. It wasn't God. It was shame. Tom was blinded by shame.'

Instead, I slap my hands on my thighs and say, 'Opening time.'

I only moved down here last year to be with Karen after we left college, so I don't have that many what you'd call mates in Coventry. The ones I did have, through work and that – the ones I used to watch football with or talk to about cars or holidays or mortgages – I've lost touch with. It wasn't their fault. I just stopped calling them after a bit.

It's not easy, either, meeting new people on the dole. You can't ask them what they do for a living for starters. 'The only thing worse than being unemployed is being nosy,' Frank told me the first time we met. 'It's a lonely old business, all right, on the dole – all three million of us.' He raised his eyebrows meaningfully. We were stood in the queue to sign on and I kept my mouth shut. Frank was a big bloke. Even balding and beer-bellied he looked hard. We shuffled forward over the rubberised floor towards the plastic window in front. Frank was ahead of me, and when he stepped up to the counter he hunched his shoulders like a kid at school not wanting anyone to see his answers. All we were doing was signing our names, but when it was my turn I covered up same as Frank.

That was the second time I'd signed on. The first time was awful. I got home and felt exhausted. It was like a day's work – catching the bus, queuing up, signing my name. I lay down on the couch with the TV on and curled myself into a ball. That was about a fortnight after Karen left.

I didn't remember him when Frank introduced himself, but he said he was Lisa's father. Lisa Chambers. We'd met at a parents' evening.

'Oh, Mr Chambers,' I said, but he stuck out his hand and said, 'Frank.'

'Chris,' I said.

Lisa was a student of mine in the fifth-form biology class I taught last year. I took over as a supply teacher the Christmas before their exams and found they'd covered most of the syllabus apart from sex education. Their previous teacher had got pregnant and couldn't bear to teach them in her condition. 'You know how their dirty little minds work,' she'd said.

Frank took me down the pub with him and then had me home for dinner. We sat in his kitchen over a cup of tea waiting for Lisa to come home from her summer job at five thirty. It felt like I hadn't talked to anyone for weeks. We started with football, but by the time we were done I'd told him so much I was embarrassed. I hadn't really talked to anyone about Karen until then. Most of our friends had been mutual and I'd somehow been too ashamed to call them. We'd been seeing each other for two years before she got the research assistantship at Warwick University. Last spring she was offered a Ph.D. place. Now she's sleeping with the head of her lab.

Frank made it easier by telling me stuff, too. He said he hadn't worked for nearly two years since Ford bought Jaguar and rationalised the plant.

'Rationalised,' Frank said. 'Like it made fuck-all sense to me.'

Frank had this whole philosophy of unemployment worked out. How to handle it. Keeping your chin up was his big tip. 'Look, there are no jobs round here. You've just got to accept it. All you can do is try and stay busy, make yourself useful, feel like you're worth something.' He cooked for Lisa every evening. She was back by then, and she rolled her eyes when she heard that, mimed two fingers down her throat, but Frank kept on. He did the shopping, he said, and the ironing and pushed the Hoover round the house every morning without fail.

'My job now,' he said, 'is being the best father I can be.'

'I hope it's not just a job!' Lisa broke in.

'More like hard bleeding labour,' Frank said, and he gave her arm a squeeze.

Since he'd not had one – or even a sniff of one – everything had become a job for Frank. Looking for work was a job. 'Just not one I'm much good at.' Being a good father was a job. Being a good mate. Keeping his chin up was a full-time job.

'Thanks,' I told him at the door when I left that night, and he said, 'For what? Listen. We have to stick together.' He meant the unemployed.

'No really,' I said.

'Here,' Frank said. 'Let me tell you. You were one of the few who ever encouraged Lisa at that school. Made her want to stay on and try for college.'

I tried to tell him it was my job after all, but he went on.

'She's going to be better than her old man. Don't get me wrong. I'm not one of those fellas who says "Why should my kids have more than me?" God knows I want her to have more than this.'

Lisa had come up behind him to see me off, and I could see her shifting her weight from foot to foot, embarrassed. I nodded to show I was listening. Frank must have sensed her, though – that or the draught through the open door. 'Well, anyway,' he said, 'she always used to tell me how biology was her favourite subject.' That made me feel absurdly happy for a moment, but Lisa just blushed.

The pub is a pit – torn seats, yellowing wallpaper, bulges of damp in the ceiling plaster – but it's empty at lunchtimes and it's got a dartboard. Frank doesn't like crowds and darts is better than bar billiards because you can play for free. Frank taught me that.

At the bar he pulls out Lisa's tenner, folds it lengthwise, making a sharp crease with his nail, and asks me what I'm having. After a second I say, 'Bitter shandy.'

'Bugger that,' he says. 'Two pints of bitter,' he tells the girl, and we wait in silence, watching the glasses fill. When she puts them back on the bar, I try to slip her my half, but Frank says, 'Gerraway! I'm getting these in.'

The barmaid looks at us blankly.

'Fine,' I say, and then, 'Ta,' and finally, 'Cheers.'

We've been coming here right through the summer, every couple of weeks after signing on, and this is the first time either of us has bought the other a drink. I take a sip while Frank pays. I should be buying him one. I got a job offer last week, but I still haven't told Frank and now's not the time. The man's buying me a drink. Besides, it's up north and I don't know if I'll take it yet.

'She made that up,' he says now, when we've sat down and he's had a good drink. 'Lisa did. About God and that.'

'Really?'

'Bastard.'

'She thinks on her feet, Frank. She's good at her job.' I try to sound bored. Frank doesn't know about Lisa and me.

'She's asking for trouble. That thing about the poll tax is something she just threw in there. She says she has to do something to make it interesting. Says it's boring otherwise. Next thing you know she'll be telling the wrinklies Peeping Tom was getting his leg over.'

I take a sip of beer and watch Frank over the rim of my glass as he raises his own. Frank needs a pint after signing on to give himself something to look forward to. He closes his eyes to drink.

Wrinklies is what Frank calls Lisa's OAPs. She says that's rich coming from him. 'Don't go lumping your dad with them,' he tells her. 'I've taken early retirement, see. Early.' Frank is forty-six. Lisa told me once that he'll never work again and for a moment I thought she said he'd never walk again.

When Frank finishes his beer I say, 'My shout,' and grab the empties quick as I can. We can't afford a tip so we take our glasses up when we're done. Frank taught me that, too. He follows me over to the bar, but I don't give him a chance to pay. Then when the barmaid gives me my change, he says to her, 'An' a couple of whiskies, luv.'

'That tenner's burnt a hole in your pocket,' I tell him, and he throws the whisky down without even bothering to take it back to the table. It makes me wince, but he just sighs contentedly.

'Cheers, big ears,' he says.

We play darts for a bit, but neither of us can hit a double to save our lives.

'You know what you need,' Frank says when he finally gets out. 'You need glasses, pal.' This is an old one. He's been after me for ever to get an eye test. They're free for the unemployed.

'My eyes are fine.'

'Next game on it,' he says, on his way to the bar for another couple of pints and two more doubles.

'You're on,' I say, taking up the darts, but Frank beats me hollow. I've not had more than a pint at a time for weeks, and the whisky's ruining my game.

A couple of Frank's mates, Tony and Don, come in as Frank is finishing me off. 'Good arrows,' Don calls. Tony has a tightly rolled up newspaper under his arm, which he waves in our direction. They get their pints and pull up chairs. Don asks, 'What's the crack, lads?'

Frank's mates are about the same age as him, and the first time Frank brought me down here they didn't like the look of me. I was young. I had a degree. What the fuck was I doing there? It was as if they didn't expect to see me again, and they hardly bothered to say a word in my direction. They've warmed to me over the weeks, though, especially since they found out I was Lisa's teacher.

'Did you ever teach that Debbie Jackson?' Don wanted to know and I said yes. Debbie had been in Lisa's class, but dropped out for a career as a topless model for the *Sun*. The idea that I'd taught sex education to a Page-3 girl entertained Frank's friends no end.

Tony's got a big grin on his chops today as he unrolls his newspaper and says, 'Got a nice picture of your girlfriend in here, professor.' He likes to let on that Debbie had a crush on me. ('Stands to reason. You being an authority figure, teaching her the ways of the world and all that.') He smoothes the paper down and we all lean forward to have a look.

The page won't lie flat, but Debbie is clearly recognisable. She's posed, topless, perched on the front of an ice-cream van. She's laughing, wearing bikini bottoms, her head thrown back, about to take a big lick of an ice cream she holds in her hand. Don reads us the caption: 'De-lovely Debbie Jackson's ambition is to be a journalist. Here she is getting her first big scoop.'

Debbie is all tits and hips, Lisa slim and a little flat-chested.

'Why do they always have to pretend that those girls want another job?' Frank says. 'It's like when they ask the beauty queens what they want to be. She's got a job. She's a model. What's she want to be a journalist for?'

Debbie's become a bit of a celebrity in recent weeks. The city holds a Lady Godiva parade every year and the lord mayor usually chooses some local beauty to ride through town in a body stocking. This year, though, a Labour councillor's put her own name forward for the job, because she thinks she can use the ride to protest the poll tax. The *Sun* picked up the story as an example of loony left politics and suggested that Debbie, as a local girl, would be the better choice. Beside the article they printed pictures of Debbie ('local lovely') and the councillor ('stick to politics').

'Your Lisa should have a go,' Tony tells Frank now. He gives Don and me a broad wink. 'She's a little cracker.'

'What's that supposed to mean?' Frank says. I feel myself tense. Tony stares at his newspaper. 'What's that supposed to *mean*?' Frank leans into the table and it rocks. Tony's pint slops a little and he puts his hand around the glass. 'I would die of shame,' Frank says, 'if that was my daughter riding around starkers. I hope I've brought her up better than that.' He looks over at me and tells me to sup up so we can get to the optician's. He raises his glass – it must be two thirds full – and drinks off the rest of his pint. His Adam's apple throbs in his neck, and a little beer runs down his cheeks.

I look at the half-pint sitting in front of me and feel sick at the thought of drinking it, but make myself anyway. Wasting it would make Frank wonder what was wrong with me. Don gives us a mock salute as we leave. 'See you in a fortnight,' he says, meaning the next time we sign on. 'Same bat-time, same bat-bar.'

Tony looks up, briefly, and goes back to studying his newspaper.

I was all right sitting down, but when we come up the steps I reel a little from the booze, and Frank has to take my arm for a moment. It occurs to me that I won't be able to tell him about the job now, and I lean on him in relief. I wouldn't be able to make a decision about it in this state and I don't trust myself to say it right. I'd start on about the job, but I'd end up telling him about Lisa and me.

Instead, I say I'm busting for a piss, and he stands guard while I go behind a skip.

I often wonder what made Frank pick me. Of course, we've got more in common than Lisa or just being unemployed. We're both big footy fans, and I go round there most Sunday afternoons to watch the game. When Frank talks about his old job he never says he was 'sacked' or 'fired' or 'laid off'. He says he was 'given his marching orders' or he 'took an early bath' – like a footballer who's got sent off. When I talk about Karen, I say she 'kicked me into touch'.

What we really have in common is that Frank's been sacked and I've been dumped. In the beginning I thought Frank's philosophy – keep busy, believe in yourself – would help me get over Karen.

I haven't talked to her for two months. She's still with him, her boss. He must be twenty years older than her. I suppose I've been hanging around all summer waiting to see what'll happen there. 'You'll get over her,' Frank tells me from time to time, but some nights, when I can't sleep, I walk out to the university and look up at her window. I wrote and asked her to explain it to me once and she just said she hoped we could be friends. I don't believe in that, though. I don't think it's possible – staying friends after you've been lovers. It's just one of those modern myths.

I suppose Frank's lonely, himself – his wife died five years ago. But he likes to see himself as a thinker. 'Boredom,' he says, 'is our black hole. The centre of the unemployed universe. It'll suck you up if you're not watching.' He's started to go down the library and the museum, but he doesn't like to go alone, and he doesn't know anyone else who'll go with him.

Lisa says her father's just a snob. 'He likes to hang out with a better class of unemployed people.' Meaning me.

The optician's is behind the cathedral, and as we're walking between the new cathedral that they built in the sixties and the ruins of the old one bombed in the war, we see Lisa again with another party. Frank waves but she ignores him, and he makes us follow her inside and lurk on the fringe of the group. She smiles at me a couple of times, but when she sees her father looking she scowls. The walk has cleared my head some, but dealing with Lisa and Frank is too much and I take a seat in a pew. The cathedral is cool, almost cold, after the sunlight outside.

Lisa is telling them about the tapestry of Christ – the world's largest tapestry – which covers one entire wall of the cathedral. It shows Christ seated, but from straight on the chair is hidden by his robes and the perspective is lost. It looks as though Christ is standing, as though his body is a long oval. Frank says he looks pregnant, but to me, when I can get my focus, it looks like Christ has a thorax and an abdomen. He looks like a great, stinging insect. That's the biology teacher in me.

Lisa points out details. Her suit jacket rides up as she raises her hand, and I catch a glimpse of white blouse at her waist. The tapestry was woven in France, where it took two hundred women over a million hours to complete.

'Waste of effing time,' Frank whispers.

Suddenly I think I'm going to throw up, right here in the cathedral. I have to put my head between my knees to steady myself.

Lisa begins to lead her group back outside, and Frank helps me up. At the door she stops and slips some coins into the donations box. Most of the tour party does the same, but Frank and I walk past quickly. Lisa gets a special allowance for this from the tourist board. It's by arrangement with the cathedral, a way of raising some revenue for the upkeep of the place.

'Fucking sheep,' Frank says as we walk away. He hates the OAPs because they're allowed to do nothing.

The first time Lisa came by my flat was about two months ago. It was a Monday, her day off, she said, and she was out cycling. I told her I could see that. She was flushed and wearing cycling shorts and a tight white T-shirt. She asked if she could have a glass of water and I helped her pull her bike inside and she followed me upstairs.

'Don't look at the mess,' I said, hurrying ahead of her to push my job applications into a neat pile and cover them with the phone book. I wasn't sure whether I was worried about what Lisa might think if she saw them or what she might tell Frank.

I offered her a seat, but she preferred to bend over and study my bookshelves.

'You have a great collection,' she said.

'I've not got much to do with myself but read,' I called back from the kitchen. 'You're welcome to borrow any of them.'

'I'd like that.'

When I came back she pretended not to be looking at the photograph of Karen on one of the shelves and I pretended not to have caught her. I passed her her glass. My fingers were wet with condensation and I dried them on my jeans.

The receptionist at the optician's is on the phone when we arrive. She is perched behind her desk, twirling a pen in her long fingers. We loiter under the bright fluorescent lights and I try on a few frames and pull faces at Frank. I'm trying to distract him. The girl is clearly making a personal call, and I can see Frank getting tense. It's not that we don't have the time, of course, but Frank hates to see a job done badly. 'There's no reason,' he hisses. 'Not with so many people in need of work.'

Eventually she looks up, covers the mouthpiece, and asks brightly if she can help us. Frank tells her I'd like an eye test.

'They're free if you're unemployed, right?' I ask, and Frank looks daggers at me.

'Uh-huh,' the girl says and tells us to take a seat. The optician is with someone. She goes back to her conversation. Frank flips through the pile of magazines on the table – back issues of *The Optician* – and finally sits back, crosses his arms, and glares at the girl.

I nudge him and whisper, 'Doctor, recently I keep imagining every woman I see naked. On a horse.' It's a stupid thing to say and makes me think that I'm really drunk, but Frank just grunts. The receptionist looks over at our whispering, but he stares her down.

Frank hasn't looked for work in a newspaper or at the job centre for six months. In one week, he's told me, he went to twelve interviews and didn't get a single offer and he doesn't believe in job creation any more. 'There are no new ones round here,' he says, 'just fewer and fewer of the old ones.' What he does now is to watch other people at work in shops or restaurants, wherever he goes, and decide if he could do their job better than them. He lives for bad service – especially if he thinks someone is treating him badly because he's unemployed. Quick as a flash, he'll write off a letter of complaint, and always at the end, often in a PS, he'll offer his own services. He thinks if he makes the complaint vicious enough, they'll sack someone and consider him for a job. I find myself defending people just to stop him sending a letter that'll do him no good and only land someone else in hot water.

The receptionist, having finally finished her call, says the optician will see me now and gestures towards a staircase behind her. Frank makes a big song and dance and insists on coming with me, and she smiles blandly and says, 'If you like.'

'That was nice of her,' I say as we go up. 'Wasn't it?'

'The universe,' Frank whispers back darkly, 'is finite and shrinking, buddy boy. There's no one creating nothing, just remember that.'

Lisa told me that she loved me last week, and then she asked me if I loved her. I said she was a lovely girl.

'You're still in love with her,' she said.

'Debbie?' I said, but she was serious.

'Karen!'

'No.'

She looked me in the eye, saw I was telling the truth, and it seemed to satisfy her. I was disappointed. This isn't the nitrogen cycle, I wanted to tell her. It's not photosynthesis. You don't have to take my word for it.

She likes to come to me in the morning of her day off, before I get up, and crawl in beside me. After we make love, she sleeps. Her lie-in, she calls it, and after an hour I slip out and bring her a cup of tea.

I'm twenty-four and she's seventeen. I think Lisa sees our lovemaking as a way of growing up, although I know I'm not her first. She's conscious, too, that somehow her having a job and me being unemployed has closed the gap. Besides, she likes the sneaking around. We hardly ever talk about her father. The subject makes me uncomfortable. 'Bor-ring,' she says. But Frank's only boring when we talk about him. When we don't, when he's this shared unspoken thing, she likes it. It's romantic. She thinks the secrecy brings us together.

'Maybe he already knows,' Lisa said once, and then, when she saw the look on my face, 'Just teasing.'

A little later, she asked, 'You could get a job, right?'

'Lisa,' I said. 'I'm a teacher. It's the summer holidays.'

'But next year?'

'Next year? Yeah, probably.'

'Thought so,' she said, and there was a glint of triumph in her voice.

Sometimes Lisa makes me wonder why I ever thought she was such a promising student. I can't tell her, but I wish she could just see that I sleep with her every Monday for something to do.

The optician parks Frank on a stool at the back and points me towards the chair in the centre of the room. I'm still feeling the effects of the beer and whisky, and when he asks me to read the letters on the screen I'm not sure if my eyes are that bad or if it's the booze. Next he switches the overhead light off and makes me look at a lighted board of letters and symbols while he slips the heavy lens support over my head. In the darkness, perched on the chair with the odd weight on my head, I'm beginning to feel the room spin.

It's quiet in the office, just the optician's voice asking me, 'Better, worse or the same?' as he clips lenses into place, and the sound of Frank's breathing. A couple of times I can't say if my vision is better, worse or the same and I make up an answer. My mouth tastes foul.

This must have been what it was like for the peasants waiting for Godiva to ride by, I think. Sitting in the dark, refusing to look out and shame her. Just listening to the horse. Then I think, maybe she wasn't all that pretty after all. Maybe that part's the legend. Perhaps Tom looked out and was blinded by her plainness.

Frank farts somewhere behind me – it's soft and so prolonged that he must be faking it somehow – but after a moment I can't help myself. I laugh so hard I lose my balance and have to put out a hand to grab the optician.

'Don't waste my time,' he hisses out of the darkness. He puts his face close to mine and says, 'Some of us have work to do.' I steady myself and sit still. I used to teach the eye.

The optician clicks another lens into place – the sound is dry and precise – and the tiny letters jump into a focus that seems almost supernatural. 'Better, worse, the same?' he says, and I tell him, 'Much better.' I hear him make a final scratch with his pen and he flicks the lights back on.

Gleaming in his white coat, he tells me I'm short-sighted and need glasses. He asks me what I do, and after a moment's hesitation I tell him I'm a teacher. He looks hard at me and says, 'Right.'

He tells me that I qualify for a discount of twenty pounds on the lenses and that I can choose frames from the selection downstairs. His voice is flat, and when he's finished he turns his back on us as if we'd never been there.

Frank and I go look at frames. He's embarrassed that this free trip is going to cost me money, but I'm still smarting from the optician's voice and also somehow elated by the memory of my improved eyesight. I try on a few frames, but the National Health ones make me look like one of my students and I find myself picking the more expensive frames. I look like someone else with each pair I try, and eventually I find one I like. I stare at myself and think, That's how I want to look. It's an odd moment of recognition. I wear them over to the girl at her desk and she smiles and says, 'They suit you.'

She pulls out a calculator and pecks away at it with her bright nails until she works out that the lenses and the frames together will cost me just under ninety quid.

'What about the discount?' Frank wants to know, but she tells me that she was including the discount. 'Bugger that,' he says. But the girl looks at me expectantly, and I say, 'Fine.'

Frank starts to say something, but then turns and walks away to look at sunglasses. The girl gives me a business card and says that the specs will be ready tomorrow after lunch.

Frank is wearing a pair of dark glasses with the price tag dangling over his nose when I go over to him. He's bent down, peering at himself in one of the little mirrors. When I appear behind him, he waggles his eyebrows at me in the mirror. It looks comic, his bushy eyebrows above the glasses. I say, 'Let's go,' and he takes the glasses off and blinks hard in the sunlight.

'You don't have to pick them up if you don't want,' Frank says out in the street, but the idea of leaving the glasses there seems somehow shocking to me. Now that I know what I'm missing, it would be impossible.

'It's fine,' I tell him.

'No really. He's a wanker, that optician. Just don't go back. All right?'

'Forget it.'

I ask him if he wants to play some table tennis. Frank is a demon at table tennis, beating me consistently with undiminished delight, but he just shakes his head. 'How 'bout going down the museum?' In the end, he suggests going back to the cathedral and climbing the old spire, the only bit of it left standing after the war.

'It's a beautiful day,' he says. 'The view'll be something else.'

Our UB40s get us in free and I follow Frank up the twisty

staircase, peering at the graffiti along the way. The narrow windows in the walls let in enough light for me to make out hearts and arrows and penises and balls. I'm relieved we didn't run into Lisa again outside the cathedral. Her tour circles every forty minutes or so.

Frank counts the stairs softly in time with his breathing. 'Two hundred and eight,' he says at the top, and we step out on to the balcony. The spire extends another twenty feet above us, but this is as high as we can go. We walk around slowly, and it's so clear we can see for miles. The breeze is stronger up here, and looking into it makes me blink. Frank points out his house, and the floodlights at Highfield Road where the City play, and the pub and the job centre and the road that leads out of town to the old plant. He points and I squint and say, 'Oh yeah.'

Now that I'm sobering up, I think I should have told Frank when I was drunk. Told him about this new job. Teaching in Manchester. Starting in a couple of weeks. Not that the details matter. Not that he needs me to tell him now. My mind is made up. I stare out at the view.

'The world is your lobster,' I say – an old Monty Python line – but Frank only looks puzzled.

I lean over one side and look down at the pitted head of a gargoyle. The university should be out there somewhere, but I can't make it out. Below and to my right the crosses in a cemetery look like a box of matches someone has dropped.

I feel like I should be trying to memorise the view.

The last time I walked out past Karen's I stepped quietly over the gravel of the car park below her window, placing my feet carefully and gradually letting my weight settle on them. I had begun a letter to her, something to say I thought we could be friends now if she wanted, but I'd never posted it. It wasn't that love for Lisa replaced my love for Karen. It was the fact that I didn't love Lisa and slept with her anyway that changed everything.

On an impulse I threw a stone up against Karen's window

and immediately stepped back into the shadows, my heart pounding, staring up at the drawn curtains. But no one came. I hoped they were in there, still, listening, their ears ringing from the snap of the stone on the glass, afraid to look out. But there was as much chance that the room was empty and that they were at his house.

Frank's looking over another side down into the walls of the cathedral itself, and I go over and stand with him. It's just after five and offices are emptying. There are figures in suits walking home through the ruins, and in the late afternoon sun they throw elongated shadows and move across the ground in complicated antlike patterns.

A tour party moves among the workers, but I can't tell if it's Lisa's. All the guides wear the same outfits. We watch as the group is shepherded from the cross of charred beams salvaged from the bombing to the site of the old altar.

'You have to imagine a wooden roof,' Frank says in a falsetto, and I realise he is reciting Lisa's script. 'The cathedral didn't take a direct hit, but when the buildings on either side were bombed, the heat was enough to cause the timbers to start to smoke and burst into flames. They collapsed into the cathedral and the fire melted the leaded windows, destroying all but a few panes of the beautiful stained glass.' In his normal voice he says, 'You'll be moving on, then?'

I nod.

'Have you told Lisa?'

Oddly, I'm not surprised. But I can't think of anything to say. All I can think is how unsurprised I am.

'Just going to leave her?' he says. 'Without a word of good-bye. What a fucking disgrace.' When I don't look up, he says, 'Not good enough for you, was she?'

I almost reply to that, but something in his breathing makes me stop and listen. It's short and ragged. I think, *he's crying*. But nothing in the world would make me look. This goes on for a couple of minutes. I watch the tour party straggle back and forth and finally stop beneath the spire.

'Too bleeding old,' Frank says at last. 'They won't climb it.'

We see their faces turn up towards us, and Frank waves. He waves like a kid, shaking his forearm back and forth. The sleeve of his nylon anorak makes a sound like panting.

'Come on,' he says, and I join him, feeling foolish until those below begin to wave back. If I had my glasses I think I'd be able to make out their faces, although the thought of leaning over the edge with ninety pounds' worth of glasses hooked over my ears gives me a moment of vertigo.

The old folks are getting tired of waving, and a few of their arms are falling. The guide is holding a hand up to shield her eyes, trying to make out against the sky who's up here.

'Come 'ere,' Frank says, and he takes my arm roughly and pulls me back against the spire. He leans his back and head against the cool, rough stone for a moment and then thrusts himself to the edge and spits.

We stay up there until it begins to get dark. It's the end of September and the nights are already beginning to draw in. I watch street lights come on below us, pink at first and then amber as they warm up. Finally we hear someone shout up from below that they're closing the spire. In the dark on the way down, Frank leads and I put my hand on his shoulder.

Freshies with Attitude
Pavan Deep Singh

Black Country

Parmjit waited impatiently. He checked his watch as he heard the chimes of the town clock strike. It was half past five, and they were late, he thought to himself. He was waiting at the end of his street, a quiet cul-de-sac with a neat group of semi-detached houses. He checked his watch again and again as he walked out into the main road. He slowly wandered along, hoping to see the shabby blue Ford van that had picked him up every morning without fail for the past six weeks at a quarter past five and taken him to work. Parmjit had been working as a labourer during his holidays from college, in a farm near Evesham. The day was Friday, his last day of work. He worked for a local businessman, an entrepreneur – Billa, who would pack his van with people and take them to work on various farms.

Parmjit stopped and thought for a moment; maybe the van had driven past forgetting him. Just as he turned back, he heard the familiar Punjabi music pumping out from behind. It was the shabby blue van at last. It screeched past him and stopped a few yards away. Seconds later a bright yellow turban popped out of the driver's window. It was Billa and he called out to him in Punjabi.

'Oi Jeeta! Hurry up, you're slowing us down.'

The back door of the van swung open. 'Jump in,' called out a voice from inside. Parmjit climbed in and pulled the door shut; the van quickly pulled away and disappeared into the traffic.

Traditional Punjabi music was pounding away. The van had no windows or seats in the back, and Parmjit found himself a place and sat down. Altogether, there were six people in the back including his friend Marik from college who sat opposite him and was preoccupied with his mobile phone.

'Kidda Parm,' Marik said as he reached out and shook hands with Parmjit.

'Safe man,' said Parmjit as he got comfortable. 'Did you check out that ADF tape? It's mad.'

'That's what I'm doing now, this stuff they've got on is nasty,' said Marik as he put away his mobile phone and plugged his earphones into his ears and began nodding his head to his music.

Parmjit looked around and saw all the usual faces. Mr and Mrs Singh, otherwise known as Karnail and Gejo, were arguing about some family matter. Gurbachan Kaur, or Bibi Bachni (BB) as everyone called her, had her dupatta tightly wrapped around her head and was mumbling away. She was trying to concentrate on her morning prayer amid the noise.

'Bibi, put in a good word for me,' came Billa's voice from the front.

Dara, the oldest person there next to BB, was sitting next to Parmjit and opposite Mr and Mrs Singh, and he was preoccupied with the *Des Pardes*, his Punjabi newspaper. Parmjit tried to close his eyes to get some sleep, but the van made a sharp turn and stopped.

'Last stops, then we on the motorways,' shouted Billa in his broken English as he momentarily turned down the music.

'It's the Freshies,' said Marik as he pulled out his earphones.

Dara opened the back door and in came two odd-looking teenagers. They both had permed hair, gold earrings, white trainers and leather jackets. Marik gave them a very strange look. The Freshies – Makhan and Pala – got in the van and quickly sat by Dara; the van whirled away.

'Motorways coming . . . coming . . . and happened,' Billa shouted as they approached the motorway.

'Look at them. What the hell are they wearing? Looks nasty,' said Parmjit with a disgusted expression, looking at Makhan and Pala who nevertheless seemed quite confident and sure of themselves.

Parmjit had never been to India himself, though he had heard much about it from his father, and living in West Bromwich he had come to see many Freshies over the years. Freshies was a degrading word, a cuss word, a local term coined by the youngsters, and it was used to describe newly arrived immigrants, usually illegal ones from India or Pakistan or wherever. There were other terms as well, such as FFI – meaning Fresh From India, or FOB – Fresh Off the Boat.

'I've got a new one: CFF – Confused Frustrated Freshies, that's what they are. They should be sent back, they're a disgrace to the human race,' Marik joked. He was always outspoken and made no secrets about his dislike of immigrants, especially Makhan and Pala.

'Yeah, they should be locked up for having bad taste in clothes,' agreed Parmjit.

'Kidda Makhana, Kidda Palaya.' Marik nodded away, trying to make polite conversation. 'Cool weather, ain't it?' He laughed.

Both Makhan and Pala nodded and smiled, not quite sure about what Marik had said to them. They tried to ignore him as they turned their attentions towards the Punjabi headlines in Dara's newspaper.

'Bit stupid, ain't ya?' Marik continued.

'Leave it out man, they don't understand,' Parmjit butted in.

'You translate then, ask them if they've ever shagged a Punjabi prostitute then,' Marik persisted.

'You boys, have you no shame!' Dara shouted as he folded up his newspaper. 'These boys are your brothers, you know.'

'They're not my brothers, mate,' Marik interrupted as he played about with his Walkman.

'Well, at least they work hard, they have manners and have had a decent upbringing, they're not latchkey children like you boys,' Dara continued aggressively.

'Parm, what does latchkey children mean?' Marik speculated.

'Dunno, mate, children with funny keys I guess,' assured Parmjit.

'Oh yes, children brought up in India are very so well behaved,' Bibi said in her usual slow and squeaky voice as she finished her mumbling. 'I was in Delhi last winter, visiting my sister – Charni – her grandchildren were so wonderful to me, always asking if I needed anything, asking if I was well and taking care of me. Children here have no respect, we have lost our children to the English ways,' Bibi reminisced in Punjabi.

'Yeah right!' said Marik. 'Look at these two, they're creeps, they're not the innocent type, they've gotta crafty look about them, you know. The kind who wouldn't think twice before robbing old ladies.'

'Yeah, but you know what these oldies are like, they love everything Indian. I bet the next thing they'll say is, Oh we should never have come to this wretched country,' Parmjit joked with a phoney 'Indian' accent.

'You know I think these guys have a serious attitude problem,' Marik went on.

The conversation continued; the Freshies kept quiet as usual, though their eyes keenly followed the action. It was more of a confrontation than a conversation, as Parmjit and Marik had their opinions and Bibi and Dara had their own set of rigid ideas, and no one was really prepared to listen or agree with anyone else. Karnail and Gejo, on the other hand, were unaffected since they had continued with their own bickering throughout the two-hour journey. It was a typical scene that took place practically every morning in the van.

As soon as they arrived at the farm everyone went off and

found a place to change into their work clothes, putting on their ridiculous aprons, gloves and caps. Billa walked towards the farmer – Mr Bevans – and began to chat with him. From a distance Parmjit and Marik looked out as they saw the two engaged in serious discussion, nodding away in disagreement and aggressively using their hands and waving their arms about.

'Billa looks stressed, man,' Marik said as he adjusted his cap, wearing it back to front.

'Yeah, looks like serious stuff happening,' Parmjit said as he looked out carefully. 'I wonder what Bevans is saying.' There seemed to be a problem.

'Never mind that, let's get some boxes and start the picking and packing, that's what we Pakis do best – picking and packing. We better start before the Freshies, you know how fast they are,' Marik said as he charged towards the stack of boxes.

They worked in teams of two and their job was to fill boxes with freshly picked beans as fast as possible. Mr and Mrs Singh worked as a team, Dara and Bibi were a team, the Freshies were a team and, of course, Parmjit and Marik were a team. Every team had been allocated an aisle, a row, which they would work on during the day.

Marik started by picking the beans from the branches, passing them over to Parmjit, who packed them away neatly. Every so often they switched over. They would make two pounds for each box if it was of the right weight. It usually took them an hour to fill a box if they worked alone, but working in a team they could fill four, sometimes even five. Working at the farms was hard work, and the boys were glad that they were only at it for another week, until their college holidays were over. It had all seemed like a good idea to work in the farms before the summer holidays, a nice little earner, some pocket money. But the novelty had quickly worn off.

The summer had started off pretty well, with the boys making about twenty pounds each a day, but then something happened. The Freshies turned up. The Freshies, well, they worked at an alarming pace, packing more boxes than everyone else, especially the boys. They obviously made more money than everyone else. What was even worse was that Billa never checked their boxes properly, saying that the Freshies were proper Jats and therefore had a natural instinct about farm work. Parmjit and Marik hated the double standards, because each time they filled a box and took it to Billa for weighing he would examine their box thoroughly, sometimes checking each and every bean. Often throwing out a few and sending the boys back to fill their box properly. The boys did not take to this kind of humiliation well, swearing back and calling out abusive names in Punjabi, with the usual mother, father and sister insults.

Parmjit and Marik had been working without a break all morning, boring and mundane work. Parmjit stopped; he looked at his watch; it was almost lunchtime, and he took a sip of his cola and then threw the empty bottle over the aisle, hoping it would hit someone. The only thing that had kept the boys going was the cussing and blazing and daring each other to steal from the other workers, especially the Freshies. But now all their enthusiasm was dead. The day was unusually hot and the sun was scorching; it was as if they were working in an oven.

'I've had enough,' Parmjit said as he wiped off the sweat from his forehead. 'This is slave labour, you know, I can't work like this.' He took off his T-shirt and wrapped it around his waist and looked across at the others.

'The Freshies, I bet they're caning it. I think we should ask them to give us a hand,' Marik said as he also looked over to see the others.

'But . . . Have you no pride?'

'They're supposed to be our brothers, ain't it. We're never gonna make any money at our slow pace.'

'OK, but you ask,' Parmjit said.

'No sweat! Just watch me,' Marik said with great

confidence and walked across towards the Freshies' row. Parmjit followed.

'Kidda lads, we brothers, yeah . . . my ancestors your ancestors same thing, yeah!' Marik began trying to level with Makhan and Pala. 'You see, me and my mate Parm, here, yeah, we thought you could give us a hand, right . . .' Marik continued as he pointed to Parmjit.

'Mak, are you sure they know what you're talking about?' Parmjit wondered, realising that both Makhan and Pala looked rather amused as they both grinned and laughed. 'Looks like they're making fun of us, mate.'

'Look, I know they know. They understand all right! They speak in English in some parts of India. Don't they?' Marik assured himself and Parmjit. He then looked directly into Makhan's and Pala's dark eyes. 'Eng-lish. Under-stand. I friend. You help friend, yes.' Marik nodded his head, waved his arms as he struggled. Speaking ever so slowly.

'You cheeky – now you've really lost the plot,' Parmjit said as he laughed aloud.

'This stuff works, you know. It's how Tarzan speaks to the natives and they always know what he's on about,' Marik stated.

'You stupid, you English Lakis, we have to make our money, don't waste our time,' Pala unexpectedly shouted out.

'Chill, man, chill, respect, I dig the attitude.' Marik danced around.

'What's a Laki?' Parmjit stuttered, looking rather puzzled.

'I . . . I don't know. But I don't think it's a compliment, you know. I'm getting some bad vibes, man,' Marik stuttered. 'We better get on with our work. These losers aren't gonna help us, they think they're way better than us.'

'There, that was a fine example of communication breakdown,' Parmjit reflected as they walked back to their aisle.

'Now, I gotta admit that was embarrassing.'

'Yes but not as embarrassing as being called Marik instead of Amrik.'

'Yeah, em, yeah, but, anyway, it's not my fault that the English woman couldn't pronounce Amrik,' Marik said, shaking his hands and getting ready to resume work.

'Karnail, Gejo, Bibi, Dara, Marik and Parm, all of you come, urgent meeting,' Billa shouted out at the top of his voice.

'I wonder what he's got to say, we better go and check it out,' Parmjit said. The boys left their work and walked to Billa by the van. Everyone except the Freshies was gathering there. The farmer, Mr Bevans, was also there, standing next to Billa. Both of them were looking very worried.

'What's the problem? You're eating into our time,' Bibi said in Punjabi.

'Yeah, Bill, what's the deal?' Marik shouted.

'There are rumours,' Billa muttered.

'What kind of rumours?' Parmjit asked.

'Well, we think there might be a raid here today,' Mr Bevans began.

'It looks like somebody has reported me to the police. There might be a raid here today, in search of illegal immigrants,' Billa started to explain in Punjabi. 'Mr Bevans has word that we could be raided any minute and when they – the police – come they'll want some kind of identity from you all.'

'That's gonna be a major problem, ain't it. I ain't got my bus pass,' Marik claimed.

'I'm not worried about you, I'm worried about Makhan and Pala. If they get caught they'll be sent back and put in prison and I'll lose my licence,' Billa said. 'I need help from you all. We must be careful, we must hide them.'

'Respect, man. I didn't know that Billa had a licence. Did you?' Parmjit wondered.

'Who cares about Billa, this is the best news I've heard all day. If you ask me I think it's for the best. Makhan and Pala should be caught and sent away,' Marik whispered to Parmjit.

'I know what you're saying, they're losers and all that, but if they get caught I'll feel sorry for them in a way,' Parmjit responded.

'You're not going all philosophical are you?' Marik asked.

'I suppose they're like us – Indian,' Parmjit continued.

'What do you mean? You're not going soft in the head are you?'

'No, nothing like that. Well, what I'm trying to say is that our parents were like them . . .'

'You mean bastards.'

'No, immigrants. We should help them.'

'One last thing. We must be very careful,' Billa shouted as everyone walked back to carry on with their work. As they walked away they all talked about the situation. Karnail and Gejo discussed various options and suggested ideas to help, while Dara and Bibi got emotional and began talking quite a lot about Kismet and Waheguru.

'Back to work,' Marik said. 'That's that then, I suppose they'll get caught. I wonder what'll happen to their boxes.'

'Come on, we will ask them,' Parmjit said.

Once again the boys went over to see Makhan and Pala, who were both busy working.

'All right, lads, we hear you're in a bit of bother,' Parmjit began.

Makhan and Pala looked bewildered.

'Yeah, both of us thought we could help you guys with your predicament,' Marik added.

'Predic-a-what!' Parmjit said, looking puzzled.

'You know what I mean. We could help; after all, I know people, Parm here knows people who know people who know people. Makhan, Pala, with us as your mates you've got nothing to worry about. We wanna help. We're brothers, ain' it,' Marik stated with confidence.

'I'm surprised that you two want to help us,' Makhan said.

'Yeah, yeah, we're just full of surprises, ain't we, Parm?' Marik laughed as he looked at Parmjit. 'And all you have to do is help us. I mean, fill a few boxes for us, helping us out and all that.'

''Cause like you we have a problem too. We've got to make money as well,' Parmjit said.

After some time, the boys saw that Makhan and Pala were not going to help them. They went back to their own work.

'It's been a while,' Marik whispered to Parmjit.

'Yeah. We've got to make up for lost time,' Parmjit responded, realising that they had neglected their work.

Marik looked around and wondered, 'I'm surprised the police ain't come yet. What did they say when you phoned them? You did ring the police! Didn't you?'

'Well, no, I thought you did. Anyway, you're the one with a mobile,' Parmjit said.

That was the last day for Parmjit and Marik working at the farm, their holidays from college were over. As far as they were concerned they would never work in a farm again. It always made them angry that Makhan and Pala never helped them out, and they never got caught. They often wondered about that day, about the mystery person who had called the police. Who could it have been if it wasn't either of them? Maybe it was Bibi, or Dara, or Karnail and Gejo. Who knows. After all, everyone was losing money because of the Freshies.

Gap Kids
Julia Bell

Norwich

They've opened another Starbucks on London Street. Haven't even put the signs up yet and there's people milling around on the cobbles, drinking lattes and cappuccinos from great white beakers that look like they were made for babies. A blur of khaki and trainers, skateboards and mobile phones. Something in me resists as I pass them, makes me want to go to the markets instead, where the coffee tastes of chicory and there's always a layer of scum on the top of the water.

I go in anyway, but I feel a bit guilty ordering a three-quid mochaccino, as if I'm doing something bad for my morals. Residual shame from the time Psycho Sue caught me in McDonald's sinking my teeth into a Big Mac. 'Oh Janis, lass, whorraya doing in hia?' There was nothing I could do to deny it. The evidence was in my hand, half chewed. 'Ya'r a Fair Weather Wendy ya are, Janis,' she said, dumping a load of Womyn's Collective 'Meat is McMurder' flyers on my table. How could I tell her about the cravings then? *I want more*, I wanted to scream at her. More than thirty quid a week and smoking Cheap Cil's slate and living in a house that has gone past being cared about, with the dole on my back every five minutes. *More*. The talk about communities and alternatives: it wasn't a political point, it was pointless.

There's a queue at the end where you're supposed to collect your drinks. The students they're employing haven't quite got used to the idea of slick service and the old ladies are confused by the system of paying and then waiting. They look anxiously at the red faces preparing their drinks as if they're being ripped off.

While I'm waiting a group of girls comes in, petite replicas of the glossy fashion pages: summer sportswear and string handbags, water bottles and books.

One of the girls waves at me. 'Hiya!'

For a minute I can't quite place her. A fellow student, I know, but name, year, subject evade me. I smile back and wave, then realise it was a mistake, she's coming over to talk to me.

'All right,' I say, 'how's things?'

'Great! Just taking it easy for a bit. Having a bit of time off, working out what to do next, you know?'

Yeah, I think, I know.

'Anyway, what d'you get?'

'Oh. A Desmond.'

'You what?'

'A Desmond. A two two. Desmond Tutu.'

She looks at me, not quite sure what to say. 'Oh, er, well done.'

'It's all right. I was pissed off about it last week, but –' I shrug.

She smiles and nods encouragingly. Now I remember: Carolyn Giles, Women and Literature, last semester. She didn't see the point of feminism. Our generation are so *over* all that,' she whispered in my ear during one of the lectures. 'I mean I *like* wearing lipstick, y'know what I mean?'

'What about you?' I ask.

'A first,' she says, her grin widening. 'I got a first.'

'Well done.'

We smile at each other. I don't have anything to say to her.

'You still writing?'

'Oh. Yeah. Just bits and pieces.' *That's* why I came into town. To procrastinate. Anything's better than pottering around the flat in this heat while the computer throbs away idly on the desk, like toothache. I promised myself that I'd finish my novel when I got my degree, but I've hardly written a word since the results.

'You going to watch the match?'

'The match?'

'England Germany.'

'Oh.' That match.

'We're having a party,' she says, 'a barbecue, tonight, to watch it. You want to come?'

'Sounds great,' I say, trying to be non-committal.

'Come on,' she says. She's being insistent, writing the address down on a Starbucks information leaflet. 'We've got Widescreen TV and cocktails.'

'All right then,' I say, more to get rid of her than because I mean it. If Fiona were here she'd be complaining. 'Football,' she always said, 'is a game men play with their balls, and since I have nothing to do with either I don't see why I should care.' She was fond of lines like this – 'His mother should have thrown him away and kept the stork' or 'Men are like rollercoasters, stay on too long and you start to feel sick' – she had lots of them stuck in her memory like fridge magnets.

'You will come, won't you?'

'Thanks, Carolyn,' I say, this time remembering to smile. Her persistence is touching. She must think I'm worth it. 'I'll try and make it,' I say. 'Sounds fun.'

On the way back from the centre, weaving through the knot of medieval streets, the whole town seems to be melting. This heatwave is unexpected; no one's had a chance to acclimatise yet.

They've done up the Slug and Lettuce, the one by the cathedral. Looking through the window, it's like a Gap advert. Beanbags and trestle tables, fake tans and sports sandals. Gaggles of red, beery boys in England shirts clog up the pavement outside.

'Cheer up, love.' One of them is in my face, livid with drink.

'Fuck off,' I say, broadening my shoulders, making myself butch.

He shouts something back, but I'm across the road now, past the cathedral. I dig my hands into my faded 501s and childishly comfort myself with the things I will buy when I sell my novel for millions of pounds. I try to smile.

I turn into Magdalen Street and the shops begin to get cheaper, scruffier. Someone shouts at me from across the road.

'Janis!' It's Kenny. Kenny lives in the bedsit underneath my flat, little more than a bathroom, a kitchen and a lounge-bedroom. 'Yar all right?' he roars, stepping out into the traffic to talk to me.

'Yes ta,' I say, reaching out a hand to steady him as he staggers on to the kerb.

'Yar going to watch the match?'

'Maybe,' I say.

'I'm going up the Ironmongers,' he says, 'but I'll be in the Tavern later.'

I like Kenny, he looks out for people. Trouble is, these days, he can't really see them too well. He used to work on the rigs out of Yarmouth, fucked his back in some accident, and now he's pissing away his compensation. Since the Tavern got Sky Sports we watch the football together, me nursing halves of lager to his halves of whisky. Man U, always Man U. Unlike the rest of the country, people round here like winners.

'Later, Kenny,' I tell him. 'I'll come and find you later.'

'Nice one, girl.'

He slaps me on the back and staggers forward. His eyes are swimming. I doubt if he'll last until the evening. Not in this heat.

He's been sick outside his flat. Down the wall by the guttering. There's flecks of blood in it by the look of it.

Once I'm in, I want to go out again. The heat is oppressive, the damp smell that rises from Kenny's flat suffocating. Fiona would hate this; living so close to men. She always said she wanted to live like the Amazons. 'Women give you all the emotional support you need,' she said. 'Men don't know what the word means.'

I lie on the sofa and try to read but the words swim in front of my eyes. It's too hot to think. Every now and then the sound of roaring – *En-ger-land, En-ger-land, En-ger-land* – jerks me out of my dozing.

I suppose I will watch the match. Since I've been living here I've got into it again. I was born in 1966: 'Best year for football this country's ever seen,' according to Dad. Which meant that I had to like football whatever. Sacrilegious not to. We watched it together on the telly. He said he couldn't afford to take me to matches, though he would go occasionally with Uncle Ted, or Barry, his best mate, in his battered gold Capri. On my eighth birthday he bought me a Liverpool scarf.

There's a commotion of coughing and swearing outside. I get up and look out of the window. It's Kenny and some bloke from the pub. I've seen him before: greasy baseball cap, slimy bomber jacket with the padding escaping at the sleeves. I can't make out what Kenny's saying; all his words are tonally berserk, like someone's messing with the pitch control.

'Fach off. FACH off. Ahll be ahrit. Yaar NO yaAR no.'

Kenny's holding a T-shirt to his head. There are big oily patches of blood down the front of his shirt. He's swaying all over the shop. He should probably go up the hospital, but he won't. Last time he went in about his back they tried to dry him out and he nearly died.

Greasy Baseball Cap gets it together to open the door. There's a crash as it swings back on its hinges and more swearing and then someone sitting down, the creak of springs. Silence. The roar of traffic from the ring road. I wonder if there's anything I should do.

There's blood spots on the tarmac, a grisly trail leading from the car park round the back to the flats. I knock on the window.

'YAAARRR?'

'You all right, Kenny?'

Greasy Baseball Cap comes to the door without his bomber jacket, showing a ripped and greying T-shirt with IBIZA SUNSHINE in faded fluorescent letters on the front.

'Kenny's indisposed,' he says in a strangely composed voice, comedy posh.

'Is he all right?'

'I'm looking after him.'

His skin is plump, fleshy, made childish by glasses that are sub-NHS: blue plastic frames taped up on one side with Elastoplast. He's got the hiccups but he's trying to hide it.

'Er, OK. I'll leave you to it.'

Carolyn's written the address in curvy handwriting. *Pottergate*, a cobbled street still inside the city walls. It's early, probably too early to arrive, but I can't face going back inside the flat. Not with Greasy Baseball Cap downstairs.

I take the long way round, following the city walls, all the way down the river, past Cow Tower and up through Cathedral Close where they film costume dramas outside the Queen Anne houses. It's so picture-postcard it hurts.

When Fiona left for London she said she'd miss the scenery. 'Norwich is so pretty,' she always said.

Pretty vacant, more like.

A lad in a red Ronald McDonald wig opens the door. I recognise him vaguely, friend of one of the students, maybe even Carolyn's boyfriend. He looks surprised to see me. We stare at each other for just too long.

'Er. Come in, come in,' he says, finally.

He steps back and leads me through the house to the kitchen. It smells of paint; the hall is a new, soft orange, the floor shiny polished wood, the kitchen a pale toothpaste green. Carolyn is opening bags of nachos, cracking the lids on tubs of hummus.

'Oh, hi.' She looks a bit surprised. 'You're here.'

'I brought some booze.' I hold up a fourpack of Stella.

'Great!' We look at each other. She smiles uncertainly. I'm beginning to wish I hadn't come. 'Everyone else is out the back. What d'you think of the house? We did it ourselves.'

I don't know what to say. 'Gorgeous.'

'We bought it between us.'

'You *bought* it?' How horribly grown up.

'Well, Nikki's dad secured it, but we've got our names on the deeds. Kind of made sense really, house prices and all that. I'll show you round.'

The house is impeccable. Her bedroom is a dark blue with stars painted on the ceiling and material draped over the headboard. This obsession with home decorating has passed me by a bit – I blame *Blue Peter* myself, all those bloody washing-up bottles and rolls of sticky-back plastic.

'Couldn't live with this colour though,' I say, trying to sound authoritative rather than catty.

'Really?' she says, disappointed. 'D'you think? Maybe it is a bit strong.'

When I was her age I was at Greenham, shivering in Cheap Cil's bender, joining hands around the fence, talking revolution over a damp campfire, people throwing stones at us from passing cars. Psycho Sue earned her 'Psycho' label for battering a copper and getting six months for it. We thought we were saving the world. We thought we were all going to die in World War Three. Now, I wonder why we cared so much. No one else seems to any more. Everybody wants an ecstasy lifestyle – doesn't even matter if they don't take the drugs.

I look at Carolyn swinging her hips in her Joseph skirt. I bet she really regrets inviting me here. I crack a ringpull off a can of Stella with a defiant hiss. Well, I'm here now, might as well get drunk.

*

They've put the telly outside on the patio. Massive great box with a screen like a cinema. A dozen kids are sat out on the grass on rugs and cushions and beanbags. I recognise quite a few of them. One of them puts a joint behind his back.

'S'all right,' I say, 'I'm not anyone's mother.' I flop down on the grass next to the boy in the red Ronald McDonald wig. 'Hot enough for you?' I ask, smiling. He doesn't look away from the screen.

Up close I can see that the wig is making him overheat – his temples are beaded with sweat.

'Nuh, boiling,' he says, nodding his head.

They're still building up to it. Shots of the crowd, wigs, warpaint, Liverpool flags, BCFC, Man U, the Gunners, even some sad bastard in a Canaries shirt.

'What's the score going to be then?' I ask.

'Two nil,' he says, definitively, his eyes drifting from the screen to watch Carolyn as she comes outside with a tray of crisps. I watch his eyes dropping down her figure, lingering on her breasts. 'I put twenty quid on it.'

'Oh.' I shift myself about on the grass and take another swig of beer. A boy in a white England shirt puts burgers on the barbecue. They hiss and spit and catch fire. They've let the coals get too hot, but I won't interfere.

'Fuckin' hell, Simon, you trying to set fire to yourself?'

'Piss off, Dan.'

Carolyn comes over and sits next to me. 'Pringles?' she asks, offering me the bowl. I shake my head,

'No ta. They make me feel like I'm living in an advert.'

'Oh.' She looks crestfallen. I wish I wasn't in such a bitchy mood. 'Dan?'

He reaches across me to grab a handful. 'Thanks, babe,' he says, winking at her.

She giggles. 'You look a twat in that wig.'

'Love you too,' he says, crunching on a wedge of crisps. Smithereens of reconstituted potato cover his England top.

'Messy bastard. You need a bib.'

'Ah fuck off,' he says with his mouth full.

This abuse goes on for ages. I pretend not to notice, watch the screen, finish my beer, open another one. The air is thick with barbecue smoke, and in the distance is the noise of chanting from the pubs. Then a roar and the players are coming on to the pitch. Someone turns up the volume. With the super-surround sound, the cheering is deafening. I get expectant goosebumps. Nothing else is happening now. The streets will be as empty as they were for Diana's funeral.

'Ooh, it's David,' Carolyn says breathily.

'You like him?' I ask.

'Yeah, don't you?'

'He's a fucking shirtlifter,' Dan says, before I can reply. 'SHE-RA. SHE-RA.'

Carolyn giggles.

They play the German national anthem. Everyone hisses, as if at the baddie in a panto.

'Send 'em off,' Dan shouts. 'Twwoooniiil, you bastards.'

For the first five minutes everyone stares at the TV. All the players are nervous. They're over-kicking the ball, marking each other too hard, neither side can settle into a rhythm. Dan shouts 'Penalty!' or 'Free kick!' every time Germany touch the ball.

England get a free kick. Beckham takes it.

'Come on, lover,' Carolyn says as the camera closes in on him kicking the ball, shorts flapping around his thighs like sails. 'Do it for me, David.' The ball lands at the feet of the Germans.

'POOF,' Dan says, giving the finger to the TV.

After fifteen minutes it gets strangely boring. We're not playing as a team. Everyone running back to defend and nobody passing the ball around in midfield. Beckham is too much the star to be a team player. He's been strutting around, puffing out his cheeks, hands on hips, waiting for free kicks so he can do his balletic little superstar turns.

Carolyn stands up to fetch more drinks.

'Get us a beer, there's a love,' Dan says.

'She's not your love,' I say, almost by reflex.

Scholes kicks the ball at goal but it flies high above the crossbar.

'OH!' Dan sits up, thumps the grass. 'You what?' He half turns towards me.

'Never mind,' I say.

At half-time it's still nil-nil. I've had three cans and my head feels tight and fuzzy.

'We're playing like fucking *donkeys*,' Dan says, scuffing the grass with his trainers.

I lie back and look at the back of the house. Must be eighteenth century or very early nineteenth. Old, anyway. The brickwork looks like it's been recently repointed and the woodwork is shiny with new paint.

'You own this place then?' I ask, more for something to say than because I'm interested.

Dan laughs. '*Me*? He shakes his head. 'The girls got it sorted. I pay the rent. Couldn't afford a place like this on my wages.'

'Here you are, carnivore.' Carolyn stands over him, holding out a burger. Her wraparound skirt flaps open, giving him a flash of her knickers. He blinks. Tomato sauce drips in a thick splodge on to his jeans.

Second half and immediately Germany get a free kick.

'Fuck off, Krauts!' Dan shouts, flinching away from the screen as Ziege boots the free kick. It floats over the crossbar.

'We won the war, you wankers.'

'You didn't,' I say.

Dan turns to me. 'Eh?'

'You didn't win the war.'

He narrows his eyes. 'You trying to be funny?'

No, I'm trying to pick a fight, I think. I take another swig of beer. 'You're all right,' I say. 'I'm pissed.'

I suppose I feel a bit guilty. There were loads of Germans at

Greenham. Made some of us look almost right-wing. Selma and Hilde; they wouldn't buy food from shops because they said it propped up the system, so they ate what they could catch or steal from other people's vegetable plots until Hilde got pneumonia and they had to go back to Berlin. Selma complained that the English countryside hadn't proved at all nourishing or fruitful, 'not like in your poems'. But the truth was that they were scared in case radioactivity had leaked out and contaminated everything. They were living on acorns and blackberries in the end, gathered from fields miles away. I wonder what they're doing now, if they're watching this game.

England surge forward again. Michael Owen could score but – *argh* – the ball won't sit down for him. I find that I have been pulling up handfuls of grass.

'Come on, come *on*.'

It happens in slow motion. Or maybe it takes so long to sink in that by the time we've realised it's a goal they're already on the replay. Beckham kicks the ball perfectly, like it's on the end of a string attached to his boot. It bounces between two bewildered German defenders and on to the head of Alan Shearer. Bang. In the back of the net. The cheering could be heard in outer space. All over town you can hear it. No one louder than us.

'OH YEEESSS. FUCKING YEEEESSSS. SHE-RA, SHE-RA.'

Germany are retaliating almost immediately. There is a different kind of urgency now, the game picks up pace and momentum. We've got to hang on; they've got to score. Germany seem to have far too much possession but they keep missing their shots on goal. We're winning because of their mistakes.

Dan can hardly watch. He covers his eyes with his hands whenever Germany get a free kick.

'Come on, one more goal. One more. OH! Ince, you fucking *tosser*.'

Ten minutes to go, and it's like we've all crawled closer to the telly. I'm surprised how much I care. If England win, I think to myself, if England win I'll finish my book, get out of here. Make enough money to skip town, go travelling, maybe even go visit Selma and Hilde, or go to Spain for a bit, get a tan, maybe even get a girlfriend.

Eight minutes to go, and still nothing is safe. Barmby gives away a dangerous free kick. Oh Christ, we can't let them score, not so late in the day.

Dan is silent, holding his breath.

'We're going to win,' says Carolyn cheerfully. 'I'll go and get the champagne.'

'Shh,' Dan says. 'Don't say that, it's bad luck.'

Countdown time – oh no, three minutes of time added on. Too much, too much, anything can happen in three minutes. I watched Man U beating Bayern Munich in the Tavern with Kenny. Two goals in two minutes.

Then the whistle. At last, we won. Dan's eyes are wet round the edges. 'Fucking hell,' he says. Then he stands up and lets out a big roar and starts jumping around with the rest of us. We're all kissing and shouting.

Dan picks up Carolyn and spins her round. He loses his balance and they fall backwards into the bushes.

'Aaww, Dan.' Carolyn gets up. 'For fuck's sake, I've got mud on my skirt.'

Dan looks at me and shrugs, then grins some more. 'SHE-RA, SHE-RA.'

I go inside to get more beer. My legs are spongy, drunken. I try not to trip over the TV wires on my way.

I fix my hair in the mirror of their cork-tiled bathroom. They've even got an old cast-iron bath, like the one in the Flake advert. I nick some expensive hair gel from the shelf above the sink. A pro-vitamin *system* for extra gloss, it says on the bottle. When I've flattened my hair into a black cap, I trace the lines under my eyes with my fingertips. I think of Carolyn and her friends with their smooth skin, and I can't stop the sinking feeling that I didn't make the best of my looks when I had them.

Carolyn's in the kitchen, rubbing at her skirt with a cloth.

'It's great we won,' she says, 'but Dan's really doing my head in.' Her cheeks are flushed, her hair is ruffled, she looks drunk. 'He would have been unbearable if we'd lost. I know you're not supposed to say this but I only ever watch football if England are playing. I can't stand it otherwise and Dan's gone mental over this tournament. He's been watching all the matches, even the ones with Eastern European teams in. I mean, who wants to watch Yugoslavia? Tell you the truth, he's pissing us off a bit.' She lowers her voice. 'Me and Nikki used to go out with him. Not together mind, but you know –' She shrugs and giggles. 'It was all right when we were students but now – I mean, he hasn't got a degree or anything and we only agreed to let him rent a room off us as a kind of short-term thing. You know? He's kind of getting in the way.'

'You've got a twig in your hair,' I say, picking it out for her.

Outside, Dan's having a heated debate about Alan Shearer with Simon, who's still trying to cook things on the barbecue.

'I tell ya, he's a fucking donkey. Worst England captain ever. You watch what happens to the team when he retires.'

'Ah, Dan man, how can you say that? He scored the fucking goal. Against *Germany*. Come *on*.'

'Here you go,' I say, dropping the fourpack on the grass. 'Beer.'

Dan looks up at me and smiles. 'Cheers, darling.'

I'm not your darling, I think, but then wonder why I'm arguing with him. I smile back. 'Shame about your bet.'

'I know, twenty quid down the Swanee. That was next week's drink money, that was.'

'You still working at the Norwich Union then?' Simon asks, sparking the tip of a joint.

'Nah, I jacked it in last month. Trying to get a bit of DJ-ing, you know.' He sighs. 'But I was thinking I might go to Essex for a bit, back to my mum's.' He looks at Carolyn, who's coming out with a big portable stereo. 'Nothing to keep me here really.'

Carolyn puts on some dance music. The kind of drubbing bass and hissing treble that they tried to ban, once upon a long time ago when young people en masse were still dangerous.

She starts to dance; swaying in her stack heels, moving her arms.

'C'mon everybody,' she says, looking at me. 'We won.'

Tides

Sarah O'Mahony

Suffolk

In the hot, dry weather, a couple of months after we'd moved into the houseboat, I was ill. I gave up painting; the blocks in my watercolour box dried and cracked in the middles. I slept on the deck under a black umbrella. When I started to feel better, I realised my period was late.

I thought it was the illness affecting my cycle. A friend of mine who'd moved to the Welsh countryside to live in a self-sufficient community had once told me this kind of thing happened. But Andy bought me a pregnancy test from a chemist in Thorpe Aspal, where he worked, the town beside the power station that rose over the coastal marshes. In the evening I stood on the creek bank clutching the pharmacy paper bag. I stared at the pylons marching towards the reactor. Cables knotted like barbed wire around the shining dome. The sun was falling, and a smell of burnt meat was in the air. People were barbecuing at the campsite further down the coast, cooking orange hot dogs and sweaty onions. Acid crawled up my throat; I thought I was going to be sick. I shook the bag. Something rattled.

'Don't do that,' Andy said, taking hold of my hand. 'It'll break and give the wrong answer. It cost ten quid. You can pay for the next one yourself.'

I did the test to stop him nagging, telling him it was a waste of money, women know when they're pregnant. You feel different, I'd heard people say. You just know.

But it was positive, there were two blue lines. I read the instruction leaflet a second time to make sure I'd understood. I tried angling the stick to catch the last of the day's sunlight. The plastic windows mirrored the wide empty sky and beneath the reflection, two blue lines remained.

The next morning Andy drove me to the doctor's. It was an open surgery, you turned up without an appointment and waited to be seen. I didn't want to wait, but Andy insisted.

'We have to do something,' he said. 'We have to get you checked out before we start to think about things.'

'Checked out?' I said.

'You know.'

I didn't feel like talking. Andy wanted to wait with me, but I told him there was no point missing work.

'It's not as if there's anything wrong with me,' I said.

'Will you be all right getting the bus home?'

'I'll be fine.'

'But I feel guilty. I ought to give you a lift back.'

I looked at my feet. Across the toes of my grey-white Reeboks the leather was cracked. 'Just go to work,' I said.

After he'd gone I sat on the padded plastic bench, watching the second hand travel round the clock. It was hot, the sun shining through the window on to my face, making me sweat. I was wearing shorts, and my legs stuck to the plastic seating. Yellow foam poked through a split under my thigh; I picked at it, tearing off little corners and flicking them on to the carpet, until I noticed a woman watching. I leafed through an issue of *Family Circle*. I couldn't concentrate on the long articles, the true-life features – 'Winning Through' – so I read the health page. Lung cancer was increasing in women. My Uncle Bill had died of lung cancer, and my father had told me that on the X-rays Bill's lungs looked pitch black because of the density of the tumours.

There was a picture of a pregnant woman eating an orange. She was smiling, a hand resting over her tight stomach. You were supposed to take folic acid supplements, available in Boots, before conceiving. I put the magazine down.

There were only a few people in the waiting room. An old woman was called in to see the doctor. She stood up and straightened herself, rearranging the bulky winter coat she was wearing. There were a couple of young people who didn't look ill. I wondered what was wrong with them. I remembered seeing a television programme about cancer in reactor towns. The scientists didn't know whether it was caused by the electricity lines or the nuclear fuel, or both, or neither. Their map of leukaemia incidence on the wall showed hotspots, red dots, near power stations on the coast.

The secrecy of cancer was what worried me. The growths were hidden; there might be no symptoms until your case was too advanced to cure.

My name was called over the intercom. I swallowed, stood up and walked through the swing doors.

'I might be pregnant,' I told the doctor.

He smiled. 'That's not really an emergency.'

'No.'

'Well, we'll just check, shall we, and I'll have a quick look at you.'

He gave me a clear plastic bowl and directed me to the toilet. In his office, I watched the urine soak along the test stick.

'Yes,' he said. 'You certainly are.'

I lay on my back on the couch while he pulled on his rubber gloves. He wriggled two fingers around my cervix, telling me to breathe in, while he pushed down on my stomach with his other hand. It didn't hurt, exactly; the nerves there, inside, didn't seem capable of pain. Discomfort was a better word. I hated being palpated, pulled around. I'd heard that in hospitals they had beds with stirrups.

'Good,' the doctor said. 'I'll leave you to get dressed.'

I went back to the consulting room.

'Now, you'll have to make a proper appointment to discuss

your healthcare and delivery dates,' the doctor said. 'There's plenty of time. Come back next week.'

'Oh.'

'I'm on a tight schedule today, I'm afraid,' he said, looking at his watch. 'It's an open surgery, emergencies only, really.' He smiled. 'The nurse can speak to you if you'd like to wait until she's free. But do pop back and see me next week.'

'Oh.'

'Are congratulations in order?'

'I don't know.'

'Are you on your own?'

'Yes.'

'I see.'

'I mean no, I'm not. I meant I came here on my own today.'

'Good. It's helpful to have some support.'

I didn't want to speak to the nurse. I walked out of the surgery and towards the bus stop. My hands strayed to my stomach. I prodded and squeezed, trying to feel where the thing was growing. I went into the gloomy public toilets and pushed my hands down the front of my knickers, trying to feel through my skin what the doctor's hands had felt. I couldn't tell the difference from normal.

Outside town, the bus stopped by the long driveway which led to the reactor. I looked at the glinting dome. The bus doors slid open and cool air blew in. I didn't like to breathe it too deeply. The driveway forked. There was the road to the visitor centre, which was signposted all over the county by brown plaques. And the road to the complex, guarded by a series of checkpoints and barriers. The sun was glaring through the window, making my head ache. I moved to the other side of the bus. I could feel the heavy air settling in my lungs. I wondered if they gave you pills for cancer, or if the treatment was always radiation, the kind that made your hair fall out. Or was it the pills that made your hair fall out? I didn't know. I'd never thought about it.

That evening I asked Andy if he knew.

He pulled a face. 'Why?'

'I was thinking about the reactor.'

'Why?'

'There were people at the doctor's.'

'Yes, and?'

'I don't know, I thought they might have had cancer or something.'

'That's morbid, Rose.'

I shrugged. 'I'm just interested.'

'It's sitting around on the boat all day that does it.'

'What?'

'Starts you thinking like this. What's happened to your painting? You haven't done any for ages.'

'I've not been well, have I? I still feel weak.'

He flicked my arm with his finger. 'I know. Listen, don't worry.'

I pulled the curtains and we went to bed. The water was low, our houseboat gripped by the oozing mud. It listed to one side, so that the bed sloped and I slid down on to Andy's half, pressing against him. I could see the yellow aura of the power station through cracks between the curtains, the lit fences and floodlights projecting a pale radiance into the sky.

When I was certain that Andy was asleep, I touched my stomach, poking a finger into the flesh. All I could feel was a wall of muscle which tightened involuntarily.

We'd found the rhythm of the tide strange, at first, but we got used to it, fell in with its patterns. We only made love when the water was high at night, and the boat dipped and swelled on the creek as we moved. Small waves broke on the hull and in the morning, when the tide had gone, a white crust of salt clung to the new paint. If there was a full moon, we always checked that the curtains were properly shut. Andy worried that people would watch us, we'd be some night fisherman's entertainment. It made him nervous when weekend tourists walked up the gangway and peered through our windows. Andy hated being watched; he said the houseboat was like a goldfish bowl. The marshes were so flat that you could see our boat from miles away. In the visitor centre, at the plant, powerful telescopes looked out over the land.

I'd wanted the houseboat as soon as I saw the advertisement. We were looking at houses in Thorpe Aspal, where Andy's firm were transferring him; we'd driven up for the weekend. I'd brought my paintbox with me, and I was pleased to discover that the watercolours sold in the tourist galleries were no better than mine.

'If we came here I could paint full time,' I said. 'I bet I could make enough money to live on, in the summer at least.'

'I suppose you could try,' said Andy. 'If it didn't work you could always get a proper job in town.'

I shook my head. 'The tourists all want souvenirs. I won't charge too much. I'll sell hundreds.'

I looked in the window of a newsagent to see what the locals were offering each other for sale. A pair of cherry red Doc Martens, size seven, barely worn; a litter of Border collie pups. A pair of children's rollerskates, extendable; and a Ford Sierra, £300 ono.

A houseboat.

I thought of my friend Laura on her co-operative farm in Wales, planting cabbages, weaving baskets. At the creek we could swim, we could fish. There would probably be blackberries at the right time of year. I wasn't sure when that time was.

'I suppose it can't hurt,' said Andy, when I suggested having a look. 'Go on, then. We'll drive down today.'

'Thank you!' I said.

He looked at me and smiled.

The owners, an elderly couple, said the boat wanted a lick of paint and the gangway needed fixing but other than that, it was in good condition.

163

'Think of the money we'll save on a house. I can set up my paints on the bank. Maybe I can sell landscapes in that café.'

'They would say it's in good condition, wouldn't they,' Andy muttered. 'For all we know it might be like a sieve underneath.'

'We can get someone who knows boats to look at it,' I said, businesslike.

'Who do we know who knows boats?'

'We can find someone.'

It was a warm spring day and the tide was in. All the houseboats were bobbing in the water, the rigging round the masts tinkling like windchimes. The owners of our boat had raised a ragged Union Jack, which was waving limply in the breeze, rising up on gusts of wind and then sagging, wrapping around the mast. Jerry's boat, moored at the next stage, had a different flag, a smiling sun appliquéd on to a red background.

In the haze of the day, the golf-ball sphere of the reactor was camouflaged against the wide white sky so that it seemed only an outline, a cloud, nothing permanent. Later I would find out that it was not a sphere at all, but a shape I didn't know the name of, a something-ahedron, according to Andy. Its surface was made up of hundreds of mirror-like facets, which was why, on that first day, it assumed the sky's colour.

We paced along the shingle beach. Pieces of green and brown glass hid among the stones. Frosted and blunt, they'd been churned around for so long that they didn't look like glass, but like lumps of a rare mineral. I put them in my pockets.

'Go on,' I said. 'Please can we?'

'I suppose it'll be a change. We can always sell up, can't we, if it doesn't work?' Andy was pretending he wasn't keen, trying to wind me up, but I could tell he was excited.

'It will work,' I said. 'I'm going to build up a proper collection of paintings. A portfolio. I'm going to take my paintings around all the galleries. I could even start a gallery myself.'

'Good. I can retire when you've made us rich.'

I squeezed his hand. We kissed. There was a faint taste of salt on his lips; I liked that. I kissed him again for longer. A fisherman was hunched near us, by the breakwater, but we didn't care. The waves spat shingle, sucking the shore as they receded.

After we moved in, we discovered that the boat owners campaigned against the reactor. We noticed posters in windows, slogans painted on the wooden shacks along the quayside. Everywhere, the symbol of the smiling sun. This disappointed me, it made me worry. We didn't put any posters on our boat, although they handed them out for free in Sal's café.

'I don't like it,' I said.

'Why not?' said Andy. 'Do you believe in nuclear power?'

I was startled. 'I don't know. I don't think so.'

'Why don't you like the posters, then?'

'They're creepy.'

He laughed, nodded.

'Do you believe in it?' I said.

'Probably not, no. But the place is already built and, in my opinion, they're not going to dismantle it just because a few people put posters up.'

'And if you use electricity, like they do in the café,' I said, 'isn't it hypocritical to complain?'

'I don't know about that. There's not much option, is there? You always need electricity for something.'

'You can make your own. In Belgium they harness the tides. And there's solar power. Or you can have a generator, can't you? Is that what they're called?'

He snorted. 'If you've got the time to spare, you can. Perhaps you should install one here.'

'Very funny.'

Our boat was moored near the ferry jetty. A leathery man spent every day rowing passengers between the banks of the creek, adjusting his trajectory according to the current, and his baseball cap according to the position of the sun. After Andy and I had been living on the boat a couple of weeks he started to nod when we passed him, lifting his cap to acknowledge us. I liked this; I always waved to him so the tourists would know I was a resident. He lived in a hut on the other side of the creek. When the tide was in at night and the boat lights pitched and sawed, throwing shapes on the walls of the houseboat, I'd try to fix my eyes on the ferryman's glowing window. Behind his hut were the floodlights of the reactor. The sky was never fully dark.

There were about thirty houseboats. At low tide they lay beached, held at angles by the mud. At high tide they rocked, flimsy gangways swaying as the ropes pulled. Our neighbours were eccentric. Greta and Pete owned goats. Rick had decorated his cabin windows with pictures of elephants and painted the hull pink. A retired couple lived in a boat crammed with plants. In the mornings, when it was chilly, their cabin steamed up like a greenhouse, the big rubbery leaves perspiring, soaking up the light. The boat looked like some kind of botanical experiment; you couldn't see the couple at all. When they did emerge, they didn't speak to us. I commented, once, on how lovely their plants were, and said that if they ever took any cuttings I'd love one or two, but they just smiled coldly, said they'd let me know and walked on.

Andy was the only person on the creek who worked in town. Most of our neighbours were retired. A few of the women worked at Sal's café and in the nearby pub, and there were the fishermen. The smell of fish was everywhere. There were buckets of silvery whiting, handwritten signs displaying the price per pound. At weekends people drove from the towns to buy fresh fish from the creek. Jerry, who lived on the boat next to ours, owned a blue-painted fish kiosk by the jetty. I told Andy he should resign from his job, buy a lamp and a big green umbrella and become a night fisherman. He laughed. Sometimes in the evenings Andy fished in the creek, but he always threw his catches back in. He said he hated to see the fish gasping, out of their element, like drowning people. I laughed at him. I said he'd never survive in a self-sufficient community.

'I wouldn't want to,' he said. 'They're for misfits, nutters.'

'Laura!' I said, angrily.

'Exactly.' He was smiling.

At first, I walked miles each day through the rush-beds and along the steep gravel bank built up to keep high tides from flooding the marshes. From the top of the ridge I could see the clean, open spaces, the geometry of the land. The place reminded me of a diagram from a school textbook: the level, rusty earth and beet fields divided by straight drainage channels, a tall windmill standing in the middle of black mud flats. Every angle seemed to have been calculated. Even the trees were all bent to the same degree by the wind.

I started to wear shorts, something I hadn't done since I was thirteen. It felt like a holiday. I stayed out until six or seven, the time when Andy got home from work. I tried to paint.

But then I started feeling ill.

The Saturday after the test we sat by the ferry jetty, watching tourists. Posters were pinned to the telegraph poles. Some advertised protest meetings, some the summer carnival on the boating lake.

Andy threw a handful of shingle into the creek.

'We'll go to the carnival, won't we?' I said.

'If you like.'

'Do you want to?'

'Dunno.'

'Well, think about it. Do you want to go or don't you?'

'I don't really care either way.'

Children dangled their feet in the muddy water and ran along the creek bank. They were collecting crabs in their plastic buckets. Two girls lay on their stomachs, craning their heads to see underneath the jetty. The creek mud had dried grey and flaky on their arms and legs so that their skin looked old, like elephant hide. The crabs hid around the barnacle-scabbed pilings. One girl was tying a piece of string around some bait. Jerry and the other fishermen left their offcuts in buckets for the kids to use.

'I've got one! Look!'

I watched the child dance on the jetty, dirty arms and legs flailing. She hauled up the line.

'Watch out, Sam,' a woman shouted. 'Keep away from the edge.'

I walked on to the jetty. The girl dropped her catch into a bucket of seawater. A clump of weed was stuck to the crab's back. About twenty crabs were piled in the bucket, some clambering around, trying to scale the sides. I stared at the girl. There was a line of snot creeping across her lip, a smear of mud on her cheek.

I saw the girl's mother watching me warily. I smiled at her and waved at the ferryman, who was halfway across the creek. He didn't wave back.

'Rose!' Andy called.

I beckoned him. 'Let's go.'

We walked.

'What were you doing?' he said.

'Looking.'

'At what?'

'Nothing.'

'Rose, how old was that girl would you say?'

'I dunno.'

'Four, five?'

'At least seven. I don't know. Why?'

He shrugged, not looking me in the eye. 'Because I can't tell, I haven't got a clue. I don't know anything about kids.'

I looked away from him, across the creek mouth to the reactor. There was a heat haze over the marshes. The dome rippled like a mirage beside the flat sea. It was as if waves of heat and light were radiating from it. Ultraviolet, gamma rays, dangerous things I vaguely remembered from science lessons.

Jerry opened the hatch in his kiosk, fastening back the shutters. He tipped a bucket of ice into the metal tray and began to lay spotted plaice over the cubes. Tourists gathered as he slapped out different kinds of fish. I could see their eyes, their slit gills.

I remembered the time I'd thrown up when I saw Jerry gutting his catch and dropping the entrails into the high creek. That must have been the pregnancy starting, I thought.

'Let's go somewhere else for the rest of the day,' I said.

In the early days I'd often bought fish from Jerry. I expected a special price, a discount, but I paid the same as any tourist. I didn't buy the ready fillets he prepared for his kiosk; I was determined to learn how to clean a fish myself. I asked him to show me, and he made me feel sick, pointing out the organs, the areas to avoid puncturing, with the tip of his knife. I remembered dissecting an earthworm at school, my unsteady hand nicking the inner tube of the digestive tract and the muck sliding out like ink, obscuring everything. Jerry whipped his knife across the scales and the tinny eye flickered, catching the light like a milk-bottle top.

We ate the fish for dinner, and I thought of the coiled intestines, full of creek debris, that had bulged inside. I prised the white flakes apart with my knife, suspicious, looking for bones.

When I was ill Andy took over the cooking. We had chicken drumsticks or sausages or cheese grills that he'd picked up from the supermarket on the way home. He never bought fish. I was glad.

We walked back from the jetty to the boat, where we sat on the deck on our beanbags.

'Where do you want to go, then?' Andy asked.

I was tired. 'I dunno. You say.'

'Do you want to go somewhere in the car?'

'I'll get sick.'

'Doesn't leave many places, then. The lake?'

I shrugged.

The power station was shimmering in the heat. The fields inland were divided by a mesh of cables that branched out, like nerves, from the reactor. The pylons and overhead wires marshalled like an army, thickening and converging as they approached the town and the dome. Jerry had told me that the overhead wires created a magnetic field that caused freak illnesses.

'You know the stories about cancer?' I said.

'What about them?' said Andy.

'What do you know about them?'

'I don't know anything, really. Just the usual stories you hear in the papers. A power station doesn't poison you overnight, Rose. Do we have to talk about this again?'

'It's important.'

'It's not, at the moment.'

We went to the boating lake in the village. It was manmade, an unrealistic shape cut out of the land, hemmed around by a small wood. Beyond the trees a five-mile sweep of flats bordered by a long, crescent beach led to the reactor. We hired a boat and meandered between the islands with their weeping willows and fibreglass dinosaurs. Swans glided, looking bored. When we moored the boat at one of the islands a vicious swan ran at us, hissing and spreading its wings. I threatened it with an oar while Andy untied the boat and pushed us away from the bank.

'It must have got some cygnets,' he said as we rowed away. 'They get protective.'

I wasn't sure if he was trying to make some kind of point. 'It's too late in the year for cygnets,' I told him, although I had no idea if that was true.

Andy said I shouldn't row in case I strained myself, so I seized the oars. I kept steering us into reeking dead ends, stagnant pockets where the swans didn't venture. Andy trailed his hand in the water, coating it with bright green scum. The summer before, Jerry had told me, the council had to close down the lake because it was full of lethal blue-green algae. A couple of children had ended up in intensive care. The council had to treat the water with chemicals before it was safe again.

'Don't eat anything till you've washed your hands,' I ordered. 'Wash your hands as soon as we get back,' I added. I wasn't sure whether the poisons could get through your skin.

Andy grinned at me and waved his slimy hand, flinging drips of green on to my trousers.

After the test, we didn't make love. We went to bed early every night, but never touched or talked to each other. I slept badly, waking often, listening to Andy's breath rising and falling.

In the mornings he went for walks, creaking down the rotten gangplank. I stayed in bed, hands creeping to my belly. Later I'd hear the engine splutter, gravel grinding under the tyres as Andy left for work. He never came in to say goodbye; he thought I was asleep and didn't want to wake me. I pretended to be asleep so he wouldn't pester me to make a doctor's appointment. In the evenings I'd tell him that I'd forgotten and I was going to make one the next day.

I hung around the creek. I didn't feel like going anywhere.

One morning I was considering going to the payphone and making an appointment, but when I emerged from the cabin Jerry waylaid me. He was standing on the path, wearing his CND T-shirt.

'Do you ever think about that place?' he asked, pointing his thumb at the reactor.

'Sometimes.'

'You should come to the meetings in the village hall. There

are things you might be interested to know. Things that concern us.'

He told me about flatfish. They weren't born flat, he said; at first they swam like other fish, but one of their eyes began to crawl until it reached the other side, and then the fish turned over: flat.

'Is that really true?'

'Hang on.' He walked on to his boat and picked a fish out of an ice-filled bucket. He held it up, waving it in the air. I could see that the eyes were asymmetrical. The second eye, Jerry said, never quite reached the place it was meant to.

'Isn't that supposed to happen, then?' I said. 'Is it because of radioactivity?'

He shook his head. 'It's supposed to happen, but it's going wrong. Pollution's making all these kinds of cycles go wrong, mutating things. *That's* part of it.' He gestured at the reactor. 'It's the hormones, too, in the fertilisers farmers use, affecting the genetics of things.'

'That's terrible.'

'They're buggering up the sex of everything. The sea's full of hormones, women's chemicals.' He looked towards the horizon.

'Really?'

'It's having a contraceptive effect on the fish. It's a bloody disgrace –'

I began to laugh; I couldn't help it. Jerry looked at me as if I was mad.

I gave up walking; I didn't feel well enough. I was sitting in the café one afternoon when I saw Greta. I smiled, and she sidled over.

'Hello, dear. Young man not with you?'

'He works all week.'

She turned her mug around, the base grating on the table-top. 'Actually, we haven't had many young people living here over the years. I suppose it's very quiet, not much happening.'

'That's why we liked it.'

'And you can't have children living on a boat, that's another reason, I suppose.'

'I suppose.'

'There was a tragedy here once, you know. A little girl was here with her mother visiting someone, and she fell off their boat into the mud and drowned.'

There was the taste of vomit at the back of my mouth. I swallowed some tea.

Greta looked smug. 'The Wilkinsons, who lived on your boat, were quite old. You met them, didn't you? They were heartbroken when they had to leave. Mr Wilkinson used to love fishing before his arthritis got bad. Have you seen my goats?'

'No,' I said, although I had.

'Daisy, Hildaberry and Margarie Marple, they're called.'

'Hildaberry?'

'The name of a great-aunt I had. First and surname. The farmer lets me tether them in the field behind the boat shed. We milk them. We could almost manage on our own really, what with Pete's fishing and the goats. I could let you try some of the milk if you want.'

I swilled the dregs of tea around my mug. The thought of drinking goat's milk made me want to retch. It struck me, too, that it probably wasn't safe for the baby, unpasteurised, full of listeria. I thought I ought to be thinking about those things.

'No thanks.'

'It tastes nice; strong, distinctive. People are prejudiced against goat's milk but they'll eat goat's cheese happily enough. The Greek stuff. They don't know it comes from goats, perhaps.'

'Self-sufficiency,' I said.

'Pardon?'

'You're self-sufficient.'

She looked pleased. 'Yes. Living on a boat's a full-time job in itself, isn't it? Pete wanted to have solar panels put in our boat, you know, but it wasn't practical. Are you going to fix your gangplank soon, by the way? I meant to ask.'

'Andy's got a calculator with solar panels,' I told her.

She gave me a look.

I felt sick but I was hungry, too. I thought of the baby stealing everything I ate, embedded there, turning from a tadpole into a frog. Andy had borrowed a guide to pregnancy from the library. The pictures terrified me. There was a whole frieze of them, progressing from a speck of red tissue to translucent creatures with webbed hands, bulging eyes and thready veins. The ninth was a perfect baby tucked into the position for sliding out. Its head was almost as big as its body. I hid the book under the mattress.

I thought about the girl, floundering quietly in the mud. My mouth went dry. I was still having headaches; they came and went. I wondered if the power station was causing them. I didn't mention it to Andy.

I came back from the beach to find him painting on a piece of wood, using the leftover gloss from the hull.

'What's that?'

He finished and held it up; the paint started to run. It was a sign declaring that our boat was private property and that we weren't responsible for the consequences if people chose to walk up the gangway.

'What's the point in that?'

Andy shrugged. 'Jerry said it was a good idea. Everyone else has got these signs, and our gangway's the worst of the lot. If someone falls through it, Jerry says we could be liable.'

'That's stupid, it's petty. Why would anyone be walking up our gangway, anyway?'

'You can't be too careful, with the summer season and all these people around. Tourists come up the gangway all the time.'

'You sound like Jerry.'

He didn't reply.

'A little girl died here once,' I told him, pausing for effect. 'She drowned in the mud.'

'There you go, then. This is a sensible precaution.' He disappeared into the cabin and I wished I hadn't mentioned the dead girl.

As it got dark, the creek drained, the moon peeling the sea back, exposing reefs of smooth rock beyond the breakwaters. I'd never seen the tide recede so far. The radio crackled. Andy fiddled with the dial but it didn't make any difference; the faint voices were trapped behind a barrier of static.

'There must be a storm around,' he said, switching it off. 'No point wasting the batteries.'

'Out to sea,' I said.

I closed my eyes and leant back, resting my head on a cushion. I thought of the still creekbed, sucked dry. The crabs had been pulled out to sea with the fish, and the mud was disclosing its secrets: old buckets, broken shells, sharp white fish bones.

I thought of the girl's body uncovered near the creek mouth. She was bloated, her stomach swollen with air and seawater. Her lips were blue. Dry seaweed stuck to her skin, wreathed her puffy mouth and nostrils. When the tide came up and pulled her out to sea, the green threads would rejuvenate, grow fat and salty, slither away. The girl would drift, deflate and sink, to be buried among the stones of the seabed.

I coughed to stop the sour taste bubbling up in my throat. I put my hand over my mouth and swallowed hard, forcing air down.

'Shall we go for a walk?' Andy asked.

'No.'

'Just down to the beach? We could walk out to the rocks.'

'You go if you want. I'm going to sleep.'

I pulled the curtains and undressed. Andy took off his shirt and trousers. I noticed him looking at me and got into bed quickly, pulling the sheets around my body and turning to the wall. I felt him hesitate before climbing in. I wondered if he'd edge over and touch me, but he sank into the mattress and sighed. I relaxed.

Neither of us slept. We lay straight, keeping a narrow strip of mattress between us. Outside, a fisherman walked down to the beach.

Andy slid a hand across on to my belly and rested it there. It was sweaty and heavy. I pushed it away.

'I wanted to see what it felt like,' he said.

'Now you know.'

'No different.' He sounded surprised.

'How would you know?'

'What's the problem with all this?' he said. 'You have to tell me, you know; I'm not a mind-reader.'

'What the hell do you think the problem is?'

He didn't say anything else. Later I heard him sniffing; there was a tug as he wiped his eyes on a corner of the sheet.

I woke before the sun had risen, needing to be sick. The creek water lapped at the bottom of the boat. I looked across at Andy, sprawled and white in the pale pre-dawn light. Without his glasses his face looked soft, vulnerable. I shook his shoulders gently and he uncurled, rubbing his eyes.

'What's wrong?'

'Nothing,' I said. 'I was lonely.'

He rolled next to me and we looked at the boat lights jiggling in the mist.

'It reminds me of the lightships,' he said.

We'd seen the lightships in the Thames estuary a few years earlier, when we were first together. I'd thought they looked like decorations, floating Christmas trees, but really they were warning lights.

'Will we go to the carnival tonight?'

'If you want.'

I reached out and stroked his back. He pushed against me and we were about to kiss when we heard a splash.

'Morning, Jerry boy,' someone shouted. 'Off to try for some fish before the hordes arrive.'

At seven, we walked along the stony beach. We passed a fisherman inside a green tent, his line glinting in the air. Pebbles wriggled down the sides of my trainers, planting themselves in the soles of my feet. We took our shoes off, grit showering out when we shook them.

We climbed over the next breakwater and saw thousands of white and grey oyster shells heaped against the wooden barrier where the sea had spat them. The day before there had been no oysters, but now they covered the whole beach. Some were still wet.

'What's happened?' I said. 'Where did they come from?'

'I don't know.'

We sat down on the bank of shells. I lay back and looked up at the brightening sky. In a couple of hours it would be a lurid blue. It was August; in the hot days every scene looked artificial, like a tinted postcard. I'd given up trying to paint the landscape because it always looked false.

Andy crunched down next to me. I felt the pressure of his hand on my stomach. I rolled over, burying my front in the prickly oyster shells. I picked one up. It was old and dull. The pearly layer inside had been chipped off.

'Let's go for a swim,' Andy said.

There was no one around, except for the fisherman on the next beach, so we stripped to our underwear. I was pocked with dents from lying on the shells. The sea chilled me, making my chest contract so that breathing was difficult. A wave crashed on me and I choked, spitting water, shaking it out of my ears. My arms and legs were grazed where I'd been ground against the oyster fragments. I liked the sharp, cool pain of the freezing water, the salt stinging my raw skin.

After Andy drove to work, I lay in the boat picking strands of dried seaweed out of my hair. I couldn't be bothered to shower. I heard people talking.

'I was in the information centre and they told me it was a Roman oyster pit, where they used to throw the shells after they ate them,' someone said.

I went out on deck to ask Jerry if it was true.

'Yep,' he said. 'The sea wore the layer off the top and opened up the pit.'

'They're really that old?'

'Yep. I see you put your private property sign up.'

'Andy did. Nothing to do with me.'

'It's a good idea,' he said. 'You never know what can happen. A little girl was drowned in the mud, once. Terrible.'

I could see her limbs, sprawled in the mud like dead eels. 'I've got to go,' I said, retreating into the cabin.

In the evening we went to the carnival, shining the torch ahead of us as we walked along the path to the village. The dry mud was cracked like crazed glazing, thin crevasses opening everywhere. People were talking, car horns beeping. Vendors wore pink and green neon tubes on their necks and arms, their faces lit by the fluorescence. Parents bought these necklaces for their children, who twisted them in their hands, chewed them, dropped them.

'I'm sure those things are poisonous,' Andy said.

We sat on damp grass at the edge of the lake. Pan-pipe music blared from the loudspeakers as tourists packed into the grounds, pulling blankets out of their bags and settling themselves on the floor. The villagers sat on the landing stage or rowed their own boats to the centre of the lake for a better view.

The music stopped; the loudspeaker spluttered. 'Here's the Thorpe-Dixon family, with a ghostly theme.'

I breathed in. The float was full of children. I'd forgotten carnivals were children's occasions. Mr Thorpe-Dixon was barely visible in the dark, propelling the float through the stringy waterweed. He wore thigh-length waders. His kids pranced in black costumes with luminous bones tacked on to the arms and legs and chests. They wore skull masks. The crowd applauded as they held hands and danced the cancan.

Another float came round: Vikings. There were eight children: five girls and three boys. One girl was dressed as a man, to make up the numbers. She was wearing a horned baseball cap and cardboard armour. Her plaits straggled down her back. I tried to imagine myself with a baby, or a young child like the girl, but I couldn't.

Andy reached for my hand. It was resting on my stomach; I pulled it away when I felt his touch. Applause rippled around the lake and I thought I felt the thing inside me wriggle. I pictured it growing in there, a hard cluster of cells. I squirmed.

'Are you comfortable?'

'No, I'm not.'

'We should have brought cushions. I should have thought of that. Are you all right?'

'For God's sake!' I said.

I looked up and saw a float decorated in red and silver. There were two children wrapped in Bacofoil. Comic-book explosions were painted on to the backdrop. There was a flash and the kids turned their torches off. When they turned them on again they were lying on their backs.

'Jesus!' said Andy.

'Make the world safe for our children,' shouted the men who were pulling the float. The villagers on the landing stage clapped. So did a few of the tourists, but not many.

I could see the pale green crown of the dome, above the trees. 'Jesus,' I said.

When all the floats had circuited the lake the fireworks began, with a barrage of stars that split into smaller sparks. Everyone gasped. I imagined, again, that I could feel the thing unfurling in my belly. I thought of the pictures in the book, the bulging eyes, the webbed hands. Ashes pattered on the water. I remembered collecting burnt-out cartridges the day after firework displays when I was a kid, sorting them into colours.

After the display had finished, Andy switched on the torch and we walked towards the beach. He shone the beam in front of me, watching to make sure I didn't trip in rabbit holes. We passed the tide-stick, a wooden pole with white paint marking the high-tide levels of the past hundred years. After the tufty grass petered out, the beach shelved steeply down. We sat at the top of the oyster escarpment and looked out over the low dark sea. The flags that marked the lobster pots, as far out as I'd ever swum, rocked in the distance. The moon had dwindled to a sliver. When Andy turned off the torch, the only light I could see was the light of the reactor.

'It never stops, not even at night-time. Anything could be coming out of it. The force fields.'

'What force fields? You don't know what you're talking about.'

I picked up an oyster, handed it to Andy. 'This is from the Romans. Jerry said it was a genuine Roman shell.'

He grunted. 'I'm sick of hearing about that power station.'

'Aren't you listening? After the Romans ate the oysters or got out the pearls, or whatever they did, they threw them in a big hole. It was sealed over. Now it's opened up.'

'What?' he said. 'What are you talking about?'

I turned the broken shell in my hand, examining the chalky crust on its frilled edge. I imagined the baby turning, flexing in its yellow lake. I dropped the shell.

'What's wrong?'

'I hate that place. It's poisonous.'

'This is unhealthy, Rose.'

I lay awake for hours. The boat rocked and the light of the reactor shone above the ferryman's hut. I rolled over, sick. It was impossible to get comfortable. I remembered Chernobyl, the reports on television, the toxic clouds they'd said were crawling down from Scandinavia. That week they kept us inside our classrooms at lunchtime.

The cooling plant was under the seabed, next to the reactor.

If it cracked the sea would boil. Somewhere there was the dead girl, tethered to the bottom by seaweed.

I wasn't sure I wanted the baby. I thought there might be something wrong with it. I'd heard Greta tell stories.

I sat up. 'It might be abnormal.'

'What?' Andy was half asleep.

'It might be abnormal. Because of the plant. Greta and Jerry were talking about it.'

'Greta and Jerry? What do they know? Ask the doctor; he'll put your mind at rest. When are you going to the doctor, anyway?'

'Soon.'

'You'll have to see him next week, you can't keep putting it off. I'll make the appointment for you.'

'No, I'll do it.'

The ferryman's light had gone out and the condensation on our window split the reactor's glow into hard yellow beads.

After the carnival weekend, the tourists started to leave. Andy worked late most days and I didn't leave the boat. I felt worse than ever. I woke up early, vomited, then lay in bed all day, keeping the curtains closed. My breasts were sore; I had to lie on my back.

Greta walked up the rickety plank and banged on the door. 'All right, love?'

'Yes, thanks,' I called.

'You ought to get this plank replaced. It'll give in winter. Are you staying here this winter? We're going to stay with our son in Ipswich.'

'I don't know.' I hadn't thought about it.

'You want to get the plank fixed,' she repeated.

'Bugger off,' I whispered as her shoes crunched on the gravel.

I went to the doctor's. I got dressed and then caught the bus to town, taking carrier bags in case I needed to be sick. The bus passed the road to the reactor. The dome shone. I wondered what it was made from. It looked like something from science fiction. I imagined the workers inside, throwing glowing tubes into some kind of furnace. Masks, silver suits, monsters. I knew nothing about science.

I asked the doctor about the reactor, whether it was dangerous.

He shook his head. 'I don't want to speculate. I know one hears things but I can reassure you on two counts. Firstly, you haven't lived here long and secondly, your partner doesn't work at the plant.'

'But I've heard lots of things.'

'You don't need to worry.' He shuffled my medical notes.

'But I don't really know if I want to have a baby, anyway.'

'Ah.' He cleared his throat. 'You're thinking along those lines, are you?'

He began to explain possibilities.

When I got back I found a sticker, a bright sun with eyes and a grin, over the O in our private property sign. I went into the cabin and sat down, thinking about what the doctor had said.

Andy came in. 'Bastards.'

'What?'

'There's a sticker on our sign, didn't you see it? Jerry's trying to make a point. I don't want him pestering us, we've got enough to deal with.'

When Jerry came out on deck to fish, Andy tackled him. 'Did you put this sticker here?'

'What sticker?'

'The smiley sun.'

'Did I?'

'You tell me.'

I shoved a finger in each ear so I couldn't hear anything.

Andy stalked into the cabin. 'Have you been encouraging him?'

'What?'

'He's crazy.' He shook his head. 'Why do you even talk to him?'

'I thought Jerry was your mate.'

'What's that supposed to mean?'

'Well, helping you with the sign and everything. I thought he was your buddy.'

'I thought he was your mate. He says you're interested in the campaign. You never told me.'

I didn't tell him I'd been to the doctor.

Andy took a day off work so we could go somewhere together, talk properly. It was a hot, cloudless day and the sea was calm. People were calling it an Indian summer.

'Where do you want to go?' he asked.

'The plant.'

'The visitor centre?'

'No, not the visitor centre, I just want to have a look around and see what the place is like. You can get to the beach nearby, can't you?'

'Yes. The sea's warmer there, apparently.'

'Is it?'

'There are plants and fish you don't get anywhere else, because of the heat.' He saw my face. 'Oh. I wasn't going to tell you that.'

'Why?'

'Because I knew you'd think it meant something.'

As we drove, I felt sick. I stuck my head out of the window and breathed in the rushing air. The reactor loomed. It was massive, skirted by multiple fences. I felt a movement in my stomach.

'It would take a chunk out of England if it blew up,' I said.

'Don't start.'

Andy took off his shirt and trousers and went to the water's edge in his trunks. I watched him, running my fingers through the gravel. The stones were smaller than those on our beach, and there were no oysters.

'Come on,' he called. 'It's nice.'

If I had the baby, I realised, it would be showing in a few weeks. I wouldn't be able to wear a swimming costume.

I shivered as I walked into the water, but after a while it was warmer to duck under than to stand up, half wet, in the breeze. The wind seemed to be blowing from the power station, not in from the sea. I didn't look at the dome. I couldn't tell, yet, if the sea was hotter than usual. I swam out beyond the breakwaters and let myself drift.

I swam further. There weren't any lobster pots, and without markers I couldn't tell how far I'd come. I started to wonder how far I was from the shore, and from the cooling plant underneath the seabed. The water felt as if it was getting warmer. I looked at Andy, a distant figure in the surf.

Something brushed past my leg.

'Andy!'

I was treading water, trying not to panic. A grey head popped up metres away from me. It swivelled, staring. The girl, I thought. I screamed, making my throat sore, but only a strangled noise came out. The head vanished.

I could hear my heartbeat in my ears, the blood drumming. I felt heavy, I thought I might sink. I was trying to swim but I didn't seem to be moving. I pulled at the water, turning to see if the thing was following.

It re-emerged. I realised it was only a seal but I screamed anyway. I kept swimming as fast as I could. My arms ached. I hated the thought of its plump bulk diving underwater, circling underneath me, faster than I could move.

I reached the shore, exhausted.

'Are you all right? You went a long way.'

'I feel terrible.'

'You shouldn't have gone so far out. I didn't realise how far you'd gone. I tried to shout but you didn't hear me.'

I lay on my back. 'Why are there no lobster pots?'

'I expect all the fishermen are scared of the place.' He snorted. 'Like our friend Jerry.'

'You can't blame them.'

Andy shook his head. 'You never used to be so super-stitious,' he said, bending over and kissing me. 'You taste of seaweed, it's disgusting.'

I lay there, bloated. I didn't say anything about the seal. My ears were full of humming, the sound of the pylons, the wires meshing together, carrying all that electricity.

When we got back to the boat my foot broke through the rotten wood of the gangway. I wobbled, almost losing my balance, clinging to the wooden rail. Splinters pierced the mud below and vanished. I yelped. Afterwards I stood on deck, shivering. I winced as Andy's hand brushed my breast.

That night I dreamt the boat's moorings had broken and we were sailing out to sea, away from the fisherman's glowing hut and the swaying lights of the creek. All we could see was the reactor, a luminous orb crowning the coastline.

When I woke up I remembered the seal watching me, diving in the murk. They came up the creek sometimes, I'd heard Jerry say.

I had to get up, to be sick. When Andy woke, I told him I couldn't stand the movement of the boat any more; it was making me ill. I was fed up of the rotten, fishy creek, the neighbours, and the reactor crackling in the distance.

'I want to stay somewhere else,' I said.

'Jerry will be pleased.'

'Bugger Jerry.'

'You can't have a baby on a boat, I suppose,' Andy said. 'It's for the best, if that's what you want to do. Or not.'

'I don't want to have a baby anywhere.'

He knitted his fingers together and then stretched them. I could hear all the little bones cracking.

We spent our last night in the boat. The weather had turned; the wind was whistling through the masts and the rigging, which chimed like xylophone keys. The moon illuminated streaky, racing clouds. Wood creaked and the sea pounded against the shore, chipping and smashing the remaining Roman oysters. I was wearing my bra in bed; I felt wretched and heavy. Andy lay behind me, fitting around the curve of my back.

In the morning we loaded the car and then walked to the beach, passing Greta.

'Moving today?' she said. 'Shame!'

I smiled stiffly and looked around for the ferryman. He was inside his hut; he'd cut his timetable after the holiday season.

Greta's goats bleated as we walked to the beach, past the creek mouth. The currents were strong, swirling fiercely enough to pull you out to sea, although the water was low. I looked at the beach, covered with oyster-shell fragments, and the long bay sweeping to the reactor. A couple of fishing boats were topping the swells and a cargo ship glided sluggishly along the horizon.

As we walked back to the car I saw the houseboats, keeling in the mud like the fibreglass dinosaurs on the lake. Behind them loomed the gleaming dome of the reactor, a monstrous egg perched in its nest of marshland and woods.

Is it a Bird?

Gemma Blackshaw

Chelmsford

I'm thirteen and skinny. So skinny, Mum says, that if I turned sideways she'd miss me. I think I must spend a lot of my time sideways. She doesn't notice much except when Wayne Fisher's dad's around.

– Look at the bones on that, she says, pushing me back by my sticky-out hip. – Whippet.

The only thing thin about Mum is her mouth, thin like the line you draw on stick men. – Blokes like something to grab, she says, don't they? He looks me up and down. Scuffed up trainers with the treads worn down flat. Jeans. A Superman T-shirt I saved up for off the back of Weetabix packets. Nothing shows through it except my collarbones. – Flat as a board, she says, certainly don't take after me.

I touch myself on the roof of the garages. There's a ledge running along the gutter rails and if you roll over it you land on a piece of flat roofing sheet that you can't see from the ground. I lie on my back like a starfish. Like I'm the only thing between the estate and the sky. No planes even. Looking down, my hip bones are higher than my knees, poking through the pockets on my jeans. I'd like jeans with badges on and zips at the ankle so you can put them on over your trainers. When I push them down the pebble-dash bites into my legs but I don't mind it. I lie there all stiff and as I'm doing it I hear things. Car doors and hosepipes, Bulldog kicking off, grown-ups shouting at kids to clear the fuck out the garden and play in the street. And then it's like I'm flying above it all. *Whooosh*.

Diana Lees wears a bra. Mum tells me this when she walks past in a T-shirt and cut-off denim shorts. I'm dragging the bins to the pavement. They catch on the raised paving slabs and I have to heave them over on a tilt.

– Look, she says, Diana Lees in a bra.

It's early but the sun's already white and thin. There's a haze across the road surfacing but no cars yet. Diana Lees sits out on the estate pavement, picking at the plasters on the backs of her heels where her sandals cut in. She peels the glue away from the edges, rolling it between her fingers and then putting it in her mouth. She treads over to the field fence when I get the bins off the pavement and haul them across the road. She'll keep to the estate all day. The garages, the front gardens, the compost bins that everyone uses for tin cans instead of kitchen scraps. She used to walk through the fields out the back. She'd be out until early evening, through Broomfield, the Chignalls, Great Waltham. As far as the Dengie Peninsula, Mum said, but I don't see how she'd know that. Wayne Fisher used to follow her. Wayne Fisher never follows me. He tries to pull my T-shirt up instead. – You got yourself some tits yet? he says.

Mum's in the back garden. The washing line's tipped over and there's dirty glasses in the long grass. We don't have any deckchairs, though it's hot enough. Blazing day after day so my freckles are spreading and the spaces between my fingers are pale and milky.

– Why don't you put a swimmie on? Get yourself a tan, she says.

I'm kicking stones against the dustbins, ding, ding, ding, listening to the combine harvester rattling out the back. The yellow off the cornfield catches on the white garage doors and makes them shine. When the wind picks up you won't be able to see in front of you for dust. You'll run and skid and it will blow up behind you like you're on the Grand Prix. Mum's always going on about farming. Fertilisers and kids born with no eyes. Fields set on fire with cigarettes. When she looks over the fence she says we'll go up like dry grass. – Like the outback, she says. – In Australia. And I think how brilliant that would be to have a bushfire like you see on the telly round the back of Berwick Avenue. Everyone would own up to it.

– Why don't you put a pair of shorts and jelly shoes on? I look at the blonde hairs on my arms, tense the thin muscle running from the inside of my elbow to my wrist.

– I'm going climbing, I say – You can't climb in jelly shoes.

– Why don't you go up the high street instead?

She waves in the direction of Dean Locker and Danny Hardwick kicking a football across the field on their way up from Melbourne. Their jeans are tight round their waists. Metal buttons and St Christophers on thin gold chains round their necks catch the sunlight so it's like they're gleaming. They've got number two skinheads and Mike Tyson shoulders, all wet and shining with sweat. They duck in and out of each other, running in bursts to stop the ball from flying into back gardens. Mum flexes her toes on the plastic chair.

– I'm off out tonight, she says. – You'll be all right.

I throw a stone ahead of me in a high arc, watch it fall on to the hard, packed mud of the field. I trek out after it, across to the garages.

– See you later then, I say.

I used to have a place in the fields. There was a gap in the scrub along the ditches and if you held your sleeves across your face you could push through the brambles. It must've been a den or something cos the mud was flat like it had been pressed down and there was newspaper pushed into the hawthorn so you wouldn't notice where the hedge had thinned. You couldn't even see it from the estate. I started just looking in at first, to see if anything had changed. Wham bar wrappers, the stopper off a roller skate, a T-shirt with The Big Es Sex on the front. I'd stand inside, peeling the bark off sticks, breaking thorns off the hedgerow so when I had them all in my hand they looked like teeth and they bit into my palm when I closed my fingers over them.

In the winter I'd lie down in my coat and I'd listen to dogs running, the smack of shoes against the frozen paddock ground, people slapping their hands together, their breath turning white so it looked like they were smoking. I'd stay there until I didn't even feel the cold. Thinking she might call me in. Thinking she might be looking out the upstairs window. Over the back garden fence.

I stopped going when they found Diana Lees, shaking like a leaf half a mile upstream. No T-shirt, no knickers, but Wayne Fisher said she never wore them anyway. I used to wonder about that.

People like to see their cars round here. No one uses the garages except for fridge-freezers and tool boxes so it's quiet when I pull myself up and fall, heaving on my arms until I think they might give out. The scabs on my knees and shins split open. I catch my forehead, then my chin as I haul my chest over the top. My nipples are sore from the scraping and I know that later I'll have to hold cotton wool soaked in cold water up to them and count to twenty until the sting goes away. I get one knee up over the roof edge and stop for a second to catch my breath. I could get a crate to stand on but I don't. I'm sweating when I get the other leg up, when I roll on to my front and feel grit and sand against my face. So tiny that you'd need a microscope to see it and then the pieces'd look like planets, like moons.

The view from the garages marks out my area. The estate hemmed in by fields on one side, the Broomfield Road on the other. One stretch of hot tarmac and to look at it shimmering you'd think it went right down to the sea, but it stops at Chelmsford. Five petrol stations along the way. People use a lot of petrol on our estate. Cars out everywhere with Arsenal stickers and flattened Orangina boxes propped up against the windscreens to keep out the sun. Skid marks across the roads from handbrake turns. Striped sun umbrellas. BMX bikes on one pedal. Stereos on window ledges. Back doors wide open and mums pegging out washing, lines and lines of sheets filling with the wind and waving like sails. It's the first bit of breeze we've had in weeks.

Mum says we're in a heatwave. Every afternoon, she gets up, snaps back the blind and narrows her eyes against the glimmer off the road.

– Another scorcher. It's another scorcher, she says.

She reaches for her cigarettes, shakes one out and uses it to point at the road.

– You could fry an egg on that car bonnet, she says.

Up this high, I can't hardly see the car bonnets. Everything dissolves into sand and petrol and split concrete road seams filled with tar. Sunroofs catch the light so you have to look to the side of them when they're passing. *Whooosh*. The glare off the garages doesn't let up and I have to hold my arm across my forehead. The sun's high, watery like you get in foreign countries, and it hurts my eyes to look at it.

I stay up on the roofs all day, eating crisps. Walkers cheese and onion, Monster Munch and KP Skips. I watch blokes ripping cars to bits. Even new ones. They stand round in Bermuda shorts and trainers, watching back seats and gearboxes pass from car to car. They don't say anything when Wayne Fisher runs past with a metal garden chair and tips it in the pond out the back. I look at the ripples until they're gone. Until the water's flat and smooth like a washed-out pebble. I watch him pulling up stubble and chucking it at his brother, at washing lines and fences. His hair's been bleached by the sun. Bright white, so it looks like he's got a number one even though the hair touches the top of his ears and the back of his neck. He's shouting but I can't hear what he's saying above the noise of the harvester. If I could look like anyone I'd look like Wayne Fisher.

– Burnt as a berry, Mum says when he tracks past our gate each morning. I look at him running round the pond with his head down and a stick in one hand, and I think how I'd like to be burnt like that.

Mum used to look like me. She told me this when I was in the bath. I was lying in the cool water with the window open, stroking the hairs down there, when she came in. She said, Wayne Fisher's dad's been talking about you. I touched the faint tan lines on my arms. I looked dirty even though my nails were clean. She gripped my wet arm.

– What do you think you're playing at? she said. – Running round late at night when I've told you to stay put.

I slid further down in the water, took a gulp of it so it filled out my cheeks. She slapped the side of my face. The water sprayed out my mouth across the bathroom tiles.

– If I hear you've been up to things I'll knock you sideways.

– I haven't, I said.

She pulled the plug on the bath and the water rushed between my legs.

– You better watch yourself, she said. – Blokes get the wrong idea. Blokes think you're asking for it.

I stood up in the bath. I could count the hairs down there with two hands.

– I used to look like you, she said. – Look where that got me.

I started running at night cos I liked the way it made me feel hard. I'd run full speed across the narrow driveways of the main road, up and down the dips in the pavement, pitching over fences and gates with coils of barbed wire that caught on my T-shirt hem and, one time, my belly. A thin, white scar tracking to my hip. I'd run over scraggy grass and beaten footpaths and car parks and bridges until it hurt to run any more and I had to hold my ribs to stop them from breaking. I'd run further every night until my muscles ached and my feet blistered and the fronts of my legs became hard, until shin splints meant I had to change surfaces. Concrete, grass, concrete, grass, until I felt that my trainers would leave the ground. Chelmsford and back, Melbourne and back, Braintree and back. Once, even Witham. Baddow Road, Springfield Road, Chelmer Village Estate, Newlands Spring.

Now that it's summer I take my time instead, stop and look at things I find in the road. Bits of car lying round from crashes, a pair of sunglasses shaped like Minnie Mouse heads, ice-lolly sticks with jokes on, cigarette lighters. One time I found three metal cowboys holding rifles. I kept them on the roof for a whole week before putting them back in the road. The next night they'd gone. I'm used to this. Things don't stay put for too long round here.

– It's hot, innit?

I squint down at Diana Lees, scuffing the sides of her sandals in the dirt.

– You hot up there? she says. I swivel round on the ledge so my legs are hanging down. I make it look easy but it's not. I kick the backs of my trainers against the wall so cement from the treads falls to the ground.

– There's a bit of wind, I say. – When you get high up there's a bit of wind.

She sticks her hands in her shorts pockets. – How d'ya get up there then? she says.

– Climb it. Don't use any crates or anything, I say. I swing back up on the roof and run along one side, skidding at the end.

– It's high up, innit?

– S'pose so. Not as high as some places.

She shades her eyes with her hand. – What, she says, like the multi-storey?

– Yeah but that doesn't count. You've got steps up that.

I hold my arms out to the side.

– Trees are better, I say. You've gotta climb trees.

– Bet ya can see for miles and miles up there, she says. – Bet ya can see all the way to Chelmsford.

– Yeah, I say, pretty far.

– How high d'ya reckon it is?

– About two Escorts, I say, like that. I put one hand flat on top of the other.

– D'ya think I could get up there? she says.

I shrug.

– Bet no one could get ya up there, she says.

I look around me, at the crisp packets and the cans of cola, the T-shirt from the scrub in the fields.

– No, I say, s'pose not.

And then I look up. There's a shout from the field. A clod of mud hurtles over and smashes against one of the garage doors, spraying her in dirt and stones. I scramble to the edge to see Wayne Fisher running over from the pond.

– Giv'us a hand!

I haul her up to the ledge. My arms start to burn.

– You've gotta get a grip, I say, get your hands up on the edge.

She scrapes her sandals on the pebble-dash.

– There aren't any footholds! Use your arms! I say.

I grab her elbows, leaning back, feet against the gutter rail.

– Come on! Kick your legs out and pull yourself on.

I catch the waistband on her shorts and drag her up. She rolls on to the roofing sheet. Her legs are grazed rough like sandpaper. We lean back behind the ledge to catch our breath, keeping low. Five minutes and Wayne Fisher gets bored kicking around, heads back to the estate.

– That was close, she says.

– Yeah, I say, close.

I crack my shoulder joints, pulling them away from my back. She screws up her face and puts a finger on the tip of my collarbone like she's trying to push it back in.

– You're skinny, aren't ya? she says.

The combine harvester's moved into the next field. Wheat chaff drifts through the air and settles on cars and pavements, dustbin lids and windowsills. The roofing sheet's warm and dusty. There's grit rolling under my hands. Diana stretches her legs out in front of her.

– Show us where everything is then, she says.

I point out Melbourne block of flats, Broomfield football ground, Angel Green stores, Shell petrol station where Wayne Fisher drops lit fags to see what happens. Then there's the model-aeroplane shop on the main road, Days of Chelmsford car salesroom and parking lot, the bridge going over the A12 to Witham where blokes drop water bombs and, one time I saw, bricks. All this stuff I look at every day cos it's always changing. Everything changes when you get some height on it. Sometimes you could near step off the roof cos you're sure you'd just swoop over it all. And I tell her that.

– Whooosh, I say, my hand like a wing on a plane. – All the way to Clacton.

We look out over the roofs, everything flat, dry fields, dry scrub, dry mud, no water anywhere 'cept the pond and that's getting lower. The Council are planning to drag it for fish, fed up with the neighbours' complaints that they have to use nets to draw the dead ones off the surface, lying belly up and glistening. As the water level sinks you find things. Petrol cans and hairbrushes, a racer bike with handles curled like a ram's horns, fishing rods, a dead bird, broken off windscreen wipers. I'm about to reel them off, about to ask, had she seen the letter from the estate in the *Essex Chronic*, when she pulls out the T-shirt stuffed in the hole between the roofing sheet and rafters.

– Where d'ya find it? she says. – I've been looking all over.

I look at the ditch, at the barbed wire down one side of it and the mud with dried in tractor-tyre marks.

– Dunno, I say. – I just picked it up.

I look back down at my hands. They're hard like I've rubbed

salt into them. The sun's slacked off. It's cool. The air's gone green, like wet grass, but she's still sweating. I can see it on her nose and the top of her lip. She's wringing the T-shirt in her hands. Bringing it to her face and then taking it away like a dog testing water for the first time.

– You all right? I say.

– Yeah, she says, yeah, I've gotta go.

And then I'm looking at her scraped sandals and her grazed shins and the scabs on her knees and the Stars and Stripes bikini top with more in it than I'll ever have. Everything sliding out of sight until I hear her smack down on the ground. I don't watch her run back to the estate. I listen to her shoes instead, fast and regular as they beat down on the paving slabs.

Later, I make my way back. The sky a blue so deep you could swim in it. Mum out and the estate dead still. The back door swinging softly on its hinges. I open all the upstairs windows, let the wind flap out my Superman T-shirt, the cap sleeves fluttering the tops of my burnt arms, the sun blisters across my shoulders cooling. Mum's sheets lift and stir, puffing out like a parachute when a gust carries through the window. I lean my chest over the window ledge, wince as the blisters stretch and spill, take huge gulps of air, drinking up the evening. I listen to the rush of the Broomfield Road out the front. Five minutes away but you'd think it was right outside your window. Like those motorway hotels abroad.

Mum's got a better view than me. South facing. Field facing. From her window I can see the corn heads sway in the breeze. The field's dark and navy, stirring like an ocean. I used to look out here for foxes, sitting on the ledge, cos I was even skinnier then, rigid with pins and needles. Not daring to move in case I missed one, running along the pond bank or across the heat-dried mud of the gateposts.

Mum came back late one night and found me there. She said the only wildlife I'd find round here was the Fishers. And as she said it I swear on my life that I saw something, thin and silver, streak along the outside of my eye. I stopped looking after that. I didn't think I'd get lucky a second time.

Mum caught me. My legs were wrapped around the sheet. The window was open but I was hot, hair plastered to the back of my neck. The air was wet and salty as I rolled in and out of it. I dug my heels down the fitted sheet, felt waves slowly rising down there. My legs were stretched out straight when she came in.

– What are you doing?

I pulled at the sheet but it was stuck underneath me.

– No, nothing, I said, I'm not doing anything.

I could smell me as she sat on the edge of the bed. The smell I carry around on my hand all day if I do it in the morning.

– It's hot, that's all, I say.

I started to gather the sheet up under my arms. I went to open the window further. She grabbed my hand, pulled it to her face. I felt my wrist give way.

– Not doing anything? she said, bending my finger back to her nose. – Not doing anything?

I wake up wetting myself. This happens quite a bit. I never catch it in time. My Superman T-shirt's soaked to the armpits and I have to peel it, still warm, from my skin. I strip the bed, putting the wet things in carriers from under my mattress to take to the laundrette when the coast is clear. I wipe myself down with a dry end of sheet but I can't get rid of the smell of wee. It will stay with me until I can get to the shower. I'm about to get a flannel for a stand-up wash when I hear something, carrying on the wind. I lean out the window, listening.

The noise is coming from the garages. Someone's dragging an oil drum or a watering can across the gravel. It's heavy, metallic, cos it sounds out when it bumps over bigger stones, sloshes over the ground every few paces. I lean further out, rest my hands against the cool concrete wall. That's when I see Mum, standing some distance off with Wayne Fisher's dad. She has her red sundress on, the hem flaps around her legs. Her heels click down the estate. Immediately I get back into bed.

Wayne Fisher's dad looks at me. I don't mind this. Sometimes I look back at him. I look at the holes in his work jeans, the dark hairs on the front of his arms, the sweat mark running across his shoulders and down to the small of his back. I look at his bicep flex and relax when he leans across me to get beer from the fridge. One time he let me drink some straight out the bottle, held it while I drained it dry.

– Don't tell your mother, he said.

I clinked the bottle against my white teeth.

– Sure, I said.

I breathed him in. BO and petrol and musty garages where the sun hadn't reached through. – You should have a wash, I said to him. I stuck one thumb through my jean loop, held the other hand up to my nose.

– You stink, I said.

– You love it, he went, grabbing my hand and putting it against his fly.

I don't know why I let him do it. I don't even like him.

Mum doesn't check on me but I lie dead still even so. I count my breaths in and out to get them steady. I'm on my side, face to the window with one hand cupped over it, fingers slack. Really, I never sleep like this. Wayne Fisher's dad told me.

– Stretched out you were, he said, flat on your back. I checked on you, your mother was out like a light.

And I looked at him smiling so wide I could see his gold fillings. One on each side.

I draw the sheet up to my neck despite the damp heat. I listen, but there's only Mum downstairs, running water in the sink, closing the back door, slipping shoes off at the stairs, leaning heavy on the banister, falling on to her bed with a low moan. I wait fifteen minutes and then I slide in socks to the airing cupboard for a clean pair of jeans. The only clothes in there. They're stiff from the wash, could near stand up on their own, and I have to fight to get them on.

I slip out the back. Past the garages with a track through the mud that leads to the field, past dusty cars and shattered glass, up through the estate and on to the Broomfield Road. I walk beside oil stains and grass, and it's quiet except for the telephone wires stirring way above me. I close my eyes and walk through a cloud of mosquitoes underneath the only tree on the road. They fly in my eyelashes and I wonder if I'll ever see the ones with lights in them, flies with sparks. I saw seagulls one summer, chasing each other up the River Chelmer. I lay back on the garage roof, looking at their huge white wings, the way they coasted, wondering what they were doing out here with no waves, no strips of sand, only gravel pits and scratchy green belts, Riverside Leisure Centre with the blocks of ice from the rink that melt in the car park and run to the drains.

It's late. There's nothing in the sky, nothing on the roads. I run with my arms stretched out, cut down the Petersfield roundabout to the dirt path snaking beside the river. I track past dark water, tall weeds that stir in the breeze, shopping trolleys tipped from the banks breaking the surface like flying fish. I reach the Broomfield bypass, skirting past the pools of electric lights. And there's no grass underneath me, no rain for weeks and weeks. And I think about Mum, waiting for the weather to break.

– Where are the clouds? she says.

I stop at the crater. I come here quite a bit. One deep crack, some way off from the river bank in a field that no one farms. It's always been here. Filling up with water or crumbling under your trainers so you can never be sure how long a ledge will last out and you have to skid down in levels until you reach the bottom. Flints and clay and cans like a lining, baked from the heat.

Wayne Fisher's dad told me about temperatures, about how surfaces shrink in the heat. You can see pictures, he said, of deserts with whole pieces of earth split down the middle, cracks so big you could lose an animal as big as a horse. I told him, I'd like to see those pictures. And I think about what they might look like, how long they would stretch, how wide, if people follow them like roads. If they use them for dumps.

And I'm catching my breath as I lean over the crater, bent with my hands on my knees, when I hear him. Behind me, and then over me, so quick. And as I hit the ground, stones in my back, a spool of cattle wire by my head, I think about my tight jeans. About how they're going to be tough to get off.

I go the back way. Sprinting over stubble fields and electric fences, dried cow-pats and ditches I don't see until I'm in them. I cut through the copse, twigs cracking under my trainers, against my chest as I push through denser parts, and it hurts and I don't mind it. I belt through Croxton's Mill and there's the rush of water from the weir and there's wet on my face from the spray.

I reach the estate from the field, one shimmering flat under the night light. I stop for a second to catch my breath, holding the place where my jeans cut in and there is wet. And that's when I see Diana, pouring petrol over the stubble. Her arms are pale and gleaming. She uses the back of her hand to push the hair away from her face, pours in one long spurt before raising it to her forehead again. She's bent with the weight of the can, walking with it in bursts. Petrol sloshes over her legs. The fumes carry on the wind. The pond surface shivers. I keep to the edge of the field, jogging softly until the flats of my hands are against the garage doors, the peeling paint. I haul myself up.

I look out across the field, at the machinery glinting among the hay bales. There's just a glow at first. Like someone's lit a cigarette and thrown the match to the ground, where it flares for a second. A tiny chink of orange that flickers, brightening as the breeze catches it. And then I see it run. Whoosh to the banks of the pond. I stand up as the stubble starts to crack, the air blowing hot and dry in my face like it's supposed to do in deserts. It spreads to the ditches, rising higher to the dead wood of the elm trees. And as the wind whips my T-shirt I see the tree explode into the sky. Hundreds and thousands of black dots cawing and wheeling up above.

Mum's at the back garden fence, standing between Wayne Fisher's dad's shirts. It's the first wash she's done in weeks and I think about that. The cotton sleeves wave from the line and across her face, trying to catch hold of her. There's a washing basket at her feet, pegs in the grass.

I hear Diana's mum calling for her, face up to the field gate. Long shrieks that drown out the birds above, and bring everyone running, rubbing sleep out of their eyes, to their back yards. The smoke billows like cloth around my head. Waving my hands in front of my face, I try to clear it, to look for Mum.

I see her bend, slowly, picking the pegs from the ground and holding them against her nightdress with one hand. She pulls the shirts one by one from the line, flings them over her shoulder. She stops at the back door, loaded with white washing. And I think, for a second, that she might call my name, might run to the fence and press splinters against her cheek. But she doesn't call and she doesn't run. She backs through the glass door and slides it shut. I see her legs through the leaf-pattern panels, heading towards the utility room.

Pondlife
Ashley Stokes

Carshalton

'I've got something for you,' Rachel says. At her hip she pats the slim, canvas shoulder bag. 'For later.' Neil smiles. He knows it is his Christmas present.

'I've got something for you too,' he says. It's more than the Paris perfume and silk underwear he has wrapped up in silvery paper and hidden in his jacket. Since he arrived back he's been anticipating this meeting. For two days he's lolled around his parents' house, staring at the same old decorations with nothing to do but eat and wait. Christmas is for children, parents and couples, he thinks. He doesn't enjoy it any more. He's restless at home. He can't smoke. The central heating makes him sweat and oversleep. He can't sit through another film that he didn't enjoy two years ago. The childhood photographs that hang in the hall and on the landing make him cringe. All day he's wanted to be with Rachel. Tonight he will make her a proposition and get her away from here.

Rachel stands in the porch in her black leather coat and a navy-blue woollen hat. Her umbrella drips steadily on the welcome mat. It is raining hard, has been for days. It battered down Christmas Eve without a break, continued all through the night and today. But she won't come inside the house. She never does. She came in once, for coffee after they'd seen *Pulp Fiction* at Sutton UCI. She complained that Neil's mother looked at her in a funny way. Neil's mother always looks at people in a funny way. She doesn't mean anything by it.

Rachel's nervousness frustrates Neil. He has to come back here to see her. She won't make the twenty-minute train journey to his bedsit in Balham, despite the perfect weekend they spent there after they met again, as adults this time.

'It's too far,' she said to him. 'It's miles away.'

They can't go to hers, let alone sleep over. Her mother, she says, is already asking questions about Neil. He isn't afraid of her. He can handle a girlfriend's mother. Unless they meet he can't be certain that Rachel is telling the truth. He wonders if he's ever going to be alone with Rachel again. For three months he's come home every weekend to see her. They smooch in pubs and alleyways, in cinema queues and in her Fiat Uno, parked in the Carshalton boondocks, the wipers fanning the windscreen, Kiss FM on low. Then he sleeps alone in his old single bed in his untouched teenage bedroom. He lies awake sometimes, listening to the trains and the foxes screeching, thinking *nothing happens here*. He is twenty-five next month. Next month it will be 1995. He doesn't want to keep coming back to Carshalton.

Out in the avenue, raindrops jump on the roofs of cars and vans. Pink and ruby fairy lights hang in double-glazed bay windows and entwine garden conifers. The treetops spasm and flutter in the gust. As Rachel tries to put up the umbrella, Neil takes her hand and swings her into the alley alongside his parents' house. Her lips are cold as he kisses her.

'Happy Christmas,' he says, breaking off. 'I missed you today.'

She says nothing, nestles her head in his shoulder.

'Was it terrible?'

'It's never a dull moment,' she says, 'with me and her.'

Neil considers asking Rachel now, get it over with. He's excited. But a car chugs into the top of the alley. Headlights angle their shadow up the fence, the two of them gelled together, their outline like a thick, leaning candle. Tyres ping and skitter the gravel. She giggles and they walk briskly away and make for the main road. At the junction, he says,

'Nowhere's going to be open.' They could stay in, wait until his parents have watched the *One Foot in the Grave* Christmas special and gone to bed. Then they'll have that soft, Prussian-blue lounge carpet to themselves.

'Let's go back,' he says.

'We'll find somewhere.'

'Always the optimist, Rach.'

'Me, optimistic? Happy go lucky, fabulous, but optimistic, come on. What have I got to be optimistic about?'

'I'll tell you later.'

'Flatterer.'

She once said that the things he says to her are for the sake of saying them, as if he only likes the sound of the words. She said this recently, and when he was sixteen. Then she turned him down when he asked her out. She says he hasn't changed much, he still has a way with words.

Neil is a junior copywriter for Cusp Medical, an aggressively marketed private health-insurance scheme. By day Neil stares out across the rooftops of Bloomsbury from his high-rise office on the Euston Road. By night he frets about a screenplay he never seems able to start. He's going to write a romantic comedy. He likes it that Rachel believes he can write a film. 'Everyone knows you can write,' she says. 'Even when we were at school, those things you used to show us.' Neil doesn't remember there ever being an 'everyone'.

'The Victory might be open,' he says.

'No it won't.'

'It's closest.'

'No it's not. The Red Lion is closest.'

'I wouldn't be seen dead in the Dead Lion.'

'I hate the Victory. That Moon pub thing in Wallington might be open.'

'I'm not walking that far on the off chance. And it's a khazi. Anyway, it's too near my school.'

'It's miles from your school and it's near the Melbourne.'

'Someone'll kill me if I go in there.'

'Paranoid, paranoid.'

'C'mon, let's try the Victory.'

'No, Neil. We'll go to the Fox and Hounds.'

She takes his arm. They huddle beneath the umbrella. One spoke sticks out from under the fabric. There's no one around. No cars whoosh past. Neil's hair is already drenched and Rachel's softened mascara racoons her eyes. As they cross the road the fissured tarmac swims with spray and glimmers of scarlet and yellow-green Christmas lights. Neil thinks that they could be crossing this road on any December night in the last thirty years. They head for the village.

Alongside the Wandle there are steep-gabled, mock-Tudor houses. They pass the cut-off wedge of land between the river and the railway that they've always called the Island. Overhead, the railway bridge's black and ruddy brickwork curves, almost twists. Neil remembers his father telling him that artisans like the men who built this bridge no longer exist. They pass bottle banks, the offices of Vinamul, and bare trees, their ivy-swathed silhouettes dark against the grey-purple clouds. The rushes hiss by the riverside. They take the narrow bridge at Butter Hill, where the chemical works used to be but now there's an estate of beige-bricked, identical houses that could be anywhere in the South of England. Neil's father says they are made from kits, like models.

Rachel is telling Neil everything about the Eagle Star office party and all the things she wanted but didn't get for Christmas. He doesn't say anything, lets her talk. Rain runs down his face, leaving a varnishy resin taste in his mouth. He realises it's the Cossack Extra Control Hairspray for Men that he spent ages clouding over his head in front of the bathroom mirror. He wants to be somewhere, anywhere dry so they can exchange gifts and talk. He knows the discussion they'll soon have will be one of the most important for him. And he likes the way she talks, always has. Liked it when he used to for-tuitously bump into her on the way to school, outside church-hall discos, the top deck of the 157, outside McDonald's in

Sutton High Street, at the parties where he watched her dance to 'West End Girls' and 'The Reflex'. Outside McDonald's in Sutton he once saw her kissing the tosser who thought he looked like Billy Idol, who relished calling Neil a cripple because he limped. Tosser Idol had his hand inside her blouse. She wore calf-length black suede boots and a pencil skirt, and Neil was in love with her knees, the way they swayed together. He was crestfallen, but he still liked the things that she said.

Now, it is her dry asides, the irony, the way she describes people, the things she wants to be. If she sees someone flash or cool in a film or a video, she'll say forlornly, 'I want to be like that.' She wants to be the little girl in *Leon*. She wants to be Justine Frischman. When she had long hair she wanted short hair. Now she has a sleek black bob she wants her curly tresses back. And then she'll say, 'I'm sorry, I am still fickle I'm afraid.' The way she draws attention to her weaknesses makes him laugh.

They carry on up Butter Hill. On one side of the road is a terrace of identically shaped shops: a solicitor's, a news-agent's, a bookmaker's, and on the other, a metallic square two-storey office block with tinted windows.

'I used to call this the seventies-eighties road,' says Neil. 'It's like seventies on one side, eighties on the other.'

'Why?'

'One side's never changed. The other has.'

Rachel shakes her head, wobbling the umbrella. 'You are strange sometimes.'

They cut through another new estate, the same beige houses built where there used to be sandhills, and enter Westcroft Sports Centre car park. It is empty. Floodlit rain lends the asphalt a mercury sheen. He pulls her closer to him and they run until they reach the building. In front of the foyer they hurry down the concrete steps, skirt the edge of the park, where the bourn runs once in a blue moon, and just before they reach the high street Neil notices. He stops and stares. Every time he comes back something has changed. It isn't the little things he minds, speed ramps and the different shops. It's the new developments.

Carshalton belongs to Sutton, the 'Green Borough'. Its Liberal council is environmentally friendly. On election it repainted all its vans and fleet cars a fresh, clean emerald and emblazoned them with a spreading oak motif. But it allows building on every conceivable open space, and it builds ugly and it builds incongruously. The fields where Neil used to play junior-school sports are now beige. The huge stretch of watery land at Beddington Corner. Slices of Grove Park. He's heard it said that only the ponds in the centre stop the whole place from being filled in for houses.

Carshalton could look exactly the same as Croydon, Sutton, Kingston, Ashford and Woking. Neil is not reconciled to these changes; he feels as if he should be consulted first. He has to sort out what this place means to him. He wonders if Carshalton is ever going to be finished. Here, where there used to be a large converted Victorian house, is another beige cul-de-sac.

Rachel pulls his arm. 'C'mon.'

'Where's it gone? That old house, the education offices.'

'Oh that went ages ago. Those houses are really pricey.'

'They look shit.'

'They look really nice,' says Rachel. 'Close to the shops, close to the park. I wouldn't mind one of them.' The rain intensifies, sounds like marbles cascading on to the umbrella.

Now in the high street, they pass the Star of Bengal, Abra Kebabra, the motorcycle showroom and the tyre centre. Neil's collywobbles rise. He's eaten too much turkey today, but his stomach feels hollow and acidic. Part of him wants to keep walking. He'll be asking her in how long? Half an hour. Once they're settled in the pub with dripping fringes and wrapping paper screwed up on the tabletop.

'Oh fuck,' says Rachel. The Fox and Hounds is shut. 'We'll try the Greyhound.'

'We won't get in there, you need tickets.'

'Neil!'

They cut across the graveyard of the parish church, opposite Carshalton Ponds, the water's surface alive with rainfall. From here the Wandle creeps through Hackbridge and Mitcham Watermeads and Ravensbury Park, undercuts the railway at Haydons Road, Merton, trickles through Earlsfield, Southfields, Wandsworth, sloshes into the Thames at Bell Lane Creek. Neil sometimes thinks the Wandle is the only thing that rises in Carshalton.

Here at the ponds, overshadowed by yews, is a small white bridge with a griffin's head keystone. Neil always liked this bridge. In his teenage imagination it was a place for assignations. If he'd had girlfriends it is where he'd have wanted to meet. Before school he would fantasise about being there with Rachel. He wouldn't leave the house until she passed his front garden. She said no when he asked her. He didn't have girlfriends until he'd left Carshalton. Two weeks ago he walked with Rachel in the park and they kissed there, above the river's beginning, duck shit on the masonry and grey squirrels cracking acorns in the undergrowth. Sometimes with Rachel, Neil feels he is living out an adolescence that he never had. The kiss didn't feel different to any other.

The Greyhound Hotel is ticket only.

'Told you,' said Neil. He is sopping now and can't feel his toes.

'Racehorse,' says Rachel in a sing-song voice, as if this is a game and she is winning.

In Festival Walk the river bed is mushy with sycamore leaves and a dribble of stream. The biggest London plane tree in Britain lines up with St Philomena's water tower. In West Street there are white, weather-boarded frontages and new beige houses in Old Swan Yard.

'Village of the Damned,' says Neil. 'Village of the Damned.'

'What are you going on about?' says Rachel.

'I was brought up here. Look at it. Look at the state of it.'

'Neil, this is normal, this is just like everywhere else. It's you that's done things arse about face. Our parents come from shitholes like Streatham and they moved out here, where it's nice. Why do you want to live in the armpit of the world?'

'Nothing wrong with Balham.' Neil thinks that he might have to be more flexible about locations. Only slightly more flexible. He draws an imaginary Berlin Wall at Tooting Graveney.

The Racehorse is shut. The Hope is open, but Rachel won't go in.

'I can't be seen in there. It's a front room. Look, it's got pot plants in the window. Look at those cactuses. I still live here, remember. Anyway, I got off with a crap bloke in there and I don't want to risk it.'

Used to her talking like this, Neil shrugs, tries to smile. The first time they went out she might as well have been reading the register in 5C.

At Carshalton station, where British Rail cut the Gordian knot of the leaves-on-the-line problem by cutting down all the trees, they switch into North Street.

'It looks like we're going to the Victory after all,' says Rachel.

'Seems that way,' says Neil. Quite soon he will know how he is going to live in 1995.

'Last time I went in here,' says Rachel, 'I ended up getting off with someone really crap.'

'Do you remember the last time you went to the Windmill?' says Neil, talking to the kerb.

'Of course I do,' she says. 'I got off with you.'

He remembers how quietly ecstatic he was that afternoon he ran into her in the Windmill on Clapham Common. He'd been bored all day, trying to write some dialogue for his screenplay. He'd ventured out at about three thirty, as the daylight began to fade. The brickwork around Balham station dusked to a deep, almost maroon russet as he passed. Aimlessly he'd straggled up to Clapham, fancied a drink. She came up to him while he was waiting to be served. At first he was delighted simply because she remembered him. He hadn't thought about her for years, apart from occasionally in masturbation fantasies when he reeled through all the girls he'd met and never fucked. When Neil left home for university and film studies she stayed behind. She said she couldn't leave her mother. Her mother couldn't cope without her.

In the Windmill she was with friends, but they left. Neil sat with her, catching up, sharing cigarettes. For once, he consciously stayed sober, drinking vodka and Coke without vodka. They swapped phone numbers. He was surprised when she kissed him in the car park. He thought he was only going to walk her to Clapham South. A brief, sharp, French kiss. His scrotum crawled. She was drunk. He was too timid to ask her back that night. She said she'd call.

She rang him the following Saturday, after he'd given up on her. She said her mother was driving her mad. Could she come over? They saw *Star Trek: Generations* at the Clapham Picture House, ate falafels, slept together afterwards.

Whenever Neil thinks of her, when he's dopey on the tube in the mornings, when he's peering out of his office window when he should be writing copy for inserts in lifestyle magazines, when he sits at his tiny desk in the evenings and notebooks his romantic comedy, he thinks, how ironic that he might after all end up with someone from home.

When she enters the pub he lingers outside for a second. He squeezes his fist and stares up at the night sky. Raindrops dive into his face.

Inside it is hot with smoke and steaming coats. Copper-coloured tinsel loops around the bar and the walls, tracing picture frames and the big brass mirror engraved with a fleur-de-lis pattern. She asks for her usual, diet Coke. Rachel rarely drinks alcohol. The calories, she says. She takes a seat at a table on the dais as Neil waits at the bar alongside a line of men about his age, all wearing bright ski jackets and jeans. Primary colour boys. Neil is suspicious of anyone who dresses like they've just stepped out of a Fosters window display. He doesn't recognise any of them. He looks up at Rachel. She is rummaging in her bag. She looks studious, preoccupied. She wears a mustard-yellow blouse that he's never seen before. The overhead lights shadow her collarbone. In profile, she lights a Silk Cut Ultra. 'A small chest,' she often says, 'that's all I have.' Then she notices him and smiles. He thinks every night could be like this, just Rachel and him, out somewhere. There would be more intimacy if they were living together. He would be able to inject some passion.

He remembers the way she clung tightly to him that Sunday morning. She stayed in his bed while he went out for newspapers and almond croissants and bagels from Safeway. While he was making the coffee she asked him if he wanted to get back in. 'It's warm in bed,' she said. She uncovered herself, put her hands behind her head, smiled her downturned, knowing barb of a smile. There was a ghost of a tan about her shoulders and thighs, teardrop outlines around her breasts that he hadn't noticed the night before. He wants every morning to be like that.

As Neil carries a Coke and a pint towards the stairs a ski jacket barges into him, slopping Guinness over his sleeve.

'Cheers,' says Neil. The ski jacket grins, widens his eyes, then jogs him again as he steps past. Into space Neil spits 'Cunt', then flinches.

'What'd you say?'

Neil turns. Acne scarred, the ski jacket rolls his shoulders and, like a skittish flightless bird, pokes forward his head. A big turquoise vein pumps in his neck.

'Drat, oh crikey,' says Neil.

'Yeah?'

Rachel calls Neil. She is standing up. The ski jacket watches as Neil climbs the stairs and sits down. If she wasn't here he'd have let it go anyway.

'You are unsubtle sometimes,' says Rachel. 'You always did have a big mouth.'

'He walked into me on purpose.'

'And he's twice your size and there's a wrap of whizz on his table.' She dips her head closer to Neil. 'He's still staring at us, keep your head down, he's still staring.'

'I'm not scared of him,' says Neil, craning to peer over Rachel's shoulder at what looks to him like KitKat foil on a table surrounded by three other skis. He remembers being fifteen and in Sutton High Street, when he'd just come out from seeing *Rocky IV* or *Teen Wolf Too*, and kids would shout: *Want a fight, you starting?* Neil limped. He couldn't run very fast. He was both scared and jealous of them. This was when his territory was delineated no further south than Sutton and no further east than the Croydon flyover, Mitcham cricket green to the north, Kingston upon Thames to the west, and London was a rolling grid of flickers and pinpricks viewed from the top deck of the 157 as it hit the high ground at St Helier's hospital, where Neil's mother suffered her protracted contractions and a plaque commemorates the birth of John Major.

'I know him,' says Rachel. 'You don't want to upset him.' Neil wonders how well she knows him. 'I don't think you'd last very long around here now. You never were very street-wise, were you?'

'Who wants to be streetwise if it means being a gibbon?'

'Shhh, keep your voice down.'

'Fuckwits.'

'Seriously, shhh. I can tell you things, stupid things.'

The ski jacket gives Neil the evil eye as he passes to rejoin his mates. Leaving crosses Neil's mind, but he doesn't see why he should. He thinks, *I am not frightened of them.* He strokes the side of his chin and holds Rachel's gaze.

'You look nice.'

'I look fat.'

Neil laughs and takes one of her presents from his jacket. 'You don't know anything about being fat.'

'Oh but I do. Look at me. Cup of lemon tea and I put on a stone.'

'Happy Christmas,' he says.

'Oh wow,' she says. 'Here, I've got something for you.' She slides a thin, oblong package across the tabletop, then slits open her gift with violet, manicured fingernails, smiles, and mouths 'thank you'. She sprays her wrists and sniffs. 'Mmm, that's nice. I hope you haven't got that.'

'Oh thanks. Thank you, yeah, great, brilliant.' Neil has read *The History of the World in Ten and a Half Chapters*. Only the *Half* chapter resonated.

Rachel's eyes glisten in the lamplight. She tilts her head. Neil slips his jacket over the back of his chair. He is going to ask her now. It is time to start a conversation about us. At some point, all couples have a conversation about us, about what they want. Neil and Rachel have never had this conversation. He struggles to find an opening. She says, 'You wouldn't believe my friggin' mum today.'

Neil sags and lights a cigarette. He's heard a lot about Rachel's mother. He remembers when Rachel was fourteen her dad moved out to Canvey Island to get away from her. He knows she has a penchant for younger men that embarrasses Rachel, and he wonders if this is why he's not allowed to meet her. But Rachel says it's because she doesn't want him to suffer one of her mother's amateur tarot readings. She's got a thing about palms as well, reckons she can predict love lives, cancers and progeny. He's heard she's on antidepressants, that she once stood on the coffee table, wine bottle at hip, singing 'Cry Me a River'. This made her seem quite a laugh, but it was eleven in the morning on Good Friday and she hadn't slept for two nights. She's addicted to horoscopes, New Age healing, Gustav Klimt, Carl Jung and Enya, holistic discussion groups, self-help manuals and lonely hearts columns. She walks barefoot in Wallington precinct. She wears Rachel's clothes, but only after they've gone out of fashion. Often, when Neil phones, Rachel'll quip, 'I'll ring you back, Mum's in.' And she doesn't call for two days. Seventy-five per cent of their conversations, by telephone or otherwise, are about Rachel's mother. They even talked about her in bed.

'Do you know what she did?' says Rachel. 'She lit this well smelly, frankincense joss-stick thing and put it on the window ledge while I was trying out my new silver trainers which she bought me, but they're the wrong size and I hate that, when someone can't be bothered to find out what size you are. I was walking up and down the hall and the smoke alarm goes off. And she runs into the kitchen because the joss-stick thing has fallen over and set fire to the curtains. And the house is filling up with smoke and she puts it out by throwing this pan of mulled wine over it. Then she was kneeling on the floor crying, saying that they were her best curtains and she bought them in Tangier when I was a baby. And it's just not true. She got them from Curtain Land on the Purley Way when she won five hundred quid on the Premium Bonds. It's not funny, Neil. Can you imagine if your mum did things like that? You wouldn't think it was funny.'

'I'd sling her in a home,' says Neil.

'A home? She's only forty-five and she's a probation officer. She thinks she's progressive. I could never leave her. Imagine what could happen to her if I left.' Rachel says this slowly and assuredly, as if she is taking strength from her responsibilities. Neil stubs out his cigarette and immediately lights another one. Rachel's problem, he thinks, is that for too long she's allowed this to be her purpose in life. And her excuse.

'If you left,' he says, 'she'd have to grow up. You're her daughter, not her mother. Look at all the things you've missed out on because of her. You didn't go to university . . .'

'I was too thick to go to university . . .'

'No, don't be stupid, you got good enough grades.'

'But I can't do maths. I couldn't get my head around the parallelogram.'

'And you're still stuck at home.'

'I like living at home.'

'No, you don't. You moan about her all the time. I sometimes wonder what we'd talk about if your mother wasn't barking.'

'She's just sad and lonely,' Rachel says. 'If she found someone else she'd probably want me to move out. I haven't got the money anyway. Do you know how much money I've got to last until the end of January? Fifty-two pounds.' Rachel spends her entire pay packet as soon as she gets it. She works too close to all those clothes shops in Sutton. Neil tries to work out how much spare he has each month, what little cutbacks he's going to have to make.

'Rachel, I want to ask you something.'

'I'm all ears, oh hang on, I forgot to show you what I brought for you.'

'No, no, the book's here.'

'No, I found this yesterday.'

She puts her hand into her bag and draws out a folded sheet of paper. She presses it down on the table and smirks as she passes it across to him. In the corner the ski jackets are shouting out 'Little Donkey' but changing the words to something about jump leads and Pollards Hill slappers.

Neil opens the paper, recognising his own poor typing, the wonky Es and Tipp-Ex smudges, and he cringes. He cringes so hard that his eyelashes feel frozen. It is 'Elegy for the Lost and Discarded', a poem he wrote when he was sixteen.

> I thank you for the autumn wind
> The dry leaves in your hair
> The fields are gaunt and dying
> The summer leaves the air
> We stand upon the ivory bridge
> The river flows beneath
> To you I give my every thought
> But you I cannot reach

He can only manage part of the third stanza before turning it over.

'Quick, burn it,' he says, sparking his lighter flint, 'burn it.'
Rachel snatches the paper.

'Don't be silly, it's good. You gave me that.'

'Yeah, when I was a fucking fat romantic twat and you had bad taste in poetry.'

'My mum really likes it.'

'Then she is a raving veggieburger. Hello sky, hello trees. Fanny farts of the goddess.'

Rachel's eyes darken. She rips the Cellophane from her fag packet and crumples it in her palm. 'Fuck off, Neil.'

'Sorry, Rachel, it's just . . . you know.'

'You're still the same, Neil, no different to when you used to give us poems on the bus.'

'Thanks.'

She wrinkles her nose at him and sips her drink. 'What were you going to ask me? You said you wanted to ask me something.'

'Nothing.'

'Come on.'

The poem remains, words up.

> I see no colours left in you
> But feeling never dies.

He reaches out and turns it over again.

'What I was going to say,' he says, 'is that I've got you another present.' Retrieving it from his jacket, he hands it to her. Without looking down, she begins to unwrap it. The paper crinkles and glints. She runs her fingers over the material but does not smile. She has the silky black bra and knickers in her hands, absently rubs the material with her thumbs.

It was uncomfortable having to buy them, to browse in a lingerie shop. He didn't really have a clue what he was looking for, but one of Neil's ex-girlfriends had told him that underwear is the most intimate present you can receive from a man. The rosy, pouting man at the cash till called him 'honey'. Neil felt part of his spinal column seep like glue. He couldn't get out of Secrets quick enough.

'Neil,' Rachel says. 'Do you think you can really have a fling with a friend?'

He blinks. She waits. She looks at her lap. Then she blushes. And he thinks, oh fuck, mistake, mistake, shouldn't have bought her those, she thinks I'm a perv, like those blokes who send canalside, tits-out pics to *Amateur Photographer*. Rachel holds up the knickers between her thumbs. She pulls them apart. The elastic keeps stretching and stretching and stretching until it's half as wide as the table.

'How big do you think I am?' she says. 'These are, like, twice my size.'

'No they're not, they're the right size.' He knew he hadn't made a mistake. He'd checked her size when her underwear lay on the floor in his bedsit, when she was in the shower. You never know when this sort of information will come in handy. 'You're being stupid, Rachel.'

'I could keep the frost off my car with this bra. Look at it. It's like a parachute.' She tosses it up in the air and starts to laugh.

The bra does not come down.

The ski jacket has caught it.

'You've got big waps, Rachel. You could use two skips and a battleship chain.'

Neil stands up, swipes at the bra. 'Leave her alone, you subnormal prick.'

The ski smirks, briefly. Then his eyes yellow. He rings a finger in his ear. He outsizes Neil, makes him feel like he is shrinking, but he can't back down. This is what you are, how you are tested, were tested, are untested, what you missed out on and where you failed here.

'My ears are burning,' says the ski. 'You want to say that again?'

It's a long way to the door, there is the table, his jacket to retrieve, the narrow staircase, a crowd, his girlfriend. Neil breathes out. Lines harden on the ski's upper lip. The lines deepen. Rachel is staring up at Neil with imploding eyes.

The ski lets his jaw fall, then clashes his teeth with a hard, bony snap.

'Fuck off,' says Neil. 'Piece of shit.'

'Oh for fuck's sake,' Rachel mutters.

The ski drops his shoulders. Neil shivers and jumps back. The ski laughs. 'Brave man, very brave, for a poof.'

His arm blurs across the table, is around Neil's head and pushing him down into the ashtray. Rachel is shouting. Pain stabs up Neil's spine as he tries to free himself. He can see the grain of the wood hovering in front of his eyes. He can smell ash. The table shifts. Chairs judder. He flings his arm but only manages to smash his pint glass against the wall.

'You fucking ponce,' screams the ski, his elbow grinding into Neil's shoulder. Neil somehow springs up. The ceiling see-saws in his vision. He slumps back against the rail. Rachel is barging the ski, grimacing and cursing. She shoots Neil a look that he's not sure of. *How did this happen?* he thinks. *How did I let this happen?* The ski's mates are now restraining him, have their arms around his stomach, but they stare at Neil with the same switchblade eyes and GBH expressions. Big men with Santa hats and false beards, bar staff, swagger past Neil and chest the ski back to his table. There isn't anywhere else they can go.

'I'd make tracks, mate,' says one. Neil is already scrambling on his jacket and making for the stairs. He turns. Rachel stands by the end of the table, clasping and unclasping her hand in the air.

'Cheers, Derek,' she says dryly. 'Cheers. Nice to see you again.'

Outside, in the road, Neil pants. The rain seems to hiss on his hot forehead. Rachel takes his arm and marches him swiftly down the street.

'I can't take you anywhere, Neil, for God's sake. I used to go out with him. You were almost as bad as him.' She swivels on her heels and falls back against the wet brickwork of the railway bridge. 'Your face.' She giggles. 'Your face.'

'It wasn't just the parallelogram,' says Rachel. 'It was also the rhombus and the trapezium.' She prods at the concrete with her feet, makes the swing lift higher. She's not annoyed with him now. And she's stopped laughing. They sit on the playground swings in the park at the end of Neil's road. He'd invited her into the house, but she fobbed him off. Then he thought he was finally heading for a rendezvous with Madame Veggieburger. Rachel was, she said, gagging for a turkey sandwich with cheese coleslaw and Hellmann's Light. But they ended up in the park, with the roundabout and the climbing frame. The swings have leather bands instead of the hard plastic seats that could smash your teeth in. It is still raining. The wind rushes in the poplars behind them. Down where the darkness hardens around the river, sycamores sway and willows flail. They could take a shortcut through those trees to Rachel's house. Neil doesn't fancy having his palm read any more. She has strapped the bra over her ears and tied it under her chin.

'Octagons were cute,' she says.

'I always found the isosceles erotic,' says Neil. 'And the words parabola and Polaris and paintbox.'

'Freak.'

'Says the girl with a bra on her head.'

'Neil, what do you think's the difference between having sex and making love?'

'Don't know. I've thought about it a lot. I reckon it's like the difference between grabbing a fillet-o-fish and going on a gourmet catering course in Versailles.'

'I thought it was more like watching Hale and Pace when *Grease* is on the other side.'

'I hate *Grease*.'

'*Grease* is cool.'

'Did you listen to those Smiths tapes I made you?'

'No, they remind me of when you used to be a goth.'

'I never was a goth. You were a goth.'

'No I wasn't. You wanted to be a goth, that's worse.'

'Do you still like Curiosity Killed the Cat?'

'You've got a nasty long memory, Neil.' She bumps his swing. The chains rattle. The wind in the poplars sounds like a tide coming in. She says, 'Neil, tell me a secret.'

'A secret?'

'A secret.'

This is what he has been waiting for. His opportunity. He has waited for something like this almost since they met. Here is a question he can turn into us. But instead he thinks he should end this now. On the walk back, while she was by turns angry then amused about what had happened in the pub, when he felt drained for losing it and because she had been out with someone like that and he had been no better, he decided that he was going to tell her that this isn't what he wants. He doesn't want to keep coming back here, not when it's like this, if it can make him like that.

He turns and looks at Rachel, the black rings beneath her eyes, moonlit skin the colour of onion, her soggy tea-cosy hat and expensive silk brassière wrapped around her head.

'What sort of secret?' he says.

'I don't know. A secret secret, I suppose.'

Neil pauses. It could still work. She might say yes. If he doesn't ask he'll never know. He's alone. They hardly know each other.

'What are you thinking?' she says.

'Do you know when I did that paper round?' he says. 'I used to get really nervous when I knew I was getting near your house. And then when I was there I'd take ages to walk up the drive and I'd take ages putting the paper through the letter box, just in case you came out, and I'd make sure that if there were cut-out coupons for Pizza Hut or something that you got tons, and I'd peer in the window just to see if you were in the front room.'

'Did you ever see me?'

'I don't remember.'

She stands up, takes both his hands and pulls him to his feet. She places her arms around his neck and her mouth to his, and she tastes of rain and tobacco. He runs his hands across her head, sliding the headgear away; it flops in a puddle and her hair feels smooth and warm as his palm travels down to her nape. She unbuttons his coat, puts her hands around his waist. She's on tiptoes now. The poplars rustle and clack. The roundabout scrapes back and forth in the wind.

Who Died and Left You in Charge?
Alexei Sayle

London

Miss Cicely Rodgers strapped her cock and balls into the Miracle Deluxe Vagina which was made from skin-like, flesh-coloured latex and came with adjustable straps to ensure a perfect fit and to hide any last sign of maleness. It was complete in every detail, including soft vaginal lips and a simulated clitoris. Over this she slipped Femme Form padded hourglass panties to give her womanly curves and on to her chest she put a lacy padded bra. Next, make-up, beard-coverer and on her head the popular page-boy wig, suitable for all face shapes. Finally, a sober women's business suit in charcoal grey and on her feet simple court shoes, though a huge size eleven, with a restrained, ladylike, two-inch heel. Cicely wasn't one of those trannies who dressed like a Chechen prostitute.

When she was Clive he wore clothes that were a bit too young for a man of forty-five: trainers like dead pigs' noses in grey and orange with reflective strips on the back, designer combat pants so expensive it would be cheaper to join the army for a year and T-shirts with 'Quack, combust, shithouse squad' or similar gibberish written on them. Cicely considered herself different to Clive, with a more innate sense of good taste. After all, they both thought, what was the point of being a part-time woman if she was going to be the same sort of woman as he was a bloke?

This transformation from Clive to Cicely took shape in a

place called Transformations which is right o[...]
station in Eversholt Street, Camden Town. It [...]
shops. Most of the shops, you wouldn't rememb[...]
sold even though you only looked five seconds ago[...]
two old-fashioned cafés that serve chicken curry w[...]
potatoes and spaghetti with chips on the side and two [...]
margarined bread for the consumption of solitary men wearing hats in all weathers.

All the main railway stations used to be surrounded with
cafés serving this kind of food, as if the first thing a fellow
fancied after coming down from the North was a weird
combination of food. As it turned out, what a lot of fellows
seemed to want as soon as they got off the train from the
North was to be a woman.

Transformations was opposite the station so that nervous
businessmen from Tring and Liverpool and Glasgow could
slip in there and be transformed into nervous women. On the
red-painted windows of Transformations it said: 'Wigs, waist-
cinchers, make-up'. There was also a big before-and-after
photo: a young man in chinos whom a market researcher
might put in the B2 socio-economic group, self-employed
graphic designer or something, and on the right, the same
man done up as a woman from a Bradford council estate who
has had a hard life on account of her daughter being pregnant
and on crack and who sings at the Trades and Labour Club to
keep her spirits up.

Once or twice a week Clive would visit Transformations to
change into a woman, then he would go out for the afternoon
with his friend Ashlee (usually Archie). They would walk
about, then go for tea and a bun or for a little drinkie in a
fashionable bar. Being Cicely out for a walk was, Clive
imagined, rather like being a slightly forgotten celebrity –
Mel Smith perhaps or Kenneth Branagh. Most people paid no
attention but one in thirty looked once, looked again, saw
something not right, a remark or a thought coming up to the
surface, by which time Cicely has passed, leaving turned

...s, pokes in the ribs, sometimes aggressive shouts or sniggers in her trail. It is similar to being a minor celebrity in that the glances are related to the coolness and hipness of the area and the inhabitants' indifference to people off the telly. In Camden Town, where in the local starship trooper Sainsbury's there were more pierced than unpierced shoppers, Mel or Kenneth would go a long time before they got asked for their autograph unless it was on their Switch card receipt. Ashlee and Cicely could walk for hours in that neighbourhood, untrammelled by any interference.

Cicely really enjoyed their walks, they had been the highpoint of her week until Ashlee pointed out the cyclists, then she never enjoyed them again. Clive and Cicely were alike in that respect – they were both prone to having things ruined by pointing out.

Years ago, Clive had loved to take long drives up the motorway in his car: a Gordon Keeble – a sixties, Italianstyled, British-made sports car. Then one day he'd been going to Leeds and he took his friend Leonard with him.

After a bit Leonard asked if he could drive, so they pulled into Leicester Forest East services and changed seats. Leonard raced straight back on to the motorway and was soon doing eighty-five in the inside lane, ahead of them in the distance a small hatchback was travelling at about seventy in the middle lane. Rather than swing across two lanes to overtake, Leonard got right up behind the Vauxhall Astra and started flashing his headlights. Clive was a very conscientious driver, he believed in keeping a safe, two-second distance between vehicles; he achieved this by watching the car in front pass an object – a sign or a bridge – and then saying to himself 'only a fool breaks the two-second rule'. If he could complete this sentence before he passed the same object then they were a safe distance apart.

He tried this with his Gordon Keeble and the Astra and got as far as 'only a f . . .' After a lot of flashing the other car moved over. Leonard passed it and moved back into the inside lane himself.

'What was that all about?' asked Clive.

'The middle lane should be solely for overtaking,' explained Leonard in a pedantic voice. 'Cars should travel in the inside lane at all other times. If they don't, it slows everybody up as it only leaves one lane for overtaking. Driving in the middle lane is selfish and thoughtless.'

'Oh, I didn't know that,' said Clive, and he never enjoyed a drive again.

From then on, the motorways, instead of being a ribbon of pleasure unrolling with merry welcome, were concrete channels of anger full of selfish dawdlers creeping up the middle lane with inflaming insensitivity; each licence-plated rump sneered at him personally. Like Leonard, Clive would now get behind them all (and there were thousands once you noticed), blip his lights and if they didn't move he'd honk his horn, get closer and blip his lights again. Often the cars wouldn't move, either not noticing or refusing to budge.

In the month after his drive with Leonard, Clive had four near-crashes, was shot at once and had two fights on a slip road. In the end, he sold the Gordon Keeble for a big loss, the bottom really having dropped out of the classic car market, and if he ever travelled outside London, he took the train.

So it was with the cyclists.

Cicely and Ashlee were walking up Camden High Street one day, chummily arm in arm. They were crossing on the pelican opposite the Acumedical Chinese Healing Centre when they were forced to jump back and apart by a cyclist riding the wrong way down the road.

'They make me so mad,' said Ashlee.

'Who do?' said Cicely, with a dizzy sensation in her head as if she were on the edge of a high diving board; she knew something bad was coming but she couldn't get out of its way.

'Bloody cyclists, especially round here,' replied her friend. 'They're a fucking menace. They ride on the pavement, they ride through red lights, they ride through red lights against the traffic, they ride through red lights against the traffic on the pavement and worst of all there's just something so horribly smug about them, like they're doing you a favour by making the world a worse place to be in.'

Instantly, Cicely saw that Camden High Street was filled with swooping, careening machines and her heart was filled with hate. She had always thought of the bicycle as a rather benign machine but now these people she saw zinging about might as well have been mounted on HIV-infected Rottweilers for all the fear and anger they aroused in her. They were very various: forgetful women on folding shopper bikes, black youths talking into mobile phones and riding no-handed, claimants on wrecks of racing bikes with the drop handlebars turned upside down so as to make sure their brakes didn't work, serious mountain bikers with front suspensions made from impossibly light alloys found only in crashed asteroids, hip twenty-five-year-olds on chrome BMX bikes (she couldn't even begin to figure out what that one was about), and messengers, messengers, messengers. These pedalling freelance postmen wore expressions fixed on their faces that said, 'Don't stop me now, bastard, last year's VAT receipts must get to the Chemical Bank ere night falls! The script rewrite must be on the desk of Tim Bevan at Working Title by yesterday morning or there'll be hell to pay! The tickets for the charity ball must get to Mel Smith right now and no old lady on the zebra crossing will stop them' – so up in the air she goes, arse over Zimmer frame.

In all her wanderings around Camden Town one of the few cyclists she ever saw who stopped at the traffic lights and pedalled on the road and behaved in a generally non-malignant way, obeying the law like in the olden days, was the writer Alan Bennett riding around on his dark green lady's bike with the wicker basket out front like something from a film about the Cambridge of F.R. Leavis.

Cicely tried to keep the thing about the cyclists from Clive, but he heard about it soon enough and his life was ruined too.

If anything, it hit Clive harder than Cicely. He was even more prone than her to taking things hard; for example, he was barred from several 24-hour minimarts and his local Blockbuster Video for arguing about things.

They had a good job. They were bookbinders. Clive had served his apprenticeship at a venerable firm of bookbinders in Bermondsey. He was among the last intake of working-class kids before that craft became a middle-class, art school shutout. Now he worked from home, surrounded by glue and card and skin, in a council-owned live/work apartment in the Brunswick Centre, Holborn, a bold 1960s experiment in concrete eyesores where a Georgian square used to be. He made a good enough living, enabling him to buy Cicely the finest in giant lace panties, by repairing ancient manuscripts, binding lectures and other modern texts for the nearby British Museum and London University, and by doing the occasional fine art job – binding a limited edition set of etchings in rat skin, that sort of thing.

On the days when he didn't go to Transformations Clive would work all morning, then, like ten thousand other lone craftsmen all around London – painters, sculptors, makers of contemporary jewellery, writers on internet matters – he would stop at one o'clock, have soup and a grilled cheese, brown bread sandwich, listen to a politician being toasted on Radio 4, then go for a walk as himself.

Every day he took the same route: past the drunks bungling round the DSS emergency payout place in Upper Woburn Place, the Kosovans washing windscreens while their women begged at the corner of Upper Woburn Place and the Euston Road, after that Eversholt Street past Transformations, then more drunks at the start of Camden High Street. Clive often thought that rather than being paved with gold the streets of Camden Town were paved with alcoholics, seeing as so many of them were sprawled on the ground. A surprising number were foreign; Clive imagined a lot of them were on drunk exchange schemes from other countries. One thing he noticed about the drunks was that many of them sported the most magnificent heads of hair.

'What a waste,' thought the almost completely bald Clive as he passed yet another comatose figure displaying a splendid mane of luxuriant jet-black tresses. Then he heard on Radio 4, while drinking his lunchtime soup, that alcohol abuse promoted hair growth and prevented baldness as it led to the suppression of testosterone production in males. Clive thought he might have given heavy drinking a go if he'd found out about its tonsorial qualities before he'd lost his hair. He suffered particular hair problems: because of his dressing he couldn't even grow a strange little beatnik beard in compensation as many baldies did, seeing as it would pretty much give the game away on Cicely.

Thirty minutes' brisk walking would find him heading west up Delancey Street then round Regent's Park Road to Primrose Hill where he would have a cup of cappuccino sitting outside one of the many patisseries and coffee bars. Just up the road was the headquarters of Creation Records, so strolling up and down was a parade of men exactly like Clive: thinning-haired forty-somewhats dressed in clobber aimed at eighteen-year-olds. Clive and his fellow coffee drinkers would stoically huddle on the outside seats of the cafés no matter what the weather. Inside, the patisseries would be empty even in the middle of a January meteor storm. Twenty years ago you couldn't get an Englishman to sit outside a gaff; even in summer temperatures of ninety-five degrees drinkers would barricade themselves in pubs behind frosted glass, glazed tiles and mahogany. Now you couldn't keep the bastards indoors, no matter what.

But even here, in this crescent of chi-chi shops, the cyclists were up to their dirty tricks. Even when he saw one doing nothing wrong, Clive would think 'fucking bastard' before he realised they were riding on the correct side of the road through a green light, not doing no harm to no one. Until the pointing out of the cyclists Clive had managed to force himself to enjoy, indeed, to revel in the wild drinkers, the dirt, the litter, the terrible record-company tosspots, the whole gritty urban schmeer – but the cyclists spoilt it all.

Everywhere they taunted him with their lawless ways and though he tried there was nothing he could do to either unnotice them or to find a way to cope with their behaviour. He tried shouting at them as they hurtled towards him at thirty miles an hour on the pavement but one person, more or less, shouting in the middle of the street in Camden Town, either at cyclists or lamp-posts or imaginary six-foot-high dung beetles, was neither here nor there and nobody took any notice, least of all the cyclists.

He tried remonstrating reasonably with them. One time while he was on a zebra crossing, traversing Regent's Park Road, a girl zipped across it behind him, clipping him on the ankles as she sped up the pavement.

'This is a pedestrian crossing not a bike crossing,' he said quite mildly.

She just looked over her shoulder at him but he caught up with her half a minute later as she stopped to look at her A–Z.

It wasn't often you got one of them stationary so he went up to her and said, 'You shouldn't ride on the pavement and that, you know. It's really intimidating for old people and stuff.'

She just looked up and said, 'Who died and left you in charge?' Then rode off, her behind waggling contemptuously at him.

Clive knew then he was going to have to kill one of them.

At nights he couldn't sleep for imagining arguments he'd have with this girl, though even in the self-justifying cavern of his brain he came off worst. She always had the snappy rejoinder, 'Who died and left you in charge?'

'You or one of your kind,' was all that he could come back

with, but you could see on her face that she didn't believe him. Well, he might not be able to kill a cyclist but he knew a woman who could.

The first thing he did was to become a member of the London Cycling Campaign: it was important to know his enemy. He soon found out that the major cause of death among cyclists was them being crushed under the wheels of trucks. Clive reckoned it would be going too far to buy himself a truck and get an HGV licence and so on. However, in another whining article about how great they all were, these pedalling pricks, he read what terrible havoc four-wheel drive vehicles – Range Rovers, Toyotas, Shoguns – carved through the pedestrian and cycling population with their big bumpy bumpers. Their huge flat fronts smacked the unprotected human form with a metal punch of bone-vaporising ferocity.

One dark evening a few days later, a secondhand car salesman in an ill-lit car lot sold for cash a Mark One Land Rover Discovery, M plate, to a tall, ugly woman.

Clive hid it in the garages underneath the Brunswick Centre. The Discovery leaked black diesel smoke from its rusty anus and the inappropriate, pale blue, clunky interior designed by Sir Terence Conran was filthy and falling to bits, but Cicely felt it would do the job. The pitted chrome bull bars screwed to the front of the Disco would be especially good at mashing up a biker.

Cicely had great fun clothing herself as a middle-class mum on the way to pick up her kids from one of the posh private schools in Hampstead, then she went hunting for a cyclist heading the wrong way down one of the streets of Camden Town.

As she drove, her eyes switching back and forth, she daydreamed about her family life, her husband, her kids, the dinner parties she'd cook for his boss at the bank.

Kate Maguire strapped her small son into the child seat of

her bicycle. She was late getting to her friend Carmel's place where she was going to drop off Milo, then go on to work on the night shift at the Neurological Hospital near Russell Square. She had been forced to go back to work at the Neuro after her husband died, and the old pig-pink Raleigh lady's bike was the most economical way for her and Milo to get around town. If she'd had to pay bus fares or, heaven forbid, own a car she and Milo would be having laurel leaves for tea every night.

Today, though, she had a problem: if she didn't somehow shave fifteen minutes off her journey she was going to be late for work. That was the thing about bicycles: you always knew to the second how long a journey took. Not like a car – in central London the same hundred yards could take twenty seconds or two hours to drive depending on what butterfly was flapping its wings in the Brazilian rainforest that day. The simplest way to make up the time on leaving her little house in Lyme Street would be for her and Milo not to turn left into the long one-way system; that was suited to fat-arsed car drivers but was an annoying detour when you are pedalling yourself as it would take her down Bayham Street, along Pratt Street, across the high street and up Delancey Street. It would be much quicker to ride the wrong way past the tube station, then go against the flow of traffic, up Parkway, the way she had seen thousands of other cyclists going. She had often sensed other cyclists' perplexity as she stopped at the lights and waited, while they bumped up on to the pavement or through the traffic lights with the little green man showing, scattering pedestrians left and right.

She buckled on her shiny plastic helmet, gave the straps holding Milo in one last safety check and set off, resolving, for the first time, to go head on into the traffic.

But she didn't, she couldn't force herself to do it; she went through the one-way system as usual and was a bit late for work.

So Cicely drove into and killed a bicycle messenger called Darren Barley who was a complete waste of fucking space and deserved to die.

Façade
Leone Ross

London

Meg raised her head from the book she was reading and listened to the shimmering quiet of the library. She'd sat at this desk for nearly a year, this old pine desk, flaxen with age, graffiti soaked into its surface. She read the words for what seemed the hundredth time. A telephone number and a shopping list of carnal delights, on offer *now* if only you rang immediately. For a small fee, of course. Sometimes she wondered if it was addressed to her. Someone had written it for her, to tempt her. They were all so free.

On Tuesdays, she skipped classes and walked the streets, watching them. Casually linked arms. Hips bumping. Tongues and teeth clashing and parting. Drunken white boys baring their bottoms, swinging from the roof of the tube, laughing. Frothy mouths and strange smells. The first time she'd plucked up the courage to get on the tube, she'd missed her stop, watching a couple touch each other, the girl's face flushing redder and redder as the boy kneaded her left breast. Big blotches of colour flooded down the girl's face, her neck, spread across her chest until Meg thought she was a splendid pink thing, topped with yellow hair. Like someone's wedding cake, or a pretty dress.

She'd gone home that afternoon and tried to hug her mother.

'What you doin'?' Mamma had looked alarmed, shook her away from her flower-print bosom. Her Bible clattered to the floor. 'What you doin'?'

Meg didn't try again. After all, you had to appreciate what you had. Mamma was a good, Christian woman, a woman who had given her morals, a roof over her head. Life. She tried not to think about what her mother must have done to give her that life. She stifled a giggle with the back of her hand. Mamma. On a bed. Legs akimbo. Oh no. She couldn't see it. They must have done something else. They must have found a new and unique and chaste way to sin. What man could have made Mamma do things like that?

She looked down at the graffiti again. Often the sentences would float through her brain as she studied, smirking between the paragraphs of Chaucer. It was all spelt wrong, she was sure. *Blujob. Arse fuck. Sweet pussy.* But she was proud of herself. The first time she sat here and read the words, it had taken everything in her to stay. People would see her leaning on these words. They'd think she was a bad girl. She wasn't a bad girl. Just a good girl with the courage to choose a bad desk.

Outside, it rained. Drops streaked silver lines across the skylight window above her. Rain in England was shy. Jamaican rain was bold; great showers of it that soaked you to the skin in five minutes and then went away again, leaving warm puddles in the potholes. London rain was cold. Cold and scared.

The clock stood at seventeen minutes to eleven. The rust and the rain in the wall had done their thing and now the clock was schizophrenic. Years before it had shone and ticked. Tocked. Clicked. Smooth. So crisp that it set your teeth on edge. Now it went mad on the hour, the clang of its seconds becoming shrieks. She drew a slow hand through her hair and decided to leave.

She could feel the librarian stirring impatiently. None of the staff liked the extra shift around exam time, and who could blame them? No one else but her stayed this late, either.

The librarian's eyes followed her, waiting for her to come

up to the desk. *Probably read every book in the fuckin'
library*, he thought. His mother said that women who read
too much were inclined to excessive masturbation. He'd
never worked out the connection, but she still phoned him
every Thursday and Sunday to tell him just that, her dentures
grinding slightly down the clear British Telecom line. One
day he'd get up the nerve to ask her for an explanation. He
looked over at Meg again. She was what his father would call
bland, my boy, bloody bland, and that God-awful blue mascara she smeared on seemed to make it worse. She always
dressed in black, swamped in the clothing like a human bat. A
Goth gone wrong. He sighed and bit his lip.

Meg climbed the tube steps at Tottenham Court Road. Her
mother never rode the tube. Her mother said that Man had
overextended himself, and that all this technology was the
work of the Devil – after all, only denizens of the Devil would
want to be so close to Hell anyway. She said that when the
Father came for the Faithful to take them Home, He would
abandon everyone who happened to be on a tube or in a car or
a plane. For some reason that Meg could not understand,
buses were just about all right with the Lord, as were boats.
Which is why they'd taken a ship to Eng-land. The final
indignity. She'd told people at college that they'd come on
Concorde, but after they'd trickled away from her, grinning,
she was struck with the agonising possibility that perhaps
her imagination had taken her too far. She'd never been on a
plane. Perhaps she'd said something wrong.

A man bumped into her from behind. She scuttered out of
the way. He hissed at her and strode up Oxford Street. She
watched his confident stride. If only she walked that way.
Passing Façade would not be nearly as hard if she walked that
way. She'd done it so many Friday nights and it still scared
her. Last week had been the worst.

'Jesus, bitch, you're not coming in here, are you?'

That had been a week ago, and she supposed that those men

weren't bad, just high-spirited, that was all, young men were like that, full of fun.

'Look at that skinny bitch, no tits, no ass. Oi, somebody stretch you thin?'

Her mother always told her it was her Christian duty to turn the other cheek, but the boys last week hadn't understood that concept and when she'd tried to explain they had been a little indecent and her waist still hurt where they'd grabbed her. Two ten-pence-sized bruises, where their fingers had sunk into flesh. She told Mamma she must have bumped herself. It wasn't the first lie she'd ever told her mother, who never understood her blue eyelashes anyway.

Meg walked slowly up the road and turned the corner. There they were, scores of them, like insects, milling around the entrance. Shouting. Breaking glass. The occasional taunt wasn't a problem. No, it was when they looked and when she looked back. They looked at her with no recognition at all, their faces blank, as if she was an alien. They were bored when they looked at her.

From where she stood she could see the walls of the club throbbing. Cars of every colour and make zipped past, heading up Tottenham Court Road. Night light gleamed off their shining hides. Images of the crowd flickered deep inside the glow of the headlamps, then were gone, carried away inside the roar. She could close her eyes and see them. Black leather clinging to hips and thighs. Green, silver and red spike-heeled pumps. Fourteen-hole Doc Martens spiralling up their legs. Taut skins. Firm breasts. Gleaming, tanned stomach muscles. She supposed they all went to tanning booths, or parts of Spain on holiday, where they toasted themselves and grabbed each other. Wandering fingers against long, tapered legs. Wet mouths. Whispers of grass and metal. The club doors opened and closed, an echo of strobe lights making patterns across the ground. They were all strange children, dancing on the moon. Carefully packaged time bombs.

She pressed her thighs together, her bladder fizzing. She

wanted to pee, and she realised that she was shaking to the beat of the music hidden behind the doors. Sweat rushed to the surface of her skin and was whisked away by the chill night air. Her whole mind jerked. It wasn't far, just over there, a few steps. One foot in front of another. Then she would be past. She cursed herself. Why did she always stay at the library so late? She could have borrowed the books and gone home before all this began. Mamma loved to see her read, would never disturb her, stepped around her as she passed through the house, cleaning endlessly. Leaving Meg in a tiny circle of dust. She started forward. One step. Two steps. A yellow Ferrari barrelled past, revving up dust and scum from the dark ground. A red sweet wrapper went giggling down the pavement, caught in the wind. It would pass them before she did.

Three more steps. A fourth. A battered VW and a grinning Chevrolet skimmed past, smelling her. She was sure her scent would go wafting over and they would all look up. The trick was to skirt the edge of the crowd as fast as possible, but there was just something about her, there always had been, something that made people hate her. Even in Jamaica. In kindergarten all the other kids got together to bash her. In high school their jokes were about her and she never seemed able to make herself small enough to go unnoticed. The more she squeezed herself small in her skin, the more they'd followed her, shouting.

She began to walk faster, tripping over her own feet. She could feel the music through the pavement. No one was paying any attention to her. Maybe she could slip by. She had never done it before. But maybe this time. A girl stood by the steps, bottle in hand. She smiled at the man in front of her. He threw his arm around her shoulders. Meg could see the perfect curve of her navel, the soft swell of her stomach, could see the white camisole she wore slashed to the waist.

The red sweet wrapper danced on in the breeze.

237

The girl had a scar on her left ankle and her boyfriend wore a raw silk coat. She shifted her weight from one golden Roman sandal to the other.

The wrapper paused, as if measuring the distance.

Meg's blood sang.

The wind smiled.

Her breasts shrank back against her ribcage. Six more steps. She was halfway around the edge of them all.

I'll go to church this Sunday, Mamma, just let me pass . . .

The sweet wrapper lurched a few feet in the air, then settled on the woman's ankle, covering the scar. She stamped to free herself of the clot of paper.

It hung on, sticky and malevolent. Meg stumbled forward, trying not to break into a trot.

I've got blue eyelashes, they'll let me through, because my eyelashes are part of them. I use Max Factor mascara every morning, they must understand, see, blue, a supplication, a prostration, an offering . . .

The girl plucked the wrapper off her ankle. Her dark eyes caught Meg, swaying past in the breeze, three heavy books under her arm. She saw the thin dress and the flat feet, the hunched back, the fear. Laughing, she drew back her hand and flung the wrapper in Meg's direction. Meg came alive and ran, hiccuping, tears threatening, wishing she were someone else, somewhere else.

Meg read books. Books about how to be beautiful and how to be confident and how to be brave. She stood in the mirror and raised her shoulders, up, down, around. The books said body language was all, posture made the man. The books said that she had to think herself confident; it all seemed a mad game, with specific rules. You sucked your tummy in and straightened your spine and held your head like a queen, and people treated you like one.

Meg made a decision about her life. Something had to brighten corners that she saw as dark and dim. They weren't so different from her. At college, they all looked normal. Not exactly like her, but safer. They wore T-shirts and trainers and their scrubbed faces were not different from her own. Were they? Surely she was part of them too.

Her fantasies tripped her up in her dreams and she lay awake, listening to her mother scratching the back of her throat, a croaking noise, like the lizards back in Jamaica. She would straighten her shoulders and lift her chin, then. She would go to Façade and light up the dance floor. The most beautiful boy would come and dance with her, snake hips and thick eyelashes. She would be like them. There would be explanations and apologies. 'We knew you were one of us,' they would say. 'We were waiting for you.'

'It's twenty quid.'

Meg stared at the doorman. She felt like cigarette ash, ready to fall, smouldering. But she had inserted a steel bar in her back and she was determined to stand tall. She stood before the belly of Façade, her pores wide open. The ground shifted beneath her. The man handed her a ticket. It was a slice of brick in her hand. Mamma would be so cross if she found out, so angry that Meg, her good girl, wasn't at the library. She had wavered at the last moment, but she had heard the music again. Too late to turn back from temptation.

A party of six young men stood behind her. Checks, stripes and impatience.

One spoke. 'Move, will you? You're in the way, you skinn—'

Oh no, not that, don't call me that, I'm one of you.

She was inside. The club stretched long before her, hot pink walks, the marble floor a roll of black shadow. A man walked past, leaving a drink in her hand. She stared until it was swept away by another. The sound of breaking glass drowned in the music. She couldn't believe how loud it was.

Panic hit her and she turned to leave, but the crowd was too thick and, not daring to swim upstream, she found a bar stool and clung to it. Across the floor, she recognised the sweet wrapper girl. She stared at her. The girl looked back indifferently and danced on. Meg let herself smile, small. The girl continued to wave her arms to the music. She didn't throw anything. Meg's lips rolled off her gums in joy. She was in. She looked at them. The multitude was self-absorbed, yet they moved in unison, every hip part of a larger truth. Predestined choreography, their skin aglow. Meg could feel the beat in her throat and thighs. Slowly, her heart began to beat time.

'What are you drinking?'

The bartender was cut from a Kays catalogue. Square jawed, corn-coloured hair, set-square teeth.

'I don't drink . . .' she faltered.

'Ah, c'mon. I'll make you my special.'

She watched him pick up a glass, letting the small of her back settle against the spidery edges of the stylised stool. A dog paced at her feet, whining. Bones jutted through fur at odd angles, and its eyes were lined with kohl. Its owner, a man with yellow contact lenses and an orange shirt, lifted it off the floor and danced with it as the animal tucked its hindquarters inwards. Meg turned back to the bartender and blinked. He was opening cans of strawberries. He slopped three of them into a blender, adding drops from small containers, his white shirt splattered with vermilion.

She stared at his hands. People in London always seemed to have dirty nails. At her first Saturday job, in a music store, the boss had told her off for being a snob. He'd noticed her taking CDs from customers with the tips of her fingers, avoiding the grime. Perhaps it was the newsprint from the papers they all liked to read, incessantly, hiding behind anything on the tube. Perhaps the grime was just the colour of their souls.

Behind the bartender, two women kissed, chewing at each other's lips, their hips rubbing. Everyone seemed choreographed. Everyone seemed to know the rules, except her. She watched as girl number one grabbed the back of her partner's head, pulling her gleaming neck back so she could put her teeth into it. Meg put her hand to her mouth as their fingers intertwined, both sets of hands diving between girl number two's long, pale legs. The couple saw her watching and smiled. The dog howled. One of the women touched her.

'Something for the weekend, love?'

It was a bright yellow plastic bag.

'Oh, thank you . . .'

The bartender thrust a glass of liquid strawberries at her as the women disappeared into the throng. Meg lifted it to her nose. Stuck her tongue into the sweetness. The liquor sat on her tongue, promising mischief. She took a swallow. Hiccuped.

The lights went off.

In the swirl of darkness, Meg stood perfectly still, shocked. The club filled with meaty silence. A raised dais stood on the dance floor, a lone spotlight trained on to its surface. The chant began, fists shaking in the air.

'DANCE-DANCE-DANCE-DANCE!'

Bass shattered into colours before her eyes: orange, red, green. The crowd began to move once more, but no one turned from the dais.

'DANCE-DANCE-DANCE-DANCE!'

He leapt on to the stage and stood before the hungry mass, his arms outstretched. Long, red, curly hair fell down his back in a ponytail, pulled severely from his face. His eyes were expressionless, black as the tolling of a bell. His face was painted white, the mouth thin and wet and lined with purple. Black hieroglyphics crawled over his cheekbones. His tongue flecked out, as if he was tasting the music.

Meg stared.

Orange and purple rags hung from his wrists and ankles. Every curve of his body lay bare for them to see, outlined in dirty white Spandex. Except his genitals. Meg strained to look. No, there was nothing there. What had he done with it? He must have tucked it away somewhere. She gazed at his face. He was quivering; she could see his whole body shaking from where she stood. Yes, he'd tucked it away. She felt absurd relief.

'DANCE-DANCE-DANCE-DANCE!'

The crowd was pleading, and he gave them what they wanted. Leaping, twisting, he became the beat. She had seen dancing before; she came from a country of dance. But never like this. Never this beautiful arrogance. Never this organised purity. He was in control of every muscle. His body obeyed him, like a machine. His haunches were pistons. His face filled with colour through the paint. Like the moaning girl on the tube. Like London.

Occasionally he paused in his wild abandon to march on the spot, trembling. He played the mannequin, counting his fingers, moving his head from side to side in curious, robotic fashion, oblivious to the roar of the crowd beneath him. And then the wilding would begin once more. Meg felt her body jolt as he leapt high in the air. She tried to catch his eye, but they were empty as he gazed at a fixed point ahead of him. They were as still as his body was alive, insane with the dance. He was an angel.

An angel from God. She dropped her glass, ignoring the liquid as it splashed her toes. This was how Mamma had lain down with a man. This was how. He had come to her in spirit; he had presented flesh as a gift, as purity. It had not been animal. It had been a gift from God.

He was flying, flying, they were flying together, over roof-tops, gardens, all God's things.

Unconsciously, she began to pray.

He was pounding, screaming, leaping, twirling.

She prayed for his hands on her as he went faster, until her eyes stopped registering his movements.

She prayed as she felt the music in her thighs and thick rain between her legs.

All she could see was the power of his body, how sure he was, how right, how each muscle bent to his will.

Sweat poured from him, baptising him, making him sweet for her.

The lights were black and he was gone.

She clung to the dais, exhilarated. People were leaving. She shook her head, trying to get control. Girls in front of her swapped jokes and cigarettes. She followed the movement towards the door. Outside, she wanted to shout in exhilaration. She had done it, and if Mamma was truthful she would have been proud.

The yellow bag fell to the pavement. She opened it. A goody bag. Three condoms: orange, green and red. They smelt of peppermint. Slender, silver pamphlets. *Safe sex. Safer sex.* A tiny bottle of oil, a square of latex on a golden card. She crouched down by a mound of sweltering garbage bags, letting everyone stream past her. She followed the instructions with shaking hands. *Press your finger against the latex. Feel how firm it is! Now squirt a drop of oil on to it. Count to five. Press your finger against it again.*

Puzzled, she pushed a gentle fingernail forward. The previously resistant rubber buckled. Her finger swam through it. Like a shark.

Oil destroys latex! Use a water-based lubricant, like KY jelly, EVERY SINGLE TIME YOU HAVE SEX!

Meg's breath caught. They had given this to her. That couple, kissing. They had given these things to her, as if it was simple. As if she would go home tonight with a man. As if she was one of them. As if she was alive.

'Hey sweet thing. Get yer coat. You've pulled!'

She looked up. It was those boys. From last week. Leering now. As if they had never seen her before. As if they liked what they saw. They turned away, staggering against each other. One of them, the one who had hurt her, she was sure, looked back. Winked. A delicious wink as he swayed down the street. She straightened her back. Her eyelashes flickered in the street lights. She smiled.

*

Meg lived for the nights. She had to find him. The memory of his face kept her in a multicoloured day-dream through the halls. She stole from her classes and ran to the toilets, shutting herself in, fondling herself harshly, rubbing her crotch against the securely locked door. Her orgasms left her sobbing but triumphant at the weakness of her flesh.

She wanted him. They could marry and he would dance and she would study and support him and believe in his art. She walked the dance floor, questioning endlessly. She forgot the shyness that had paralysed her. Someone had to know. Who was he? A tall man promised to tell her and she didn't protest as she knelt between his legs, watching him unzip himself. His genitals smelt like rubber as she moved forward and blew on to his skin, unsure. He cackled.

'Yer having a laugh. Suck it!'

She took him in her mouth, his movements jerky and careless against her cheeks. She swallowed like a pro and went for another strawberry drink when he laughed at her unanswered questions.

The dancer's androgyny worked on her blood. Meg shook. Her hands, her lips. Shook. And still, feverishly, she passed through the place, asking.

'Can you help me, the dancer, do you know his name?'

When he was on stage she subsided, gaunt, to the very edge of the dais, drinking in his madness, longing for his empty eyes. They all knew her now. She saw them smile in recognition as she stepped through the crowd. They called him the Dancer, or the Dancer Bloke.

'You want to know who the Dancer is? We all want to know.'

She would find out for them. She would know, she would be the keeper of the secret. The blue of her mother's Bible drove her out of her mind. The gentle cleaning, the moan of the clock worked at her. Her body shrank, skin to the bones, the hair to the scalp. And she shook and waited.

*

The impervious walls of the library greeted her as people tried not to recoil from her burning face. She was skeletal. The graffiti on the desk reached out to embrace her, delighted. It was good to have a friend.

In one fist she crumpled her exam results. She ran her fingers over the stacks of books and lifted down a heavy encyclopaedia. She sagged under its weight. It was so heavy and she was so tired, oh tired, Lord, yes, but she had to study. Maybe he visited the library sometimes, maybe he would be hanging out somewhere near it, please, oh please.

She wiped her face, thinking of how she would walk up to him and how he would remember her. Blue mascara filled the pouches under her eyes. She took down the books and piled them behind her on the floor.

She hugged them to her chest and began to rock on the floor, the rows of shelves high above her. She watched the tears soak into the page, like his sweat, yes, watching the mascara streak into the tears and fall across the leather covers. Her nails fell on to the page; jagged, accusing, white crescents. She picked them up and put them on her tongue, tasting herself. He would come to her now, using the beautiful coloured rags at his wrists to wipe away the tears, and to wipe the dust off the dictionaries.

The librarian grinned at the clock. Time to go. What was that witch doing back there? God, he hated ugly women.

'Excuse me, it's closing time!'

He sighed impatiently as she shuffled past him, mumbling. Not his problem. His shift was finished.

He hummed as he lifted his bag and signed out. Bag full of soiled spandex, orange and purple rags. He took off his baseball cap as he stepped out into the night. A girl walking past smiled at the fire in his curls.

The click of his heels echoed on the pavement as a blood-red sweet wrapper danced after him in the wandering breeze.

By The Sea We Flourish
Julie Burchill

Brighton

The Brighton motto was In Deo Fidemus – In God We Have Faith. Pretty cheeky for what must be one of the most godless towns in England. Funnily enough, a couple of years ago I suggested to the then mayor a new motto for Brighton & Hove, something like Ab Mare Floreamus – By The Sea We Flourish. I think they have used this in the current motto, which is, in English, Between Downs & Sea We Flourish. Anyway, the real motto should be whatever the Latin is for We Have It Away By The Sea, and the crest would show two burglars loading an old table into a van, the interior of which already includes a mixed group enjoying multiple acts of love.

e-mail from David Gray to Susan Raven, June 2000

Annalee knew, before she had been in Brighton for an hour, that he meant to shag her.

And wouldn't a 'shag' be what it was, too! Shags made her think of naff things like loose tobacco and thick, dirty carpets and bad hairdos. And wouldn't doing the deed with Jhon – or was it Jonh this week? – be about as special as one of those nasty little fags he was forever rolling, let's not forget the attractive bits of tobacco which habitually decorated his front teeth, and his pubic hair, about as appetising as a deep-pile carpet in a public area that hadn't been vacuumed for a month? And the day after you'd done it, well, you'd feel as though you'd been given the worst haircut of all time. So 'shag' was really appropriate, when you thought about it.

Of course, Annalee had always used the word 'shag' herself, ever since she was thirteen and first doing the deed. But recently, since she'd put sex on hold, she was starting to think that common acceptance of the term had been rather a bad idea. She suspected that it had made men sexually even lazier than they had been before. After all, when you were 'having sex' at least it sounded quite like hard work, something you'd have to put your back into a bit, and as for 'making love', Jeez, then you *really* had your work cut out for you. But 'bonking', which had preceded 'shagging', sounded like something silly you'd do on a bouncy castle, just stupidly bumping into someone and almost accidentally sexually connecting with them. And now we had 'shagging' – which basically sounded like someone falling on you and not having the energy to get up again. Was it any wonder that she'd left sex on the side of her plate for Mr Manners for the past six months?

But Jhon was determined to put it back on the menu this weekend, it seemed. *He meant to have sex with her!* – the idea made her smile and gasp, but out of incredulity rather than excitement. Of course, she had always known he *wanted* to, ever since she'd started his course at college – film, media and youth culture studies; yeah, *right*, whopper and regular fries, please. His give-away intake of breath when she'd turned up first day in class wearing a T-shirt two sizes too small with SLUT written in hard black letters across the front, just to establish her feminist credentials; and that nasty gulping sound when she had announced the title of her latest essay – 'Teenage Kicks: Pussy Power Goes to High School', for God's sake. But gasping and gulping was one thing; poking and prodding were two whole other things altogether, and she was damned if ever the twain would meet.

What was it with Ugly Old Guys, anyway? Didn't they have mirrors in their houses? Was there something going on she didn't know about? Perhaps when a man reached the age of forty in this country, or grew nose hair – whatever came first – the Nice Police came in the night and took away all the regular mirrors, replacing them with trick ones which showed reflections of, like, Josh Hartnett and Heath Ledger. It had to be something along those lines or UOGs wouldn't prance around thinking the world was their oyster and every girl their pearl, ripe for the plucking.

Sometimes when Annalee felt Mr Sage's ('Call me Jonh. That's Jonh with the H on the end. Not before the N. To show how redundant the letter is.' Pretty sexy stuff, eh?) eyes on her, she felt like doing a De Niro: 'Are you lookin' at me? Excuse me, but are you lookin' at me?' She couldn't really blame him; Annalee knew she was beautiful (whatever that meant), though God knew she did her best to spoil it. Not many days passed when she didn't squint hopefully into a grubby, communal looking-glass in a halls of residence bathroom to encourage the promise of a zit with a dirty safety pin, or to pluck thirty hairs out of one eyebrow in order to hasten the ruin of the sumptuous symmetry of her face. She had ruined the honey sheen of her hair by constantly backcombing it (excellent) and dulled the bright blue bloom of her eyes by sleeping in mascara each and every night, instead of praying, she applied make-up before going to bed and left her room without checking it each morning. But her mouth still looked like a kiss, her brow like a baby's and the arrangement of her eyes, lips and cheekbones haunted her ceaselessly, like an irritating tune she couldn't shake or like some cruel algebra of fate. Fucking *beauty*!

So she *didn't* blame him for wanting to shag her – but, equally, could he in any way blame her for not wanting to be shagged? *Do as you would be done to – The Water Babies* had always been her favourite kids' book, and the more she saw of men the more she couldn't help thinking that it should be made compulsory reading for all men over the age of thirty. Let's be logical here for a minute; if *he* was in her position, would *he* want to lie on his back and have twelve-stone-plus of middle-aged man, complete with nose hair and halitosis, lie on top of him and stick six inches of gnarled purple flesh into a sensitive orifice, thence to have the burden wriggle and groan and prod until a quantity of fetid slime was forthcoming? Would Jonh really want that, right here, right now? Annalee couldn't swear to it, but she doubted it, she really did. So why was she supposed to be wetting herself with glee over the idea? Just because she was beautiful she was supposed to want sex. But surely being beautiful was the best reason ever for not having to have sex. You had so much to keep nice.

'We're almost there!' Jonh exclaimed as the train slowed down through a station called Preston Park.

'Don't bet on it,' Annalee muttered, crunching down defiantly on a fresh Parma Violet.

So what was she doing in Brighton with Dog-Man? One little word – skint. And for the first time in what seemed like eight years the sun was shining and it was shamelessly, brazenly hot. She'd hit her parents for the last shekel she'd ever get out of them this term and the appeal of sitting in a scummy room in Clapton with a Pot Noodle and daytime TV for company was no longer pungent with bohemian glamour the way it had been when she'd been at her posh day school in Cheshire. Since she'd stopped having sex with her fellow students she noticed that they were much less eager to pay for things, which made her all the more determined never to shag any of the tight bastards again, actually. So when Mr Sage had asked her if she had any plans for the weekend . . .

Annalee had never been to Brighton before, which John – sod it, he could spell it like everyone else – had refused to believe for three wearisome days. Like it was some cute, charming, little coyness – why the fuck would she lie about it, eh? Why should she have been to Brighton? – she had grown up in Cheshire. Her parents had been fond of

Snowdonia and Corsica for family holidays; later, with friends, she'd been to the Greek islands and, of course, Ibiza. Why would she have sought out what was basically one big gay bar with stones where its beach should be?

So she wasn't expecting all that much. Nevertheless, she kept her eyes down to the ground as they descended the steep hill from the station, Dog-Man chattering happily enough all the while. He obviously thought she was planning to stay the night with him or something disgusting, as he kept commenting on the prices outside various hotels as they walked – in your dreams, Face-Ache! She had her sweet little return ticket ('Oh, pleeeze, John, let's go first class – make it *special* right from the start') snug in the back pocket of her jeans, and when the sun went down, she wasn't. She'd be back on that London-bound train, fed and watered and thoroughly sunned up, tucked up in her own single bed by midnight. No problem.

But then John said, 'Well, here it is,' and she looked up, and she was lost.

Annalee had always been annoyed by the American phrase 'picture perfect' to describe anything pretty; what the fuck did it *mean*? Lots of pictures weren't perfect at all, but obviously meant to portray ugliness and disarray. What about *Guernica* or that poor Cambodian kid running down the road on fire?

What the dumb Yanks meant, obviously, was *postcard* perfect. And now as Annalee looked up, she was confronted with such a blue-sky-golden-sun-turquoise-sea moving postcard cliché that she felt like running back up the hill screaming in defiance. But then she turned to John and saw him sneering, and her heart went out to the pitiably beautiful thing in front of her.

'Look at it,' he announced with a nasty little laugh. 'London-on-Sea in all its shabby splendour. The grand old whore of the South Coast. The –'

The lights turned green and she bolted across the road to the esplanade.

'Annalee! Wait.'

She pushed herself right up against the pale green railings and looked out at the incredible horizon. To her left, the glittering pleasure domes of the Palace Pier; to her right, the broken-down dignity of the West Pier. She could definitely feel a cheap metaphor coming on.

'Annalee!' John was next to her. 'What happened, babe? Why d'you bolt like that?'

'Just had to be – here –' She leant over the railings towards the sea and closed her eyes. 'Just can't believe how beautiful it is. Jesus, is it the luckiest thing in the world to live on an island, or what?'

She felt spasm after spasm go right down her back from her neck to her butt as she breathed in the air. Suddenly the idea of going back to London that night seemed almost surreal in its silliness. Next to her, John was perfectly still and silent. Even he, it seemed, was speechless in the face of such gloriousness.

She opened her eyes to smile at him and saw that his eyes were fastened to her nipples which, of course, were pointing through her SLUT T-shirt all the way to France in her excitement at being here. Her smile slipped away, unnoticed. Well, if that was what she had to do to stay here, she'd bite the bullet and do it. As long as he didn't expect her to kiss him.

As they stepped on to the Palace Pier there was a crackle from a row of speakers above them and then an old song that Annalee knew from seventies nights at various discos began. 'You're a dirty old man,' sang a black woman who didn't sound a bit put out, but rather relishing the thought of a major scuffle. 'You better keep your hands to yourself! You're a dirty old man – go fool around with somebody else –'

She began to laugh and looked sideways at John. He was scowling, bless him! Obviously the soundtrack wasn't quite to his liking. She was starting to feel quite affectionate towards him. At least she knew he'd be a bad fuck, so she didn't hate him; it was the good fucks a girl couldn't forgive.

'Look, John! Let's go on this!' A booth with a sign: SECRETS

IN YOUR SIGNATURE. 'How much?' she asked the kiddie behind the counter, who swallowed his chewing gum in lust and pointed at a sign. 'Oh, please, John, pay for me!' As he was doing so she wrote her name carefully: Annalee Cross. The kiddie fed it into a machine and handed her a sheet of paper. She grabbed it and ran to the railings to read it.

> You do not value yourself enough, even though you are arrogant and conceited. For the sake of fleeting comfort and pleasure you are willing to give up that which, in the long term, will be the making of you. In other words, Don't fuck him, you lazy bitch!

Annalee gasped, and as John reached for the paper a gust of wind twisted it up and flung it into the air. It danced in front of them for a moment, then fell into the sea below.

'Very fucking funny!' she snapped at the shocked-looking kiddie, walking quickly up the pier.

'What's up?' John caught up with her.

'Nothing . . . well, Lurch there in the booth. Wrote something bitchy on that paper –'

He laughed. On consideration, he was most unappealing of all when he laughed. It didn't seem right, somehow, that someone that ugly should have fun. 'That's impossible, Annalee. Those machines are an utter con. The predictions are in them already, all stacked up, and they just come out at random – ' She sped up again. 'Come on, slow down!'

'Why?' She stopped, hands on hips. 'Can't keep up? Too old?'

He looked sad then, and she felt sorry for him. She took his arm. 'Come on, let's go on the ghost train.'

She walked over and jumped into a car; he gave some tokens to the boy in the booth and went to jump in next to her but, as he put one foot in, the car jolted and moved away, leaving him sprawling backwards. Annalee and the booth boy both laughed instinctively, and her last sight of him as the car jolted forward was him getting up and limping into the car behind.

The Brighton ghost train was nothing special; pretty much like her parents' marriage really, with masses of slamming doors and eerie silences. Unlike her parents' marriage it was over mercifully quickly. She clambered unsteadily from the car and stood there, ignoring the booth boy and waiting for John. But after three minutes he hadn't emerged, which was mad because he'd set off straight after her. She looked at the booth boy, he looked back and nodded, then pulled a lever and disappeared through the double doors that led to the alleged frightfest. Five minutes later he reappeared, shepherding an indignant John.

'It's a disgrace – I shall certainly write to the proprietors about this – breaches all known standards of safety – all the way to Brussels if I have to – '

He was covered in dust; Annalee walked over to him and started brushing him off. He went quiet and looked pleased.

'Calm down, eh? What happened?' she asked.

'I went in just after you and it was going fine until the second skeleton – the one with the top hat that leaps out at you? The stupid bugger didn't just leap out, he fell right on top of me. Pinning me down like he was trying to shag me or something.'

Annalee started to laugh.

'Yes, OK, but it wasn't that funny at the time, in the pitch dark, with the car stopped.' He stomped over to the booth boy. 'I want my money back.'

'Weren't money. Tokens.'

'My tokens then.'

The boy looked at him, then reached in his pocket and retrieved the tokens. He gave them to John. Annalee had the distinct feeling that, even though he was a lowly fairground-ride attendant and John a book-learned bourgeois, the boy felt that John was just a poor old thing. And what did that make her? A poor old thing's thing. Her bright mood

253

vanished and she turned away, walking quickly back down the pier.

John was running after her, still bleating. 'Bloody gimcrack town – full of losers. What sort of person would ever chose to *live* in a place like this, that's what I can't understand. Like living in a brothel. This isn't a place you live – it's a place you go and play, and then you go home again. It's just a simulacrum – '

'Please, John, not simulacrums,' she said automatically.

'Look at it!' He gestured at the glittering coastline stretching away in a blur of hotels and high, white houses on either side. 'Bloody old tart, Brighton! Look at this and then look at London!'

'Do I have to?'

'What d'you mean? Who could not love London?' He was genuinely baffled.

'I don't know.' She looked out to sea. 'Someone who wants to live in a place that isn't just a machine for making it in? That isn't just a repository for people's shagged-out, old dreams?'

'You can't seriously tell me you'd live here – a girl with ambition, with ability? It's a washed-up town, Annalee, full of washed-up people with washed-up dreams – fuck, what was that?'

'I don't know,' she said slowly. They were standing on the pier looking towards the white houses of Kemp Town where they had just seen something like a huge piece of lightning, yet soft and rippling in the heat haze, spring out from the shore towards them. No one else appeared to have seen it. 'But I think you made it angry.'

'What? Made what angry?'

'Brighton,' she said and smiled to show she was kidding. But she wasn't. All day she had been conscious of a feeling that Brighton seemed to be somehow flashing, winking at her. As if it was beckoning; she was conscious of shadowy places behind the tourist façade, of rich dark curtains momentarily lifted slightly at the corner and then dropped mockingly when she turned her head quickly to catch it. Come on, little girl . . .

'I'm going,' she said suddenly, striding off the pier on to the heaving esplanade.

'But why? I thought you liked it here –'

'I do. I'm just sick of being a tourist. I'm sick of not knowing anything about the place I'm in.'

'But what's to know?'

'And that' – she sneered – 'is the exact statement that perfectly illustrates my point.' She started to walk back the way they had come, to climb West Street and Ocean Boulevard to the station and thence to the delights of London. Better the devil she knew than the bright shining angel she was obviously never going to be allowed to get a handle on.

'Annalee, wait!' He swung her round and shoved a piece of paper into her hand; six numbers. She looked at him and he smiled as if he had already shagged her.

'What's this?'

'Cocaine, Annalee,' he whispered. 'We're going to get some cocaine.'

So that was why, six hours later, they were sitting in a café on the seafront watching the tourists go home and the afternoon grow dark and chill. It always amused Annalee when you read those surveys in newspapers which claimed that people spent three years of their life asleep or a year on the toilet or six months picking their noses; what about waiting for drug dealers to call you back? Six hours' wait to buy a gram of coke and it was all gone in thirty minutes. If only that shimmery, shiny feeling wasn't so addictive, the way it hardened all your emotions and made sorrow just slip off of you.

She was just about to go off on a right royal one when John's mobile bleeped and he muttered into it with a crocodile smile.

Mission accomplished, he was knocking back the dregs of the most recent long-lasting beer and getting to his feet, gesturing to her to follow as he left the café quickly. Then they were in a turquoise and white taxi, speeding along the seafront, as John said, 'Whitehawk Way, please. Top of the hill.'

The cabbie looked back at them, raising an eyebrow. 'You sure?'

'Ye – es. Why?'

'You sure you wouldn't like to go to West Street back there instead? "Little Beirut" the coppers call it. Or you could always go out on to the old pier without a hard hat and risk having your brains stoved in by a falling rafter. If you like to live dangerously, why not? Only you sure you want to go up Whitehawk? I'm just asking.'

'Rough, is it?' asked Annalee, interested.

The cabbie laughed. 'You could say that.'

'Rough, here?' John gestured at the tall white houses lining the seafront past the pier. 'What's the Brighton idea of a slum? Only two bathrooms and no bidet?'

The cabbie laughed. 'Have it your own way.'

They turned off the seafront and began to ascend a steep hill; beside the road were fenced fields as far as the eye could see. John laughed. 'Look. That must be where all the Brighton slum kids keep their ponies.'

The cabbie laughed, but Annalee knew he didn't find it funny. 'Here we are. Top of Whitehawk. Don't look down.'

They got out and John paid the driver. No sooner had the tail lights disappeared than a group of figures emerged from the shadows. They were boy-men – those peculiarly working-class young English males who at one moment have all the knowing vulnerability of a child, and the next all the menacing strength of professional bouncers. There were five of them but four hung back, joined and similar like a line of cut-out dolls. The one who stepped forward was slight and slippery, with a quantity of dark blond hair in a vaguely retro quiff and a leather jacket that looked older than he was.

'You the one down from London,' he said, looking away from them. It wasn't a question. God, was it that obvious? His voice had a slight marbling of a rural accent, yet also seemed slightly American. What was a Brighton accent anyway? Was there such a thing? Or was it all washed away with the fishermen, or buried somewhere under the hotels?

'That's right,' said John, surely with more aggression than was entirely necessary. 'Have you got the Stuff?'

The Stuff! Good Lord, any moment now he was going to start talking about 'charlie' or 'snow'.

'Yeah, I reckon I do.' He looked at Annalee for the first time, at her face, then at her SLUT T-shirt, then at her face again. 'Why you want to wear something like that for.'

Again it wasn't a question; she had the feeling that this boy had never asked a question in his life, or looked for an answer. He shook his head and for one moment he looked very old; no longer a teenage drug-dealer but an Amish elder shaking his head more in sorrow than in anger over the folly of a beloved granddaughter.

'Annalee,' she said, holding out her hand.

'Johnny,' he murmured, touching it.

'Come on!' barked John. Annalee could see suddenly that he was scared stiff; not of being in a strange working-class district at night trying to buy drugs from a gang of boys who didn't read a book from one month to the next but of losing her to someone her own age. Why did he think it was either or? If he had an iota of sense, surely, he'd realise he should be scared of both. 'We haven't got all night,' he added for good, suicidal measure.

Johnny turned and murmured something to his boys and they began to laugh. Their laughter sounded like the colour the sky goes before it rains. He turned back and smiled at John, his peculiar, slippery eyes sliding away to one side again. 'In't that funny. Because we've got all night. All this night an' all the next one an' all the next one too. In fact, all night's all we got.'

'That sounds like a Bon Jovi song,' said Annalee instinctively. Sometimes she was amazed and slightly appalled by how much pop culture ran in her very veins, she who had wept over *The Faerie Queene* when she was ten.

Johnny laughed but John shot her a poison look. He fumbled in his pocket and took out a roll of notes. 'There you are. Two grams. Make it quick.'

Annalee looked at him, amazed. He wasn't exactly David Niven but he certainly wasn't this rude in the normal course of things. He was a tight tipper and he was anti-pets because he couldn't see 'the point' in springing 39p per day for a tin of Kattomeat – 'What's in it for me?' – but she had never dreamt he could be so out and out, sitcom rude. She realised that, faced with the young man, a man with the genuine, livid, flagrant youth that he and all the other middle-aged men yearned for so much these days – as much as any ageing Hollywood siren in a black and white film – rudeness was the nearest he could get to a demonstration of virility. She had seen it before in other UOGs when she'd been waitressing in the school holidays; she'd always thought it a bad mistake, but she realised that this time it was worse than that. It was bad manners. And things like that meant a lot to boys like these.

Johnny turned and looked at his chorus again; again, that rippling laugh like infant thunder. He turned back. 'Why don't you say please,' he murmured.

John glowered. 'Come on. Stop messing about. Take the money.'

'Take it,' said Johnny over his shoulder. One of the boys stepped forward and did so.

'Now give it to me.'

'Give it to him.'

They were on him like Roman lovers, pushing him softly to the ground and then doing God knows what. Johnny stood and watched them for a second, frowned, took two wraps from his jacket and dropped them on the undulating heap. Annalee watched, fascinated. She knew she should feel sorry for John, lying there, gurgling and crying out on the ground, but that was what he'd wanted for her, wasn't it? At least he wasn't going to get pregnant.

The boy turned to Annalee and she saw that his hair, which had looked dark blond like Eddie Cochran's, was in fact black like Elvis's, and that he was tall and hunky like a rocker, not small and wiry like a mod. Then he moved under the street light and seemed to change back again, shimmering. He smiled and it was like every great intro to every great pop song, ever.

Annalee stepped under the lamplight to look into his face and she gasped as she saw his eyes properly for the first time; not only were they changing by the second, from the blue to the green to the grey of the sea, but the irises were rippling like waves. He laughed aloud at her surprise and drew a hand across her breasts. She looked down and saw, with no surprise this time, that where the word SLUT had screamed in black, the words TEEN ANGEL glowed in starlight.

'You want to see Brighton?' he whispered into Annalee's mouth, and she could taste Juicy Fruit and poverty and sex and everything that had made the English working class the very scary ride indeed that they now were and for ever would be. 'Or you already seen it?'

She was on the back of the motorbike, laughing. 'I haven't seen anything,' she told him, although he knew that already. He gunned the motor, she kissed his neck and they rode down the high hill of Whitehawk to take their town at last.

Cider
Neil Grimmett

Somerset

We had not been able to attend Ernest and Sue's wedding and
judged that may have caused them to take offence. Then after
the way my brother – who had made it, had been the best man
in fact – continued to get treated we put it down to deeper con-
siderations. I mean – long-time best friend and a new wife, the
best friend's family – all those connections and memories; oil
and water with too many possibilities forming shapes after
each swirl.

And of course there was his problem and the way she had
managed to deal with it. Which at first had seemed as unlikely
as this relationship working out any better than all the others.
'Ernest is off the pop,' always followed on the heels of a new
lady, before she crept away to leave him alone and staggering
after another departure. No difference to start with; only that I
liked this Sue from the first moment I'd met her, so had my
wife, Julia. Sue seemed genuine and full of hope, for both of
them. I had easily managed to put my brother's assessment
and description down to the fact Ernest had gone and picked
the middle of the fishing season to fall in love and ruined their
sport. I could not see any other reason, not at that time.

Our holiday was already booked and paid for when they
announced the date of their wedding. There was nothing that
we could do about it. And besides, Ernest was truly my elder
brother Robert's friend. I had only got to know him since
Robert's marriage, when Ernest had suddenly started turning

up on our doorstep, usually drunk, with some very young, pale girl jittering and giggling in his arms, always having already been sent packing by Robert for daring to turn up in that state. But theirs was the real bond – and one that had always seemed, to me, unbreakable.

But by the time we got back from our trip to Boston it was all over: thirty years of friendship. Robert could not believe it. He was on the phone the very day we got home. 'Have you heard anything from Ernest or Sue?' That was his first question – asked before we knew anything about him having been banned. It was the same question I got asked almost daily for the next three months. It was as if he suspected me of knowing something or maybe even being in league with Sue. Robert knew it was all down to Sue. He had tried to phone Ernest many times since the wedding and on each occasion got through to his wife. By degrees her responses had become more hostile, until the last call when she had told him, 'We do not want to hear from you any more.'

Robert told me that he could hear Ernest in the background, whimpering away like a new puppy. 'If he was half the mate he should be,' Robert kept on telling me, 'he'd call up from work or somewhere behind her back, and just say: "Don't worry, old friend. You know what women can be like. Things will get better, just hang on in there."'

I could see that Robert was hurting and very lonely. I guess that is why he started making up and then repeating bits of gossip during each of his phone calls: 'Did I tell you that I saw them? Walking along like two ageing hippies on their way to a pop festival. Caroline spotted Sue the other day and said she's as fat as a blimp, sat in a car and propped up by a couple of overstuffed cushions and unable to get up without being helped. The landlady of the Angel said that they had been in and had sat in the corner of the pub with a glass of lemonade for an hour, tittering away and looking unwashed. One of the tractor drivers thinks he saw her in a van with a gypsy heading out towards the woods.'

He rolled these notions around, trying to gauge some opinion or comfort from me. It was only a matter of time, he knew, before Ernest saw through her. 'He is slow,' Robert said, 'but he'll get there. It will be like the finger that points. Then he'll be back, tapping on my door.'

Then I got a card from Sue and Ernest. It had this note pinned to it, written by Sue and announcing their move to a new house. She'd put down the phone number and said to give them a call and arrange a get-together. I thought that probably Robert would have received the same; and yet there was such a hope that he had not that I could hardly wait to get to the phone.

'Did *you* get a card?' I asked. And there was a silence that made me wish I had not mentioned it or had any of those feelings in the first place. It was just that I had been shut out for so long. How many times I'd stood and watched as they left to go night fishing for sea trout on some stream in Devon, or pike fishing or duck shooting on one of the fens with peat fires and good malts to fill the evenings. Deer stalking, sailing trips and, apparently, girls girls girls. With never a single invite for me. There was less than a year's difference in our ages and we shared the same interests. So why? That is what I had always been left wondering. And now, as my wife and I drove along, following Sue's directions to their cottage, I had an idea I was going to find out; or even better, that it was going to be *my* time.

Their home was a long, white cottage set back from the edge of a busy road. 'Cob walls,' Ernest said as we stepped into the cool silence, 'over four foot thick in places.'

We sat in the front room drinking tea and eating snacks, catching up on each other's lives as if it had been days instead of months. Sue was no bigger or in any way noticeably different from the last time I had seen her; Ernest, though, had changed. He was no longer jerking between timid and aggressive; he seemed to have found a calmness or confidence.

'Cider?' Ernest asked a short while after lunch had been

finished. I was shocked and tried to catch Sue's eye as he went out to the kitchen. I did and could see nothing to say that he was breaking any rules, or that there was anything unusual about him being allowed to drink. But cider! Of all the stuff you might trust and claim a familiarity with, this had to be the most treacherous. I had never got used to it; not after living in Somerset for thirty years and being introduced to its charms early on. One day you drank it and it was a refreshing apple drink with a faint tang of oak and blossom, calming to the mind and spirit; the next time it was evil and bitter with a charge that was notorious for causing arguments and violence.

A lot of the local pubs had a two pint rule to protect the tourist who did not understand the potency of the stuff. Always there were stories of Americans or Germans who knew all about 'apple juice' and could drink it all day; always they left the support of the bar and sank on legs that had been cut off from brains. 'Knee Trembler', 'Knee Knocker', 'Knee Cracker': just a few of the local names.

This stuff was the extra dry, flat, murky brew of the farms. 'It is made down the road,' Ernest said, 'but the apples come from the old orchards on this land.' Their cottage belonged to the remnants of a country estate, crumbling and clinging. 'I'll take you out in a while for a walk and show them to you.'

He had finished his drink and was up on his feet before I was halfway through, hurrying me along so that he could go and fetch more. Was he going to get out of control? I wondered as he snatched my empty glass. Was this going to be my fault, my turn to be banished for ever?

Above the deep fireplace there was a huge wooden lintel. It was over two foot thick and ten foot long and had a grain that you could have lost a finger in. The more I looked at it, the more its age and wear became apparent. A thousand wormholes had punctured it and what I had thought to be natural texture turned out to be tunnels and chambers exposed by the gnawing of centuries. Life that had crawled away in its own world, unseen until the damage was done and the call to flight had betrayed everything. 'That beam is amazing,' I said to no one. Both the girls turned to look at me.

'It is over three hundred years old,' Ernest said, arriving back with the drinks, 'and that's three hundred years in this house, not counting how long it took to grow or be cured. The back wall of this house is joined to a barn that is over six hundred years old. If you hurry up with that drink, I'll give you the guided tour.'

From the outside, the barn looked as if it was sinking back into the earth; the walls bulged and holes cluttered the roof. As we moved to the door four jackdaws shot out of one of the spaces, then another four. 'Safe, is it?' I asked. Ernest pushed open the heavy, studded door and stepped aside. Inside, everything changed. The vastness and intricacy of the place had kept all of its power intact; the unmistakable age made you feel too young and fleeting. And the silence listened.

'It was a tithe barn that used to belong to the abbots,' Ernest explained. 'But look at the size of it and imagine how much corn they were demanding. The power they must have had.'

The floor was like a sponge made of straw mixed with layers of bird and bat droppings; each step was an effort and released another breath of ammonia and choking dust. 'But that wasn't its only purpose.' Ernest pointed a finger at a wall. 'It was also the court. They held all the trials here. Look at that doorway and those alcoves.' Gothic arches had been carved out of solid stone and were clearly visible above bricked up doorways and recesses. 'And those windows – they are for firing arrows out of during a siege.' Long, thin slits of light shone in from the end of dry funnels. 'You feel what it must have been like to be in here back then, trapped and without hope of being rescued.' Ernest had started whispering. 'Hearing lies about yourself falling from someone's lips. How helpless you would have been to stop what was happening and what would follow.' I moved towards another door that was leaning open. 'Look at that roof,' he said, grabbing my arm to hold me back, 'some of it still has the original thatch.'

The holes shone like lights and made it possible to see. The roof was a web of beams and joints that must once have meant more to those that laboured to produce such a structure than a mere support.

'Great place,' I said, getting out of the door and breathing deeply.

'Now stand back,' Ernest said, 'and take a look at it from here. You can really see it as it was.'

This section, the opposite end to their cottage, had all its original shape and stones intact. It rose out of the remains of an old pond and looked like the watchtower of a castle, brooding and still occupied. We walked away and down into the orchards.

The land below the barn was divided into irregular shapes by low hedges and gates that dangled from wire or string. Inside each enclosure were the trees. Some of them, I noticed, were surrounded by their own cage. A heavy, ornate iron structure that must have been placed around the immature tree to protect it – judging by its size – from something large. Now they embraced the trunks like honeysuckle and in places the wood had begun to pour and deform around its constraints. A lot of the trees were leaning and all of them played host to clumps of mistletoe. A scent of fermentation squeezed out of the ground.

'They just let most of the apples fall and rot,' Ernest said, explaining the smell. 'All that lovely drink going to the worms. If it wasn't for the local farmer making a few barrels there would be nothing. What a waste, hey? Shouldn't be allowed.'

'Do you know what varieties of apples they are?' I asked. Something in Ernest's voice was changing and made me need to keep him focused.

'Bloody Butcher, Chisel Jersey, Cockagee, Cup of Liberty,

loads of different ones – there are probably some types growing here that are no longer in existence anywhere else. These are very old orchards. Some people think cider was what was meant by the apple being of the tree of knowledge.'

I followed him through another gate into what looked like the end of the orchards. This piece of land was circular in shape and some of the trees had fallen over. Someone had started cutting them into logs and sawdust covered the grass. Ernest sat on one of the fallen trunks.

'This is very hard for me,' he said. 'After all, you are . . . I mean, he is your brother.'

I stood in front of him, waiting for what I guessed was going to be some sort of message for me to carry to Robert. This had been about setting me up as a go-between.

'Though,' Ernest said, 'you are nothing alike – only in looks. If it wasn't for that I would not believe that you were in any way connected. It is no good; it has got to be said – even if you are not ready.'

He reached down behind the trunk and brought out a clear plastic bottle full of what looked like cider. He struggled to unscrew the top as if it had been wound on by someone stronger. 'I put this here last night,' he said, 'just in case we got hot on our walk.'

Ernest took a long pull on it, collapsing the bottle with each gulp, before handing it to me. I drank. The liquid was warm and plastic tainted and I could not help visualising what might have slithered over it during the night, searching for a way in, desperate to taste.

'Do you know that I was used by him?' Ernest asked, taking the bottle back from me and then swallowing what I had left. 'From the start of our friendship until the end, every single chance he got I was only ever there to make him look good or help him get what he wanted.'

He was staring at me and there was a look on his face that I did not recognise. His voice was strong and unslurring.

'He tried it on and made a pass at every girlfriend of mine.

He even had a go at Sue after he knew we were getting married.'

I wanted to say something. But there was this memory of Robert bragging about an incident. I had put it down at the time to showing off and had not believed a word. It had concerned a Christmas when Ernest and his girlfriend had been staying with Robert and his wife, Caroline.

Robert claimed to have been downstairs alone, enjoying the log fire and a late-night glass of port. He heard the stairs creak and had looked up expecting it to be his wife. Instead, it was Elizabeth, Ernest's girlfriend. She was wearing a baby-doll nightie and she had sat next to him on the sofa. As she crossed her legs, Robert said, the orange silk had ridden up her thighs and revealed a glimpse of pubic hair. She asked him if he had a drink for her as she was hot and could not sleep. Then, according to him, they ended up under the Christmas tree humping away for the rest of the night. He finished the tale by adding the little details that he got pine needles embedded in his knees and Elizabeth had them in her butt.

All the time this memory was coming back to me, along with the fact that Robert had mentioned many times that Ernest could never satisfy the women in his life, I could hear Ernest telling me how each attempt of Robert's had been rebuffed and then reported to him by the angry and offended girl. It was all down to the fact that Robert was inadequate, Ernest explained. 'I even know,' he said, 'that Caroline is not happy with him in that department. She told Sue that Robert was a poor and inconsiderate lover.'

The need for me to protect my brother had become stronger than any other desire. Just to have to stand and listen made me feel low and treacherous. I decided to tell Ernest about the Christmas tree scene, give him all those green needles my brother had stored and shared.

'He even tried it on with me,' Ernest said, freezing the words in my mouth. 'He did everything he could to get me into bed with him one time. Your brother is a sick liar.'

I understood what it was in Ernest's look that I had not recognised earlier: cunning. He was as unhappy with his new life as anything before, and he was looking for someone to blame for where his weakness had brought him. Now he wanted me to betray my own brother to help his cause. I turned to go.

'The reason I'm telling you this,' Ernest said, 'is that I know he is deeply jealous of you and that he will do the same to you as he did to me.'

'You are dreaming,' I told him. 'This is the drink talking.'

'He is coming to you soon,' Ernest said. 'That is why you have to know these things. Caroline has told Sue that she is going to leave Robert. She has had enough of him at last. He knows he cannot come here; so it will be you. It will be a perfect opportunity for him. It won't bother him that you are his brother; or Julia is your wife.'

I had heard enough and walked away. In the distance I could see the two girls coming down the slope towards us.

'Sue has warned Julia,' Ernest shouted. 'She has told her all about him.'

I could see Sue and Julia glaring at me as if I was guilty of something. Behind me I heard Ernest trying to get to his feet and follow. But I knew that he could not and that his legs had gone. He was going to have to crawl to catch up. If he wanted to be there as I told them the real truth.

Sound of the Drums
Courttia Newland

Off the M4

We were walking. Six of us along the empty stretch of dual carriageway, with the black tar of the road glistening like snakeskin. All talk was kept to a bare minimum. The beam of the tall street lamps periodically illuminated us, like it illuminated the Catseyes along with the hundred other young men and women walking the same route.

The road was silent, save the low chatter and murmur of youths. The police had blocked the road about a mile or so behind us – all five cars of them. Even though they were powerless to stop the crowds of street youths, travellers and suburb-softened rich kids marching past their pitiful little blockade like some powerful non-violent army, at least . . . Well, at least they'd managed to stop the vehicles. For all the fuckin' difference it had made.

I wondered if they were pleased about their shabby little display of authority, or if they felt frustrated by the powerlessness of their situation. I tell you something for nothing – it had been like coming up on E to walk past that barricade with my fellow ravers – even though I only knew five of them. The policeman had made vain noises to try and stop us, but come on, man – I mean, how the fuck eight policemen are meant to tell a country of over a million full-on music lovers that they can't party and take drugs until they drop has been beyond me for the longest time. And beyond them for that matter.

It was cold, but our quick trot had peppered our foreheads with sweat, so we didn't really notice the chill. The sky was clear and the moon full, hanging high above us in bright, awe-inspiring detail. Up ahead there were a few other scattered groups of people, more eager to reach the location. They were blowing whistles and foghorns. Every now and then we would catch the hint of whatever drug they were consuming, riding the wind beneath our noses – we'd all sniff and look at each other knowingly when that happened. I turned to Filo and reached out a hand.

'Lemme draw some green nuh.'

Filo had been quietly puffing to himself before I disturbed him with my request, more concerned with brushing herb ash from his new Nike puffer. He inclined his head my way and blasted the spliff once more – hard. There were snaps and pops that reminded me of a forest fire I'd seen on TV one time, when I was bunking off school as a kid. The head of the spliff sent a reddish-orange light dancing across Filo's face in a way that has stuck in my mind ever since.

'Huh?'

I stepped closer without realising it, relishing the feel of the switchblade in my back pocket, knowing I'd use it if pro-voked. Fuck, I'd use it even if I wasn't provoked.

'You heard me, man. I ain' gonna say it twice.'

Filo stopped and held his arms out by his sides before he pointed a finger at me with the hand that was holding the spliff.

'Wha' d'I tell you about the way you chat to me, Shivan? Didn't I warn you about dat shit star?'

He was eyeballing me angrily, offering me out with his body language, knowing he couldn't just come out with it like he wanted. Bunny rapidly put his tall, skinny body between us, his shoulder-length locks swinging back and forth wildly, betraying the swiftness of his manoeuvre. While he separated us, the girl pushed her hand into mine and grabbed it force-fully, even as my mind grabbed at her name. Sandra . . . No,

Susan . . . No . . . If I have to be honest, I still can't remember that fuckin' girl's name. All I can remember is that she said her parents were Iranian and she lived in Acton. Her name wasn't important then.

'What'm to you, man?' Bunny was saying, with a look of annoyance that was definitely real. 'Why you lot affa argue all the while?'

'Yeah, man, why you arguin' for, yuh fushin' fools!' the girl's drunken friend spat, stumbling even as she turned to face us.

I covered my eyes with my free hand and walked away from Bunny and Filo. I was pulling the girl past her tanked up friend and on past Cat: a tubby black guy who was ignoring us all, choosing instead to sit on the kerb and build another of his brain-shattering skunk spliffs. I walked further on, trying to take my mind away from Filo's words, which were replaying in my head. Trying to take my mind away from the fact that he'd disrespected me. Again.

'*Ow!* You're squashin' my fingers, Shivan!' She pulled them from my clutches and carefully inspected each and every one. 'They're all red now.'

She had a squeaky Minnie Mouse voice that made me squirm each time I heard it. When she realised I didn't give a fuck about her fingers, she turned back towards her friend, who was now being helped along the road by Bunny. Filo and Cat were bringing up the rear, no doubt busy smoking that zook Cat had built. I kept walking. She struggled to keep up by my side.

'How come you lot don't like each other den?'

I ignored her. Pretty soon she gave up annoying me, dropping back to join Bunny and the others, troubling them with her irritating little voice instead. I was grateful for the solitude of the road – I breathed the cold country air deeply once she was gone. It'd been a long night. Though it'd been profitable so far, it was one in the morning and we were still trying to get there. This was not what I'd envisaged back at mine, when me and Bunny had caught wind of the rave, planning this little excursion.

It was the girl's fault, I told myself, burning holes in my own pride with the words. *The fuckin' butters girl had made us waste too much time.*

The large group ahead of us started whooping and blowing assorted instruments once more. Then, all of a sudden, they started to run. I tried to see where they were going, but a few of them ran off the side of the road into some thick bushes, and were gone in the blink of an eye. I stopped and strained my ears to listen over the sound of my friends talking.

I could hear music. It was faint, tinny and far away – but it was definitely music. And I liked what I heard.

'I can hear music!' I yelled back as loud as I was able. Within seconds they were all crowding around me, eager to hear too. Bunny was smiling my way, his grin almost lighting up the dark. I smiled back eagerly.

'About fuckin' time, man,' he grumbled, looking around himself to make sure everyone was there, trying not to shiver – as it was cold and he was wearing no jacket. Confident and fair-minded, Bunny was the natural leader in our little group of friends – a role that I knew he often despised. But at times like these his inbred ability to take charge was an undeniable reflex that worked like his lungs or his heart or the blinking of his large dark eyes.

I had a lot of respect for Bunny, so the constant fighting that occurred between me and his cousin Filo was a deep and painful thorn in my side. I tried to like the brer – but every time I tried, he'd say something else that would piss me off – and by the end of it all we'd just about keep from coming to blows.

'Fuck dis weather . . .' Bunny muttered detachedly, raising an eyebrow at me as I'd warned him to put on a jacket back in London. 'Suh Shivan, yuh sure it's dese bushes dem people . . .'

A thickset white youth detached himself from his cluster of friends and approached me with a friendly look on his face.

'Any idea were the rave is, mate?' he asked me, his Northern accent a surprise to my London ears. I nodded at the thick bushes.

'Dem people ahead of us ducked t'rough dere I think,' I told him, suddenly thinking of this bloke in monetary terms. I tried to make my voice jovial. 'What, you sorted fuh Es, mate?'

The Northern bloke smiled knowingly – but before he could speak one of his friends waved and whistled.

'Oi, wha yuh got geezer, I might 'ave summa dat like . . .'

Bunny made a gesture to indicate he'd wait a little further on, then he left me to walk over to the group and get on with business. Four sales later, we came back looking pleased with ourselves. I nodded at Bunny. Without another word we formed a neat and orderly line, following Bunny's towering figure into the bushes. Pretty soon we found a worn and beaten trail. It led us upwards; within seconds we were all panting for breath, solidly cursing all the B&Hs and weed spliffs we'd been smoking since our teenage years. The music got louder as we got closer. Bunny broke through the bushes ahead of us; one by one there were gasps and shouts of exclamation as the others stepped into the field after him. When it was my turn, I looked over the expanse of low-cut grass, joining in with my friends' words of excitement whenever I could.

The sight was simply amazing: thousands of people (I later learnt it was something close to fifty thousand) – all talking and dancing and rushing and drinking . . . Looking like some great assembly of silhouettes in the dark. Mangy mongrels running and barking between the legs of ravers everywhere I looked. Bonfires blazing from numerous points. Caravans, tents and vehicles of all kinds forming a loose ring that covered at least five acres. And as for the sound system . . .

The sound system was built into the trailer of a large HGV. The organisers had obviously just driven the huge truck on to the field, then peeled back the trailer sides to reveal speakers piled as high as a house. The infectious, don't-dare-sit-down beat of jungle spread like a fire alarm across that field – sending shivers down my spine and movement through my whole body. It was all I could do not to start barrelling towards the speakers screaming with the sheer delight of it all. For one moment, the sound of the drums was all I heard.

It was time for me to go to work. We quickly began moving towards the large crowd, each of us knowing the other's routine. I told Bunny I was 'missing' and disappeared into the crowd as swiftly as I could manage – thoughts of the pills in my pockets foremost in my mind. People were dancing all around me – huge strobe lights bathed them with a mystical type of light and the bassline shook me deep within my torso. I wormed my way into the middle of the jostling crowd, then stood there, taking it all in, before digging out my bag of pills and swallowing my second for the night, grimacing hard at the unbearable taste. I was ready for anything now.

By 4 a.m. I was fucked, but still conscious. The fifty thousand were fucked but still conscious. Some mad kind of jungle mixed with ambient was blasting out over the field and they were still raving, still going for it as hard as they possibly could, sweating and blowing plumes of steaming breath from their overworked bodies. Other people sat by fires, either zoned out or reasoning over large spliffs. I watched all this from where I was sitting – a little hill, quite far away from the main bulk of the ravers giving it some in the middle of the field. I motioned at the thick line of coke I'd placed along the centre of a flyer, then looked over at the girl lying on the floor next to it.

'Oi – oi, d'yuh want dat or not?'

She struggled into a sitting position.

'Huh?'

I have to admit she looked terrible. I'd met her dancing with a group of friends near the car they'd driven here, and secured our lust with a large wrap of powder. When I left her friends, she'd left too. The girl's red eyes and smudged make-up, crumpled T-shirt and wild hair were the first things you noticed about her – the things you saw before you realised she could have been pretty without them, and began to imagine her that way. Of course, I wasn't really bothered with looks at that time. I was in the middle of an intense rush; the only thing on my mind was relieving the sexual tension heightened by the MDMA and other assorted drugs inside my body. I motioned at the line once again.

'D'yuh want dat?'

She nodded silently. I gave her a rolled up note and she bent over the flyer, snorting loudly. I watched the crowd moving. A pinch of daylight was slowly emerging from the eastern end of the field – on the west (where we sat), the sky remained dark and full of stars. She sat up, leaving only tell-tale smidgens of coke dust on the flyer. We looked lustfully into each other's eyes. I leant over, grabbing the back of her head roughly and forcing our lips together, until I felt the switchblade in my front pocket digging into my leg. Tugging it free, I placed it on the grass in front of us, feeling the way she followed it with her drugged up eyes.

'Wha's dat for?' she slurred drowsily.

Protection, man, don't worry yuhself wi' dat . . .'

We kissed again, then I laid her on the grass and turned my attentions to her body – running my hands across her breasts, hips and inner thighs, lingering once I got down between her legs. After long minutes of playing and probing, I looked up to see what reaction I was causing.

Things were not as I'd expected.

'Fuck!' I cursed aloud, just about resisting the urge to slap the bitch to her senses. She'd fallen asleep on me; she was spark out with her arm over her head in a very unnatural angle. Her legs were still wide open, although motionless. I gave her a routine shake. She moaned and stirred a little, but stayed exactly as she was. I cursed again, wiping my sweating forehead with a loose hand – I needed some shit badly, even though I knew it wouldn't do the hard-on in my jeans any good.

Picking up my switchblade, I decided it was about time I went looking for the others. I'd seen them around during the course of the night; Filo and Cat had been selling rocks like crazed jewellers. Bunny had been circulating dud Es and hugging us with a loved-up grin on his face within an hour of our arrival. I'd noticed Filo talking closely with the Iranian girl back then. It niggled me to see him touching her arm, smiling in her face, placing an arm around her shoulder, even though I didn't want her myself. It was a pride thing and I could see it clearly; but the fact of the matter was I hadn't hung around to watch proceedings because I hated Filo too much to see him near any girl I'd talked to – however briefly.

I know that sounds crazy – it sounds crazy to me as well. Now. But where we come from, the way that we'd been brought up, we didn't have a lot to be proud about. So the little things that meant nothing to others meant the world to us. Fuck, man; sometimes those little things were all that kept us going.

I left the comatose girl and wandered past the remains of the crowd until I bumped into some London guys I knew. I stopped and asked if they'd seen any of my friends. Frankie, a light-skinned, goateed, South London youth, passed me his skunk zook and shrugged.

'I swear I see Filo an' Cat boppin' past us a while ago, but dem man could be anywhere by now,' he told me in his flat, toneless way.

I took a blast of the skunk. My buzz (which had receded to the back of my brain) burst open like a flower catching first light of day.

'Was they wiv couple gyal?' I managed, taking a few more puffs. Frankie nodded.

'Filo was wiv one big-tittie, Arabic-lookin' suttin,' he offered cheerfully, grinning and showing off his gold caps. I tried not to let the fact that I was fuming show too much.

'What about Bunny?' I asked as I handed back the spliff. Frankie nodded in thanks.

'Yeah blood, I seen my man a minute ago lookin' fuh Rizla – he went off over dere . . .' He pointed at a large cluster of bushes, much like the ones we'd clambered through to get to the field. 'I tell yuh wha' though – I think I see Filo an' dat Arabic gully goin' dat way too . . .'

'Yeah?'

I was looking off towards the darkened bushes; thinking about that fucker thinking he'd got one over on me. Frankie saw that I wasn't really listening to anything he said after that, so he left me well enough alone.

The bushes were moving in the wind. Thick leaves were rustling sibilantly, seeming to call me in song as the sound of the drums accompanied and echoed from behind. If Filo was in those bushes with that girl from the pub, I decided, he was a dead man. If Filo was in there, I was gonna fuck him up.

I told Frankie and his friends I was leaving, then walked resolutely towards the cluster of bushes. My mind was filled with thoughts of the violence I'd inflict on Filo when I saw him – telling the story now, I don't even know how I managed with all the pills I'd been swallowing. If there was one emotion I wasn't feeling, it was one of being loved up.

The bushes waved and swayed and beckoned at me to come closer. I obeyed, feeling that hard look come over my eyes, the look that told people I wasn't joking around, don't fuck with me, don't even try to talk with me – it would all be to no avail. When I was in a mood like this, nothing could stop me behaving in exactly the manner I desired. When I was in a mood like this, God alone knew what the outcome would be for the victim of the anger I carried within.

A sudden noise came from behind me – it took a second for

my ears to realise the noise was screaming – then I spun around quick as I could to see what the drama was about. I blinked in shock, not believing what I was seeing. A hippie-looking guy sitting with a few of his mates shouted the words that almost everyone in that field was thinking.

'Shit! The fuckin' pigs!' he screamed, jumping to his feet and emptying all his drugs on to the grass in one quick motion. 'Fuck ya, ya fuckin' wankers!'

A police van was barrelling across the field a mile a minute, heading directly towards the large speaker/trailer. Like most people, I was staring straight ahead, looking into the bright headlights like startled deer. More vans appeared, spreading out on either side until eight TSGs made a tight V formation, the first vehicle forming the tip. A searchlight lit up the area from high above us, appearing simultaneously with the sound of helicopter blades. Everywhere I looked people were running, screaming, holding their friends and dropping large amounts of drugs. Soon, the ground was a carpet of wraps, self-sealed bags, KitKat wrappers and pills.

I ran for the safety of the bushes. Even though I'd done well enough on my Es, three of the fifteen I'd brought out with me were left – enough to land me back in jail as I was treading the tightrope of probation. There was no way I was throwing those away. Ducking my head, I pushed my way into the greenery, embedding myself deep in its leafy foliage, then I watched and listened to proceedings out in the field.

It was mayhem. I backed further into the bushes as the police methodically chased and arrested dealers and punters alike; some of them people I'd had brief transactions with. I saw Frankie and his crew being forcefully led away, struggling, fighting and cursing with every step. I crept into the thick of the leaves.

It was strange – the swaying and rustling all around me, compared with the noise, destruction and loud music – which played on despite the raid – from behind. There was stillness in those bushes that seemed to massage my mind. Though anger and fear of the police still reigned inside me, it wasn't the all-or-nothing, unable-to-see-anything-but-red madness that usually overtook me. It was a controlled, cunning, watchful type of rage. And it was much worse.

If a policeman had jumped out in front of me in those terrible moments, he wouldn't have lived very long.

Despite the noise, I couldn't fail to hear the soft sounds of a woman moaning a little way from where I was. I slowed, then stopped, turning my body as silently as I could; then I saw them – a man and woman together on the earthy grass not thirty feet from me – the man thrusting deep, causing her moans, his trousers pushed down around his ankles.

The smile froze on my face when I recognised the girl's voice. It disappeared completely when I focused on the Nike jacket – Filo's Nike jacket – bobbing up and down in time with her moans. I squinted. It was hard to tell. Filo had his back to me, so I couldn't see his face and his body completely blocked her from my vision. But the moans . . . It was her voice, I was sure of it, even though I'd only met her that night.

So I watched them. I watched them wriggle and squirm.

At first I didn't notice that my breathing was more laboured. Didn't feel it when I freed the knife from my pocket, clutching the weapon in one tight, cold hand. The sound of the drums went on behind me – and the harder they went, the more they moved, the louder they moaned, the faster thoughts ran in my mind; but none of it had anything to do with the girl. Filo was the prevailing thought in my mind. All I could see was that Filo had disrespected me. Had disrespected me. Disrespected *me*.

I was moving before they knew it – before *I* knew it. Clicking the blade open and bringing my arm down again and again – muting her screams, muting his cries – giving vent only to my will. His arms were flailing wildly, but I crouched over him, my larger body holding him down so he couldn't move, couldn't turn, couldn't stop the deadly blade from falling. Blood began to fly; somewhere inside me I could hear the girl's hoarse voice go into overdrive. But I didn't stop stabbing until the body beneath me stopped moving.

The first time I told the police what I'd done that morning I cried for the next two days. I still cry every time I think about it. Of course, their sympathies were reserved for others more deserving than me, so I received no pity – though they knew I'd committed a crime spurred on by rage, not nature. I hope they also knew I'm really not a killer.

I stood over the bleeding corpse and watched without really seeing it – arm aching, chest heaving, the girl shuddering and gobbling like a goose beneath my shadow, her eyes eating away at my face. I dropped the knife. The girl's breath caught in her throat. I leant down and callously turned the body over, wanting to see Filo's face *now* . . .

Then the sound of the drums came to a sudden halt. And as my hands grasped thick black locks I came to an even swifter realisation . . .

Bunny's face stared blindly up at me, his eyes rolling back in his head, exposing pure white and making me yelp. I let go of the jacket – Filo's jacket, I kept telling myself. But now it made perfect sense that his cousin might have borrowed it through the night – I knew how cold he had been.

Bunny fell bonelessly to the ground as I stumbled and fell. The smack of him hitting the earth was more than enough to start the girl screaming again, but I couldn't find the voice to tell her to stop. All I could do was look into the dead eyes of my best friend and know I'd just made the most terrible mistake of my pitiful little life.

'Bunny, man . . .' I began to sob. His arms seemed to be reaching out to me, his mouth held for ever open in an expression of outraged shock. 'Ah Bunny, I didn't mean it to be you, man – c'mon Bee, get up from the floor . . .'

But Bunny wouldn't get up because the deed had been done. He was dead. There was nothing more for him to say. It was *all* he could say – and he shouted it from every limb, every muscle and every pore.

That's how it was when police came crashing through the bushes and found us.

Hark at Him
Rachel Bradford

Bath

Our mother was using a leaflet from Help the Aged to funnel Co-op instant coffee granules into the Nescafé jar when the doorbell rang. 'Please, Wallis, just try to act normal!' She was flapping her not-quite-dry nails, shooing me out of the kitchen towards the front door. Act normal! As if it's normal to get picked up by a bloke twelve years younger than you while you're rummaging around in Waitrose freezers for garlic bread. Normal, like mooning over the Elizabeth Duke section of the Argos catalogue, checking out the cubic zirconas and single sapphire clusters when you think your daughter's watching *Emmerdale*. Normal, my arse.

He had an old pair of daps and no socks on, standing on our step with his mouth open, in his red corduroy jacket, holding a bunch of limp carnations. Before I had the chance to even start acting normal our mother pushed past me, gushing. 'Joseph, hi! Come in, come in, just throw your coat down anywhere. You must excuse the mess, it's always total chaos here.' Bloody pants on fire, lying cow. She'd done nothing but clean and exfoliate since Wednesday. I'd come in the day before to find her under half an inch of Japanese rice scrub scattering Shake'n'Vac on the lino.

I watched them all through dinner. She touched her hair thirty-two times. He said 'absolutely' forty-three times. When they ran out of amusing holiday stories, accident and emergency stories and Asti Spumante they tried to take me hostage to their conversation.

'Wallis is interested in photography, aren't you?'

'No.' She shot me daggers for that.

'Well, you've got a camera, haven't you?'

'Have you, Wallis? That's cool, I bet we've got simply loads in common.'

I bet we simply bloody haven't.

'Hey, why don't we hook up some time? Hang out and get to know each other.'

Yeah right.

'How's about this Saturday? We could go into town, maybe take a few snaps. What do you say?'

Out of the corner of my eye I could see our mother standing at the draining board doing frantic Lassie-type nodding behind his back.

'Yeah, town. Right. Saturday, yeah. Smart.'

Sold. One perfectly good Saturday to the vino-glow man, stretching his legs, pushing his daps even further under our kitchen table.

The black magic-marker scrawl vibrated on the seats as the 179 from Paulton slid through the drizzly villages on its way to Bath. 'Cas loves Nash', 'Bex woz ere' and 'Tight Tindell nobbed a heifer, July 98'.

Being up on a Saturday before the *Brookside* omnibus. Bloody scandalous.

God. Please don't let him try and hug or kiss me hello. And please God don't let me see anyone from the fifth year or the lower sixth form. And please, please don't let him be wearing those trainers. Or a hat.

The sheep on the hill past the Camerton Inn looked well pissed off like they were soaked through and too heavy to move up under the trees. It used to be such a laugh going into town. All ice cream and photo booths and laughing at the French exchange students' clothes.

Our mother had tried to dress me up like a librarian that morning.

'Oh, Wallis, do you have to have your hair hanging in your face like that? It looks like a valance sheet. And why you think that purple make-up is a good idea is beyond me. Mind you don't sit still for too long when you're in town, someone'll think you've had a turn and call the doctor out!'

I want to slap her silly face when she does that horsy laugh. Like she can talk. They'd have their work cut out for them if she ever went on *Style Challenge*. I swear, some of her earrings could have been car-booted by Pat Butcher.

As the bus swung into the station I saw an orange-waterproofed figure standing, foot up on a rail in a Marlboro poster pose with – oh no. A camera round his neck.

'Hey kiddo! How's it going?' I cringed. Tosser. In my boots I was almost as tall as him.

'All right, Joseph.'

'Oh dear, you make me feel old.'

You are old.

'Please, call me Joe.' He'd fastened the popper of his jacket under his chin; it made the hood stand up and gave him a big pointy head.

'Thought we might stroll by the abbey. Promised a pal of mine I'd take a few snaps to show the guys back home. They keep threatening to visit but they never actually make it past the M25.'

'That's where you're from then, London?'

'That's where I was living before I came back here. Pimlico.'

I'd never heard of it, could have been the name of a petrol station for all I knew.

'Best move I ever made, coming out to the sticks.' He looked up at the thick yellow sky, taking an exaggeratedly deep breath before stepping off the kerb backwards and almost slipping over on a half a Big Mac that lay by the bins outside British Home Stores.

His whistling echoed through the underpass behind Marks & Spencer's; the *Big Issue* vendor stuck a paper in front of him, not shouting like usual because he was talking on a mobile. Call Me Joe took my arm and hurried me past. I jerked it back and shoved my hand in my pocket. A short woman with a golfing umbrella almost took my eye out as we turned the corner by Fishy Evans.

Every time I passed there I thought about that murder. I was still at little school when it happened, it was all over the *Evening Chronicle* and HTV West for ages. The manager, or the owner, I don't remember exactly, got found stabbed to death in the chippy. I could remember being so shocked I dropped the milk bottle in my bowl of Rice Krispies and it went all over, made a right mess. Our mother was well peeved. Turned out that this man who worked there had got the sack or something, but he never meant to kill no one. He broke into the shop and got surprised and killed the bloke.

When they caught him it turned out that this girl from my class knew him, he used to babysit for someone on her estate. Imagine. A real-life murderer in our village. When we used to go in there with our dad after, I used to think I could see blood on the floor but it was really just red flecks in the fishy mosaic. I wonder if fewer bad things really did happen then or if it's just that I never saw the news because I was out playing after tea.

I could have told Mr Please Call Me Joe from Pimlico about it, if I wanted to be interesting. But then I expect he'd probably just have a bigger story anyway. After all, they have murders all the time in London, don't they?

He stopped in the Abbey Green to take a picture of the Crystal Palace.

'Spent my eighteenth birthday in there.' He was fiddling around with his lens thingy, pushing buttons here and there.

'Got drunk as a lord on cider and black and threw up in the taxi on the way home!'

He caught me staring, burnt up bright scarlet and went back to hiding behind his camera.

'I don't know, eh Wallis? What it is to be young and foolish!'

Hark at him.

The rain had stopped but the Japanese tourists still had their hoods up, crowding round a street performer outside the Pump Room doors. I'd seen him in town before; he wore rainbow braces like Mork and did an impression of a turkey meeting Bernard Matthews in the afterlife. He was shouting at the punks on the courtyard steps.

'Oi! What are you looking at!'

They were laughing and jeering back. He pulled a pink Marigold glove out of his pocket, blew it up and held it to the top of his head like a mohawk, then started jumping up and down screaming out Sex Pistols songs.

'We're so pretty . . .' the punks joined in, 'we're VACANT!'

The Japanese tourists had stopped watching the busker and seemed more interested in the punks, who had started pushing each other off the steps.

' . . . we don't care.'

A little Japanese bloke in a tartan cap was trying to take a picture of a girl with pink dreadlocks and a rat on her shoulder. One of the punk boys, this lanky effort with two little red spikes like devil's horns, steamed across and was looming over him, shouting about invasion of privacy and demanding money.

'Wallis.'

I pretended not to hear even though he was talking so close to my face with his fried egg breath.

'Come on, kiddo, let's go and have a cuppa, eh?'

God. There was going to be a bloody fight here and he wants tea. We could at least wait till the filth show up. Maybe the tourist would suddenly throw his mac down and turn into a karate expert and kick the punk's head in.

But Call Me Joe had his hand in the small of my back, pushing me through the crowd. I knew I didn't really have a choice. After all, our mother could strop for England, and if I lost him there'd be hell to pay.

Back on the main drag, in the stream of Saturday shoppers, I wondered what the time was and how long I had left before I could go home.

'Let's see then, where's a nice café that's not too far?'

'I know somewhere.' I knew if I left it up to him we'd end up in some posh place where you feel stupid because you just ask for coffee and they've got thirteen different kinds.

'Well, lead on, Macduff! This is your town.'

The market smelt like a pet shop, sawdusty and damp. The silver shop lady sat behind her Perspex window with one bar on her fire; she was too busy with her knitting to notice all the people passing that looked but wouldn't buy. Ladies in hats and old men with small children were milling around the sweet stall; there were candy canes and fairground-coloured lollipops in Christmas-tree-shaped stands, large jars of stripy humbugs, Pontefract cakes and fudge. The kinds of sweets old people buy for kids because they think bubblegum is vulgar and spacedust is dangerous.

'Do you know, I don't think I've ever been in here before.' Call Me Joe was trying to get past a pushchair without waking a toddler to get to one of the booth seats in the café.

'You have to go to the hatch and order, they don't come and ask.'

'Oh, OK. Tell you what, why don't you go and order and I'll save a seat. Here' – he gave me a two-pound coin – 'that should be enough, shouldn't it?'

Standing at the hatch, the smell of bacon rolls was making me hungry. I thought about the chips and curry sauce I could have for tea as I slid his change into my jacket pocket.

'Ah, there we go, just what the doctor ordered.'

He'd put his jacket on the seat next to him but didn't take the camera from round his neck. On the table next to us a greasy-haired man reading the *Mirror* was dropping chips on the floor for his dog.

'Well, I'm glad we've had this time together, Wallis.' He cleared his throat and picked nervously at the crusted top of the salt cellar. 'The thing is, you see, I really do like your mum . . .'

Here we go.

' . . . and I think it's really important that we get on, and I em . . .'

I was listening to the old couple on the table behind bickering over a red blouse that she'd bought but apparently didn't need because she had three others exactly the same hanging in the wardrobe.

' . . . and I'd really like it if we could be, well, erm, friends. I think that people should have friends of all ages. After all, what's age? Just a self-imposed restriction, right?'

I pulled a half-empty packet of Lambert & Butler out of my pocket; his sheepish grin fell right off his face. I offered him one.

'Oh, I er, no. Thank you, I don't.'

I lit one and blew a smoke ring across the table; it floated until it touched the handle of his mug, broke and was swallowed into the steam.

It was raining again and the light was fading as we walked out through the passageway and on to Pulteney Bridge. Across the road a large party of Americans was blocking the pavement to photograph each other to the backdrop of the weir.

'Bus is due in a bit.'

'Oh, rightio then, I'll walk you down to the station.'

On the bench by Bog Island the sherry drinkers were playing I-Spy under a big bit of tarpaulin.

'Something beginning with P.'

'Pigeon!'

'He always says bloody pigeon, stupid great eedjit, I'm not playing if he doesn't try.'

'Try? I'll try you in a minute if you don't pass that bottle on.'

Call Me Joe moved off the pavement to get round them.

'Something beginning with T.'

'Pigeon!'

'Tourist.'

'Ah well, there you go, boy, you've got me again.'

Just as we passed the postcard stands outside Peacocks, a tall thin woman walked out of one of the tall thin buildings and stopped dead, staring at us. I realised Joe had stopped too. She reset her smile, sly like a cat, and walked slowly towards us. Joe didn't move.

'Joseph, darling, well, here's a surprise. I could have sworn Sally said you were away this weekend, something to do with a seminar, was it?' Her hair was perfect under her umbrella. She stretched her neck out, put her bony cheek to his sweaty red face, not close enough to touch though, and kissed the air.

'Vanessa, hi! Yes, yes, that's right, it was cancelled. The weather. Cancelled, or postponed rather, due to the weather.'

'The weather?'

'Yes, that's right. Floods, you see, down in the valleys, makes it rather, you know. Difficult.'

'Ah.' She turned to me and flashed a big movie-star smile. 'And who's this pretty little thing then?'

'This is Wallis, she's the daughter of a friend.' Vanessa smirked behind her lipgloss. 'Well, a colleague actually.' Vanessa just raised her eyebrows. 'I was just walking her down to the bus station, then I'm going home, so if I can drop you anywhere?'

'No, no, Joseph, that's quite all right, you two carry on. But do give my love to Sal, we simply must get together soon, it's been absolutely ages. Maybe I'll give her a ring later. Anyway TTFN, darling.' She looked at him, then at me, gave a snorty little laugh, turned on her kitten heels and stalked off.

289

I started walking, quickly.

'Wallis, wait, please.'

My boots were making a strong click click on the stone. I could hear his floppy flat shoes squelching behind me, trying to catch up.

'Wallis, let me explain, that was just a . . .' He was spluttering away behind me but with the wind and rain in my face, and everything in my head, I could hardly hear him at all.

It crossed my mind to cause a scene. The police station was right there. I could run in and tell them I'm being stalked by this man who's been following me round town saying right dirty things to me. But I never. And I never let him catch up to me neither. Instead I just ran and ran.

Roadkill
Jackie Gay

Lancashire–Devon

'Where you been to get that pint, fucking Scotland?'

'It's the bar staff, man. Slower than a week in jail.'

Leon and Jack were having an early pint in preparation for the hitch south. They felt they needed it. It'd been a while since they'd come out of the valley to Lancaster or even Hornby, let alone all the way down to Devon, where Jan was, in a fucking council house of all places. *The kids think it's great*, she'd said. *Slamming each other into the windows, sticking their fingers in the leccy sockets. They were safer in the bender, at least it'd break before they did.*

'She'll never get them out of that house now,' said Jack.

'Poor Jan, man. Stuck it out longer than most, though.'

'Yeah. Fancy another one before we go?'

'Yeah.'

Leon and Jack had both fathered Jan's kids; Leon the first two, Poppy and Joe, and Jack the third, Katie. So when they wintered on the same site in the Forest of Bowland they'd had to talk about her eventually. They were hard men, hard travellers, no roof over their heads for a good fifteen years, Leon even longer – he'd been with the convoy in the eighties, when the stones were still free and it was whisky and cocaine for the whole of June.

The eighties as the golden age. It made everybody laugh. Early eighties though: before the act, the poll tax, the bean field. Leon's gorgeous silver and red fire truck smashed to fuck by truncheons and boots, the stones razor-wired off. He'd never had a vehicle since then. What you don't have they can't take away, he'd said, and Jan agreed. She was happy with a piece of tarp to make a bender, to sleep outside curled up with Poppy and the dogs for warmth. Tougher than the pair of us, Leon and Jack agreed, during the months they'd been frozen into the valley; no electric, no telly, shoring up tepees against knife-sharp winds, chopping wood and sliding around on frozen ruts, thinking of warmth and rest.

Some days, though, when the wind calmed and the air hushed, their teeth stopped chattering and their fingers warmed through and they stood outside, snagged by the magnificence of the oak woods they were camped by. Ancient, giant trees, shattering the ice-grey sky with jagged branches, frozen still as if in a kids' game of statues, mist and dead foliage draped over the branches like used-up party-streamers.

The first lift they got was on the back of a flatbed truck with a 'Mighty Mayo' sticker in the window of the cab. Inside were six labourers singing 'The Flower of County Tyrone', fighting for space and harmonies. Leon and Jack hung on as far as Forton services and then shivered on the slip road, hoping for a nice warm lorry to whisk them south to Jan.

Leon flipped up a squashed hedgehog off the tarmac and kicked it into the gutter. He was thinking about his daughter, Poppy, and how she'd been the previous summer, fussing with her hair all the time and looking at him with pure disgust when he'd staggered back to the bender early one morning, still tripping, eyes like kisses, reeking of cider and streaked with dirt. He'd tried to talk to her – what do you want, love? – and she'd said, A *house*, Dad, like fucking normal people. Can't you tell Mum? She wants to go back to squatting that shack on Exmoor this winter. Half a fucking mile to the stream for water every day. Fucksake, I'm *fifteen*.

As if that explained everything.

'Here,' said Jack, nudging Leon. A lorry was moving out of the car park. The driver flicked his headlights and an array of lamps on top of the cab flashed in time to 'Brown Sugar' which blared out of the open windows.

'Come on in, lads,' said the driver. 'It's your lucky day, I'm going all the way to Brum.' Jack and Leon exchanged glances – he'd chew their ears off for two hundred miles but it was a good lift. They scrambled up and pulled the heavy door to; the driver hardly paused for breath until they were well past Manchester.

' . . . meet a lot of your types, I do, on the road, like. And worse. Have to check the whole rig every time I come back from Europe these days. You call yourselves travellers but I tell you I'm up and down these roads every day of my life. That's the way to see the country.'

'If you're into motorways and service stations and loading bays,' muttered Jack.

'Backbone of England, mate. Me, I can go anywhere. Fit in anywhere. Suss people out straight away, I do; one look round the pub and I know what's what. You have to be adaptable these days, a chameleon, like.' The driver shivered exaggeratedly, wiggled his bum on the sticky plastic of his seat.

'I'd adapt him back to the Stone Age for nothing,' Jack whispered to Leon, who pressed his nose against the window and thought of Jan, sitting miserably in her council house while the kids left lights on for days and ran bath after bath, mesmerised by the water spraying out of the taps at their command.

Still, it was warm in the cab, Leon thought. Radio 1 and a wrap of baccy and a couple of pints in his belly. There'd been times over the winter when he'd wondered about getting a house himself; smashing a log on to the pool-ice for water, splitting kindling all day, numb-knuckled. The site kids were always up in the trees, calling to each other from the high, creaking branches; whistles and bird calls, drumming against the trunks, messages up and down the valley. *Why shouldn't we live like this!* he'd thought, although he'd never bothered with theories – leave all that to someone else. Me, I'll just get my boots on and get out there. A way of life, just like any other. Stonehenge, Glastonbury, the Albion Fairs, the Hood Fair, the Elephant Fair. Up and down all of England for the summer, serious R and R. Then back to a valley or a field somewhere quiet for the winter; odd-job man, farm labourer. He could always get by. And anyway, who'd give him a house? He hadn't existed officially since the poll tax and liked it that way. Jan did too, although it wasn't so easy for her with the kids. The shack reclaimed by its owner? Leon could hardly believe it. It was uninhabitable by most people's standards, but he'd been repossessed and Jan got shunted. Shelterless on Exmoor in the middle of winter, the kids turning up at school blue and social workers sniffing, there wasn't a lot else she could do.

Jan in a council house, man. It felt like the end of the world.

'Oi! Watch what you're doing,' yelled Jack suddenly. Leon's head rocked on his neck like a boat on a wave. The lorry was all over the road.

'Sorry, boys,' said the lorry driver, safely in the inside lane again. 'Someone's lost his load further up, there's stuff everywhere, didn't you see it? Whoa . . .' He swerved again, a piece of foam bounced off the windscreen. 'No need to worry when you're the biggest thing on the road, eh?'

'If you say so,' said Jack, glancing at Leon. *Let's get out of here*, in a millisecond exchange.

'You wouldn't believe what shit I see on these roads every day,' said the driver. 'Bits of tyre, trim, spilt loads, pallets. Animals too. Badgers and foxes, rabbits, hares, everything. Every day up and down the country, thousands and thousands of them, splat! Eyes still staring upwards, all innocent, like. You'd think they'd learn, wouldn't you? I mean, if you were a fox would you try and cross the A1?'

'They don't have much choice,' said Jack. Leon could feel him bristling. Jack was always rescuing animals; birds with broken wings, car-stunned hedgehogs. This winter it'd been a fox. Jack had spied him sleeping in a patch of sunlight during the day, this old blind fox who needed warmth more than safety. Jack wasn't adverse to taking out chunks of his fellow man, though. This could all get nasty if they weren't careful.

'I need a piss,' said Leon. 'Drop us at the next services, mate?'

'Not a good idea if you ask me. I've known people spend three nights solid there.'

'*We'll* worry about that,' said Jack.

There were four other people waiting for lifts and as they walked over to the slip road one broke away and ran towards them. 'Hey, boys, good to see you. I knew there'd be a few of us out on the road today. First hint of spring and we have to get moving, heh . . .'

It was Mary, one of the old school. She was a bit of a legend, famous for having hitched with a cooker all the way from Canterbury to Manchester when a load of travellers were squatting in Hulme one winter. The gas bottles in the vans had run out, everyone was skint, so Mary said she'd fetch her mum's old one, slid down the embankment at the side of Princess Parkway as if Kent was just past Southern Cemetery.

'Where you off to?' said Jack, as they passed tobacco between them.

'Just *anywhere*,' said Mary. 'I've been staying at a mate's all winter, my back was bad, you know. But I just start feeling choked after a while.'

'Not you as well,' said Leon. 'Jan's in a council house. We're on our way to see her.'

'Jan?' said Mary.

'It's the kids,' said Jack. 'Katie's got this PlayStation. It's all she ever talks about. Sits there with her thumbs twitching if you take it off her, Jan says.'

'God, I remember those kids when they were little. They could make cash out of a festival before the rest of us had even got our stalls up.'

'Yeah, well, they're growing up now.'

Mary, Jack and Leon settled down in a patch of sunlight and carried on smoking. They might as well wait until the other hitchers had lifts, and it was warm enough to just squat, blow smoke, chew the fat. A bit of nostalgia, Leon realised, for the times since the kids were old enough not to need watching every second and now, when they seemed to hate everything him and Jan and Jack were about. Every time Leon thought about it he shifted uncomfortably – in his sleep, while stoking a fire or tinkering with the old Land Rover they had up at the site. Like he needed a shit but there was nothing doing – it was the only way he could think of to describe it, but then he couldn't even *think* that because Poppy's face, twitching with revulsion, would swim in front of his eyes. Joe would laugh too hard; at least with boys there was that toilet humour thing to connect over.

Mary and Jack were heavily into reminiscences. 'It's something we should be proud of,' Jack was saying. 'It's unique, man, like punk and mods and all that. Remember all those French and Spanish heads who used to come over to Glastonbury every year? *Ve haf nusink like zis in our country.*'

'What about when all the ravers started turning up at festivals?' said Mary. 'Couldn't get their hats on that we'd been dancing in fields for fucking years.'

They'll start on about the human chessboard at Stonehenge in a minute, thought Leon, feeling suddenly sick. No food and too many roll-ups. 'Listen, I'm splitting,' he said. 'I'll see you down at Jan's.'

Mary and Jack stopped chatting and blinked up at Leon. 'OK.' They shrugged. As Leon set off across the fields Jack shifted a little closer to Mary and asked her if she'd been there the time they'd nicked a generator and set up a sound system in Savernake Forest.

Leon felt better after walking for a few miles. He was somewhere in Staffordshire, he thought, and had this mad idea that he'd walk to Devon, cross-country to the border, then down Offa's Dyke and over the Severn Bridge, like he had once as a boy with his mates from school. But Jan needed him quicker than that, perhaps that was why his stomach kept turning; she'd always been so capable bringing up the kids, had them washing their own clothes and fetching water and wood as soon as they could toddle.

But what could he do? The things he was good at – physical stuff: building, carrying, digging, walking for miles without breaking into a sweat – the kids thought were a bit weird. When they were younger they'd all been so tough; running around naked most of the summer, they never seemed to get cold even in winter and if they did they knew what to do. Down the charity shops with a couple of quid, fetch some wood and make a fire. He remembered them taking off for the day across the fields, flanked by dogs, him and Jan watching them disappear for ten hours without even a twitch of worry. Now the slightest thought of Poppy plunged him into deep, gut-wrenching anxiety. They turn into these girl-women, he thought, curled up with her mum sucking her thumb one minute and the next up in your face saying, Who are you to tell me anything? Leon could have stood it if she didn't seem so frail, almost like a baby again, tottering around, falling into things that'd hurt; pushing back his hands when he reached out to try and stop her.

Two more lifts and he was in Malvern. He'd jumped out of the last one at the traffic lights, belatedly realising that the middle-aged woman – stout and proper, her scarf pinned to her coat collar with a brooch – was actually coming on to him. 'Ooo, you look so strong,' she'd said, 'I could do with some muscles around the house.' She'd even leant over and patted his leg at one point; that was when he started looking for the way out.

Blokes'll do that to Poppy, he thought, as he charged straight up the hillside to the ridge; and little Katie, and there's fuck all I can do about it. How shit does that make me feel? Mind you, she can defend herself, her mum made sure of that. Her mum's taught her lots of things: be honest, look people in the eye, trust your instincts. But . . . Leon couldn't help feeling that something was missing. Protection; certainty, maybe. Some gentle way of teaching her that all the answers don't suddenly come, like flicking a switch for electricity or running water.

He walked along the ridge. There was mist in the valleys below him, obscuring the towns and distant city, just a spire poking through here and there, a few low hillocks which looked like sleeping animals. The sun broke through the clouds in shafts, buzzards hovered over cross-hatched grass. From up there the landscape seemed to fall into place, hills and valleys and towns next to rivers. Agriculture; planting, harvesting, stocking up for winter. Him and Jan had worked these valleys for years when they were on the road, picking strawberries and asparagus, living in old caravans among the apple trees. Now the farmers shipped in illegals from Brum, so he'd heard. Vans full of them every morning down the M5, the cheapest of cheap labour and no worries about dogs or kids messing up the orchards. 'They don't want us to be people,' he said aloud, suddenly, his voice startling some birds out of the grass. 'They don't want us at-fucking-all. No wonder the kids are after Adidas and Sky telly. That way they might even gain the right to exist.'

A creature darted out of the long grass in front of him and straight into the wood's undergrowth. A rabbit maybe; a hare. Leon just caught sight of a pair of startled black eyes as it headed for cover.

Jack and Mary, squashed into the back of a transit van, caught a glimpse of the Malverns as the van rattled past. Mary had decided to visit too, she had plans for the summer which might cheer Jan up. A stall at Glastonbury; they could start tie-dying T-shirts and sewing hats in preparation. Mary knew the people who were running the bicycle-powered rave up in the Green Futures field; they'd get everyone in for free.

'Let's all go,' said Mary, 'nothing like sitting in a field for a week with your mates, off your box.' Mary never missed the festival; had watched it grow year on year, more and more people wanting to be a part of it, to join the restless, uneasy tribes from all corners of the country, roaming around the site in the half-light dawns, wrapped in blankets like a scene from the Bible. 'Everything gets better come spring,' she said. 'Anyway, I can think of worse places to have a council house than Lynton. At least Jan's got some countryside around her.'

'I don't know,' said Jack. 'Jan says all the other mums avoid eye contact. On Katie's first day at school the kids in her class trapped her inside a circle and skipped around singing, "Your mum's a hippie, your mum's a hippie." Poor kid. I went down the pub and rang her up when I got her letter. She was in bits.'

'I bet Jan was spitting too,' said Mary. 'She never could stand all that peace and love shit. Too many evenings of listening to boring blokes called Willow spouting off about spiritual fucking harmony.'

'Yeah,' said Jack. 'She was more like know your enemy than love them.'

'Exactly.'

Jack remembered when he'd first met her. On a site near Salisbury racecourse one winter, she'd been lashing containers on to the lorry ready to go down to the stream for water. Leon had recently left, saying he was going to Spain for the winter and Jan had said, *If you're off then don't bother coming back to me.* Everyone admired her, so practical and unsentimental and Jack fell head over heels in love, the first time in his life. He remembered talking some bollocks to her about song lyrics suddenly making sense; her smile, just one side of her mouth creeping upwards. Later that night he'd played the guitar outside her bender, as the smoke twisted out from her chimney pipe.

He must have sung the right words because she'd opened up and beckoned him in.

Nine months later Katie was born and six months after that Jan kicked him out. He was supposed to have been minding the kids while she had a break – they'd had a hard winter on a lay-by being pestered by locals and police, and she'd gone out dancing with a mate. When Rog turned up with that gallon of cider he'd thought that Katie would be OK with Poppy and Joe – she was, but Jan didn't see it that way. Told him to piss off in no uncertain terms. 'Never again, I promise,' Jack had said, but Jan wasn't having any of it.

'You can't argue with a woman like that,' Jack said to Mary. 'She doesn't even let the shit *start*.'

'I might ask her for some lessons,' said Mary.

Jack looked sideways at her. Was that a hint? He'd been alone long enough to take it as one. No one serious since Jan, really. Jack had stuck to life on the road to prove something at first, bumping into Jan at sites and festivals, whittling toys for Katie. *I mean this*, he was saying when he dug another shitpit, rebuilt shelters after a storm. And after a while he did, his body uncoiling each morning ready to work, his mind staying with the day.

Mary yawned and Jack shuffled a little closer in case she wanted to doze on his shoulder.

Reluctantly, Leon came down off the hills and carried on hitching. Close to, the cars and roads and straggly housing estates seemed scrappy, half finished, roads trailing off into dead ends, traffic going round in circles like flies in a bottle. He got a lift though, to just past the M4, and he could already feel the thump of Joe's head hitting him in the stomach, his bristly hair and pale, tidemarked neck. The boy had always attracted dirt.

Leon sat down on the slip road to eat the bread and apples he'd brought with him. The air was still, an afternoon haze of dust and exhaust dwindled all around, but the hedge behind him was rustling and shaking. Glancing over his shoulder, Leon caught a glimpse of two dark eyes staring at him, bright with fear, before they blinked shut and vanished. He thought there must be some creature in there, injured maybe, and he crouched down to try and coax it out, thinking, *Where's Jack when you need him?*

By cupping his eyes with his hands Leon could just make out a body shape, crouched in a hollow, branches pulled across the front of the makeshift den. The shape was quivering – Leon imagined it was trying hard not to – and the air was sour with fright.

'It's OK,' said Leon, holding out some bread, still not quite sure what sort of creature he'd found. 'Here.'

The eyes reappeared, glinting in the gloom. A hand inched out of the hedge and curled around the bread. Leon waited, hardly breathing, rocked back on to his heels, blinked and glanced away – non-threatening behaviour, Jack had told him once, every creature responds to it. To Leon it felt like some sort of test; he wanted to say, 'Hey, I'm the last person you should be scared of, us lot, we spend our lives living in lay-bys.' He waited some more. A police car appeared at the top of the slip road and crawled past. Leon munched on his apple and tried not to fidget, feeling waves of tension ebb away from the den when the Old Bill accelerated off into the stream of traffic below.

A few moments later, a hand touched Leon's, then a body slithered out, one shade of brown from head to toe – hair, skin, clothes, boots; eyes on the rest of Leon's loaf. He passed it over. The man ate steadily, took long swigs of water. He looked like he might fade back into the landscape, the scuffy brown of the dirt-splattered hedge. But he didn't; he looked up. The hope and fear and exhaustion in his eyes made Leon flinch. 'What are you hiding from?' said Leon. 'Where are you going?'

The man choked and coughed, failed to speak. Brake lights flared in the haze in front of them.

A lift.

'Come on,' said Leon. 'Jan's got a house now.'

The man curled his head into his collar for most of the rest of the journey, but when they turned off the motorway and drove across the moor he started to look cautiously around him. 'Aleks,' he said, thumping his chest. 'You?'

'Leon,' said Leon. Aleks's voice was foreign, Slavic. Leon had hitched over that way a few times before that part of Europe was torn up by war. He'd loved it – wild country, empty spaces, no one around to frown at fires or rough camping.

'Do you speak English?' said Leon.

Aleks held up his forefinger and thumb close together. His shoulders and chest were still held high; he twitched, took shallow breaths.

'It's OK,' said Leon. 'Relax. Where we're going it's safe.'

Aleks's eyes crowded together. 'Safe?' he said.

'Yes,' said Leon, suddenly proud; proud that he could turn up at Jan's with a refugee, that his children could judge this man for themselves, that the moor rolled out purple and black all around, that wild horses clustered on the horizon, well away from the road.

They walked the last few miles to Jan's house. Jack and Mary were already there, holding hands, slightly sheepish, Katie on her dad's shoulders. Joe butted Leon and even Poppy managed a flicker of a smile on seeing him; a great big beamer and rapid hair-smoothing when she noticed the young man by his side.

'This is Aleks,' said Leon to Jan. 'I think he's from Kosovo, one of those places. I found him on the side of the road.'

'I thank you,' said Aleks, solemnly, hand on his heart. Poppy had to steady herself on the kitchen counter.

'Can he stay, Mum?' she said. 'There's no one interesting round here.'

Jan was looking at Leon. He spread his hands – what could I do?

'I ask you to come and help and you bring me waifs and strays,' she said.

'What else d'you expect to fill your house up with?' said Leon.

Later that night all eight of them walked across the moor to the sea. There were no roads or even paths between the house and the ocean. Poppy kept stumbling into Aleks even though she had cat's eyes in the dark, the best in the family. The ocean boomed and crashed past the horizon. 'What are you going to do about the house?' said Leon to Jan, trying to get back to what this journey had been all about in the first place.

'Use it, I suppose,' said Jan. 'There's only that or moaning.'

'Can't argue with that,' said Jack.

'Don't even try,' said Mary.

They built a fire on the beach and listened to the tide pulling on shingle until a briny damp settled on them all. Back at the house Poppy offered to make tea, still thrilled by kettles and switches and gushing taps. 'We forget they've never had those things, I suppose,' said Jan, which was about as close as she ever got to a concession.

Out in the garden, shapes were moving in the mist, everyone crowded around the kitchen window to look. Joe's football rolled across the lawn, followed by tumbling fox cubs, their coats brightening from grey to red as the sky coloured. One broke off from the rest and snapped its jaws around a plastic bone belonging to next-door's dog. The bone squeaked and the fox cubs dashed into the scrub at the end of the garden where it merged into the moor. Everyone stared at the place they'd vanished into; their escape fluky, fragile, personal.

I Shake When He's Gone from My Door

Paul Farmer

For Andy Anderson 1919–1999

Cornwall

I look out of the window and I see the signs. A quick white van slips down the Cornish estate like a foreign tongue. There are strangers on the street. I duck but they aren't looking my way. They've come for Nigel, the next worst news. A dozen blue suits now, some with hats. They run into his house and Alison bursts out past them with the smaller kids, stands watching, the youngest clutching into her shoulder. The van moves forward to block my view. I tell myself to get out through the back, over the bank, into whoever's lost garden, fighting through the brambles and dog shit I've thrown over the hedge, out of any gate but my own. Then over the road, through the old farmyard, along the stream, across the fields and round about to town. I've often thought of that getaway, never tried it, the danger seemed always unreal.

It must be business.

The kind of business we share with the Blues.

They'll come for me, and I just stare out of the window at the white van. *Devon & Cornwall Police*. It rocks as boxes of evidence are loaded from the house. It must be business. Nigel and me, our 2 a.m. business.

I can't leap up to start running. I sit for a while, stare at nothing, drink tea stale as an old dog. I tell myself that the slow, blank lie is the better way. To stick to my story, no matter what evidence, pictures, hints of information they produce. Interrogation is better if everyone lies. The truth stands you out like a scene-of-crime suit. It's unstable, the truth. There's no end to it. Anything less than everything is a lie, it's all a part of it all. But Blues won't talk about important things – the quiet kids and the empty bed, phone calls with their mother full of grunts and angry pauses, the shock of new circumstances.

I go back to the window. All quiet. Nothing. No van, no blue suits, no Alison. No knock at my door.

This time, boy. Not this time.

I go out and walk three miles along the old railway line into town. If they want to follow me here they'll have to get out of their cars and walk. They wouldn't do that just for business. Steady. I go to Nigel's workplace by the river, cautious and familiar, look in through the secret dark way out of our business hours, the moonless hours, when we carry plastic-wrapped fascia boards to my three and a half tonner parked in deeper shadow.

He isn't there.

Everything seems everyday.

His work friends have already got used to no Nigel.

I have to walk back quick to get the kids from school.

That's the way of it for days. I don't see Alison, she doesn't like me anyhow, and why should she? Me and Nigel are just business, and her Nigel is gone. They don't like me here now. It was different when we were a family, but now I've become a character, big, dark, fierce; my clothes gone soft and my hair falling out. Smash it all off I say to barber, so you can't tell where crop ends and bald begins. No one talks about Nigel, but they won't up this end. Down there it looks quiet, but if Blues aren't watching some neighbour will be, holder of some twenty-year grudge. We should hate the phone here. It's too easy. Calls to the Social, calls to Blues, calls to the Council, Social Services and dog patrol. Often at the same time. You can be evicted, arrested, have your kids taken off you and your dog put down in one smooth operation.

It is good business to sow a bit of fear around. You put on a look that says 'I know it was *you*' and lay it like machine-gun fire, shredding lace curtains. My skill is to make each watcher believe the threat is just for them.

During the day I wait, listen to Hank Senior. Nights I wait, watch television, the kids quiet in bed. Good kids, say nothing about their ma. They talk to her on the phone in grunts and pauses of their own. It's hard to take what you should from moments, but I know this is a pause. She'll get them soon. Letters arrive, the courts closing in – straight into fire, so I can't be tempted.

They won't let me keep them. Not even one. I know it. I live here, in this Cornwall. I've seen all lead to nothing for people better than me. I've seen lives end in shit by the age of forty. Like Anthony who took his life when Moira come back from holiday with her mates to tell him she'd found herself through better sex with strangers. Like Mark who's flit for years round his ex-wife like a moth beating at her window. Sometimes he's her lodger. Sometimes she calls the Blues. And it was him who left her. Some go on to other lives but they never believe again. Too often they're shouting drunk off the last bus in the yellow light. The council won't like me alone in a three-bedroom house and that's this life gone like it never happened.

I like to have a complete evening's viewing planned in advance. I write it down on scraps of paper, lists I find later, real history. Country Music Awards, *Grafters*, *The Bill*. I drink one small bottle of strong lager, 49p at Costcutters. I sit up until two, three in the morning. Still they don't come.

Wrong. They do, once, and take me by surprise. With no word of Nigel for ten days now, seconds of forgetting have stretched into minutes. Later there might be hours and days. I'm already opening the door when I realise this is a blue suit complete with hat. A tall streak of piss he is. Moustache. Younger than me, but never been young. I'm looking behind him for others and vans but there's nothing. He says, Can I come in? and I say, No. He says, It's raining, and I say, Yes. What do you want?

Drips off the canopy soak into blue serge polyester, no doubt proofed against petrol bombs, milk bottles full of piss and other just deserts. It's a darkening evening, high wind, the sky like a circus, and the kids are curious, outside and in. He says, Do you know Robbie Thomas? I say, Course I do. There he is now. Little shit.

Raised voice for Robbie Thomas, ten, who laughs and runs off down the estate, blue around the eyes. I told him off yesterday for hitting my middle one and busting his toy. I followed a trail of jigsaw pieces like drops of blood up to Millennium Park, and there he was. Robbie Thomas is a fucking little psycho I say to blue boy. So what?

His mother says you gave him that black eye, the Blue says.

I say, That was his mother herself give him that, you stupid cunt. Don't you know better than to listen to that mazy twat? You've been round there often enough. You giving it one?

He says, Would you make that allegation against her official?

I say, Fuck off, you dozy cunt.

He says, That's offensive language.

I says, That's offensive accusation. And next time you can help push the van.

Shut the door. Applause from tired eyes which are mine in the mirror.

Yeah that's obscure. That'll puzzle him. It was a year ago, the others at home with their mother, biggest boy, thirteen, and me in the van. Gear linkage snaps in neutral by the roundabout next to the police station, near Shell garage. I'm blocking the outside lane but it's seven at night and running rain, no one about. There's a blue light behind me and the blue streak of piss at my window. He says, You can't leave this here. I says, Thank you for the information, officer. I was about to put the handbrake on and melt into Tinners. He says, I shall radio for a breakdown lorry to remove you at your own expense. I say, No need, we'll push it on the garage forecourt and I'll fix it in the morning. The boy goes with him round the back and I steer the van, but we can't make it up the tiny slop into the garage. I think they're making their blue boys weak these days. Too much wanking, no doubt. I get out and go round the back and there's no one there except my boy. The cop car is already parked up in front of the bin. They're on their way home or laughing at the window, happy to have left thirteen-year-old boy pushing a Leyland Daf.

But I'm shaking when he's gone from my door.

I look at my youngest asleep in his bunk bed. There's no peace on that pillow. Little marks from the day, tired-ness in the sockets round the eyes untouched by this deep sleep.

The kids know all I do about what will come. They seem to get born with the information these days. Ma goes off, Dad waits for Blues, fades away, failure. It's not in the genes but it is in the water, in every book in school, in the car park among the Land Rover Discoveries and Dutch Volvos. It's printed in the security coding in the child benefit book, and every tiny bit of business.

I don't feel right even being in here.

I take them to school, come home, drink tea. Wait. I'm at the window again. No one about. Above the woods a pair of buzzards soar the slopes. Behind the house rooks crow over 'little man' gardens. It's another ripped up day and the sea-sky rats have come in to shriek their hymns to bins. The estate feels undefended, exposed on its hill. They've got air super-iority and the freedom of the roads. No-go areas in our heads alone.

I can't stand it, waiting for vans. Me and the dog walk a long downhill past Chapel to the dead river valley and mine wastes. You can walk up on to the Carns and see no visitor. Only gorse grows on the attle. The smell of dust even in the rain – I swear you can feel the arsenic aching in your hips. Chill creeps under clothes, like drying sweat. The dog shits at will and nobody knows where I might be – brown envelopes or blue lights can't find me, neither wife nor Nigel can drop the word that gets me touched here. The Old Men ripped tin and copper from the scorched hills around this valley and left them looking like the arse end of World War Three. Now the veins are dry, running back to the Cornish heart of us, what once nourished us gone back under the earth leaving only this quicksilver poisoned river. The ruined engine houses were full of steam, now they're empty boxes to write your mind on, Kernewek slogans of separation from England – *Kernow nyns yw Pow Sows, Kernow bys vykken!* – the black and white Cross of St Piran. They sell postcards of these ruins from racks in Spar, and daily they draw my eyes, personal as the names of my nest of places; the estate, the village and Cornwall, as me as my own handwriting. If I bought all the cards and posted them to Blues they would have everything they need. They would know me to my empty heart.

Scuffing feet come to me round a headland of spoil near the red-banked river. A man appears, running loose, long stringy legs under short shorts. He's old, late sixties, in a white vest, white hair streaming in his own jogging wind, otherwise smooth and tanned. I watch and he stops, bends to pant, trying to hawk up something deep beyond gobbing. Tight humpty face.

All right you, I say, and he nods, slapping sounds in his mouth as he achieves gob. He sits on granite. I take a rock near by for a desert meeting of two like animals. I offer him a fag. He holds up a hand and says, No, death. He points to the back of a scrawny leg and the stripping skill of the triple heart bypass.

We sit. I say, Should you be running?

He says, I got to run, but I gave up the surfing.

I think, I bet the surfer boys loved you with your scrawny

legs and your old man's gut. I say, What colour was your wetsuit? and he says, What wetsuit?

Me and Nigel, he always had a boat when we were younger. We went fishing. We'd come back up the beach, walking dark heavy clothes through holiday crowds.

The old man talks. He starts off medical, I don't listen. I feel my clothes on my skin. Twenty minutes on, I realise he's telling me his thoughts about film stars. Film stars?

He says, All are beautiful, magnetic, the women, the skin. He wishes we had one here with us. I look around dead hills and reckon the chances as slim. He tells me what I would say. It seems I would say, This, this is beauty. She is beautiful. And what would he reply to me? Of course she is. She's a film star.

Sometimes a man is glad he can still smoke. He swills from a bottle of spring water. I don't know where he had it hidden. He comes equipped for the Tour de France, lacking only the bicycle. In the spirit of trade I say, You ever see French film stars, Pappy? They have these dirty dating shows on telly now late at night. Drive you fucking mad. All hair perms and uplifting bras. They say they grow up young now, but bollocks. They stay children for ever with fucking thrown in. I turn over to Channel 4 unplanned and there's some French film. This mademoiselle, looks like she's been raised in a veal-calf stall, drip fed on milk then thrown into the world with a little black dress and no knickers. Times she has, boy. Sitting up in bed smoking with her little tits out, some fat tosser in a towel walking up and down shouting that his life is like an ashtray. You say, *This is beauty* because she's a film star. You know how many women on our estate look like her? Fucking fat zero, boy. What would she look like with one in a pram, one on a string and one on the way? The next scene would be razor on wrists. Those fat fuckers upcountry can put on their glasses and have a wank staring at her little Postman Pat because she's nothing like us. We watch this shite telling us what is beautiful and once again that's us sure we're shit.

I don't know why I'm so angry. I stand on my rock and raise

my hands to the blind-eyed buildings, the raped hillsides, the corpse of our heritage and I shout, This! This is beauty!

That creases his busy brow. He swigs from his empty bottle and wishes he still smokes. See you again, we say, and part into our separate parts. I worry about him running on sticky legs when it should be myself I worry for. This is my lack of imagination. I reach the school by the roundabout route and take the kids home. Another night's wait.

Once this estate was full of youth. They swarmed smoking in the bus shelter. From the safety of street crowds they smashed footballs through windows. They sneered each other into courting on the corner. Surprised, they found theselves in love, pushed their prams early from their parents' homes, walking little aunties and uncles to primary school.

People from the big houses outside the estate, come from upcountry for the salaried jobs, campaigned against youth. They said women were afraid to go out at night. They said the village was becoming an inner-city ghetto. They had a petition. There was an article in the *West Briton*.

One Christmas – me, the wife and kids off to Mousehole lights – I saw men standing round the dark estate in twos where no one would ever stand, pretending to be innocent bystanders and bypassers here on the blind estate where only we stop still. I started the van and turned full beam on two of them. They stared down my headlights like snakes at rabbits. The colourless Blues. That stare, like big boots. We stayed out long past midnight, kids asleep in the back of the van. Meanwhile, police went into most houses on the estate and took away all males fifteen to twenty-five. Mothers who argued spent a night in a cell too. They searched houses, sheds and garages and found fuck all, but they'd make some charge which they'd only drop if each youth swore he'd move away.

That was how they broke this place. The kids were a pain in the arse, but it's some sad place without them. I even miss their rain of dog shit and laughter as I walk by the woods. It's like we're ethnically cleansed. There's no fight left. What the police did to the estate, English money does to Cornwall. Youth leave for work, for education, rich Tories retire here with their lump-sum Audi and upcountry pension, up go house prices, youth can't return, school closes, shops close, retired Tories open antique shop, campaign against Cornish youth.

Some filth moved in from Bristol into that vacuum, injecting downers and stabbing Stevie one afternoon when he comes back from football to find Louise beaten up in front of their kids. People phoned the Blues after she was attacked but they never came for two hours, to find Stevie bleeding on his own splat. He was the one they prosecuted. They'd been after him a while.

Fuck them.

I'm carrying the *West Briton* out of Spar. There's a hiss. It's Alison in the alley. I stand at the bus stop as though awaiting an 88A and she talks secretly to the back of my tactful head. Act like there's no one there, I tell the dog, but he's got no feel for the secret game.

I say, They got him? Alison says, They got him. I say, They coming for me? She says she don't give a fuck, it's just her and the kids now, all of them, however many, I forget. I say, It's business? and she says, No.

No?

It's not business?

It's not the fucking business, you selfish cunt. Nothing to do with you, you big bald fucker.

What the fuck is it then?

Fourteen-year-old robbery.

Nigel robbed a fourteen year old?

The fucking robbery is fourteen years old. Not the fucking victim. Building society. They say they've got genetic fingerprints.

Should have worn genetic gloves.

The Blues know about business. Nigel will tell it all, locked up in a cell. They can come when they want. So it's all worry or none.

I'll choose none like the other wankers and live like a veal calf.

Blues like a clear deal. They understand the criminal mind because they've got one. We entertain each other our whole lives, staring each other out, eyes for nothing else. That's how they do their job. These are places cold war never ended. I stand at my gate, arms folded, daring them to come, brown dog growling at my knee. One day they will. But I should have looked beyond, to those that send them, to the cut-up bastards who sow hate and harvest votes.

I ranted simple stuff in bitter evenings until she took it no more, obvious in all I did.

Fourteen years ago Nigel was thirteen. He was some skinny little kid, and he used to hang around my garden trying to buy things. He liked boats. He might have robbed a boat. 'Genetic fingerprinting.' Another tool to prove we are shit. Infallible as popes.

I'm at the gate, arms folded, while a white van cruises. We should defend ourselves, but we not only blinked first, we've got our heads down a hole and our arses in the air. You can't hide on our estate now, so you hide in yourself. You find other enemies in there, running, hiding, growing cancers. It won't be like this for ever. I want to live where love holds sway. I salute the people with their black and white flags. Let's dig the fucking ditch and cast off.

Notes on Contributors

David Almond lives in Newcastle. His story collection, *Counting Stars* (Hodder, 2000), is set in his home town, Felling-on-Tyne. His novels are *Skellig*, *Kit's Wilderness* and *Heaven Eyes* (Hodder Children's Books). His many awards include the Carnegie Medal and the Whitbread Children's Book of the Year. His work is translated into over twenty languages. His novel, *Secret Heart*, is published in March 2001.

Andrea Ashworth is Junior Research Fellow in English Literature at Jesus College, Oxford. Her bestselling memoir, *Once in a House on Fire*, won the Somerset Maugham Award and has been translated into nine languages. It is soon to be made into a feature film, produced by Kevin Loader (*Captain Corelli's Mandolin*). Andrea is currently working on her first novel.

Alan Beard's stories have appeared in numerous magazines, anthologies and on radio. His first collection, *Taking Doreen Out of the Sky*, was published by Picador in 1999. Married with two daughters, he lives and works in Birmingham and is a member of Tindal Street Fiction Group.

Julia Bell is a writer, editor and tutor based at the University of East Anglia. She is the co-editor with Jackie Gay of *Hard Shoulder* (Tindal Street Press, 1999), which won the Raymond Williams Community Publishing Prize 2000, and she co-edited the *Creative Writing Coursebook* (Macmillan, 2001). Julia is also co-editor of the UEA literary magazine *Pretext*, and has just completed her first novel, *Massive*.

Gemma Blackshaw was born in Essex in 1976. She divides her time between teaching creative writing at the University of Birmingham, studying for a Ph.D. and working on a collection of short stories. 'Is it a Bird?' is taken from a collection of stories, which are all based in her home town of Chelmsford.

Rachel Bradford was born in 1971 and studied English literature at the University of East Anglia. She is currently working in her village paper shop where try as she might she cannot get the hang of the Lottery machine.

Julie Burchill is a columnist for the *Guardian* and the *News of the World*.

Julia Darling lives in Newcastle upon Tyne and writes plays and short stories and, more recently, novels. Much of her work is inspired by the landscape of the North and by Newcastle. She has published a short-story collection, *Bloodlines*, as well as writing many stories for radio. Her first novel, *Crocodile Soup*, was published by Anchor at Transworld, and she is currently working on a second novel. She occasionally teaches creative writing.

Peter Ho Davies is the author of two collections of stories: *Equal Love* and *The Ugliest House in the World*, which won the PEN/ Macmillan and the John Llewelyn Rhys Prizes. His work has appeared in *Granta*, *Atlantic*, *Harpers* and the *Paris Review* and has been selected for *Prize Stories: The O. Henry Awards* and *Best American Short Stories*. Born in Coventry, he now divides his time between Britain and the US where he teaches creative writing at the University of Michigan.

Joolz Denby has been a professional performance poet for twenty years and is considered Britain's premier woman spoken-word artist. In 1998 she was awarded the first Crimewriter's Association New Crimewriter Prize with her much acclaimed novel *Stone Baby* (HarperCollins). She is currently working on her second and third novels, a collection of short stories and her autobiography. When not travelling the world, Joolz lives in Bradford.

Paul Farmer was brought up in South London and lives in Cornwall. He gave up a highly successful career as a bus driver to help form the political theatre company A39. Now he is a writer, performer and community arts worker.

Jackie Gay was born in Birmingham and travelled in Europe, Asia, the Far East and Africa before returning home to write. She is editor of the prize-winning anthology *Hard Shoulder* with Julia Bell, and her first novel *Scapegrace* was published by Tindal Street Press in April 2000. She is currently working on her second novel.

Lesley Glaister lives in Sheffield and writes novels, short stories and radio drama. She teaches on the MA in writing at Sheffield Hallam University. Her first novel, *Honour Thy Father* (1990), won a Somerset Maugham Award. Her other novels include *The Private Parts of Women*, *Easy Peasy* (shortlisted for the Guardian Fiction Prize), *Sheer Blue Bliss* and *Now You See Me*.

Neil Grimmett has had stories published in, among others, *London Magazine*, *Stand*, *Panurge*, *Iron*, *Ambit* and *Sepia*. In the US, *Fiction* and the *Yale Review*; in Canada, *Grain*; in France, *Paris Transcontinental*; in Australia, *Quadrant*; in South Africa, *New Contrast*. Neil lives and writes in Chania, Crete, with his wife Lisa.

Tina Jackson is the arts editor at the *Big Issue*; her journalism has appeared in the *Guardian*, the *Independent*, the *Mail on Sunday* and many other publications. She was formerly features editor at the now defunct, Leeds-based magazine, *Northern Star*. Her short stories have appeared in various magazines and anthologies and she has just finished her first novel, *Cast-Offs*.

Harland Miller was born in Yorkshire in 1964. After an MA in fine art at Chelsea, he has lived and worked mainly abroad, both as a writer and painter. His first novel, *Slow Down Arthur, Stick to Thirty*, is published by Fourth Estate. He now lives in London with his wife and daughter, where as well as writing he carries on his work as an artist. He is currently working on a new show of paintings: *First I Was Afraid, I Was Petrified*.

Courttia Newland is the author of two novels, *The Scholar* and *Society Within*, and is also the co-editor of *IC3: The Penguin Book of New Black British Writing*. He has had short stories published in numerous anthologies. Courttia is currently working on a new novel and a book of surreal short stories, including the one published here.

Sarah O'Mahony was born in 1977 and was brought up on the East Coast. She studied English literature and creative writing at the University of East Anglia, graduating in 1999 with first-class honours. Sarah is currently teaching English in the Far East and is working on her second novel.

Jane Rogers is the author of six novels, including *Mr Wroe's Virgins*, *Promised Lands* (winner of the Writers' Guild Best Fiction Book Award), and *Island*. She has also written and adapted her own work for TV. She has two children and lives in Lancashire. She gratefully acknowledges that 'My Horizons' owes a debt to Charlotte Perkins Gilman's story 'The Yellow Wallpaper'.

Leone Ross was born in Coventry in 1969. She left the UK when she was six and went to live in Jamaica. She returned to London to do an MA and work as a journalist. She has written two novels, *All the Blood Is Red* (ARP, 1996), and *Orange Laughter* (Anchor/FSG, 2000) and her short stories have been anthologised in the UK, USA and Canada. In 2000 she received an Arts Council award and was identified by US magazine *Interview 1>* *as one of seven new writers to look out for in the future. She teaches fiction writing at the City Literary Institute in London.*

Kevin Sampson started writing for legendary Liverpool fanzine the *End* in the late eighties. This informed his first novel, *Awaydays* (Jonathan Cape, 1998), set in a world of unemployment, easy sex and soccer violence on Merseyside. Kevin has written two subsequent novels, the infamous rock 'n' roll bestseller *Powder* and an unusual package-holiday fable, *Leisure* (Vintage, 2000). His story 'Diamond White' returns Kevin to the tough Birkenhead stomping ground of *Awaydays*.

Alexei Sayle is a comedian, actor, presenter and writer. His television work as a writer and performer includes *The Young Ones*, *Alexei's Stuff* and *The All New Alexei Sayle Show*. He has written regularly for the *Observer*, *Independent*, *Time Out*, *Car Magazine* and *Esquire*, and he has appeared in numerous films, from *Indiana Jones and the Last Crusade* to *Gorky Park* and *Swing*. His collection of short stories, *Barcelona Plates*, was published by Hodder & Stoughton in 2000.

Pavan Deep Singh was born and raised in Smethwick in the West Midlands. He graduated from the University of Wolverhampton with a degree in media, art and design. He is currently employed as a community development officer, working with the local community at grassroots level. He draws his inspiration from Punjabi folk legends and experiences of growing up in a culturally diverse community.

Ashley Stokes was born in 1970 in Carshalton, Surrey, and educated at St Anne's College, Oxford and the University of East

Anglia. His writing has appeared in various journals and anthologies. He teaches creative writing at UEA and reviews paperbacks in the *Daily Telegraph*.